TERROR TALES
OF THE OCEAN

TERROR TALES
OF THE OCEAN

Edited by Paul Finch

TERROR TALES OF
THE OCEAN

First published in 2015 by Gray Friar Press.
9 Abbey Terrace, Whitby,
North Yorkshire, YO21 3HQ, England.
Email: gary.fry@virgin.net
www.grayfriarpress.com

Typesetting and design by Paul Finch and Gary Fry

ISBN: 978-1-906331-98-6

TABLE OF CONTENTS

STUKA JUICE
Terry Grimwood

1 *938 ...*
Tonight it started. You could feel it. Something that burned through the music like electricity. All your doubts about the bargain were gone now. The moment you closed the deal and the amulet was pressed into your palm by that coloured blues singer, Johnson, that was his name, you had felt it coming, like a storm building. The coloured was drunk, making all kinds of wild claims. No harm in trying though, even if you believed it to be the ramblings of a whisky-sodden fool, but you and your band were going nowhere, so what was there to lose? You gave him the bottle of Bushmills you had bought him and held out your hand, and at that moment, in that grimy back alley, in that hot and humid little Southern town, you heard it, the music, and you felt strong and knew what you had to do. Johnson had said he was giving it away because he was scared. There was, he said, a price; your soul, to be checked-in before your time was due. Well, to hell with your soul, because tonight the music was alive and hot and the world was going to be yours.

1: GOD

It was when the old man looked up, and Dietrich saw the fury and the fire in his eyes, that he recognised him and understood that he was in the presence of his god. The realisation sent him to his feet with such violence he knocked his chair backwards to the floor.

"Heil Hitler!" Dietrich snapped, arm extended.

"Sit," said the Fuhrer. "Major, please, sit."

Dietrich did as he was told, after first retrieving the overturned chair, an action that made him feel clumsy and foolish.

"Thank you Mein Fuhrer," he mumbled. *Mumbled!* He was a major in the Wehrmacht.

He had fought for the Fatherland since the invasion of Poland. He was a leader of men, had survived the apocalypse in Stalingrad, and suddenly, a mere table-width away from the deity he had worshipped for almost his entire life, he was as tongue-tied as a love-sick boy.

And what was that god, but a sick, tremulous old man? Dietrich could hear the Fuhrer's every breath, see every line etched into his face.

And he could feel his power.

A table-width. That was all.

The Fuhrer leaned forwards. "You are a hero Major Dietrich," he said. "An Iron Cross, yes?"

"At Kursk, Mein Fuhrer."

In Hell, Mein Fuhrer, a hell of flame and smoke and shattered flesh, of endless slaughter and ignominious, bloody defeat.

The Fuhrer closed the distance between them further still, his eyes bore into Dietrich, and when his face suddenly became animated with rage, it was if the walls of the Bunker were drawn in around him, suddenly transformed into a halo of concrete and shadow. "I was betrayed," the Fuhrer growled. "Generals they called themselves. Hah! Cowards, incompetents, all of them. They would not listen to me. *Me*, their Fuhrer! And when I am betrayed, my soldiers are betrayed. Is that not so, Major?"

"I do my duty Mein Fuhrer." A careful answer.

"I know." His hand came to rest on Dietrich' arm. *His* hand, the Fuhrer's hand. Dietrich could feel the man trembling. "How are the defences?"

"Strong Mein Fuhrer. The men are in good spirits."

The *old* men and young boys assigned to Dietrich on the eastern borders of Berlin *were* in good spirits. Afraid, but confident that they would hold the city against Stalin's peasant hordes. Dietrich had been relieved to be called away, here, to the Bunker. He had not relished witnessing the swift destruction of his rag-tag command.

"Good. Good," the Fuhrer said, and smiled for the first time since Dietrich had been in his presence. "Now, Major, you have a special duty to perform for the Fatherland."

Dietrich felt his strength drain away. He was exhausted, sick of war. He longed for the Americans and the British to break through and put an end to this nightmare. Treacherous thoughts, he knew, but he had seen what the Russians did to the conquered. And Germany *was* conquered. Only a fool would think otherwise.

"There is an artefact, lost, now found," the Fuhrer said. "You must fetch it."

"An artefact?"

"To be returned to its owner, who has promised his help, has promised victory."

"Forgive me, but I don't understand Mein Fuhrer," Dietrich said. Careful again.

2

"This war, this total war, is only the surface of an even greater struggle. Forces you can never imagine, wrestling for supremacy, armies that could crush an entire world if unleashed. And they will be, when we return this lost possession to its rightful owner." The old man's grip tightened. "I have seen this …this being, and I have seen his armies. The only advisers I can trust, they have shown me."

The rumours were true then; a cabal of charlatans who called themselves wizards or some such, whispering magical nonsense into the Fuhrer's ear.

"Your name will go down in history, Major, as the saviour of the Thousand Year Reich."

The Russians on the outskirts of Berlin, cities pounded to rubble day and night by Allied bombers, and he, Major Paul Dietrich, a soldier of immeasurable experience, survivor of an entire war, was to be sent on a fool's errand to fulfil the fantasies of his broken, deluded leader. He should refuse, he should drag this idiot out into the rubble and show him the truth –

"I will do my best, Mein Fuhrer."

"I know you will, Major, because you are a true German."

The Fuhrer smiled and spoke with such fatherly warmth that Dietrich's anger instantly dissolved and he almost wept with love and gratitude.

2: STUKA JUICE

There was darkness, made worse by the stunted beam of his waterproof torch, darkness that pressed into his eyes. Darkness that had debilitating, bone-crushing *weight*.

There was also cold, absolute, blood-freezing cold.

And there was loneliness, down here under these millions of tons of water. A loneliness so intense, he found himself believing that he was not alone at all.

She's here …

Stirling brought himself up short. This was the bloody English Channel, not the Pacific or the Atlantic. It was a ditch, a few miles of cold grey water.

Besides, Christine was up there, waiting for him on the *Fox* with the rest of the boat's crew. And he certainly wasn't adrift. Connected to his heavy, brass diving helmet and waving gracefully in the icy currents far above him were the pipes through which he breathed and had his being.

So, Stirling my boy, you have nothing to be afraid of. You've spent most of the war underwater; folded in half for hours-on-end in sweaty, stinking mini-subs, sneaking round the barnacle-encrusted keels of enemy shipping with Buster Crabbe, crawling out of the waves to recce the Normandy beaches on the eve of D-Day. Took it all in your stride, didn't you. So don't go getting the frighteners now, not when the bloody show is almost over.

He trudged on, Frankenstein boots sinking into the soft, sandy seabed. The cold seeped through the heavy canvas suit and into his flesh. Into his nerves, his thoughts, his soul.

Traitor ... she knows ... did you really think she wouldn't find out? Do you think she's going to forgive you? Unfaithful, murderous bastard ... All she has to do is snip that pipe ... cut the cord ...

It's the Stuka Juice. It's not the truth. Stirling repeated it over and over, made it his prayer. Breathe enough of it and it sent you mad. They warned him when he volunteered for this. Hold your nerve, they said. Keep your thinking straight, laddie.

But you did betray her, Christine, your wife ... while she was in France, playing the hero ... Do you know what the Gestapo would have done to her if they caught her? You can guess, can't you? You can see it, here in the dark ... Weren't thinking about that though, were you, laddie? You'd found yourself a bitch in heat and you were sniffing at her like a mad dog ...

Sixty metres. Bloody deep, and he needed to go a lot deeper. So breathe it in, breathe in the old Stuka Juice, that magic mix of helium and oxygen. It was the only way to survive at this depth. They *had* to get it right. Before the Yanks did, before the Germans. So he had to stay down here until the test was over. He had drop into this icy black hell over and over again until they got the mixture right and the monsters stayed under the bed.

Who is the monster, laddie? ... She knows what you did that night ... she's going to leave you down here, alone, with the ...

He could feel them now, moving towards him. Slithering through the thick, thick water, coming out of the darkness. Hungry. Whispering. He jabbed the weak torch light about him, punching its beam into the darkness, seeing them flit aside, hiding.

She's bloody angry ... and she has a knife, laddie ... she will *do it ... you'll breathe in and there'll be nothing but cold water ... and the dark and the loneliness and* them ...

There! And there. Circling him, human faces, featureless black eyes, rotten white skin. And she was going to leave you here. The slut was going to abandon him to those things.

But why shouldn't she?

Get me out of here! He yanked at the lifeline.

4

To hell with you, Christine screamed back. You can rot down there forever you bastard …

"Get me out of here, please, please …"

3: CHRISTINE AND HELEN

He lay on the deck, stripped of the cumbersome suit and helmet, wrapped in a blanket and shivering. Faces looked down at him. Then Christine came into focus.

"To hell with you," she whispered. "Next time I'll leave you to rot down there forever you bastard."

"No." He felt like crying, like a baby. "Please Christine, don't do that."

"Do what my darling? What's wrong?" She looked at the others. "This is the worst he's been. How many more times does he have to do this?"

"We have our orders, Ma'am –"

"But look what it's doing to him."

"Sir, are you all right?" Harper now, the *Fox's* skipper. Big man, beard, gruff.

"Yes, yes, it's wearing off." Stirling struggled to sit up. Christine crouched beside him, hand on his shoulder. "Bit of a bad show, that one," he said to her. "Seeing things, hearing voices."

"Do you think you'll be able to go down again tomorrow?" This was Walpole. The boffin. In charge of mixing the Stuka Juice, trying to get it right. He was skinny, pale and out of place on the *Fox,* which was a fishing boat, a rough-and-ready vessel at the best of times. The crew were no fishermen though. Royal Navy, in mufti, half a dozen of them, hand-picked for the job.

Stirling felt Christine's hand tighten on his shoulder, but he still said "Yes, of course I will."

*

"Why?" She wasn't angry exactly, but the question was like a whiplash. Stirling had known it was coming.

"You know why," he answered. "You of all people."

They were below decks, in the cramped space laughingly called their cabin.

"Yes, me of all people. But you can stop this, at any time. What I did, what you did back then, neither of us had a choice."

"You volunteered."

"I was asked. Do you seriously think I could have said no?"

5

"I can't say no to this Christine."

"You can and you must. The war's almost over, you could be tucked up safe behind a desk. You've done your bit, Jim. You've done everything that was asked of you."

Christine sat on the bunk, a slight, dark-haired woman. She looked deceptively delicate, fragile, the effect heightened by the heavy Navy-issue pullover she wore. She was the only person Stirling was afraid of, and the only person he trusted with his heart.

Christine's mother was French, her father English. She had spent her childhood in Brittany until the early death of her mother drove father and daughter home to London. When war broke out, Christine joined the Royal Navy as a WREN. It didn't take long for the SOE to find her. A year later, Christine was parachuted into a night-dark French meadow. She came back, whole and hearty, or so it seemed. When she slept, though, the memories clawed their way to the surface and into her dreams. Her midnight cries still woke Stirling and he would hold her tight until the terrors went away.

She agreed to go again.

Somewhere between those two operations, she met Lieutenant-Commander James Stirling. They had married quickly and quietly. If you wanted something in these times, you had to take it. There would probably never be a second chance.

"I'm sorry," Christine said. "A tiff is the last thing we need right now. It's just that … I'm afraid of losing you. I always have been. Even when I was in France, with other … things to think about."

"It's alright," Stirling said and pulled her to himself. "Look, the whole thing really is a piece of cake. It's like going to see one of those ridiculous Bela Lugosi films, only it seems as if it's real. But if you keep telling yourself that it's all nonsense, well you can get through it."

"I'm hardly in a position to interfere am I?" Christine said. "I shouldn't even be here."

She was along as an 'Observer', strings pulled, favours called in.

"Darling, one more try and then no more, I promise," Stirling said.

He flopped onto the bunk behind her. She turned and stroked his hair.

"I love you," she whispered.

"And I love you."

*

He always had, from the moment he saw her.

6

So how could he have been in love with Helen Howard as well?

He had been at a US Eighth Airforce base in East Anglia that day, invited in to lecture aircrew on survival after ditching in the sea. The Bomb Group had completed their first one hundred missions the day before and, to celebrate, the Glenn Miller band were booked for that evening.

You wanna come, lootenant? Sure it's okay. Don't need no tickets for this one. Hey, you'll feel right at home. We invited a bunch of local girls, all in the interest of co-operation with our British allies, you understand.

Helen was a 'local girl'. She was pretty, knowing, fun. No harm in a dance. God, Christine was probably holed up with some charmer from the French Resistance at that very moment. So it was only fair.

Wasn't it?

The music was loud and exciting. They danced, drank too much, and danced again. They both missed their respective lovers. They were both lonely.

It was wartime.

*

Stirling woke, suddenly, confused. There was shouting, thuds, footsteps, then the bark of weapons, a scream.

"What is it Jim? What's happening?" Christine mumbled

There was a rattle of automatic fire. Another shriek of pain. More gunfire.

"Schmeisser," she whispered. "Bloody Jerries ..."

Stirling rolled off the bed, thankful they had gone to sleep fully clothed, scrambling for his kit bag and the revolver he kept hidden there. Christine was up as well, now crouched at the foot of the cabin's short ladder, unarmed. Stirling moved across to join her. Still a little befuddled by sleep, he climbed the ladder to the door itself.

"Ready?" he said. Christine nodded, directly behind him.

He opened the door, carefully. The night dark was a confusion of movement, muzzle flashes. Stirling saw another vessel drawn up alongside; fishing boat, like the *Fox*. Then he saw a body, another, a third, sprawled on the *Fox's* small deck.

A figure rushed out of the dark, sub-machine gun in hand. Stirling fired. The figure grunted and fell backwards. Before he could stop her, Christine scrambled past Stirling, to crouch by the body, scrabbling for the weapon.

7

And was suddenly bathed in white. Searchlight, on the other boat.

Stirling saw her freeze, saw three men move in, weapons aimed at her head. Two he didn't recognise, the other was Walpole.

"Throw down your weapon, Stirling," the taller of the two strangers said. His English was only slightly accented. "I won't hesitate to shoot her."

4: SOLDIERS

Sometime later, in the small hours, two members of the German boarding party hauled Stirling up from below decks. His arms and legs ached from being trussed-up with his wife in their cabin. Christine was still down there.

Stirling was shoved into the tiny chartroom behind the wheelhouse. The boarding party's commander was seated at the table. Stirling was forced down onto a chair opposite. The men were dismissed.

The officer was thin, almost gaunt, his dark hair streaked with premature grey. Like his men, the German was out of uniform, dressed as a merchant seaman. He regarded Stirling with deep-set, blue-grey eyes.

"You dive at first light," the German said.

"Where are the crew?"

"They were enemy soldiers and we are at war."

"You haven't answered my question."

"They were given as decent a sea burial as is possible out here, Stirling."

Dumped over the side then.

"We are not barbarians."

"That's a matter of opinion."

The German sighed, then repeated "You dive at first light."

"No I don't."

"You must. Otherwise ... Well, your wife is on board, need I say more?" Matter-of-fact, no sadistic pleasure, just weariness at the prospect.

Stirling sighed. He had known that there would be a threat to Christine and that, in the end, he would have to do something like this. Why else would the German boarding party have kept him alive if not to go down into the water for them?

Into the cold dark. Christ, down there, *breathing that bloody nightmare juice. He couldn't ...*

"Look, what do you really need me for?" he said. "The new gas mixture is on the boat, for the taking. The boffin, Walpole, he's

8

yours anyway. All you've got to do is haul the tanks aboard your ship and it's done. Bit of bad news though, the stuff doesn't work."

"I know nothing about the gas mixture. That is Walpole's responsibility."

"Bloody traitor."

"Is he? He is being true to his beliefs. After all, he did march with Oswald Mosely."

"He'll hang when this is over."

The German shrugged. "None of my concern. Or yours. You simply have to dive and retrieve an artefact." The German lit a cigarette. "From the wreck of an aircraft, to be precise."

"Secret weapon is it?" Stirling sighed. "I need a smoke."

The German held out the pack.

"Can't you untie Christine? There's nowhere for either of us to run." Stirling's hands and ankles still ached from returning circulation. He noticed that the skin of his wrists was bruised and rope burned.

"She stays where she is." The German regarded him for a moment. "Why bring your wife out here? The war isn't over. The sea is still a dangerous place."

Stirling didn't answer, but drew deep on his cigarette and concentrated on working out how he could get them out of this fix. So far there were no ideas forthcoming.

"The wreck should be directly below us," the German said. "It is a small aircraft, a Curtis Norseman, which crashed last December on its way to France. There was a passenger, an American bandleader named Glenn Miller, you have heard of him?"

Glenn Miller? Glenn Bloody Miller?

Heard of him? Was this some sort of divine joke, God paying him out for what he did that night?

Like a dog sniffing at a bitch on heat.

But that wasn't the worst of it, was it …

"I thought no one knew what happened to his plane."

The German ignored the comment. "Miller came by the artefact, many years ago. He was struggling, going nowhere as they say. He met someone, struck a bargain. His soul in exchange for fame and fortune. The bargain was sealed with an object. An amulet. That is what you must retrieve for us."

Stirling took another deep drag. He stared at the German. "You don't really believe that rot, surely."

"What you or I believe is not important." The German looked directly at him and Stirling saw the depth of his weariness and realised that it must mirror his own. "I promise that both of you will be released if you bring the artefact back from the wreck."

9

"Why should I believe you?"

"You have my word, soldier to soldier."

*

"I assumed you would like tea. You're British, the British like tea." Dietrich offered the mug. Christine turned her head away.

"Untie me and I'll drink it."

"I'm sorry, I cannot. Not until your husband has completed his task."

Christine sighed and strained forward to sip at the drink. She was lying on her side on the bunk, hands behind and bound, in turn, to her ankles, legs bent double. "My last meal?" she said.

Yes, it is. You were a spy, and, as such, condemned to death. The Fuhrer's orders.

"Not if your husband is successful."

She spat out a cynical laugh, which was surprisingly painful to him. Why should he care about the opinion of an enemy?

Because there had been another woman, just like this one. You shot her in the back of the head as she knelt by the grave she and her fellow partisans had been forced to dig. You pulled the Luger's trigger and the bullet smashed a hole in the back of her skull and tore open her face. She was still alive and screaming when she pitched forward into the trench.

He was feeling pity, for *partisans*?

Then there were the villages selected for reprisal. The men and boys shot out of hand. The women thrown to your men as a reward for their dogged heroism. Mothers, sisters, wives, daughters, screaming as their houses burned and their humanity was ripped away –

Dietrich stood, abruptly. He was breathing hard, drenched in sweat.

"I give you my word," he growled. "As a soldier."

5: THE DARK

Stirling slammed boots-first into the sea, and the old panic tore at him like a thousand knives. The water closed over his helmet; there was grey, bubble-fogged gloom.

Then came the cold.

It seeped through the thick canvas suit to wrap itself about his flesh and mine its way down into his bones. He gasped for breath, afraid, panicked, fought to claw back up towards the surface. But he was falling into the dark.

He could not stop falling –

He flicked on the torch and its beam sliced into the murk. He aimed it downwards and it was worse. Nothing for an eternity, until at last he glimpsed a dim-lit circle of seabed.

He landed, softly but firmly, his boots kicking up an explosion of silt that billowed through the torch beam and surrounded him like gritty fog. He panted for breath and was already fighting the urge to remove his helmet.

Stirling relaxed a little, tasted rubber-tainted Stuka Juice. He was alive. He could breathe.

Because the enemy *were keeping him alive, the bloody Germans, cranking the pump and squirting gas into his lungs.*

Which way to walk?

The ocean bed was a vast, empty wilderness. The chances of finding the wreck were remote. He would walk in a leftward spiral, slowly working outwards. Carefully, because disorientation came quickly down here. But he had to try –

Christine, dirty, bruised, clutching her sten-gun, face white.

Down here, pounding through the water, closer, closer.

He twisted round, the movement slow and cumbersome.

And there was empty blackness.

But she is down here, laddie, plenty of places to hide out there in the dark …

Who was down here? He struggled to remember, thought made difficult by the music racketing through his skull. Bloody Glenn Miller. It was giving him a headache He grabbed at his helmet.

No … Stop you bloody fool … STOP!

He let go. The darkness swirled in. He calmed. Lifted the torch and resumed his walk.

He could still hear Glenn and the boys. *Chattanooga Choo-Choo.*

Distant, close, waxing and waning. They'd danced to that, hadn't they, Jim and Helen, the dog and the bitch-on-heat. They'd danced, then rutted and suddenly Stirling was plunged into a desperate, breathless affair. Ravaged by guilt, consumed by his need to be with this woman until he wanted it to stop. He told her, in a cheap hotel in Brighton as the grey sea raged outside and cold November rain pounded the window.

She shouted and swore and tried to scratch his face. Then she cried and pleaded, went down on her knees. He turned away and walked out. A week later she was dead; wrists hacked open with a bread knife, the bed in her cottage, the one on which they had made love for the first time, sodden red with her blood.

*

There was light, wavering in the swirl of dark water. Light, where light shouldn't be. And the music, rolling through Stirling's head, big band, dance music yet hard to name, dissonant, discordant.

None of it was real. It was the Stuka Juice, it-was-not-real –

Stirling resumed his trudge, heading now towards the uncertain, shifting glow. He sensed, *felt*, others walk beside him. Yet when he looked round, there was only darkness. They were there all right, moving in closer with every step.

Who are they, laddie? What are they? Is she *among them? The* other *woman? Is she, eyes a-bulge, wrists all torn and bloody?*

Shapes began to form in the gloom. Christ, shapes, figures, people. Moving in time to the beat of the music. No longer dissolved by the stunted reach of the torch beam, yet at the same time insubstantial.

Faces erupted out of the black, excited, laughing, shouting, men and women. They rushed at him, then shattered into tornadoes of spiralling bubbles.

Turn back.

Now.

Yank on the life-line. Get out of here, scram and scarper. Save your sanity, laddie.

He stumbled on, making for the dancers, starting as more of them ran by, shrinking from their terrible faces. But it was the only way to keep Christine alive. So he trudged through the madness, until he saw what was in the light.

*

Dietrich paced, smoked, then went to the rail and looked out at the cloud-heavy morning sky. A few feet from where he stood, Walpole oversaw the men who operated the pump, their exertions keeping Stirling alive via the pipes trailed over the boat's side and into the choppy, foam-flecked water.

A black, rotten dread sat in Dietrich's belly. Was this moment of insanity really the salvation of the Thousand Year Reich? He barely believed that Stirling would even find the wreck down there, let alone locate the amulet in the dark and mud. Dietrich knew little about Glenn Miller, had been aware of his music – condemned as

12

degenerate by the Party – remembered something about the man's disappearance, but had cared little, if at all.

His briefing had been detailed, much of it given by one of those charlatans he had come to despise once he discovered that they were real. The man had worn the uniform of the SS, though Dietrich doubted he had ever held a rifle, let alone seen action. He was intense, fervent, and Dietrich had wanted to break his nose. "The amulet was stolen centuries ago," the man declared. "Bought and sold by the unscrupulous, its energies abused for personal gain. But now it is within reach and can be brought home to its rightful owner. The rewards for the Fatherland will be uncountable." The man opened a map on the table, general co-ordinates, taken from the report given by the fighter pilot who claimed to have downed Miller's aircraft. And, more precisely from the magician's own "inner searching and questioning". His long finger stabbed down onto the chart.

"Here," he said. "This is where you will find it."

Dietrich threw the last of his cigarette outwards over the water. It trailed a brief stream of red sparks then vanished. Like us, Dietrich mused. Like all my old comrades. So few of them left now.

Stirling and his wife would join them soon, a bullet in each of their skulls. The thought of it sickened him, odd since he had killed so many over the last five years. Why trouble his conscience over two more?

Dietrich pushed himself back from the rail and lit another cigarette.

It had to be done.

Duty, he told himself. And expedience.

And the saving of his own neck.

6: IN THE MOOD

It was an aircraft, silhouetted against the glare. Whole and undamaged by the look of it, sitting on the sea bed as if brought in for a perfect landing.

The music was loud here because of the band arranged around the aircraft. The musicians could be glimpsed between the dancers. All were indistinct in the wild mix of ocean dark and blazing light, but Stirling could see that the men were in US Airforce uniform, and the women in dresses that swirled in the water as they moved and settled slowly when they were still. The dancers' polished boots and high heels billowed the silt around their legs and then upwards to hang over the scene like the fug of cigarette smoke.

13

Stirling came to a halt at the edge of the dance floor. He had to get out of here, he should turn round and walk away. This was dangerous. This was so bloody bad. He fought for breath. He lifted his hand to wipe the sweat from his forehead but met brass and glass instead. The sweat trickled and itched. If he could just get this bloody helmet off –

Then a woman emerged from the dancers and stood about six feet from where Stirling waited. She smiled.

Helen. He had known she would be here –

No, not her. She was dead. He knew she was dead because ...

Because you killed her, laddie. Remember that, do you? Remember her face as you swung round and walked out of that hotel room? You knew what she was going to do. In your heart, you knew, and you still walked away.

I couldn't betray Christine any longer, don't you understand? I couldn't do that to her.

Of course you couldn't. You did what was best.

Helen's eyes were bright, lips red and slightly parted in that way that had driven him mad. Her skirt, and her hair, unpinned and loose, undulated in the water. She held out her delicate, white-gloved hand.

But it's all right. Dance with me.

Stirling's breath caught and he realised that he was crying. "I'm sorry ... I didn't mean ... I couldn't stop myself ..."

Dance with me, Jim, hold me close.

He reached out and felt her hand in his and followed her into the whirl of dancers. The music filled his head. He pulled Helen to himself and felt her close, despite the heavy suit, despite the helmet. They were together, crushed together. He saw the band now, their leader, conducting with one hand, trombone at the ready in the other. Light glinted from his glasses. Glenn Miller of course. Who else could it have been? The band roared on behind him. Stirling couldn't see their faces. He didn't want to, because there was something wrong with them, something too shadowed.

Then there was nothing but the music and the swirling crowds and Helen and they were dancing, dizzy, buffeted by other couples. Stirling could smell cigarettes, beer, perfume and sweat. The music roared and filled everything; *In The Mood*. Helen clung to him, hot and soft and sweet-scented.

The bandmaster's conducting grew wilder with each beat, until he resembled a jerking, frantic puppet. He turned to the audience.

Dead. His face was dead, eyes wide, mouth an open black hole.

Stirling saw the band then, human, yet not human, bestial, red-eyed, perversions torn from mediaeval images of Hell.

14

"Kiss me." Stirling felt Helen's breath on his face, inside the helmet, a butterfly wing dancing on his flesh. "Kiss me, please, kiss me …"

Despite his terror of the monstrous band, of the shadowed darkness hiding the dancers' faces, Stirling wanted her. He grabbed at the helmet clasps.

*

"I'm doing it now," Dietrich said.

"Sir?" Sergeant Baeker looked up from the pump.

"I'm dealing with the woman now."

And I don't have to explain myself to you, Sergeant.

"With respect sir, the Britisher won't co-operate if she's dead."

There was a look in Baeker's eye; he saw it in all of them. He'd known the handful of infantrymen he'd picked for this mission a long time. They were his men, yes, but they were also his friends. The three sailors who had been assigned to him were strangers but also war-hardened and reliable. A fine team.

But now he heard their muttering, whispers. Saw their unease.

Because something has happened down there, something has been disturbed –

Nonsense. He was a soldier, not some superstitious old peasant woman.

– which means that he's found it. Which means we can go back to Berlin and fight for what is left of the Reich. And if the Fuhrer's magicians are right …

"Your respect is noted, Sergeant. Your job is to keep the bastard alive, do you understand me?"

"Yes sir."

Dietrich crossed the deck. He paused outside the door to the tiny cabin where Christine was being held. He swallowed dryly and pulled the Luger from its holster under his coat. He had to do this now, before his nerve failed and it was too late. It would be simple, quick, painless.

A bullet punched into the back of her skull, her face ripped open by its exit. Still alive and screaming as they pitched her into the sea …

He opened the door.

No ...

Stirling pushed himself back. Helen stumbled, her hair and dress billowed. Her face twisted into shock, then hurt. She threw herself at him but Stirling shoved her aside and drove into the dancers.

Jim, don't. Listen to me, please listen, you mustn't ...

The dancers crowded in, spinning impossibly fast, bodies pressed together. Stirling battered his way through, each blow, each punch delivered with dreamlike slowness. He glimpsed their hell-horrible faces, felt teeth and claws tear at his suit and beat at his helmet.

Then he was through, hauling himself along the fuselage of the aircraft, until he found the door. He leaned in and saw what looked like a pile of sticks. Bones, picked clean. A pair of glasses. And there, a chain, a pendant, caked with silt.

Jim, please. Helen, her arms about him, cheek against his back. *Don't –*

His hand closed around the pendant. The music stopped, the light went out and he was alone. But that didn't matter, because he was filled with a joy so intense it ripped a howl of ecstasy from his throat. He saw a glorious, vast, unstoppable army, and glowing, golden hosts singing songs that pierced deep into his soul. He felt strength flow into him, the strength and the will to fulfil any desire, to bring any dream to fruition, and understood what it had given to Miller and a thousand others before him.

He reached up and grabbed the lifeline. One tug and his feet would lift from the seabed and he would be on his slow journey back to the surface, out of the dark and the cold.

*

Dietrich stepped into the cabin. Christine had turned herself over so that she had her back to him. He saw her cramped, bent-double legs, her hands, purple from loss of circulation, and grazed from what looked like determined efforts to free herself.

"Do I get a last cigarette?" she said.

Dietrich couldn't find an answer.

"At least let me stand up and face you. I don't want to die like this."

"It makes no difference," Dietrich said and moved to the bed.

She grunted, and twisted over onto her back. "Yes it does. It makes a great deal of difference."

16

Dietrich brought the weapon up. Christine watched him, unflinching, even when he placed the muzzle against her temple. Her eyes never left his. Dietrich wetted his cracked, dry lips. He blinked away a trickle of sweat from his eyes.

"Do it," Christine whispered through gritted teeth. "For God's sake get it over with."

His finger tightened, he felt the trigger give under the pressure –

*

The amulet pulsed in Stirling's hand. He could feel its energies, its power. He could feel what it might do.

And that couldn't be.

Even for Christine's life – which was lost anyway. He had never believed the German's promises.

Christ, Christine ...

"I sorry my darling," he wept. "I'm so sorry, for all of it ..."

Stirling turned away from the scattered, rotten remains of the aircraft and opened his fist to let the amulet drop slowly into the darkness. The band immediately struck up and all was light and music once more. Stirling let the dancers whirl around and imprison him. He waited for Helen to step out of their ranks; hair and dress a-swirl in the currents, arms out, red, red lips apart, awaiting his kiss.

The moment she did so, Stirling began to unclasp the big brass helmet.

*

Can you hear them? Women thrown to your men as a reward for their dogged heroism. Screaming as their houses burn and their humanity is ripped away –

Now. He must do it now. He could hear Christine's laboured breath, hissing through her clenched teeth, could feel her shaking, waiting for that final, explosive fragment of pain.

Can you hear them? Can you? All of them? Men, women, children, soldiers and civilians, clawing their way into your soul, daubing it with the blood you shed from them. Can you hear their rage –

Dietrich relaxed his grip on the Luger's trigger and slumped back to kneel on the wooden floor. He heard Christine's gasp of shock; half sob, half laughter.

A moment later, someone pummelled at the door, shouting. "Sir! Sir! The Britisher has gone. We have lost him!"

17

*

"Why didn't you shoot me?" Christine asked him. She and Dietrich were in the wheel house, watching as the last of the German's party boarded their own boat. She hadn't cried. Dietrich could see her grief clearly, but knew she wouldn't weep for her husband until long after they had gone and she was steering the *Fox* back towards England.

"A change of orders from Berlin," Dietrich said.

A doomed city. There would be no demonic armies to save her now, only exhausted soldiers, their ranks swelled with young boys and old men.

And nothing to save you *when the Fuhrer hears of your failure.*

"You're lying," she said.

Dietrich shrugged and made to go.

"Major."

He stopped, halfway down the steps to the deck. "Yes?"

"You do know that if it had been you lying there, I would have pulled the trigger?"

He looked back up at her. "I would have expected no less."

SHIP OF THE DEAD

Numerous so-called 'ghost ships' trawl the oceans of the world. At the last estimation, at least 30 crewless wrecks were known to be afloat on the high seas, in some cases under observation by concerned coastal authorities, in others out of sight and out of mind, only glimpsed occasionally during their endless, purposeless circumnavigation of the globe.

There are countless mundane reasons why so many vessels reach this strange, ignominious fate. For example, the 230-foot freighter SS Baychimo patrolled the Arctic Ocean unmanned throughout the 1940s, '50s and '60s (and maybe still does today), but only because its crew abandoned it in 1931 when it briefly became stuck in pack-ice. Likewise, the former Russian cruise liner Lyubov Orlova crossed the Atlantic in 2014 occupied only by cannibal rats after sitting rusting in a Canadian shipyard for two years and finally slipping loose from the tug transporting it to the breakers. But there are still the oddballs and curios, the once-happy ships reduced to derelicts by circumstances so shrouded in mystery that their drifting skeletons would become long-lasting bywords for oceanic horror, even though viable explanations might have emerged in the meantime.

The 100-foot British brigandine Mary Celeste caused so much sensation in 1872, when it was discovered under sail near the Straits of Gibraltar with its cargo completely intact but no sign of any crew or passengers, that even a very plausible theory – namely that everyone had abandoned ship for fear of volatile substances in the hold and had then drowned when the lifeboats foundered – failed to dim its appeal. Even today, it remains the big daddy of all maritime spook stories. Likewise, when what appeared to be an unregistered 'old world' schooner, Bel Amica, was spotted in 2006 floating down the Sardinian coast with no-one on board, the initial perception that it was an antique vessel adrift for over a century was disproved when it was discovered to be a modern yacht probably unregistered for tax evasion purposes, but worldwide interest persisted for years afterwards anyway.

However, then we have the perplexing case of the Ourang Medan, a Dutch-owned tramp steamer, which still sits at the centre of our scariest 'true' tale of oceanic mystery.

The outside world first knew the Ourang Medan had run into trouble in Indonesian waters when in June 1947 it sent out the following distress call: "All officers including captain are dead lying in chartroom and bridge. Possibly whole crew dead." Shortly afterwards, a final message was sent. Horrifyingly, it read: "I die."

Rescue parties from two American craft, the Silver Star and the City of Baltimore, were shortly despatched, and when they boarded the Ourang Medan found a truly macabre scene. All the crew were present, including a dog, but all were indeed dead, lying on their backs and twisted in cartoonish agony, eyes glazed as they stared at the sun, arms outstretched. Some were allegedly pointing, but at what there was no clue. More baffling, there was no sign of violence on any of the bodies or any trace of a struggle on board.

No explanation was offered until 1948, when an article appeared in the Dutch-Indonesian press claiming that a missionary had discovered a survivor living on Toangi atoll in the Marshall Islands. The man, an unnamed German, was reputedly very ill and only lived long enough to tell the missionary that his crew had been carrying an illicit cargo of sulphuric acid from China to Costa Rica, but that escaping fumes had poisoned everyone on board. He only escaped himself because he dived into the sea. While the Ourang Medan did later explode with unusual force, this story is still questioned. Modern writers have never been able to trace the missionary, while on first messaging for help, the Ourang Medan was 400 nautical miles southeast of the Marshall Islands, an impossible distance for any human being to swim or even be pushed in tidal currents and still survive, especially given that these are shark-infested waters. Moreover, experts have expressed doubt that any leakage of toxic gases, such as carbon monoxide or even World War Two nerve agents, could have acted so quickly that only one man, or no men, might escape alive (especially as someone still had time to send out mayday calls).

If one discounts the paranormal, which is increasingly difficult, the only other possible explanation is that the whole tale is a hoax. Researchers have failed to locate entries for the Ourang Medan in the Lloyds Shipping Register or in any existing registration documents held by Dutch authorities, though both those anomalies might be explained by the boat's apparent illegal status – it could simply have been renamed when it embarked on smuggling operations. And it isn't as if there is no actual evidence for these events. The full incident, almost exactly as reported here, is logged in the May 1952 issue of the 'Proceedings of the Merchant Marine Council', which was published by the United States Coast Guard.

It isn't just the Fortean crowd who regard the bizarre fate of the SS Ourang Medan as the greatest and perhaps most troubling mystery of the ocean.

THE END OF THE PIER
Stephen Laws

"You thought I got these burns in the war?" asked my Grandad. "And the limp? But I never said that, did I? No – I got these when Brinkburn Pier burned down in 1931."

These were the first words he said when I switched on the tape recorder. It was a Philips 4-track reel-to-reel with a hand-held microphone.

It was 1969 and I was fourteen years old. Grandad was very old by then and living in a retirement home. He'd always been a distant figure, not particularly close and I sensed that there had been some kind of family difficulty that had led to an estrangement between him and his son – my Dad, that is. Nothing hostile, just that 'distance'. Dad never talked about it. Mum didn't know – and I'd never known my Grandma, who had died some years before I was born, so I never got a chance to ask her.

But when my school class had been told to write a family history project of some kind, my own immediate family history was so boring that the only person I could think of was Grandad, who had fought in the First World War and must have had some kind of traumatic encounter that had led to his limp and the burns on his shoulder and back that I'd seen once when he was changing his shirt.

Except that now, of course, he was telling me that he hadn't got those burns in the Great War. He'd got them as a result of some pier burning down.

"You really want to hear what happened?" he asked. "I've never told anybody about it before. I couldn't. Because what happened was so…" Then he broke off, shaking his head, before continuing: "And I did a terrible thing. A *terrible* thing."

He stopped, and looked at me hard with those flinty-green eyes.

"So do you want to hear what happened?"

Did I? "Yeah!"

"It's true."

"Well yeah, Grandad. If you say it's true and it happened. Then it's got to be true."

He kept on looking at me as if still making up his mind and when his eyes glazed over, I thought he was going to fade off into one of his 'sleeps' again. But no, his gaze focused again, and he told me what happened on Friday 13th July 1931 to Brinkburn Pier, Raby-on-Sea.

He told me the whole thing, beginning to end, and later – when I listened to the tape again – I decided to transcribe it, word for word. No editing, no chopping and changing around; just the exact words that my Grandad used – except for one thing. I took out the 'F' word when he used it and put it something less 'F' instead. What I always liked about Grandad was that he talked like 'one of the blokes' but he also had a really vivid way of describing things. I was told once that he'd written some stuff, but I never saw or read it – so what you have in this account is that strange 'mixture' of the everyday and the vivid. When I submitted the transcript to my English teacher, it came back with a three out of ten mark and a red pen comment: *"You were asked to undertake an oral family project based on real life. Not create a written horror fiction."*

I was thoroughly pissed off and didn't know what I was going to tell Grandad if he asked me how it had been received. Sadly, perhaps fortunately, I didn't have to; because a week after I'd got it back and paced my bedroom floor wondering what to say – he died in his sleep.

He told me that he'd told no one about the end of Brinkburn Pier, not even his own wife and son, so I kept that transcript to myself. I realize now after all these years that I somehow felt that the low mark and the comment must have mysteriously finished the old guy off, even though he knew nothing about it. The manuscript went into an old box of childhood things under the bed. I moved on, got married, had kids, my parents died.

And then I came across the box again, the old reel-to-reel spools – and the manuscript.

What the hell? I thought.

So here it is – my Grandad's account; this time with the 'F' words reinstated.

Make of it what you will.

*

Your Grandma Ruby lived with her parents, Joe and Eileen, in a boarding house on Carson Street in Raby-on-Sea. I say 'lived there' – what I mean is that Eileen ran the boarding house; had been running it when she met Joe. They got married, ran it together and your Grandma Ruby was born there. It wasn't just an ordinary boarding house, though. It was one of those places that 'specialized'. There were two proper theatres in town back then and a little concert theatre at the end of the pier. I can't remember the names of the first two, but the one on the pier was called the 'Tivoli'. And the 'turns', the actors, the musicians, the dancers, the acrobats – all that lot who were in touring productions, plays or shows that arrived at Raby-on-Sea – they used to stay at their boarding house. It was the same all over the country; certain small hotels and boarding houses would get a reputation for being 'accommodating' to the entertainment trade, word would spread and that would be where the bookings were made in advance. Nice, clean, cheap, good grub – and Eileen's Place was a place with just such a reputation; perhaps able to put up with eccentric behaviour better than most.

I'd originally met Ruby when I was on leave during the First World War, and she wrote me letters. But she ended up marrying someone else, which just about bust my heart – so I moved away. Then years later, when I heard that the marriage hadn't worked out, her husband had done a bunk and she'd moved back in with her Mum and Dad, I deliberately moved back to Raby-on-Sea, got myself a job. There'd never been anyone for me but Ruby, so we started to see each other again and – well, you know how it goes.

Anyway, lots of stuff I could tell you, but that's not part of what happened at the end of the pier. So – me and Ruby were going steady and I was drumming up the nerve to ask her to marry me, when something happened at the boarding house that caused a ruckus. There was a bloke staying there, a comedian called Ronnie Pye – a biggish name back then in the music halls and theatres. He had these catchphrases: "Just what you need, a nice piece of Pye," and "Here's Pye in your Eye." People thought he was hilarious back then. Don't know why. I didn't think he was funny. He was top turn at a variety show that was then at the Tivoli. Singers, dancers, music – and him top of the bill telling his rotten jokes. He'd been in this awful British film back then, so he really thought he was Jack the Lad. Anyway, I got back from work (Did I tell you I'd landed myself a job at a greengrocers back then? Yeah, a greengrocers it was) and Ruby was in floods of tears in the back room. Turns out, this Ronnie Pye had… well, he'd put his hands on my Ruby, so to speak. Tried to kiss her and stuff. Just as he was getting ready to go do the matinee at the Tivoli. She'd told him no, he'd got heavy-handed and… well, there was a right to-do. Ruby wouldn't tell her Mum and Dad what the matter was, so they didn't know what the hell was going on. But she told me. And when I told her what *I* was going to do, she begged me not to; but wrong is wrong and right is right. So I got myself off down the High Street and headed for the pier. Believe me, son – my dander was well and truly *up!*

It was a beautiful thing back then, the pier, with a bandstand and little (what you call them?) kiosks all along the walkway either side, selling trinkets and seafood and those Test Your Strength machines, and daft cardboard cut outs where you could stick your head through and get a photograph taken. Fortune tellers, a little tea room place – and then, right at the far end of the pier, the Tivoli Theatre. Quite big – well, biggish – beautiful old Victorian building with seats for maybe a couple of hundred or so. But I wasn't in the mood to admire it that day. All I could think about as I marched down that walkway was the walks me and Ruby had done while we were courting on sunny days (and rainy days!) with her eating a toffee apple or candy floss and laughing, and then thinking about years back, with me in a Godforsaken trench in France with all Hell being let loose and never thinking I'd get out of it alive or seeing her again – and that bugger Ronnie Pye with his hands on her.

By then, it was about half an hour or so before the show was due to begin, so people were still making their way in through the big old double doors at the theatre's entrance. But that wasn't where I was headed. Instead, I swerved off to the right hand side of the building and the walkway and rail there that led to where I knew that big headed bastard was going to be. He'd bragged about it often enough when he was having his breakfast or dinner at the boarding house, holding court over the other guests. Just before and after each of his performances, he would make an appearance at the Tivoli's stage door to sign autographs for 'adoring fans' who, in his own words, "Couldn't get enough Pye".

And sure enough, just up ahead were half a dozen or so deluded idiots hanging around under the 'Stage Door' sign – and when that door opened, I'd be cutting off a slice of that Pye for myself. Below the wooden struts of the walkway, I could see dark, choppy water and there was a cool wind coming in off the sea now as I strode on, grabbing angrily at the handrail with every rigid step that I took.

I seemed to have timed everything perfectly.

Because now, the stage door was opening and a couple of teenage girls with autograph books at the ready began to twitter nervously.

I could hear voices from inside the theatre, but couldn't make anything out because a bunch of seagulls began squawking just then. I remember thinking: *I'm going to make that bugger squawk, alright!*

And suddenly there he was, stepping out through the stage door into this 'crowd' of six stupid fans with his arms held wide like there was six hundred there, all clamouring for his autograph.

I haven't described him yet, have I? I think I've been putting it off. Well, you couldn't quite tell how old he was, but older than he made out I reckon; certainly older than Ruby's Dad, Joe. I always thought he had this wide, squat face – like a Toby Jug, right down to his big jug-handle ears. With his pancake stage makeup on, and his eyebrows and lips done up really red like a tart, it made his mouth look even wider than it was. Just too wide, as I say – like a bloody frog. And with these beady, glittering, *greedy* eyes. Greedy for the *attention*, like – and for anything he could get. I bet those eyes looked just as greedy and glittery when he tried to put his hands all over my Ruby. He was wearing this big checked black-and-white jacket, baggy trousers and a little homburg hat that was deliberately too small ('To get the laughs, see?' I remember him saying). It was pinned to a shiny black, patent wig that looked like it was painted onto what I knew was a semi-bald head, which also made him look not only like a Toby Jug but also like one of those ventriloquist's dolls. Remember the kind? Used to sit on the bloke's knee, with a swivel head and a clack-clack-clack mouth.

I pushed past these two girls who were still twittering around him and elbowed this little lad who was desperate to shove his autograph book under Ronnie Pye's nose out of the way, just as he was signing a piece of paper for this old bird in a big pink dress. "Hey mister!" squawked the kid, sounding like one of the overhead seagulls. "Watch who you're pushing!"

And Ronnie Pye looked up, just as I reached him and said: "Remember me?"

It was all there, in that one brief moment.

I saw that glittering, greedy humour vanish out of his eyes.

Because he knew who I was, since he'd seen me at the boarding house often enough and he knew that Ruby and me were stepping out with each other. I saw that look in his eyes turn to fear when he realized what I'd come to do.

That's when I made my big mistake.

I'd seen that look before. In France, in the trenches. I'd seen it on the face of my pals as we crouched there, and the shells were coming over. I'd seen it in the eyes of boys even younger than me, crying like the youngsters they were when the whistle blew and we all had to go over the top. I'd seen it in the cracked glass of my own pocket mirror on the rare occasions when I tried to shave and wondered whether I should use that blunted razor for another purpose. And I saw it in the eyes of that German soldier, that poor young kid no older than me when I took the bayonet and…

So, instead of taking Ronnie Pye by the collar and smashing his nose with my fist, I hesitated.

And he blundered back, arms wide, mouth open. The two twittering girls screamed, the kid got tangled in my legs and the lady in the pink dress was right between us, arms in the air.

But I was not letting this moment go for Ruby.

I lunged forwards.

Ronnie Pye had teeter-tottered a further few steps back past the stage door and into the building, but I somehow managed to get past the pink lady and got my hand on his jacket lapel. He dragged me back with him as he retreated, slapping at my hand with fingers that felt like cold putty. Still dragging me with him off-balance, I stumbled and tripped on the lip of the doorway and sprawled forward.

There was a long *ripppp* as his lapel came away in my hand. I hit the ground hard with a *whump* and it knocked all the breath out of me. The stage door slammed. Now I couldn't hear the sea, the seagulls or the autograph hunters I'd just scared the hell out of; only me now, in an enclosed space, gasping for breath and trying to get up on my hands and knees.

Which is when Ronnie Pye put the boot in.

I didn't see it coming, and I didn't hear or really feel the impact. But I knew that the bastard had kicked me in the head. I didn't even feel the pain. (Not yet, anyway). I just remember falling off my bike when I was twelve and hitting my head on the pavement – and it felt just like that.

There was a jumble of raised, angry voices and a lot of 'movement' that I couldn't make out. Then I heard Pye shout: "*Alfie! Get him up!*"

I was hauled up by both elbows and held, and when I looked – still gasping for breath – I saw two hulking blokes with squashed noses either side of me. The air in there was hot and stale and smelled of old tobacco smoke.

Pye was looking at where I had torn his lapel off.

It's like he couldn't believe it. Couldn't believe what I'd had the gall to do. He looked at my hand, still holding that torn lapel, and then grabbed at it. But I wasn't letting it go, even though my arms were being held by these two bruisers who looked like boxers wearing their best suits for a funeral. So when Pye grabbed at it, it tore again in my hand – and he couldn't believe *that* either. His stupid look of outrage and disbelief just got stupider, with his big open mouth and those glittering eyes, that white powdered face with his penciled black eyebrows and his red painted mouth.

"You…" I struggled to get the words out, but I *did* get them out, and Pye knew exactly what I meant when I said: "You fucking *clown!*"

"Hold him tight," snapped Pye. Those eyes were glittering with something else now as he angrily threw the shred of lapel to the floor. He stepped forward, and I knew what was coming. He spat on each hand, rubbed them together, then went to roll up the sleeves on his jacket. You know? The old fashioned way – to show that you mean business and that you're going to do a really good 'hands on' job? But he was wearing his baggy stand up comedian's jacket. The sleeves were too big and long for him (for comic effect), and when he rolled them up, they just kept falling down over his hands again.

I laughed in his face.

But there was no humour in my laughter. Just out and out derision for this miserable bastard and his need to have peoples' worship. And by God, he didn't like it. His lips were trembling, and his bunched fists were shaking when he stood right up to me, holding them up so that the sleeves fell to his elbows.

I just kept laughing.

I felt the first punch, but not any of the others.

I remember this roaring sound. First it sounded like the sea around the pier, the way me and Ruby would sometimes hear it when we went for a walk there on windy days. Then it somehow sounded like a big audience laughing. But then it sounded like artillery; like the sounds of a bombardment, with the horrible roar and *whump* of those shells going over and hitting muddy ground. And Good Christ, the shock of that brought me around, crying out – because in that moment I really did think that I was back in that trench again. When the pain hit me, I sobbed. Had my arms and legs been blown off? Was I lying there in the mud, dying? I could feel the cold wind, hear that roaring and God I was hurting all over. But the ground under me was hard and didn't feel like mud or soil, and when I opened my eyes I could see metal and the grain of wood. I rolled over and I could smell the sea.

Thank God, thank God...

I wasn't back in the trench. I was lying on the walkway outside the stage door of the Tivoli Theatre, behind the rubbish bins where I'd been dumped. It was darker now, and I'd no idea how long I'd been lying there. I pulled myself up, groaned at the multiple pains, propped myself against the theatre's outer wall and threw up.

I'd been given a pretty good duffing-up.

My nose was busted, I felt pretty sure that a rib had been cracked and my jaw ached like someone had tried to yank it off. Droplets of water fell on my face, but I wasn't sure whether it was a light rain or whether a wave had thrown spume up from the below the walkway. Whatever, it felt good enough for me to pull myself away from the wall. The stage door was firmly shut and the autograph hunters had gone. The kiosks on the pier had closed up and lights were gleaming from the landward side of town as dusk closed in. I steadied myself on the handrail, listened to the deep hush of the sea and then launched myself off the rail to head back along the walkway. My head swam, my ribs hurt and my nose felt like a big aching blob in the middle of my face. And there was a big explosion of laughter from inside the Tivoli. Ronnie Pye was obviously 'on' and the audience obviously loved him. But it felt as if they were laughing at *me*. Filled with pain and shame, the humiliation forced me on – and I staggered homewards back down the pier to the landward side, with late night stragglers and courting couples avoiding me like the plague and like the mad, drunk, stumbling man that I appeared to be.

*

Ruby and her Mum and Dad were in more of a to-do than I was when I turned up at the boarding house. Her Mum opened the door and made this sound that was more like a shout than a scream when she saw me hanging in the door frame, with blood all over my face.

Eileen's 'shout' brought her husband Joe running and when she said to him: "Quick! Get him inside before the guests see," rather than "Oh dear, what happened to you then?" I was a little bit put out. But frankly, I was in too much of a state to say anything other than to ask for: "Ruby…?"

"Not before you're cleaned up lad!" exclaimed Joe; but again, I was in no state to complain.

They got me into the parlour, one of my arms around each of their shoulders and lugged me past the kitchen before any late night tea drinkers could see me, like they were lugging one of their bloody sides of beef that they got delivered every Wednesday. I tell you, though – those sides of beef were less bloody than me that night.

Halfway through cleaning me up, with a chunk of sirloin steak on the bridge of my broken nose (just to make me more like that side of beef), makeshift bandages made from old torn bed sheets around my midriff for my ribs, and yellow iodine tincture spotted all over me – Ruby walked in, yawning. Before that yawn could turn into a scream, Joe clapped a hand over her mouth so as not to wake the boarders. (See how practical my prospective in-laws could be?) When he let her go and she rose to hug me, I nearly woke them all up anyway, gritting my teeth to keep in a yell of agony. I'm sure Ruby broke another rib. Turns out she'd been worrying herself sick

28

all night and had fallen asleep exhausted. Of course, she'd never told her Mum and Dad what I was up to – but it all came out now.

So the rest of the night was full of *"Oh my poor darling,* "and *"My lovely boy"* and *"Well done, son"* and *"What's right is right"* – but I was filled with shame, because no one asked directly what had happened, just assumed that I'd done what had to be done and I couldn't find a way of telling them the truth. The more sympathetic they became, the more *loving* they became, the harder it was to tell them that I'd had the tar beaten out of me, rather than the other way around. And, of course, I could see something like hero-worship in Ruby's eyes, and you can imagine how *that* made me feel.

I refused a doctor. The more they fussed me, finally getting me to one of the spare rooms and tucking me into bed, the worse I felt. I had lodgings of my own back then, in a flat above the grocer's shop where I worked. They'd previously wanted me to move into the boarding house, but that didn't feel right, me going out with their daughter and that. I had to have – well, my own 'independence'. I didn't have the strength to argue that night, though; and I slept like a log.

I was woken next morning when Ruby, Joe and Eileen suddenly burst into my room. I woke with a start (and a groan or two), thinking: *Bloody hell! They've found out what really happened!* But when I saw the glowing smiles of pride on their faces, I knew that wasn't the case and wondered what the hell was coming next.

"He's moved out!" Eileen was the first to speak.

"Had someone come round to pack his bags for him and he's moved to other lodgings," beamed Joe.

"Never came back after last night's performance," added Ruby. Her face was really glowing. "Like Mum says, he sent someone round from the Tivoli to get his stuff."

"And good riddance," Eileen declared.

Joe nudged her out of the room. Pushing Ruby inside with me, and winking as he closed the door. "Given them some time together, Ma."

"He's got a week's lodging's left to pay," complained Eileen as she was pushed out.

I squirmed as Ruby came to my side.

"Aye," continued Joe. "Well it might be worth it to be shot of him. But come to it – we'll just send the lad here round to see him, eh?"

And all I could think was:
Oh, bloody hell...

*

29

One thing I'd learned after being demobbed from the army was how to heal, and the next two or three days didn't bother me too much from that physical point of view. I developed two black eyes around that busted nose of mine, and my rib throbbed but it was bearable. At least I hadn't been concussed. But that other stuff was *very* hard to handle. I mean, Ruby and her folks thinking I was a hero or something when I was anything but, and them continuing to fuss me.

I tell you, it was driving me crazy.

That – plus the fact that Ronnie Pye had got away with it – and that he was still somewhere around at another boarding house, most likely bragging about how he'd knocked the stuffing out of some upstart who'd got jealous over a star-struck girlfriend. The posters were still all over town, advertising *An Evening of Dance, Fun and Laughter starring Ronnie Pye* or *Tivoli End of the Pier Presents: Pye in Your Eye* or *Have a Slice of Pye*. The show was into its second and last week, with only two nights to go before the touring production packed up and moved to another small town theatre or pavilion somewhere further up (or down) the coast.

I couldn't take any more.

I had made up my mind.

On the day before the show's closing I made my way down to the end of the pier, following the same route I'd taken on the night I'd been flattened. Nothing like as purposeful in my stride now, mind. Now my guts were churning. Not out of fear. I still hated that gurning clown and the fact that it had taken two of his hired help to hold me while he did the dirty on me. No, it was that sense of shame and 'not rightenedness'. I just hoped that no one would see me when I finally got to the ticket office at the main entrance of the Tivoli and also that tickets for the final performance that night were still for sale. They were – and I bought one of the best seats in the house that suited my purpose.

Third row – Seat 9.

It was a long working day at the grocer's shop on the following day.

I'd checked and rechecked the time of the last performance at the Tivoli in the local newspaper, closed up shop as usual, and made my way into the yard at the back of the property to get ready. I was wearing my Dad's old greatcoat which had mainly stayed in the wardrobe for years, with its sleeves too long and plenty of bulk to keep out the cold. But that's not what I wanted it for. That bulk was going to keep something *in.* I checked that there was no one overlooking the yard from the surrounding buildings, and then moved quickly to the waste bins by the yard gates. Those bins were going to be collected and emptied on the following day – and they contained exactly what I wanted for my purpose. There were also a bunch of empty vegetable sacks there. I took two of the smaller ones, checked they weren't ripped – then pulled out a length of rope from where I knew it would be, stripped it, and cut it to length with a saw blade I'd taken from under the counter. It didn't take me long to fill both of those small sacks with semi-rotting cabbages, cauliflowers and other assorted semi-liquid rotting fruit and vegetables. Tying the bags tight at each end of the rope, I hauled the rope across the back of my neck so that the sacks hung on either side of my body, tucked them in under the greatcoat and then buttoned up. I looked like I'd put a lot of weight on, but the bags were hidden.

Perfect.

I did not smell good.

And by the time I'd locked up again and got back on the High Street outside the greengrocers, I was already beginning to smell worse.

I'd seen those Tom Mix westerns back then, with the long gunfighter's walk down the main street on his way to a showdown, and I should have felt ridiculous with my long greatcoat weighted down, not by six-guns, but by a load of semi-rotten fruit and vegetables – but I didn't. And to this day, I don't know why.

This was the third time I'd made that walk down the pier to the Tivoli theatre. The first time I was filled with the need for outright vengeance. The second had been a lot slower, more painful, but filled with shame. But this time I had a plan and a purpose, even though I smelled like a rubbish tip. I was aware – or rather a part of me was aware – that I was being ridiculous, but before that part of me could talk me out of what I was about to do, stop me in my tracks and turn me around and send me back home in what I knew would be a deeper and more burning shame – there was a surge of seawater beneath the pier walkway, breaking against the iron stanchions and pilings, sending spume up through the wrought iron girders beneath my feet. It was like the sound of laughter I had heard from the theatre on the night that I was beaten up. But this time, somehow, it was not a mocking sound. It was a surge – urging me onwards. Don't ask me why I felt so overpowered with my intention then; but I saw the spume splash on my shoes, and I remembered the droplets of blood splashing on my shoes from my broken nose. I strode on, faster than before, somehow embracing that nagging pain in my ribs and knowing that what I'd planned to do was not only the right thing to do, but the *only* thing to do. The sacks hanging hidden beneath my coat at my side felt heavy – and that felt *good*.

My footsteps rang on the walkway, sending echoes down to be swallowed by the sea.

And then I was at the box office, proffering my ticket to the white haired old lady sipping tea. She looked up in surprise, then down at my ticket again.

"You've missed most of the show."

The way she gulped her tea, she looked afraid that I was going to make a complaint.

"I know."

"All the acts have been on except …"

"I know."

"Well, there's only Ronnie Pye left now. He'll be on in five minutes, but he's the last."

Something about my smile was frightening her now.

"But my seat's not taken?"

"No, no – 'course not. You paid for it, dear. It's yours."

"Good."

Hastily, she punched the ticket and pushed it back across the counter to me.

"Row Three, Seat 9. One of the best seats in the house for a good view."

"Yes, I know."

There was a new expression on the old girl's face when I picked up my ticket and headed into the Tivoli. It was a puzzled look, as she wrinkled her nose in disgust and wondered where on earth that smell was coming from.

*

There were Can-Can dancers on the stage when I made my way down the aisle in the darkness. But I don't think the Folies Bergère had anything to worry about. There were only four of them. Three were managing the high kicks in a wobbly spotlight as they tossed their frilly dresses and whooped with each kick. The fourth was a lot older than the other three, seemed to have a breathing problem with her 'whoops' and it was clear that her high-kicking days were over. A small band of four musicians (billed as an 'orchestra' on the posters outside) gamely galloped on with *Mademoiselle of Armentieres*, with a trombonist who seemed to have made his mind up to sabotage the whole thing with blaring raspberries of sound that seemed to have nothing to do with the high kicks.

I stumbled down to Row Three, scanning the silhouetted heads and shoulders of the audience. I needn't have bothered to book my ticket in advance; the place was only half full. Ignoring the grumbled complaints of the people I pushed past, I found Seat 9.

Perfect. I had two empty seats on both sides of me, and a clear centre view of the stage. The high kicks of the three dancing girls seemed very close. I wasn't threatened at all by the fourth.

The 'band' came to a blaring halt, and three of the girls gave a last French *"Whoop!"* – and then went down on the stage into the 'splits' position. The noise they made when they landed made me wonder if the planks might give way and they'd plunge into the sea. The fourth girl didn't bother and just walked off. No one seemed to mind, and there was a smattering of applause. I didn't look up when the three clambered to their feet and thundered offstage with frozen smiles on their painted faces.

The band blared again, the trombonist made some kind of blurting noise that could be a warning to ships passing too close to the pier, and a fellow in a black suit and bowtie skipped onto the stage. He looked so cheerful that he needed a punch.

I reached into my greatcoat – left and right – and twisted open the tops of each sack.

The smell was bloody awful, leaking up through my collar and making my eyes water.

"And now, ladies and gentlemen! The act you've been waiting for. The Cheeky Chappy who makes you happy! Here's a bit of Pye to bring a tear to your eye! Yes, it's your own – your *very* own – *Ronnie Pye!!"*

The band blurted out a ramshackle version of Ben Slevin's *Happy Days Are Here Again* as the compere skipped out of the spotlight. The bloke operating it didn't seem to know whether to stay on him, or flash back to the other figure now coming onto the stage, hands held wide in expectation of massive applause.

After a mini-Zeppelin search all over the theatre, the spotlight fixed on the newcomer, zoomed in and out until it had got a proper fix – and there he was, that familiar, hateful sight, throwing his arms wide as if overcome by the applause he was now getting, but was expecting as his God-given right anyway.

He was dressed the same way as the night he'd duffed me up. Same big black and white checked suit, same hat, same pancake makeup and glittering eyes.

"Everybody want a piece of Pye? I bet you do! Just want to eat me up, don'tcha? Eat me up!"

Bloody hell, I thought. *He's using the catchphrases, hasn't told any jokes yet – and they're laughing already!*

"Here's one for you! Here's one you're going to love…"

And I'm just not going to tell you any of the jokes he came out with because they were older than the theatre and just like him – rotten. But everyone in the audience – except one – did seem to love every moment of it and, to use one of his catchphrases, seemed to want to eat him up.

I wanted to give him five minutes, until he was in full flow – but I couldn't stand it. Resisting the urge to jump up on that stage and finish what I'd planned to do the night I had the tables turned on me, I reached inside my greatcoat, fumbled in one of the bags – and withdrew a nice, mushy cabbage.

He was going to get every last piece of fruit-and-veg. In time honoured fashion.

With a nice good grip and with the stench now enveloping me, I began to rise. Pye had them in stitches of laughter now and was again holding his hands wide to soak it in, legs braced – and making a perfect target for my first missile.

I was aware of people around me reacting to the stink as I raised my hand, and then…

The entire building shuddered and roared.

Clouds of plaster dust suddenly billowed down from the roof, the spotlight swung crazily away and I staggered in the aisle as the floor beneath me jerked and buckled left then right. The sound of squealing metal and ripping timber joined with the shrieking panic of the theatre audience, who rose as one into a mad panicking scramble for the exits.

I gripped the seat in front of me in shock, staring upwards as cracks chased each other across the ceiling, and waited for the whole bloody thing to come down. In a flashing instant I was yet again back in the trenches, but I shook my head to clear myself out of that place. It was a bomb. It *had* to be a bomb. But I'd heard no explosive impact, just this great roaring and shuddering and rending – that even now was beginning again; like an earthquake tremor, making the walls shake and crack. The plaster columns all around the interior were toppling inwards, overhead mini-chandeliers swinging, snapping and crashing down on people as they ran screaming and running everywhere. Something flashed and sparked, and curtains at one of the exits began to burn.

Someone clawed and blundered against me in the flight, nearly sending me over the row of seats in front, and as I gripped the edge of that seat to steady myself I was astonished to see that all of those rows were *moving* – juddering back and forwards with what seemed to be an independent life of their own. I hung on for dear life as they clattered up and down, then heard and felt the wooden boards beneath my feet split with a great crunching *ripppp* that sent white spikes of jagged timber shooting up from below as the seats peeled back. I saw a tangle of those spikes splinter apart from each other, and then as another juddering seizure rent the building, they snapped back like a jagged bear trap, impaling a man trying to run through the tangle. I saw not horror or agony on his face but a look of *surprise* as his white shirt turned red, the floor split open and those jagged white spikes tore apart again, instantly pulling the poor fella apart with a *crunch* and a shining red spray.

I've told you already a few times about how the memory of things that happened to me during the Great War would sometimes overwhelm me; how ordinary things could remind me of terrible events, catapulting me back to those trenches. I don't like to go on about it, but this is part of the story you wanted me to tell you and it's also the only way of explaining what happened next. The Tivoli Theatre was falling down and somehow being pulled apart around me, and I'd just seen a man, well – *disintegrate* – before my eyes. There one moment, gone the next! And you see, son, I'd seen that sort of thing on the battlefield often, when the shelling started. There'd be this hellish blast and somehow you'd survived again, but the bloke next to you had been blasted to nothing like he'd never been there. Or there'd be another roar that would throw you flat, you'd feel the devil breathing on your back and there'd be arms and legs falling all around. Well – when that bloke disappeared and blood spattered all around – I did a crazy thing.

I just sat back down in my chair.

That's right.

The floor was cracking, splintering, lifting – a jagged spear of wood could come any second right through my seat and straight up my jacksie. The ceiling could have caved in on top of me. A chink from one of those falling columns could smash my head in at any second. More of the exit curtains were burning.

But the noise and the screaming and the devastation and the poor look of surprise on that chap's face before he ceased to exist – well, I knew I wasn't in the trenches, but it *was* like being in the trenches; so I just sat and watched… and watched… overwhelmed by that same something that sometimes hit me before, during and after combat.

I was paralyzed, son.

Just paralyzed.

I watched as a massive section of the Tivoli's flooring and row upon row of seats simply collapsed away, tearing loose from their shoring on the steel girder-work of the pier beneath, crashing down in plumes of roaring spray into the sea. Steel screeched and roared

35

as the Tivoli swayed and rocked like a ship at sea, and I watched as the two rows of seats in front of me simply spun away and fell apart beyond and below. Row Three was now on the edge of a crevasse and clutching the arm rests of my chair, I looked down through the bent and twisted steelwork that had once supported the pier and the theatre at the black-green sea thrashing and roiling, as debris – and people – fell twisting and screeching into that churning mass.

The *boom* of a gigantic wave sent geysers of seawater back up into the now partially hollow shell of the Tivoli and the cold sting of the water on my face made me reel back to see –

Survivors of the audience who had not made it to the exits (if *any* of them had) were clambering up and away over the still disintegrating rows of seats, trying to escape from the gaping maw that had opened up, that was *still* opening up. I saw a woman dangling by one hand from the end of a shattered row, a young man desperately reaching down for her free, extended hand – only for the whole row to come away, and they fell together in a twisted embrace into another greedy explosion of spray from below.

I had a grandstand seat on this vision of destruction.

But the horror of what I had seen, what I was seeing, didn't prepare me for what was to come.

Because what I really had was a grandstand seat overlooking Hell.

At first, I thought the entire shell of the theatre was descending into the sea.

The vast, churning fury of the sea below me was getting fiercer as it raged and exploded around the supporting pier girders. My knuckles were blue-white, gripping the arm rests as I prepared my paralyzed body for a rollercoaster descent into that terrible frothing mass.

But a tiny little voice inside me was crying: *This can't be right, this isn't RIGHT!*

The Tivoli was going *down...*

No, continued that voice. *This can't be happening. The sea just isn't as deep as this at the end of the pier!*

The surface of the sea was less than six feet below the shattered row in which I sat. A young woman with hair like seaweed across her face swirled past my feet, gasping for air, and was gone again.

The pier isn't sinking, hissed the voice in my head.

"What, what, what...?" I heard myself garble, as the sea churned and thundered.

The sea is RISING!

But no, it wasn't the sea rising at all. As the waves troughed and rolled away, torrents of it exploding aside and furling in glittering spray back down the twisted ironwork of exposed pier struts, I could see that the Tivoli hadn't fallen into the sea and that the semi-destroyed pier was still standing on its now twisted iron pillars and girders.

Something else was rising, and the seawater was falling back and away from it as it came. Something was coming up out of the sea, rising in the foam of the hollowed-out theatre and the sheer size and *impossibility* of it further cemented my already paralyzed body into my grandstand theatre seat.

The surface of the sea, pierced by those bent iron pillars and girders, was boiling. But that sea was icy cold. All I can tell you is that it was boiling with *activity*.

And as I watched, these... things... came wriggling and writhing out of the water. I say things. But I don't know if they were lots of things, or one big *thing*. I know that sounds mad. But imagine not one, but lots of big grey-green snakes, bigger than those (what do you call 'em?) boa constrictors or ana-whatsists – anacondas. Yes, those bloody big snakes from the Amazon. But bigger, much bigger – and much, much longer. And with no heads. That's right, no heads. But where there should be heads (at the tip, like) there'd just be this rippled, scaly grey-green skin – like the rest of it – that would just suddenly open up, and when it split open there'd be these curved yellow sharp things like teeth, all champing and gnashing and foaming. Then the skin would suddenly just cover up again like there was no mouth there at all. Peeling open, sliding shut. Peeling open, sliding shut. Ten, then fifteen, then maybe twenty of these things, thrashing around like they were being held by their tails under the water and trying to get free. Twisting and lashing and flopping. But like I say, it was impossible to say whether they were... well... like tentacles, bloody big tentacles of one bloody big thing, bigger than a house, just under the surface of the sea. If it was, I don't see what *kind* of thing it could be; not something that size. If they were tentacles, I'd never seen a picture of an octopus or a squid with tentacles like that. But if they were snakes, I'd never seen snakes like them either; snakes without eyes and with horrible mouths that were there one moment, then gone the next.

As I watched these things, more of them came out – God knows how many now – not possible to count 'em. Thrashing around in the foam, coiling and twisting in the air; now somehow growing *longer* and reaching up past me, while others kept breaking from the surface and flopping around. Some of them were coiling around the girders below, bending them and pulling them apart. These things were pulling the theatre to pieces.

And then I heard something that jerked me in my seat.

It was the sound of a *whiplash* – very sharp and very loud – followed by the unmistakable sound of a human voice. And that voice was screaming in a way that I'd never heard before; impossible to tell whether it was a man or a woman.

In the next moment, those snake-tentacles stiffened in mid-air. They stiffened and swayed as that horrible screaming went on and on, from God knows where; shrill and agonized above the hollow booming of the sea down in the newly opened shaft at the heart of the Tivoli Theatre.

And then the snake-tentacles began to hunt.

I could only sit and watch as –

A snake-thing fastened on the leg of a young man who had been teetering along the top row of the seats towards an exit. Its hideous hidden mouth seized him and flipped him up in the air. He cart-wheeled, shrieking; that shriek cut off when the snake-thing caught him again in its mouth, swallowing him to the waist before twisting back into the sea with its prey.

Two young women holding hands were struggling up another shattered aisle on the other side from me. Two of the things snatched them apart and up into the air and I saw to my horror that the legs of both women had been left behind in the aisle.

A shower of blood soaked me and when I looked up, I saw a human form disappearing into the gullet of a snake-tentacle directly above me; both of its victims' hands grasping and clawing from that horrible 'mouth' and now disappearing into its maw completely as the grey-green flesh bulged and puckered as its victim was swallowed.

A severed head spun crazily over my own head, hair flapping as it bounced and spun into the roiling ocean below. A snake-thing twisted and coiled past me, the head's owner clamped in those horrible curved yellow teeth.

Two of the things fought over another victim, both of them fastened on to the ragged torso of something that was impossible to recognize as once having been human, separating only when the trunk split in two.

Another *whipcrack* and a falling woman was snatched away by one snake-thing, only to be angrily pursued by another snake-thing wanting to claim her as its own.

That's when something slammed into me and I was knocked out of my seat by something from behind. My rib was on fire again and when I saw the 'head' of one of those snake-things move into my sightline above, I knew that I was next on the menu. It's horrible 'no mouth' slid open and I could see those curved yellow teeth

38

vibrating with pleasure. When that head snapped down at me, I threw my hands up instinctively and that's when I realized that I was lying on one of those sacks of garbage and the other one had twisted around so that it was lying on my chest. So when I threw my hands up, I was surprised to see that I was clutching that other sack. The snake-thing's 'teeth' fastened on the sack instead of me, the rope was instantly severed and the head flew up again. The bag ripped, the rotting fruit and vegetables spewed out all over the place.

Now completely free from my paralysis, I scrambled on my hands and knees, panting like a terrified dog, with the rope tangled around my body and dragging that second stinking sack with me. When I looked back I couldn't believe it.

The snake-thing that had snatched up the sack was completely still, frozen in place just as they all had been when that first *whipcrack* sound and the scream had started this terrible slaughter. It's 'head' or the tip of its tentacle – or whatever – was curled over like some gigantic bloody cobra and was covered in the remnants of rotting fruit and vegetables.

And the thing was *trembling*.

Now I realized that all of those other snake-tentacle-things had stopped hunting and were also completely still. Don't ask me how I knew, but I *knew* that the snake that had almost got me was trembling with *pleasure* – and all those others were now reacting to it somehow.

I kept crawling on all fours, quietly now, to the crushed remains of the staircase at the end of the row. There were cracks and massive gaps there, but if I was careful I might make it up to one of the exits. If only I knew what the hell was going on and why those snake-things had suddenly stopped. I reached the end of the aisle and was just about to make a scrabble for those stairs, when all Hell broke loose again.

The snake-tentacle-things had gone into some kind of frenzy.

At first, I thought they were attacking the thing that had gone for me. All the others were certainly coiling and squirming and slithering around it. But when some of those things broke away and began biting and champing at the seat that I had just vacated, I realized that I was wrong. The thing that had ripped the vegetable sack apart had scattered some of the contents on its skin, but now it was all gone – licked clean by the others – and the things were now going wild for the remnants of the sack that had been scattered in the aisle; mad for the rotting fruit and vegetables that I had intended to throw at Ronnie Pye.

39

Terrified that they might sense me moving and come after me, but too terrified at the prospect of staying where I was after they had finished snaffling up the garbage, I started up the fractured staircase, still on my hands and knees. The snake-tentacle things were in a writhing mass in the aisle, the water below foaming and churning where they emerged from the sea, and there could surely be nothing left now of the very little that the sack had contained. But there was something about that stuff, perhaps only the smell of it, which had driven them into such ecstasy.

God, I thought. *Is that smell on ME?*

Half a dozen steps further up from me there was a broken pillar, still with four feet or so of its base in place, the rest of it collapsed and strewn about. But enough to hide me as I scurried behind it, blocking me from the view of those snake-things. I looked at the shattered stairs beyond, and quickly planned what route I'd take if I made a mad dash for the exit at the top. I'd seen how quickly those things could move. The curtains there were still burning, casting mad and dancing shadows that made this terrible place look even more like Hell.

And as I peeped around that shattered column, that's when I saw Ronnie Pye, sneaking along the top row of seats towards the same exit I was aiming for.

But there was something wrong about his movement that I couldn't make out; something furtive as he kept low, aware that those things were down below him. He seemed to be struggling with something that was impeding his progress. At first, I thought that maybe he had been injured, had a gammy leg or something. But then I moved to get a better view, and I could barely believe what I saw.

Pye was holding a struggling child – a little girl, maybe seven years old – close to his chest, one arm around her waist, and his other hand clamped over her mouth. She was flapping her arms and kicking her legs as Pye moved, desperate to get away.

The bastard was using her as a shield, so if one of those things came after him, he could throw her to it while he made his escape.

Something came over me then.

To call it 'rage' just doesn't do it justice. After everything that had happened, and being flung into this hellish nightmare, and now seeing what Pye was prepared to do to save his skin ... well, I just, what do you call it these days? I just lost the plot. I was so overwhelmed that I just didn't seem to care in that moment about those horrible snake-things or about my own safety.

I stood straight up on the staircase, and shouted.

"PYE!"

40

Startled, he fumbled in his hold on the girl as he stared down at me.

"Let her go, you miserable wretch!"

I don't know if he knew that it was me, but he tried to hang onto the girl, stumbled against the seats – and the little girl pulled free with a shriek, dashing to the exit and through the still burning curtains.

I clawed up the steps, put my foot into a crack between them and fell to my hands and knees again. The second sack was still under my coat, the rope tangled around my waist.

The sound of multiple *whipcracks* came from below, and I looked down to see that the snake-things were still in a twisting mass, had finished hunting and were now attracted to the sound of my voice.

And that's when I did the terrible thing I told you about at the beginning.

"THERE he is!" I yelled, ripping open the second sack and grabbing a rotting cabbage. *"Up THERE!"*

I'd always been a good bowler. Fast bowler in the cricket team at school, and later in my battalion. Throwing that cabbage was the best 'shot' I ever made.

It hit Pye full in the chest. He was caught off balance in the aisle, tried to ward it off as it exploded there in a wet green splash.

I advanced up the stairs, grabbing handfuls of whatever came out of that sack.

An onion smacked into his shoulder, A cauliflower exploded on the seats in front of him – and when I looked down, I could see that I had definitely got the snake-things' attention.

"Have a nice piece of Pye!"

I cannonballed another cabbage straight down into that writhing mass as they swarmed over the seats and waved in the air.

"Come on Ronnie!" Another green explosion on his shoulders as he waved his hands in the air and tried to stumble on towards the exit. "Give them one of your catchphrases!"

A handful of green mush splattered his ridiculous black and white coat.

"Pye in your eye, Ronnie! Come on son – tell us a *joke!"*

I knew that smell was all over me, and I was in as much danger as Pye, but I tell you – I was so filled with outright rage, I can honestly say that I didn't care as I just kept advancing up those stairs, making every shot count – as huge wriggling shadows covered us both.

Pye screamed.

His moon face and its pancake make-up was somehow even whiter than before; his eyes like glittering marbles and his mouth wide in a red 'O' of terror. His hands went up over his head. Just as one of those terrible snake 'heads' descended on him, completely covering the top half of his body, right down to the waist. His screaming was muffled now as he was lifted clear from the aisle, legs kicking madly. And I'm ashamed to say that I yelled:

"They're eating you up tonight, Ronnie! They're just eating you up!"

I began to laugh and cry then. In that moment, I think I might have lost my mind.

"You're going down WELL tonight, Ronnie!"

And then, suddenly, I did care what was happening to me and I was filled with a terror that almost burst my lungs when something seized me by the leg and everything started whirling around. I slapped out with my arms, felt horrible wet slimy skin. I knew that another of those things had me as I saw the holes and cracks in the ceiling, then the stairs again, then the sea as I was tossed around like a dog shakes a rat or something. I saw the exit at the top of the stairs, and suddenly – *whack!* My legs tangled in the burning curtain and dragged it away from the exit. Sparks and smoke surrounded me. I heard a hissing sound, felt searing pain in my shoulders. Still spinning, I realized that the burning curtain had tangled around my head and shoulders. I clawed at it, knew that I was burning – and oh God, I didn't want to die. I could smell my hair on fire and the pain in my leg was agonizing as I whirled around and around.

And suddenly I was free and falling.

I saw the churning sea rushing to meet me, and just managed to drag as deep a breath as I could into my lungs.

Ice cold water exploded all around me, and I knew in that one moment that all the breath would be knocked out of me. I'd gasp in seawater and drown. I was in agony, pain wracking my body and the sounds of a great *rushing* in my ears.

I have no idea how it happened – but the next thing I knew, my head was out of the water and I was clinging to something hard and cold. I clung there, gasping and with my eyes screwed shut as waves sloshed up over my head and I struggled to keep myself afloat. I still hurt like hell, so I knew that I was alive. When something crashed into the water and made whatever I was clinging to vibrate like hell – I opened my eyes and saw that I was clinging to an iron rail; a fragment of the supporting girder work of the pier.

I had fallen straight into the sea where those snake-tentacle things had emerged and had somehow been sucked through to the outside. There was another crash, and I saw that the Tivoli was finally imploding, falling inwards on itself as smoke gushed through the girders and the falling masonry. Sparks flew in the air, sizzled on the water, and now the remnants of the theatre's four walls caved inwards in an explosion of dust and hissing sea spray.

There was no sign of the snake-things.

Whatever they were – whatever *it* was – they or it had returned to the ocean, or been buried under the falling theatre rubble.

My hair on one side had been burned off. The burning exit curtain that was responsible had also probably saved my life, making the snake-thing drop me. My body was freezing in that icy water, but I could still feel the pain in my leg where the thing had grabbed me, and I hoped to God that I didn't have a severed artery and was leaking my lifeblood into the sea. Planking and scraps of stuff were bobbing in the sea beside me, and I realized that I'd better push away from these pilings, grab something and try to get back to the shore before anything else decided to collapse on top of me.

I was just grabbing for what looked like a Tivoli poster-board advertising that night's show, when the surface next to it began to bubble and froth.

I grabbed back at the piling in panic, swallowing sea water and choking.

Those snake-tentacle things *hadn't* disappeared.

I waited in terror for one of them to emerge, writhing and wriggling, with its horrible 'no-mouth' sliding open and swallowing me whole like Ronnie Pye. Maybe the same one that had grabbed me in the theatre had perhaps pulled me out here and was ready to finish me at last.

The water exploded, I yelled in fear – and something came out of the sea. It flew in a foaming mass over my head and hit the pilings and girder just above where I floated. Again in panic, I kicked away from the pilings. The poster-board bumped against me and I grabbed at it, getting ready to kick at whatever came back at me again.

But it wasn't one of the snake-tentacle things.

Something had been coughed out of the ocean and was, even now, sliding and dripping down the girder and pilings in a thick, jelly-like mass.

I recognized the gaudy black and white jacket.

And as the liquefied remains of the Cheeky Chappy ran and dripped into the foaming waves, the melted-candle mass that had once been a face seemed to grin and leer and run and melt. One glittering eye squeezed out and *plopped* into the sea foam.

I kicked with both feet, hanging on to the poster-hoarding as I pushed myself away and back towards the shore through the choppy water as the jacket and what it contained at last fell into the sea and disappeared.

That, son, was what happened to Brinkburn pier on Friday 13th July 1931.

I was there, at the end of the pier, and I know.

You won't find any stories about sea monsters. They were still finding bodies washing up weeks later, but no sea monsters. Most people assumed that the theatre collapse was caused by a fire in one of the stage lights. Those that managed to get out were gone before those things came out of the sea. No one ever mentioned a little girl – the one that Ronnie Pye grabbed – and if she did survive she doesn't seem to have told anyone about it, or what she saw. I do so hope that she *did* manage to get away.

So – you've got it all now.

Not that anyone's going to believe you, mind. I've never told anyone before now, but it's so long ago I don't suppose it matters anymore.

You can check out the obituaries for Ronnie Pye, and it'll tell you that he was one of Britain's most popular and best loved comedians who died tragically in the Tivoli theatre incident.

I beg to differ on the 'best loved' aspect.

Even the thing that swallowed him couldn't stomach him in the end.

THE SWIRLING SEA

The phenomenon of the Bermuda Triangle is one of those great paranormal talking-points that persist for decade after decade, somehow defying all serious analysis. There is almost nobody on the planet who hasn't heard about this mysterious stretch of ocean and its voracious appetite for ships and planes. However, though it is a deeply feared region where countless mariners are said to have inexplicably vanished, hard facts seem to be few and far between.

Even the Triangle's specific location in the west of the North Atlantic is disputed. The general consensus is that it lies between Bermuda in the north, Miami in the west and San Juan, Puerto Rico, in the south-east. But its size fluctuates wildly from one source to the next, ranging from 500,000 square miles in some accounts to an incredible one million in others. And yet it has no official existence. The Bermuda Triangle appears in no US Navy documentation, nor in any publications or maps issued by the US Board on Geographical Names. The Worldwide Fund for Nature doesn't even regard it as being among the world's most dangerous waters for shipping. At the same time, numerous authors – Allan Eckert, Charles Berlitz and Richard Winer, among the most high profile – have been accused of producing overly sensational books and playing hard and fast with the Bermuda Triangle truth.

But what is the truth? Is it the case that nothing strange has ever occurred within the so-called Devil's Sea? The answer to that is an emphatic 'no'.

Despite a now accepted explanation for the fate of Flight 19, the squadron of TBM Avenger bombers that was mysteriously lost over the Bermuda Triangle in December 1945, providing one of the biggest scare stories ever to fuel Triangle mania – namely that it went missing through the inexperience of its trainee pilots – there have been many bizarre and unexplained occurrences in this curious corner of ocean. Some pretty significant vessels have suffered disasters in the Triangle, and of a type that are not easily explained.

In 1918, the USS Cyclops, which was loaded with metallic ore and manned by a crew of 309, completely vanished while en route from Barbados to the US. In 1921, the five-masted schooner, Carroll A. Deering, was found grounded on the North Carolina coast with its entire crew and compliment of passengers missing – whatever happened to it (and the question was never answered) *happened in the heart of the Triangle. In 1968, the US Navy lost contact with one of its nuclear subs no less – the USS Scorpion, which was also never seen again. Airborne casualties include the Star Tiger and Star Ariel, which vanished whilst traversing the Triangle in 1948 and 1949 respectively, the former while it was shortly due to land at Bermuda airport – even then no wreckage was ever found.*

In total, about a thousand major losses have been recorded in the area during the last three centuries, though perhaps the oddest event of all occurred in 1881, when the Ellen Austin, while sailing across the Triangle en route to New York, encountered another ship that was completely bereft of crew or passengers. Noting that the mystery ship was seaworthy and sailable, the skipper of the Ellen Austin posted crewmen on board it and instructed them to follow him to port. Both ships proceeded, but were later separated by deteriorating weather. When they re-acquainted some time later, the mystery ship was again empty of personnel – the new batch of men placed on board had also disappeared, and none of them were ever seen again.

All kinds of paranormal explanations have been offered, ranging from UFO attacks, to sea serpents, to death-rays emanating from the ruins of Atlantis as represented by the genuinely strange Bimini Road, a linear, tabular rock formation, which looks manmade and yet lies along the seabed near Bimini Island in the Bahamas. Skeptics have responded with explanations of their own: that the region is wracked by hurricanes and tropical storms, that variations in the Gulf Stream can cause unexpected currents and riptides, that electromagnetic anomalies can interfere with compasses, even that methane hydrates exploding from the ocean floor can turn the sea to a boiling cauldron and cause sailing vessels to lose their buoyancy.

Needless to say, none of these prosaic theories are quite as sexy as the alternative, so the mysteries live on.

As a footnote, classic horror author William Hope Hodgson (1877-1918) added a whole new dimension of terror to the Bermuda Triangle by emphasising the deadliness of its northernmost edge, the infamous Sargasso Sea. Students of 'golden age' weird fiction will be very familiar with this floating landscape of thickly enmeshed weed, a graveyard of ships from all centuries and a concealment for indescribable monsters lurking just under the surface. Thankfully, the real Sargasso is not nearly so horrendous, but it is sporadically choked with weed. A gyre, a vortex of rotating ocean currents in which a massive compost of seaborne vegetation naturally gathers, the Sargasso was a region Hodgson knew well during his days as a merchant marine, and there is no doubt that he saw wrecks entangled there and was aware that some had even lost their crews during unexplained circumstances: the Rosalie in 1840 and in 1857 the James B. Chester. But the majority of Hodgson's horrors stem from his ultra-fertile imagination. Books like 'From The Tideless Sea' (1906) and 'The Boats of the Glen Carrig' (1907) are filled with nightmarish but fictional images of this hellish realm, which had a lasting impact on readers at first publication – and ultimately, even if perhaps indirectly, provided yet more grist for the Bermuda Triangle mill.

LIE STILL, SLEEP BECALMED
Steve Duffy

It was a night trip, and the thing to remember is no-one's looking for surprises on a night trip. You ride at anchor, out where it's nice and quiet; kick back, chill out, talk rubbish till sunup. No surprises.

Back when Danny had the *Katie Mae* we often used to take her out of Beuno's Cove at ten, eleven p.m. and head for the banks off Puffin Island, near the south-east tip of Anglesey; *we* being Danny, who owned the boat, Jack, who crewed on a regular basis, and me. Jack was a great big grinning party-monster who'd do anything for anyone; anything, that is, except resist temptation when it offered itself, as it seemed to on a regular basis. Any other owner but Danny would probably have sacked him, no matter how good he was with boats: the reason Danny didn't would never have been clear to an outsider, really. Claire, who was always quick to pick up on that sort of thing, reckoned that Jack – Mr Happy-go-Lucky – represented something that Danny – Mr Plodder – had probably always dreamed of being himself, but had never quite worked up the nerve to go for. It was a classic case of vicarious wish-fulfilment, apparently.

"And I'll tell you something else about Danny," she'd added, "I bet once you get past that Big-I-Am act he puts on, it's Jack who does all the hard grafting – am I right? It's the same with you: if you didn't sort out all his tax returns and VAT for him, they'd probably have taken that boat off him by now. He likes to think he's running the show, but he'd be sunk without the pair of you. It's quite funny, really." I remember her whispering all this in my ear as we watched Jack and Danny playing pool in the basement bar of the Toad Hall, not long after we'd first started dating.

That was the summer of '95: on dry land it was banging, hammering heatwave all the way, long sundrenched days and sticky muggy nights. Out at sea, though, you got the breeze, cool and wonderful, and whenever the next day's bookings sheet was blank Danny needed little enough persuading to pick up a tray or two of Red Stripe and take the *Katie Mae* out for the night. Jack would turn up with a bag of Bangor hydroponic and we'd make the run out to the fishing banks west of the Conwy estuary; we'd lie out on the deck drinking, smoking, chatting about nothing in particular, or maybe go below to pursue the Great and Never-Ending

Backgammon Marathon, in which stupendous, entirely fictional sums of money would change hands over the course of a season's fishing. Good times; easy, untroubled. I look back now and think how sweet we had it then.

One night in early August, Claire said she wanted to go out with us. I can't really say why I was resistant to the idea. Part of it, if I'm honest, was probably to do with keeping her well away from Jack until I was a bit more confident in the relationship. Remember I told you about Jack and temptation? Well, if I'd gone on to mention me and insecurity that would've given you the whole of the picture. Over and above that…I honestly don't know; nothing like a premonition, nothing that dramatic or well-defined. Just the feeling, somewhere under my scalp that things might be on the cusp; might be changing, one way or another, and changing irrevocably. The fact was I always made an excuse, put her off; until that particular night when it had all the potential to turn into an argument, which would have been our first. Fine, I said, yeah, come along, no problem.

It had been another scorcher. Walking down the hill to the harbour you could feel the pavement underfoot giving out the last of the day's heat to the baking breathless night; under the cotton of her t-shirt the small of Claire's back was slick with sweat where my hand rested. Danny was waiting for us on the *Katie Mae*, and Jack came by soon after; he'd been away for the weekend at a festival, got back only that morning, slept till nine p.m., and now here he was ready for action again, invincible. It was just gone half-eleven when we fired up the engine and cast off; I remember Claire squeezed my hand in excitement.

The last of the sunset was gone out of the sky, and it was very dark, very quiet; a still, calm night with just a sliver of the waning moon swinging round behind the headland. The beacon winked one, two, three as we eased out beyond the end of the breakwater, Claire and I sitting out on the foredeck, Danny and Jack in the wheelhouse. As always when we were putting out on a night trip, I felt that little kick of expectation: I'd get it in the daytime, too, but at night particularly. There was a magic to it, some song of the sea, pitched between shanties and sirens.

"It's the ocean, innit?" Jack once said. "You never know what it's going to throw at you," and soon enough I'd learned this to be true.

Tongue in cheek, I told the same thing to Claire as we rounded the Trwyn y Ddraig and pulled away from the coast.

"Listen, I don't care what it throws at me," she said, arching like a cat in the first stirrings of a sea-breeze, "just so long as it's this temperature or below. Oh, that's good. That's the coolest I've been all day." She stretched out on the foredeck, head propped up in my lap as I sat cross-legged behind her, absently ruffling her hair with my fingers.

At this stage you probably need to know a bit about the layout of the boat. The *Katie Mae* was thirteen metres stem-to-stern, pretty roomy for a standard fishing vessel, with reasonably poky diesels (in need of an overhaul, but fine so long as you didn't try and race them straight from cold). The wheelhouse was amidships, the centre of the boat; behind that, on the aft deck, were the gear lockers, the bilge pump, and the engine hatch. Up towards the stem, there was the foredeck and the Samson post. In the wheelhouse we had VHF ship-to-shore, GPS, radar, and also the "fish-finder", the sonar that not only showed the sea-bottom but tracked the shoals. Down below, bench seats followed the shape of the hull for'ard of the wheelhouse above, curving with the prow around a drop-down table where we kept the beer and the backgammon set. Hurricane lights hung from the bulkheads between the portholes, posters of mermaids were tacked up on the ceiling: all snug as a bug in a rug. And outside, where Claire and I were, you had the best air-conditioning in all North Wales, entirely free and gratis.

Claire snuggled her head in my lap, enjoying the cool breeze of our passage. "This is nice," she said, letting the last word stretch to its full extent. "Just like you to keep it all to yourself – typical greedy pig bloke."

I dodged her playful backward punches, one for every slur. "Keep what to myself? A bunch of sweaty geezers sitting round getting smashed and talking garbage all night? You should've said – I'd have taken you down the rugby club, back in town."

"Getting smashed and talking garbage? Is that all there is to it? It's got to be a bit more cerebral than that, surely – big smart boys like you, university types and all?"

"You'd think so, wouldn't you?" Danny had joined us on the foredeck. "Well, you'd be wrong. No culture on this here tub."

"If it's culture you want," I pointed out, moving over to make room, "I believe P&O do some very nice cruises this time of year."

"Do you want the guided tour then, Claire?" Danny settled himself alongside us. "That's Llandudno – see the lights round the West Shore? And that's the marina at Deganwy over there."

Not to be outdone, I chipped in my own bit of local colour. "This stretch here is where the lost land of Helig used to be, before the sea came in and covered it all."

"Helig ap Glannog, aye," Danny amplified in his amusingly nit-picking way, at pains to remind Claire just who was the captain on this boat, and who was the guy who helped out now and then.

Danny's dad had fished these waters since the 1940s; he'd been delighted when his eldest dropped out of Bangor Uni and picked up a charter boat of his own. Since then, Danny had been busy proving Jack's adage that you could take the boy out of university, but you couldn't take university out of the boy. It was just a way he had. You couldn't let it get to you.

"Helig ap what?" Claire seemed slightly amused herself – remember, I told you she'd already got Danny figured out.

"Way back," Danny explained, "sixth century AD. There was a curse on the family, and a big tide came and covered all their lands, and everybody died except for one harpist on the hill there crying woe is me, woe is me, some shit or other. And nowadays hardly anyone moors a boat out there – "

"Except for Danny," I chipped in, "because he's big and hard and don't take no shit from no-one, innit, Danny lad?" He tried to punch me in a painful place, but I rolled over just in time. "Who's steering this tub, anyway?"

"Jack," said Danny, waiting till I'd resumed my former position before trying, and failing once more, to hit me where it hurt. "We'll keep going for a bit," he went on, ignoring my stifled laughter, "till we're out of everyone's way. Then we'll drop anchor and get down to business." He rubbed his hands together in anticipation of the night's entertainment. "So, do you play backgammon then, Claire?"

Claire smiled sweetly, her blonde hair blowing back into my face. "Well, I know the rules," she said, and nudged me surreptitiously.

*

Several hours later, Claire owned, in theory at least, the *Katie Mae*, the papers on Danny's house and fifty per cent of both my and Jack's earnings through to the year 2015. Down below Danny and Jack were skinning up and arguing over who was most in debt to who; Claire and I were up in the wheelhouse, enjoying a little quality relationship time with the lights out.

"Mmmm," she said into my left ear. "That was easy enough."

"What?" I said. "Me? I'm dead easy, me. You should know that by now."

"Oh, I do," she said, "I do. No – I meant those two downstairs."

"*Down below*," I reminded her, in Danny's pedantic voice. "What – you mean you get up to this sort of thing with those two as well? I'm crushed."

She chuckled, and moved her hand a little. "There – is that better? Didn't mean to crush you. Are they always that dozy?"

"Well, you had an unfair advantage."

"What?"

"You were distracting them all the time."

"Me? What was I doing?"

"Nothing," I said, burying my face in her neck. "You were just making the most of your natural advantages: this, and this, and this…"

"Mmmm…ooh. What's that?"

"You mean you don't know what *that* is? Here, let me show you –"

"Not that." Firmly, she brushed the possibility aside. "That thing behind you. It's beeping."

"Beeping…?" I disengaged myself awkwardly and looked around. "Oh, that. That's the fish-finder. Didn't think it was me."

"The whatter?"

"Fish-finder: it's sonar, like in the movies, ping-ping, ping-ping? It shows you the sea-bed underneath the vessel – down here, look – and then where the shoals are. Look, there's something: that blob there, coming up now."

"So is that fish, then?" There was another ping. The target was rising, moving closer to the boat, so far as I could tell. Or it could have been the boat was sinking, I wasn't an expert.

"Must be, I suppose. Hang on, Jack knows this kit better than I do – Jack?"

Jack's grinning head popped up from below: the original Jack-in-the-box. "Aye, aye, mateys – here you go, I've done up a little dragon each for you, all classy-like." He swarmed up the short companionway to join us in the wheelhouse. "Hell's teeth, now, what's this?" He flipped a switch up and down on the fish-finder. "Have you been pressing buttons again, Billy-thick-lad? Bloody cabin boys, Claire, I tell you –"

I dug him in the ribs, and we wrestled amiably for a moment. "It's nothing to do with me, that – I never touched it. It just went off."

"I see. Big boy done it and ran off, is that it?" He smiled at Claire. "No, you're in the clear for once. I'll tell you who'll have left this on – bloody Captain Birdseye down there. You can't trust him to do anything properly: that right, Will?"

From down below came a smothered counter-accusation: Jack showed it his middle finger and grinned again, even more roguishly. I put an arm around Claire, just so Jack didn't get carried away.

"Claire wants to know is that a shoal or what?"

"Let's have a butcher's...what, that there? No, that's not a shoal." He bent over the screen. In its faint green glow he looked a little perplexed. "Too small, see? And it's right up on the surface, practically – I don't know what that is. Sometimes you get seals round Puffin Island, off the Orme even...I dunno. It might be a seal, I suppose." He glanced up, through the cabin window. "There isn't any moon, worse luck, but if we look over, lemme see... *that* way – " he pointed out on the starboard side, "– we might be able to see something, if we get out on deck and stay quiet-like."

Which we did, joined by Danny, who'd just appeared from below decks with more beer; and perhaps I should mention at this point that Claire and I had only had a couple of cans each by that time. I'd been hitting on the majority of the joints as they went round, Claire hadn't, but we were both completely on the case so far as our shared perceptions went. Given what happened over the next hour or so, it's important you know that.

Out on the aft deck, Jack explained to Danny what we'd seen on the fish-finder. We were all of us whispering, in case we scared the seal; we were still expecting seals at this point. Danny nodded, and pottered over behind the wheelhouse on the port side.

Claire cupped her hand around my ear and whispered, "What's he up to?" At that time I didn't know. Soon enough it would become clear.

The three of us on the aft deck – Jack, Claire and I – gazed out over the waves. It was difficult to make much out on the surface, even with the light in the wheelhouse switched off and our eyes accustomed to the darkness. Away off in the far distance was a glitter of shore-lights: Anglesey to the north-west, Penhirion and the mainland south-west. Between the lights on land and where we lay at anchor was mile after mile of still dark ocean. The green navigation light danced on the tops of the soft sluicing wavelets near the hull; all the rest was a vast murky undulation, slop and ebb, slop and ebb, featureless, unknowable.

Suddenly light sprang out from the *Katie Mae*, swinging through the darkness, settling on the waves in a rough rippling ellipse. I jumped a little, tightened my grip on Claire, looked round: there was Danny, all but invisible behind the spotlight on the wheelhouse roof, directing the strong beam through and beyond us to light up the slow dark waves.

"Shit," swore Jack under his breath, then louder, hissing: "Turn it off, man, you'll frighten it away! Bastard's left his nav-lights on as it is," he added *sotto voce*.

"I thought you wanted to see!" Danny sounded a bit smashed already. Claire looked at me, and I read the same judgement in her eyes. The harsh light from the *Katie Mae*'s spot made her look even paler than usual; almost translucent.

"We *do*, but we're not gonna see anythin' if you frighten it away, you knob! Turn it off and come back here – no – wait a minute…" Jack's voice trailed off, and I turned back to the water, trying to see what he'd seen. If anything, the spotlight made it harder; it was total illumination or total blackout, vivid purple after-images blooming on your retinas whenever you looked outside its magic circle. I squinted, tried to shield my eyes.

Beside me Jack was doing the same thing. "Hold it steady, over there – look – what's that?"

A slumped low shape in the black water; dull and dark, the waves washing over it as it dipped and rose on a tranquil tide. Claire gasped and dug her fingers into my arm as a slight swell lifted it far enough out of the water for us to see a gleam of white. A face, all tangled round with lank dark strands like seaweed.

Jack had seen it too. "Christ almighty," he breathed; then to Danny: "Hold it! Hold it there!"

"What?" shouted Danny.

"Look where you're pointing it, man! Forget about the bloody seal – there's someone in the water!" Abruptly Jack was gone from beside me, over to the aft lockers, flinging them open one after another. His voice came back on the quiet night air as Claire and I clung to each other and watched the body floating towards us in the spotlight:

"…find anything on this *bastard* boat…" Then he was back, a long boathook under his arm like a jousting lance. "Right," he called to Danny, "listen up. Claire's gonna come up and get that light, okay?" He glanced at Claire; she nodded. He smiled briefly at her and resumed: "You get down here and give Will a hand. I'm gonna hook him when he gets close enough in, then you two'll have to pull him up."

And we did just that: Danny and I knelt down in the scuppers, braced against the capstans while Jack leaned perilously far out from the side, one hand grasping the side of the boat, the other waving the boathook back and forth till the waterlogged shape drifted within reach. All the way in, until it was so close to the boat the spotlight wouldn't go far enough down on its mount. Claire never wavered; she knelt on the wheelhouse roof and trained the light dead straight on the bobbing body in the waves. Danny had got a torch from somewhere, and that gave us light enough for the last part of the job.

Jack's hook snagged in the clothing of the body; he hauled it in like a fish on a gaff, and Danny and I managed to get a grasp underneath its arms. Together we dragged it out of the water and up on to deck, where it plopped down as if on a fishmonger's slab, a cold dead weight of waterlogged clothing and wrinkled flesh.

I think we all thought at that time it was a dead man. It had been lying, after all, face down in the water; it was clammy cold to the touch and we hadn't felt anything like a heartbeat as we heaved it aboard. The three of us stood around it as the saltwater drained off into the scuppers; no-one quite knew what to say, or do. A hand touched my shoulder, and I nearly jumped off the side.

Claire had come down from the roof of the wheelhouse and was standing behind me.

"Jesus," I muttered fretfully, and she squeezed my arm remorsefully, peering around me at the body on the deck.

"Sorry," she whispered, then quite unexpectedly she buried her face in my shoulder. "Has anyone looked to see..." she began, and couldn't finish. Danny just looked at me, his tanned, weather-roughened face as pale as Claire's. It was left to Jack, as ever, to take care of the practicalities.

"She's right," he said, grimacing, "suppose we'd better have a look who he is and that. Do us a favour, Danny boy, get that torch down here, will you?"

He knelt on the deck, and gently turned the body over by its shoulders. What we'd thought was seaweed around the head we could see now were long, damp locks of hair. Danny brushed them away from the face, a thing I doubt I could have done myself right then. He wiped his hand several times on the leg of his jeans, and straightened up a little. We could all see the face now: it was a man in his early twenties, unshaven, startlingly pallid.

"Shit," Danny said, and the torch he was holding wobbled for a moment. "Just look at his face a minute, Jack..."

"I'm *looking* at his face." Jack sounded stressed. "What the fuck d'you think I'm *doing* down here –" and then he drew in his breath sharply.

"It's him, isn't it?" Like the torch beam, Danny's voice was wavering slightly. "That lad we were talking to in the Liverpool Arms on Regatta Day that time, what's his name..."

"Andy." There was a slight roughness, a catch to Jack's voice. "Andy something or other; crews on that boat out of Bangor these days, doesn't he? Andy, Andy...Christ, I must be going senile in my old age." He slapped the side of his head, and Claire jumped a little at the sudden noise in the midst of all that illimitable stillness. "Andy Farlowe, that's it. His old feller used to have a fishing boat in Conwy harbour; he's retired now, lives up Gyffin somewhere. Christ. I'll have to go round, I suppose, tell him what's happened –"

"*Wait*." Claire's nails dug into my arm. "Wait. Look at him, Will."

"What?" I looked at her instead; she was staring fixedly at the body, her mouth slightly open. "*What*?" I asked her again, and she whispered it, no more, so quiet you would have missed it in the normal run of things:

"He's *moving…*"

I was going to say, "Impossible, you're imagining it", but now as I looked I could see the limbs twitch, just a little. The hands clenched, unclenched, the head moved ever so slightly from side to side. It – he – gulped a little, and his jaw sagged open. A little trickle of seawater came out in a splutter. All at once his eyelids opened, and the eyes rolled back from up inside his head. He blinked once or twice, and seemed to be trying to speak.

Jack was down with him in a shot, finger probing the airway for obstructions, ear pressed to his mouth to gauge the breathing.

"Fuck," he said, looking up as if unable to believe what he was seeing or feeling, "he's still alive, you know."

*

Not only that, within a few minutes he was conscious, talking, the lot. With Jack and Danny helping him we got him on his feet and down below decks, where Danny had the best part of a bottle of rum held against emergencies, like when we ran out of lager. He coughed and spluttered a bit, but it seemed to do the trick; he looked round at us, shook his head and cleared his throat.

"Who are you lot, then?" he croaked. We all burst out laughing, I think from sheer relief as much as anything.

He couldn't say how long he'd been in the water: "I must've been spark out of it," was all he could manage.

"You were that," said Jack, one arm round his shoulders in a bracing grapple. His attitude to the younger man seemed almost fatherly, most un-Jack-like: it was altogether more responsibility than I could remember him showing towards anything or anyone before.

"How about the boat?" asked Danny, and it suddenly occurred to all of us: how had he got out there in the first place? We looked at him: he closed his eyes briefly, as if trying to remember.

56

"We gone out…" he began, and paused. Jack nodded encouragingly. "We gone out in the evening…in the straits past Beaumaris…" Every word seemed to be an effort; not so much physically, though he still looked very weak, but an effort of remembrance. It was like watching someone being asked to remember what he did on his birthday when he was seven.

"What happened, Andy? Did you fall overboard, or did the boat go down?" Danny seemed anxious to clear up the technicalities of it all.

"I was out on deck," Andy said slowly. He pushed his lank black mane of hair back, looked round helplessly for words. "It was…it was cold." Jack nodded, as if Andy had just given him the temperature down to the nearest degree centigrade; Andy hardly noticed. "In the water. It was cold."

He shivered a little, and Claire said, "Have you got any spare clothes on board? We should get him out of those; he'll be freezing. He's probably in shock already: we should get him warm. Get some blankets round him as well if you've got them."

Jack sprang to it. "Shit, why didn't I think of that – see that locker under the seats there, Claire? You have a look in there; that's blankets. I think I've got a few things, jumpers and that in there, too. Have I?"

Claire rummaged down in the locker, came up with a thick fisherman's sweater and a couple of blankets.

"Right, mate," Jack rapped out a little paradiddle on the table-top. "Get you into these, shall we? Danny – let's have the engines on and home James, what about it?"

"Yeah…" Danny was a little slower to react; he was staring at Andy as if he was having trouble taking it all in. At first I put it down to him still being a bit smashed; I'd have thought what had happened in the last ten minutes would have sobered anyone up, but it all depended on what sort of state he'd been in in the first place – he was always a pig when it came to spliff. "Yeah. You come up too, Will. Get on the ship-to-shore, just in case, let them know there might be a problem with the…with the…what is it, Jack?"

"Wanderley." This over his shoulder as he turned the balled-up sweater right way out. "Better get on to them; nice one, Danny boy."

"The Wanderley, out of Bangor. Okay?" With one long last look at Andy, he turned and went up the companionway to the wheelhouse.

I went to follow him, stopped and said irresolutely, "Claire?" She looked up at me, reached instinctively for my hand.

"Never mind Claire – it's crowded enough in here." This from up in the wheelhouse. "Get up here, Will, I need you."

"You can give us a hand, Claire," said Jack, "give our boy here the once-over." He nudged Andy. "How about that for luck, eh, Andy lad? Floating in the water all night, and the first boat to come along's got a posh lady doctor on it!"

"I'm not a doctor, Jack," Claire told him patiently, correcting this mistake for no more than the third or fourth time that night. "I work at the hospital. I'm a junior pharmacist."

"Well, it's all the same, innit?" Jack wasn't listening. He smoothed the last of the folds out of the sweater, turned to face us with a determinedly bright smile. "You've done all the first aid and that, haven't you?"

"I might not have been paying attention, though," Claire said, in an uncharacteristically small girly-voice; but she knew she was beaten. Better women than her had been powerless in the grip of a full-on Jack attack. I squeezed her hand and turned to go up the companionway. She held on to it for a moment longer than I thought she would; I glanced back, and she was looking at me, her violet eyes dark and smudgy-looking in the lamplight.

I raised an eyebrow, *what*? She bit at her lower lip, shook her head slightly, *nothing*, and gave my hand one last squeeze.

I squeezed back, and smiled encouragingly. "See you later," I said.

Jack, overhearing me, said, "Yeah, yeah, get up there Will man."

Beside him on the bench, Andy looked up, silhouetted in the lantern light, running a hand through his sopping merman's mane. He did seem to be in some sort of shock; bewildered by it all, withdrawn almost, as if part of him was still floating out in the water, in the long night reaches where no boats came. He tried to smile; I smiled back, then trotted up the short companionway to join Danny in the wheelhouse.

"About time, Will." He sounded edgy, about half a beat off a full-scale Danny fluster. "Ship-to-shore, there. Get a move on."

There was a limit to how much I could stand of Danny playing Captain Bligh, but this was not the time to bring it up. I said nothing, and flipped the switch on the radio. Nothing. I tried again: still nothing.

"VHF's down," I said in a neutral tone, hoping Danny wouldn't take it the wrong way.

He did, of course.

"*Down*? It can't be *down*, no way, I had it up and running this afternoon. Here –" He pushed past me in the constricted space. "It's

58

simple, look. On, off…" He did exactly what I'd done: joggled the switch a few times. No grey-yellow glow on the LED frequency readout; no power-up, no nothing. Danny swore, and tried the other great standby of the non-technical layman, slapping the top of the set. The handset fell off its rest and dangled on its cord; besides that, nothing. That was Danny finished, then.

"Bollocks," he muttered under his breath. "Bollocks, bollocks, bollocks…" He seemed disproportionately panicky, I thought. After all, it wasn't the first thing that had ever gone wrong on his old tub of a charter boat: most of the equipment was second-hand or obsolete, or both and something or other was always conking out on us. So how come he was so hyper now?

He shouted down the companionway: "Jack?"

"What?"

"Ship-to-shore's out."

"Out? What you mean, out? Channel eight for comms, channel sixteen for emergencies. Have I got to do everything on this poxy boat?"

"It's not coming on." Panic rose in Danny's voice, sending it high and querulous.

Silence for a second down below decks. Then, Jack's exasperated head thrust up the companionway:

"Is it the batteries?"

Quickly I tried all the rest of the gear. The fish-finder, our newest piece of kit, ran off its own nickel-cadmiums, but everything else came off the main batteries, and it was all down, no power on board the whole of the *Katie Mae*.

"Oh, brilliant," I said under my breath.

"There's no juice," Danny told Jack, who had watched me all the way round the wheelhouse and didn't need telling.

"What you think I am, Blind Pew? I can bloody see there's no juice – get your arse down that engine hatch and find out *why* there's no juice, Danny. Make yourself useful for once, 'stead of standing round giving other people orders."

That last bit didn't go down too well, but Jack had already vanished back below. Danny stood a moment by the wheel, breathing heavily, then barged past me out on deck. The engine hatch was in the stern: I could hear Danny swearing as he banged it open and clattered down the short ladder. A few seconds later, Jack came swarming up the companionway and out on to the aft deck.

"Bloody typical," I heard him mutter, before he let himself down through the hatch to see what he could do.

I stood in the dark wheelhouse and tried to work out our options in this, our newly powerless state. Down below decks there were the hurricane lamps, and right now they were the only light we had, apart from Danny's torch. I looked at the inert console: without electricity, the head-up radar wouldn't work, and more to the point neither would the ship-to-shore VHF radio. Most worryingly of all, we could forget about the electric starter motor for the diesels; and without the diesels, we were going nowhere in a hurry. True, we might be able to start them using the auxiliary power supply, but we'd had trouble with that before when the main batteries had run down flat – which they had a habit of doing. It had been one of the things Danny had been meaning to get around to, for which read: one of the things he was going to get Jack to do for him.

At least there was the fish-finder, I thought sarcastically. That was still doing a grand job there on the side of the console, beeping away occasionally, mapping out the gently shelving bottom below the boat. Here and there on the display stray sonar returns stirred lethargically; if we'd been on a charter the punters would have been wetting themselves in anticipation of a big haul. My attention was distracted from the slow drifts and patterns on the electronic screen by Claire coming up the companionway.

"All right?" I smiled to show her everything was okay, just a few minor hiccups here, absolutely no-problemo; the dauntless crew of the *Katie Mae* coping with an emergency, just watch 'em go. "How's Andy?"

She didn't answer me straightaway.

"Danny's gone to sort the batteries out," I explained, assuming she was worried about the power being out; then I looked at her more closely, and realised it was something more than that. She was shaking from head to toe – quite literally shaking, gooseflesh standing out on her bare skin.

I was ashamed of myself. It had been a long fifteen minutes or so since we'd first had an inkling of something floating out there in the water: we'd all been through the mill a bit, emotionally speaking. No wonder Claire was still a bit freaked. I put my arms around her, but she didn't stop shivering.

"What's the matter?" I muttered into her soft-smelling hair. "No need to worry now. It's all right."

She put her hands on my biceps and held me slightly away from her. "No it's not, Will," she whispered urgently. "It's not all right – you don't know the half of it."

"What is it?" I could tell it was bad from the intensity of her response. "Why are you shaking like that?"

A huge reflexive tremor shook her all over. "It's down there." She indicated the short companionway with a glance. "It's…it's *cold*. Don't you feel it?"

Now she mentioned it, I did. It was pleasantly cool in the wheelhouse, but standing at the top of the companionway was like being in front of an open walk-in fridge.

"It's water-level down there," I explained, less than sure of my own explanation, "the water's always a few degrees colder than the ambient air temperature."

"It's not that." Claire shook her head vehemently, lips pursed. I had the feeling she knew very well what she wanted to say, but couldn't quite bring herself to say it; it was like watching someone with a stutter trying to spit it out. "It's…" she glanced back down the steps, "it's *him*." She hissed the last word, lips almost touching my ear.

"What do you mean?" I was whispering too.

Again she glanced down below, shook her head. "Not here," she said, and practically manhandled me backwards out of the wheelhouse: I had to brace my foot against the gutters to avoid going overboard. From aft came the clashing sounds of metal on metal, and of Jack and Danny arguing down the engine hatch. Claire and I went and knelt down on the foredeck, face-on to each other, knees touching.

"Should we be out here?" I wanted to know. "I don't think we ought to leave Andy on his own."

Claire took a deep breath. "Listen," she said, "that's the trouble. I've been down there with him just now, and there's something not right."

And here we were with the radio down, I thought. Brilliant. "How do you mean? Is he injured? Has he gone into shock or something?"

"Worse than that," she said, and my heart sank. "Didn't you feel anything down there?"

I looked at her, trying to work out what she was getting at. "Feel anything? Like what? I don't know, I was still a bit hyper from getting him out of the water and all that, you know?"

Claire frowned. "You were sat the other side of the table from him, weren't you?" I nodded. "So you couldn't –" A seagull swooped low over the boat sounding its harsh staccato alarm cry, a flash in the darkness over our heads. Claire jumped; if I hadn't been holding on to her she'd have probably gone over the side. She held on to me for a moment or two, then tried to tell it another way.

"Listen. When you and Danny went up, Jack was fussing round him like an old mother hen. He got him to take his clothes off and put dry ones on, towel himself off and what have you. I picked up the wet clothes; I was going to put them in one of the lockers, but I didn't like to – the touch of them…" She paused, controlled herself and carried on. "They were coming apart, Will; they were rotting away."

I didn't know what to say. "We were grabbing on to his clothes when we were trying to fish him out. I think we tore a few of the seams…"

"I didn't say *torn*," she said, "they were rotten, Will. Like they'd been in the water…I don't know. A long time."

"How long?" The voice behind me made me flinch. Danny had crept up on me again. I wished people would stop doing that; it had been a long night already, and I was getting edgy. Claire looked up. I could see the whites of her wide round eyes.

"The fabric was…disintegrating," she said. "A long time."

Danny nodded. He seemed to be about to say something, but Claire went on:

"And that's not all. Jack got me to look him over, see if he was injured at all." Again the full-body reflex tremble. "It was like touching dead meat: he didn't have any warmth in him whatsoever. What his core temperature would have been…I was shivering just touching him, *but he wasn't*." She glanced between the two of us, to make sure we registered her emphasis. "He wasn't shivering, the way you would be if you'd been hauled out of the water in the middle of the night. He never shivered, not once. He was just sitting on the bench, looking at us…" She started to shake again, and I tightened the grip of my arm around her. She squeezed it gratefully, and continued:

"Then Jack followed you up into the cabin thing, and I was left down there with him." She clutched at both her shoulders, arms crossed tightly across her chest. "He hadn't put the dry clothes on or anything; he was just looking around, as if – as if he'd never seen anything quite like that before, you know? As if there was something he couldn't get his head around; like when you're in a dream, and the details are just, I don't know, *out*…wrong somehow. And everything's slowed down, and your reactions are like you're trying to move, but everything's going like *this* –" She mimicked slow-motion, moving her head laboriously from side to side.

Yes, I thought, that was it; Claire had put her finger on it. I could see it now, the way he'd looked with a stupefied sort of incomprehension from one to the other of us as we'd gathered round him down below; the way he'd gazed at the lanterns hanging from the bulkheads, at the pictures of mermaids on the ceiling up above. Beside us on the deck Danny was nodding; he'd recognised it too.

"So," Claire resumed, "I said to him, 'come on, better get these dry clothes on, or you'll catch your death'. And he just…he looked round at me, and he nodded, but it was as if he couldn't really work out what I was asking him to do. I thought he might've taken a knock to the head or something, maybe he was still concussed, so I said, 'here, I'll help you', and I went over to him and sort of got his arms up above his head, you know, like when you're trying to put a jumper on a little kid?

"I was trying not to touch him too much, 'cos..." she looked at me, and I nodded, *yeah, go on,* "and I got the dry jumper and slipped it over his head, and then..." She started shivering again, her voice suddenly tremulous. "And then I felt the back of his head, and there was all his hair, you know, all long and wet, and underneath it –" the words came out all in a rush, "underneath it there was this big dent in the back of his head. It was huge, like the size of my fist, and it was like the whole back of his head had been caved in, and you could feel the edges of the bones grinding together." She wrung at my arm, as if to make my own bones grind. "And I snatched my hand away, and I thought there'd be blood, but there wasn't any blood, and he just kept on looking at me, like he didn't understand..." She was crying by now, and I hugged her, as much to stop myself from shaking as to stop her.

Danny was still nodding his head. "I was trying to tell Jack down the engine hatch just now," he said slowly, and if he'd been drunk or stoned before he sounded dead straight now; scared out of his wits, but straight. "I heard something about a lad going missing off one of the Bangor boats – I couldn't think of the name, though. It might have been the Wanderley." He stopped.

"When did you hear that?" It didn't sound like my voice; it sounded like the voice of someone much younger and much, much more nervous.

"...Two or three days back," said Danny miserably, and none of us said anything for a minute or two there on the foredeck. Eventually I broke the silence:

"He can't...that can't be him. No way."

"You didn't touch his skin," said Claire stubbornly. "I did. He's been out the water fifteen minutes now, and he still hasn't got *any* body heat. That's not natural. Even in the middle of winter that wouldn't be natural. It's summer, a hot summer night. And he's freezing."

"You saw him," was all Danny said to me. "You saw what he was like."

"So he's still cold – so he's a bit out of it still – so what?" I was only resisting for fear of what might follow, because even to admit the possibility of what Claire and Danny were suggesting would be to kiss goodbye to anything resembling sanity, or safety. "He can't get warm. It doesn't make him a fucking zombie." Well, the word was out now.

Danny was shaking his head. "You don't last three days in the water, Will. If he went off that boat Saturday night, he'd've been dead for Sunday – Sunday at the latest – even then he still wouldn't've been lying round waiting for us to come by. The coastguards would've been crawling all over this stretch, and the choppers from RAF Valley; they'd have got him if he'd been floating on top of the water, man…what is it?"

My mouth must have been open; it's a bad habit I have. I was thinking about back before in the wheelhouse, when Claire and I had been necking and she'd asked me what that thing was going beep. The fish-finder, I'd said; and now I remembered it, that large echo we'd all thought was a seal. By the time we asked Jack it was already up on the surface, but before that – I swallowed. Before that, it had been rising, slowly, from off the sea-bed. That's what corpses do, after a day or so. The gases balance out the dead weight, and they rise…

"*What*?" We were all extremely nervous now, Danny as much as anyone. "Spit it out, for Christ's sake."

"This is the Llys Helig stretch, isn't it?" My voice was steady, just. "We were talking about it, just before. What was it your dad used to say about this stretch?"

Danny was nodding before I'd finished. Clearly he'd been thinking along the same lines.

"It was all along the banks here." He gestured out across the waves. "All the old fishermen said the sea was twitchy from here out to Puffin Island." Twitchy, that had been it; strange word to use. "They said…they said it would spit out its drowned." He glanced back towards the wheelhouse unhappily.

"Yeah," I said, looking straight at Claire. I was going to tell her she was right, if I could find the bottle to come out with it, but in the end I just nodded. She didn't say anything; but she put a hand to my face and I held it, very tight.

"What are we gonna *do* –" began Danny, but then Jack shouted from down the engine hatch:

"Oy! Knobber! *Hand* down here? Jesus…"

"Okay," I said, deciding I'd be the grown-up on this boat. "Look, whatever we do, we've got to get moving again. You go and get those diesels started up, Danny."

He was half-way over to the hatch before he remembered who was supposed to be playing captain. "What about you two? What are you going to do?"

"We're going to take care of the other thing," I said. In all my years on boats I'd never been seasick; but I came close to it then, thinking about what the two of us would have to do next.

*

Claire and I talked it over for five minutes or so. It wasn't that we disagreed on the crux of it – I think part of her had sensed the truth about Andy almost from the start, and I was all the way convinced by now – but she wasn't happy with what I proposed doing about it.

"It's murder," she said.

I said, "How can it be? He's dead already." Saying it like that was awful; as bad as touching him would have been, knowing what we knew now, as bad as the thought that what you'd touch was...not alive, not in any way that you could recognise. But something in her balked at doing the necessary thing. I tried to argue my case, to convince her, but the trouble was what I wanted to do had nothing with reason or logic. It was as instinctive as treading in something and wiping your foot clean; as brushing a fly off your food.

But she knew that as well, every bit as much as I did. More so, because she'd been down in the cabin with him, had laid hands on his bare skin and felt...what she'd felt. I think those scruples we were both wrestling with were actually something more like nostalgia, a longing for the last few remnants of the everyday shape of things. Maybe in situations like that you'll hang on to anything that says 'this isn't happening, everything is perfectly normal, you can't seriously be going to do this...'

But we were going to do it, because it had to be done. We couldn't have taken *that* back to harbour with us – we couldn't have walked him off the boat, taken him back to his dad in Conwy and said, 'look, here he is, here's your lad Andy back safe and sound'. That would have been a hundred times crueller than what we were about to do now. So yes, I felt bad; but it was the lesser of two evils. I was completely sure of that, just as sure as I was that come the daylight I would probably feel like the shittiest, most cowardly assassin in all creation. But it was hours yet till the daylight, and below decks we had a dead man who didn't know he was dead yet. So I went into the wheelhouse, stood at the top of the companionway and called:

"Andy?" The first time it got swallowed up in a sort of gag reflex; I gulped, and called out again, "Andy?"

No answer from below decks; just the slow pinging of the fish-finder. This was what I'd been afraid of. Gingerly, I grabbed the

65

woodwork of the companionway hatch, and lowered myself into the space below decks. I was ready to spring back if anything happened; what, I didn't know. But I knew that I didn't want to do this; didn't want to look now into the lantern light and see –

He was sitting just as we'd left him. The jumper Claire had tried to put on him was ruched up around his chest; he had one arm still caught in the arm-hole, and I think it was that – something as banal and stupid as that – that finally convinced me, if I'd really needed convincing. A child could have poked his arm through that sleeve – *would* have done it, out of pure reflex; but Andy hadn't.

I stepped down, till there was just the table between us. "Andy?" I said again, and he looked up. I was already making to look away, but I couldn't help it, our eyes met. His eyes were so black, so empty; how could I have looked into them and thought him alive?

I'd meant to say something else, but what came out was, "You all right?" It was crazy enough on the face of it, but what would have been normal? He nodded; I could see him nodding, as I stared down at my feet.

"Cold," he said; that was all.

Then, out of nowhere, I found myself saying, "Come on: let's get your arm through there."

Considering what I had in mind, it seemed like the height of hypocrisy; but I think it was a kinder instinct than I gave myself credit for at the time. Steeling myself, still not looking him straight in the face, I reached across and lifted the folding table up. I stretched out the wool of the jumper with one hand and slipped the other into the sleeve. Feeling around inside, my fingers touched his: he was making no attempt to reach through and hold on, which was probably just as well. Cold? More than cold; it was as if he'd never been warm, as if he'd lain on that ocean bed for as long as the sea had lain on the land. Fighting to keep my guts down, I dragged his arm through and let go the jumper. Released, his arm fell back down by his side; dead weight.

Doing that helped me with what came next, with the physical side of it at least.

"Right," I said, in a ghastly pretence at practicality, "let's get you up on deck, shall we?" He looked up blankly. I had to look, had to make sure he was going to do it. Those eyes: I couldn't afford to look into them for too long. God knows what I would have seen in there; or what he might have seen in mine, perhaps. "Come on," I said, turned part-way away from him. "They're waiting for you up on deck."

In the end I had to help him to his feet. He was like a machine running down, almost; I hate to think what would have happened if we'd actually tried to take him back to dry land. Even through the layer of wool I could feel a dreadful pulpiness everywhere that wasn't bone. Again the gag came in my throat; I clamped my jaw shut and took him under one arm, and he came up unresisting, balanced precariously in his squelching shoes. A little puddle of rank seawater had collected around his feet. The smell – I was close enough to get the smell now, but I don't want to talk about it. I dream about it sometimes, on bad sweating nights in the hot midsummer.

I motioned him ahead. Obediently, he stepped forward, and as he passed me I saw the horrible indentation in the back of his skull. The hair which had covered it before had flattened now, and the concave dent was all too clearly visible. No-one could have taken a wound like that and survived. Just before I looked away, the bile rising in my throat, I thought I saw something in there; something white and wriggling. I came very near to losing it entirely in that moment.

If he'd needed help getting up the companionway, I would've had to have called Danny through – there was no way I could have touched him, not after seeing that wound in the back of his head. As it was, he put one foot on the steps, then, after what seemed ages, the next, and trudged up into the wheelhouse. I tried to focus on the normal things: on the feel of the wooden rail as I stepped up behind him into the wheelhouse; on the brass plaque that said *Katie Mae*, there beside the wheel; on the ping of the fish-finder in the silence. As Andy paused, silhouetted against the dim starlight of outside, waiting for me to tell him what to do next, I took several deep breaths.

"Now?" I said, and waited for Claire's voice.

"Now," she said, a small voice from out of the darkness, and I ran forwards with both arms straight out in front of me. Andy was in the act of turning round, and I just glimpsed his eyes; there was a greenish phosphorescence to them in the dark, and Claire said later that I screamed out loud as my hands made contact with his shoulder-blades.

He was standing in the wheelhouse doorway. Ahead of him was just the narrow stretch of deck that linked fore and aft, and then the low side of the boat. Claire was crouching beneath the level of the wheelhouse door; on my signal she'd straightened up on to her hands and knees as I came up on Andy from behind. My push sent him careening forwards; he flipped straight over Claire's upthrust back and out over the side of the boat. There was a solid, crunching impact as he hit the water; Claire was up off her knees and into my arms as the cold spray drenched the pair of us.

"What the *fuck*?" It was Jack. He was standing in the engine hatch; clearly he couldn't believe what he'd just seen. "You stupid bloody – what the *fuck*, man?" He clambered up through the hatch and started towards us. Claire tried to get in his way, but he pushed her angrily to one side; she went sprawling into the wheelhouse. Jack squared up to me, fists clenched: no matter how smoothly it had gone with Andy, I saw I was in for at least one fight that evening. He swung away, cursing, and dropped to his knees; I realised he was scrabbling around down in the gutters for the boat-hook he'd used earlier, so that he could fish Andy out of the water a second time.

I was backing round on to the foredeck, trying to think what to do, how to explain it to him, when several things happened more or less simultaneously.

The spotlight on top of the wheelhouse glowed dully for a moment, then blinked sharply back into life; it caught Jack in the act of rising from his knees, boathook in one hand, the other shielding his squinting eyes as the beam shone full into his face.

Danny's voice rose above the engine sound: "Got you, you bastard! Batteries up and *running*!"

And in the wheelhouse, Claire was shouting: "Will? *Will*!"

Heedless of Jack, who by then was down on his knees plunging the boathook into the black water, I pushed past and into the wheelhouse.

"What? What is it?"

Fist up to her mouth, Claire just stood there, unable to speak. Then she pointed at the console. The fish-finder was beeping still, more frequently than before, more insistently. I looked at the traces on screen and my mouth went dry.

Down underneath the *Katie Mae*, fathoms down in the dark and cold, big sluggish blips were rising; detaching themselves from the sea-bed, drifting up towards the surface. I didn't need Jack to interpret them for me this time; I recognised them all too well. Before, we'd thought they were seals. Now, we knew better.

"...Stay here," I managed to get out. Claire nodded, and I turned back to the doorway of the wheelhouse. There was Jack, bending over the side of the boat, his back to us. The stretch of water beyond him was brightly illuminated by our spotlight, still pointing where Claire had left it earlier. One look was all I needed. I grabbed Jack by the shoulder: he'd managed to hook a shapeless mass in the water, and was struggling to bring it in to the side of the boat.

"Jack, Jack," I croaked in his ear, "wait, no, look out there…"

He pushed me away with a curse, went on trying to raise up the body in the water. I thumped his back, hard, and he swung round, ready to hit me.

"Fucking *look*," I hissed, and almost despite himself he turned round.

There they were, caught by the spotlight on the still surface; bodies, rising up out of the sea. Five or six just in that bright ellipse of light; how many others, out there in the dark where we couldn't see? I'd counted at least a dozen on the fish-finder; there might be more by now. A low, unspeakably nasty sound came back to us over the waves, somewhere between a hiss and a gurgle. At the same time a stink hit us from off the water, like nothing I'd smelled before nor want to ever again. Jack turned back to me, round-eyed, horrified; opened his mouth to say something. Then it happened.

A hand came up and grasped the boathook. It nearly pulled Jack in; quickly he steadied himself, clutching at me and letting go his grip on the wooden shaft. The thing that had grabbed it – the thing Jack had thought was Andy – disappeared under the waves again, taking the boathook down with it, then bobbed back up to the surface. Whatever it was, it had been down there far longer than Andy had. Most of what had once made it human was rotted away; what was left was vile beyond my capacity to describe. It rested there on the swell awhile, goggling up at us as we stood petrified on the deck. Then, without warning, it swung the boathook up out of the water.

The metal hook ripped a long hole in Jack's t-shirt. Within seconds, the whole of his chest was slick with blood. He staggered back, and the hook caught on the belt of his jeans. It nearly dragged him into the water, but I grabbed him just in time. He was screaming, wordlessly, incoherently. So was I; but I held on tight, arms round his body, feet braced against the scuppers, straining backwards with all my might.

I managed to call out Danny's name. I felt him grab on to me from behind and yelled as loudly as I could, "Pull!"

We both strained away, and then all of a sudden the pressure was off and we all three of us went sprawling backwards, me on top of Danny, Jack across both of us. We disentangled ourselves, and Jack pulled clear the boathook from his belt. Before he flung the whole thing as far away as he could, we had just enough time to see the hand and lower part of an arm that still clung to the other end.

Meanwhile Danny had seen what was happening out on the water, the bodies coming to the surface all around. From the look on his face I knew he was going to lose it unless I did something drastic, so without thinking I spun him round and practically threw him into the wheelhouse.

"Get us out of here," I told him, and turned back to where Jack was kneeling on the deck. There was blood all over him, and over me too where I'd held on to him: I knelt down alongside him to see how badly he was hurt, but he pushed me away. I knew it was because of what Claire and I had done to Andy, but there was no time for that now. I looked round for something I could use to defend the boat with, yelling over my shoulder, "Danny! Move it!"

A throaty grumble came from aft as the diesels turned over, choked momentarily, then caught.

"Get us out," I shouted, as there came a clang from the foredeck. I clambered up around the wheelhouse, spinning the spotlight around to face for'ard as I went. There was the boathook that Jack had thrown away, snagged this time on the prow. Something was using it to clamber up and over the rail: without thinking I ran towards it and kicked out hard. My foot sank part-way into a soft crunching mass; the momentum almost sent me spinning over, but I managed to steady myself on the Samson post as the thing splashed backwards into the water. There was something on my foot, some reeking slimy filth or other – I was scraping it frenziedly against one of the cleats, trying to get the worst of it off, when I became aware of Danny hammering the glass windscreen of the wheelhouse.

He was yelling something about "haul it in": I didn't understand what he was saying at first, but then I realised. We were still riding at anchor; Danny had revved the engines to loosen the anchor from its lodgement on the sea-bed, but before we could open up the throttle and head for clear water it needed to be winched all the way back in.

I edged back round the side of the wheelhouse, with no time to stop for Claire as she pressed her face to the glass, her lips forming words I couldn't hear. Below me, down in the water, things were moving up against the side of the boat. We had to get clear.

The capstan was on the starboard side, by the door to the wheelhouse. I gave a tug at the anchor-rope: it wouldn't shift.

"Again," I called up to Danny in the wheelhouse; he engaged reverse thrust again, and the rope creaked, then gave a little as the anchor cleared the sea-bed. I threw the switch that turned on the electric motor of the capstan, but just at that moment there came a vicious tug on the rope. Sparks flashed beneath the motor housing, and an acrid gout of smoke rose from the capstan-head; I tried it again, and again, but the motor had burned out. Frantically, I tried to use the hand-bars to winch up the anchor, but the whole thing seemed to be fused solid.

"Jack," I shouted; he looked up from where he lay cradling his stomach, saw the problem, and struggled over to help.

Five fathoms, maybe six; that's thirty-six feet of rope first, then chain, and a heavy iron anchor at the end of it. It took Jack and I all the strength we could muster to raise it, arm over arm, winding the slack around the useless capstan-head. It wasn't the first time we'd had to haul up an anchor manually, but it seemed far heavier now than it ever had before, impossibly heavy, and when we'd got it almost all the way up, as far as the ten foot or so of chain before the anchor itself, I looked over the side to see if we were still snagged on anything.

Have patience with me now, because I have to tell this a certain way. In the village where I used to live as a child, near Diss in Norfolk, there was a pool out in the fields which was absolutely stiff with rudd, a freshwater fish related to the roach. We used to tie a piece of string around a five-penny loaf and throw it in, and then we'd watch the water boil as we pulled on the string to bring the bread back up, the whole thing completely covered in a huge squirming feeding-cluster of rudd. That scene, that image, was what I thought of as I peered over the side of the *Katie Mae* and saw the anchor just below the surface.

Clustered round the anchor, hanging on to it in a crawling hideous mass, were maybe six or seven of the bodies, dragged up from the oozing deep, up from long years of slow decay down where the sun's warmth and light never penetrates, there on the chilly bottom. Green phosphorescent eyes stared back at me, and a billow of putrescence erupted in bubbles on to the surface. I dropped the anchor chain as if it had been electrified, and the gruesome mass sank back a foot or two into the water.

"Hang on!" Jack grabbed at the chain quickly before the lot went down again. "Keep it tight!" Out of his pocket he pulled a hunting-knife; I didn't get what he meant to do with it until he began to saw at the anchor-rope above the chain where it was wound round the capstan. Understanding at last, I pulled on the chain to keep the line taut. All the while, I was hearing things: sounds of splashing and gulping from over the side where the anchor was banging against the hull, and that awful gurgling hiss rising off the water again. Out of nowhere, words came into my head: *the voices of all the drowned …*

I didn't dare look down there; only when Jack sawed through the last strands of the rope and the freed chain rattled over the side did I risk one quick glance over, just in time to see the anchor with its cluster of bodies receding into the deep. Hands clutched vainly up towards the surface, and those greenish eyes blinked out into cold fathoms of blackness.

Sick to my stomach with fear and disgust, I turned away to where Jack was clambering to his feet. I tried to help him up, but he brushed my hand away and went foraging instead through the storage box where we'd formerly kept the anchor and its chain. He came up with an old length of chain about four feet long; he took a couple of turns around his fist, and swung the rest around.

"You take the for'ard," he said, wincing as he held his wounded stomach. "I'll get the aft. Get something from in here –" he kicked the storage box, "and use the spotlight if you can, so's we can see what we're up against. *Danny!*" He roared the last word in the direction of the wheelhouse. "What's with the fucking hold-up? They're all around us, man: Will and me can't keep 'em off forever, you know!"

The boat was hardly moving in the water. From aft came the sound of spluttering, overstressed engines; Jack swore and looked at me narrowly.

"You just keep your eyes peeled back here," was all he said. He tossed me the length of chain and stumbled off into the wheelhouse to get the *Katie Mae* moving again. Around us in the water, the shapes multiplied: there must have been twenty of them now, more maybe. Drawn by God knows what – the promise of dry land, perhaps, or some primal impulse more atavistic, more terrible than that – they were converging on the boat. And all I had was a four-foot length of chain to keep them off.

Maybe not all: suddenly there was the beam of the spotlight shining on to the aft deck, picking out the white painted railings, the glimmer of the sea beyond and below. I heard Claire's voice:

"Over that way, Will." The beam swung round, then steadied on a ghastly greenish arm slung over the port side.

I swung the chain at it. It cut a rent along the length of the arm, laid bare the glint of white bone, but the fingers didn't relinquish their grip. A head and shoulders hoisted up above the side of the boat. I gave it another swing of the chain, and this time the contact was good. It toppled upside-down, its head in the water, its feet caught up in the tyre buffers slung around the hull, and with a few more slashes I managed to dislodge it entirely.

But by then Claire was screaming, "Behind you, behind you," and when I turned round another of the creatures was already halfway over the aft rail. Again I let fly, but not strongly or viciously enough. The chain only wrapped around its arm: it caught hold of the links, and began tugging me in towards it. Repulsed, I let go immediately; the thing teetered there a moment, then the engines kicked in at last. It was caught off balance and fell backwards: a horrible splintering noise and a shiver that went clean through the boat told me it had hit the propeller.

We began to pick up speed, pulling away from the writhing mass of bodies on the surface, but there were still a dozen or more of the things hanging on to the side of the boat, arms twined in the tyre buffers, hands clutching on to the railings, hammering at the clanging echoing hull. If we slowed down, they would try again to get up on board. We had to shift them somehow. I was leaning over the side, whacking away with a wrench from down the engine hatch, when Jack appeared at my side. The blood had dried black all down him, and he looked like he should have been in a hospital bed; instead, he was sloshing diesel oil from a big jerrycan over the side of the boat and on to the clinging bodies.

"What you doing?" was all I could get out between panting.

"Kill or cure," he said grimly, edging all along the side of the boat emptying out the diesel on to the creatures that hung leechlike to the hull. In a minute he was back round to my other side. He dumped the jerrycan straight down onto the head of one of the things, sending it sinking beneath the waves, then reached in his pocket and brought out his cherished old brass Zippo with the engraved marijuana leaf. With just a trace of his usual flamboyance, he flicked open the top and ran the wheel quickly along the seam of his bloodied jeans, down, then up, like a gunslinger's quick-draw. The flint struck and the flame sparked bright, first time every time; Jack held it aloft for a second, then dropped it over the side.

I snapped my head back just in time, feeling my eyebrows singe and shrivel in the sudden blast of heat. Immediately, flames sprang up all along the waterline, lighting up the ocean all around us a vivid orange. For a little while we could see every detail of the things in the water; how they writhed and bubbled in the flame, how their mouths opened and closed, how they charred and blackened as the fire licked up the hull, blistering the paintwork, setting light to the tyre-buffers. I heard a hissing indrawn breath from Jack beside me, thought for a moment *oh no, he's fucked up, he's got it wrong with the diesel, the ship's going up*, and then I saw where he was looking down in the water. One of the burning bodies was Andy's: arm upraised, face still recognisable amidst the flames, it slowly rolled off the side and was lost in our wake, along with the rest of the corpses of the drowned.

*

73

It was already brightening in the east as we brought the *Katie Mae* back into harbour. All her sides were scorched and black and battered and we, her crew, were similarly scarred, though in ways less obvious and maybe less repairable with a sanding-off and a fresh lick of paint. Jack had refused our help with his stomach wound on the way back; he'd sat out on the aft deck hugged into a fetal tuck, not talking to anyone, not looking anywhere except backwards at our lengthening wake. Claire and I sat squeezed up on the wheelhouse bench behind Danny, who stood at the wheel staring for'ard all the way home to Beuno's Cove. We didn't try talking to each other; really, what was there to say?

When we came alongside, Jack scrambled up on to the quayside to tie us up. He stood looking back at the boat for a second, silhouetted above us in the predawn light, then without saying anything he turned away. I glanced back at Danny and saw he was crying. Perhaps I should have done something, I don't know what, but Claire took my hand and more or less dragged me up on to the quay. We left him there on the deck; I wanted to say, are you going to be okay, but perhaps Claire was right. It was the last time I ever set foot on the *Katie Mae*.

Back home Claire ran straight upstairs and turned the shower on. I went up after about twenty minutes and she was squatting in a corner of the stall with the hot water running cold, arms wound about her knees, sobbing uncontrollably. What could I do? I got in there and fetched her out, got her dry, got her warm; but I couldn't stop her shivering, not until she finally fell asleep on the bed, hours later, after we'd tried and failed to talk through the events of the night just gone. We tried several times again, in the days and weeks that followed, but it never came to anything; we felt the way murderers must feel, and so, I suppose, did Jack, because not long after he moved away and no-one ever saw him again, not Claire or me, not even Danny.

Back to that first morning, though, the morning after; I stayed with Claire for a while till I was sure she was properly asleep, then I eased off the bed and went downstairs. There was a book I'd borrowed from Danny's old man, a collection of maritime myths and legends of North Wales: I went through it and found the entry for Llys Helig. A curse had been laid on Helig's family and their lands, vengeance for old wrongs, a whispering voice coming out of nowhere, heard all around the great halls and gardens of Llys Helig prophesying doom on his grandsons and great-grandsons, and one day the floodwaters came and washed over everything. And ever since, said the legend, the drowned have never rested easy in that stretch. As if. I preferred Danny's dad's unvarnished version myself: that the sea was just twitchy out there, no more, no less. Nothing you could explain away with spells and whispers and fairytales, a condition no story would cover; just a state of things, something you knew about and left well alone, if you knew what was good for you.

But there was something else; something that had been at the back of my mind ever since I'd first heard those hisses and gurgles out on the waves. I didn't have nearly as many books then as I have now, but it still took me the best part of half an hour to lay my hands on it: Dylan Thomas' *Selected Poems*. And I read there the poem, the one I'd half-remembered:

Under the mile off moon we trembled listening
To the sea sound flowing like blood from the loud wound
And when the salt sheet broke in a storm of singing
The voices of all the drowned swam on the wind.

Upstairs Claire moaned a little in her sleep. I got up, climbed the creaky stairs as quietly as I could, and eased myself on to the bed beside her. The curtains were pulled to, and the little bedroom under the eaves was getting stuffy in the full heat of the day. The paperback was still in my other hand, finger marking my place, and I read from it again:

We heard the sea sound sing, we saw the salt sheet tell
Lie still, sleep becalmed, hide the mouth in the throat
Or we shall obey, and ride with you through the drowned.

I shivered, and beside me Claire shivered too, as if in unconscious sympathy. The sun was hot and strong through the bright yellow curtains, but I felt as if I'd never be warm again.

MEG

Is a humungous super-carnivore still lurking in the ocean's depths? Is it possible there is a shark out there measuring somewhere between 60 feet and 90 feet from nose to tail, with a body mass weighing in at 50 metric tons, and a mouth some seven feet across lined with rows of sabre-like teeth, each one averaging eight inches in length?

If that thought isn't terrifying enough, the real-life monster fitting this bill – a denizen of the ancient oceans known to science as 'Charcarodon megalodon' (plain old Megalodon to the rest of us) – could apply a crushing 41,000 lb bite, ten times the bite attributable to the largest known great white shark of today. In an age when our seas swarmed with nightmare beasts, Megalodon was the apex-predator. It rightly held its place among the killer elite of the prehistoric world.

And yet maybe, just maybe, the story doesn't end there.

Officially, Megalodon lived up until about two million years ago. Yet in evolutionary terms that is not an especially long period of time. The last dinosaurs died out 65 million years ago, some 50 million years before Megalodon even appeared. Moreover, there is a lack of consensus among palaeontologists as to why it might have become extinct, or even if it became extinct at all. The Coelacanth, another bony fish of the early Earth, was believed to have died out in the late Cretacious period, but turned up again, very much alive, in 1938. Perhaps it shouldn't have been a complete surprise then that in 1872, crewmen belonging to the Royal Navy corvette, HMS Challenger, dredged up a Megalodon tooth that only seemed to be about 10,000 years old (a blink of an eye in fossil terms). And it goes on. Throughout human history, etchings and cave paintings have depicted encounters with monstrous fish, in some cases showing human captives being sacrificed to these horrors of the deep.

But perhaps we don't need to venture so far back to find such unnerving evidence.

In 2004, a Japanese research team was observing deep sea wildlife in Suruga Bay at the north end of the Mariana Trench in the Western Pacific. The Mariana is the deepest realm in the world's oceans, plunging to a mind-boggling seven miles (36,000 feet). Suruga Bay itself is only about a mile deep, though that is still over 5,000 feet, which makes it a rich hunting ground when it comes to new species. At the time, the team had lowered a tray of chum to the *bottom of the bay, with cameras affixed, and was busy tabulating the varied creatures that partook of the feast. Most specimens fled when a school of six-foot sharks turned up, though a few minutes later these six-footers also sped away as though alarmed by something. The researchers were then stunned to see the snout of another shark nudge into view – because this one was a giant, an absolute colossus. Only a small portion of it almost completely filled the lens. This, along with the muddy, grainy quality of the film, made it difficult if not impossible to identify the creature, but later analysis estimated that it was an incredible 62 feet in length – no known shark today grows to such a prodigious size. It didn't take long for the story, and the footage, to circle the world via the internet, and for the name Megalodon to start cropping up.*

Also in 2004, the Commonwealth Scientific and Industrial Research Organisation's white shark satellite tagging programme was interrupted off the coast of south-western Australia when one of the animals, a nine-foot white-pointer that had been tagged four months earlier, suddenly vanished from the screens. A short while later, the tag was recovered by a beachcomber in nearby Bremer Bay. According to its data, the tagged animal had inexplicably dived 1,903 feet before expiring, while the ambient temperature registered by the tag had immediately shot up from 8°C to 26°C. At the same time, the tag itself appeared to have been bleached as though by stomach acid. All of this suggested that the powerful great white had been swallowed by a much larger animal. Several culprits were suggested, from another great white (which idea most researchers found inconceivable – how large would the other great white have to be?) to an unusually sized orca, though it was argued that the interior of a mammalian stomach would have been much warmer than was shown in the data. Clearly, whatever ate the white-pointer was another fish – a very, very big one.

Common sense dictates all kinds of reasons why Megalodon can no longer be prowling our oceans. It would need to live in the ultimate depths to have avoided detection for this long, and yet reconstructed skeletons suggest it preferred warmer, shallower waters, particularly during the nursery stage of its life cycle, when it would need plentiful prey. This would most likely take it along the continental shelf and even up to coastlines, in which case it is impossible to imagine that it wouldn't be spotted and filmed more regularly. But as so often is the case with rumoured undersea life-forms which appear to defy all the conventional rules, there are few who will say for certain that this fabled 'tyrannosaur of the ocean' is not still down there, biding his time as he watches us from the inky darkness.

77

THE SEVENTH WAVE
Lynda E. Rucker

1

Do you know the story about the girl who walked into the sea?

Did she drown?

No, she didn't drown. They pulled her out.

That's good.

No it's not. It was the worst thing in the world they could have done.

I want to begin this story in this way: I have always loved the sea. But then I stop and I think: which sea? There are so many of them. There is the sea of my childhood: the flat blue glass of Florida's Gulf Coast, the dirty ocean off Galveston Island in Texas. There are the seas of my later years, the freezing Atlantic smashing against the shores of western Ireland, the windswept grey waters of the Oregon coast outside my home right now. And there are the seas of my imagination, the seas I read about in books and never saw, or saw and was disappointed by so that the sea remains forever extant only in my memory. There is the sea of the Greek isles, a sea I somehow always thought would indeed be *wine-dark*, and it was not. There is what I think of as the Gothic sea: it is somewhere off an English coast, surrounded by cliffs and moors and castles with family secrets and brooding men lurking about. This sea, too, does not exist except in my mind.

Then we have the metaphorical sea: we can be all at sea, which is bad, or in a sea of love, which is good, I guess.

But my story is about the sea, and about love, and it is not a good story at all. Or rather, the story itself is a good one, I suppose, if you are not in the story, because the things that happen in it are very bad indeed.

Because I am old, and because tonight I *feel* old, and because it is forty years to the day from another, terrible night, I am going to set down here the story of myself and the sea, and all that it took from me.

Every thing and every person that I ever loved taken from me.

Do you know the story about the girl who walked into the sea?

Women and men have been throwing themselves at death on account of love for as long as there have been humans and some concept of love, or maybe for longer: when I was a child, I had a dog who mourned the passing of its mate by refusing food for so long it nearly died itself. Before our not-yet-human ancestors were capable of the kind of planning that hastening death requires, they probably still starved themselves, or lay out in the elements, or let themselves get eaten by sabre-toothed tigers rather than bother trying to carry on.

Anyone who isn't terrified of love is either a fool or has no idea what it means. For myself, I'd sooner be flayed alive than fall in love again. You might say there is little chance of either of those things happening. At four score and five I am supposed to be preparing to die, but not from love, and certainly not from *la petite mort* – just from ordinary decay. At my age, the capacity for that quickening of the heart and the spirit and the loins is supposed to be long gone. And yet it happens. It happens to those my age and even those older than me, the ninety-year-olds, the hundred-year-olds. The human heart is never too old for passion. It is the very young who believe otherwise, but then, the very young believe everything is for them and them alone. There is the old, true adage that every generation believes it has discovered sex for the first time: and yet there is no act, no position, no method of penetration or manner of stimulation or path to ecstasy or perversion that men and women have not been doing to one another in various combinations for at least as long as they have been dying for love.

I find this extraordinarily heartening. I wonder how different humans might be if we wrote history as a chronicle of significant orgasms rather than political intrigues, poisonings, betrayals, battles won and lost. I take a wicked pleasure in saying this sometimes to people because it shocks them. *"Abigail!"* they tut, or *"Mrs. Brennan!"* if they are on less familiar terms with me, clearly believing I am one of those elderly people who has taken leave of my senses and is now just saying any old thing that pops into my head. And none are ever so shocked as the young. For all their posturing, the young really are terribly conservative, because they *are* so young, and so hopeful, and so they've yet to figure out that nothing at all ever really matters much in the end.

But where was I? I am old, you see, and I digress so readily. Ah, yes. The sea. The ghost story. Lost love. And the girl who walked into the sea, the girl they pulled back out again.

You may or may not have surmised by now that the girl was me, and if so, you are correct. Had they not pulled me out again, *I* might have been the ghost in this story. And a terrifying, vengeful ghost I would have been as well. I'd have smashed ships against rocks, rent sailors limb to limb, drowned swimming lovers. I was so consumed with sorrow and pain on that day that I walked into the sea. Those things would have felt almost like an act of mercy to me, as though I were doing those people a favour, showing them the true face of the world, and that at the end of it all there is only suffering and fear. Sparing them one more single agonising second of living.

Despite all this, it would, as I said, have been better had they left me there to drown.

I am certain as well that you do not need to be told *why* I walked into the sea that day: for love, of course. For the sake of a man. I was twenty-five years old, a late bloomer, as they say, but then I was possessed of a lethal combination of being both intelligent *and* unattractive. These days a woman can buy permission to be smart or talented or successful with good looks, for as long as she remains young at least; in my day, being pretty meant you couldn't possibly be bright while plainness was just an affront to everyone. By everyone, of course, I mean men.

I must have been almost unfathomably easy prey for Philip, the married man at the office where I worked who set his sights on me. (Philip, how funny to think of him now! He is either very old or, more likely, very dead. I cannot imagine encountering him now, doddering and senile). In those days, for me, both virginal and naïve, he was the height of dashing sophistication. I had never even kissed a man, had presumed I would be a spinster my entire life, and as for sex, that was something I gave little thought to, and never in connection with myself. The result of all this was that a man I later came to understand was very ordinary was able to seduce me and convince me that without him, my life was worthless. After two months of surreptitious rendezvous in his car, twice in the office, once in a hotel room (I told myself then he must *really* love me), he informed me that he had no intention of leaving his wife; two weeks later it was clear he'd taken up with the nineteen-year-old secretary hired a week before he dumped me.

I was, as I said, naïve. I had imagined that there was something extraordinary in what passed between us, in the pleasures of sex, that anything that seemed so intimate must surely *be* intimate. I was in love, though not with him – people say *in love with love*, and that's wrong too. I was in love with the man I thought he was, and in those short two months, I believed I was the best version of myself I have ever been although in fact I was alternately neurotic, terrified, giddy, hopeless, and consumed. Love can do that to you. And then it ends.

When it became clear to me that I had been no more than a passing fancy that he quickly tired of, I resolved to kill myself, both to send him a message and because I truly did feel that I would not be able to live with my pain. Better that he had cut me open and literally torn my heart from my body than this agony of drawing breath after breath. I did not yet understand how the most appalling pain can recede over time even if it never goes away. Time doesn't heal, but enough of it and it begins to tell us lies that let us live in the present, if we allow it.

If the past does not come to you. Did you hear about the girl who walked into the sea? Did you hear what became of her children?

The story of my suicide that wasn't is routine and not very interesting. I did very little planning. In those days, I lived in Savannah, Georgia, where my family had moved to in my teens, and so I drove to Tybee Island, and found what I mistakenly believed to be a deserted bit of shoreline. Fully clothed in a skirt and a sweater and heavy shoes, I walked out into the ocean. Had I put more thought into it, I would have chosen a more reliably empty beach; I would have weighted my pockets to ensure I did not bob to the surface. I would have forced myself to drink the salt water into my lungs. That I did none of those things, however, was no indication that my suicide attempt was merely a cry for help. I was serious; but with suicide as with sex, I was a complete novice.

Novice that I was, I was spotted, and saved by a nearby fisherman. I spent two nights in the hospital, and I believed that Philip would come to me there, having seen the error of his ways. When he did not, I understood at last that I had been a very silly girl, and that I was no different from many very silly girls who had come before me. I quit my job and found a new one and resolved to stay far away from men for the rest of my days.

I told myself that I had survived not because of my rescuer, but because as I loved the sea, the sea loved me back.

I have, you understand, been mistaken about love throughout my life.

Do you hear that? Some would say it is only the howling of the wind and the crashing of the waves, but I know the sound of my children's cries. I must move along and finish my story for you before they come for me.

81

3

I had sworn to stay away from men, but the revolving door of dull office jobs that were available to no-longer-so-young women in the 1950s eventually brought me into the path of an even duller man named Bernard. He was everything Philip had not been; where Philip had been charming and smooth, Bernard was awkward and fastidious. But he had other qualities. He was steady and dependable. And we did have one thing in common: Bernard loved the sea as well. The first time he took me sailing, I thought this was a man who would never betray me as Philip had, because there was no room in his life for another love.

And so it was that almost five years to the day after they pulled me from the sea, I walked down the aisle with Bernard. No one could say that I had not done well for myself. In those days, I was considered an old bride, and fortunate to snag such a reliable man. Bernard's boring nature extended to the bedroom. I told myself I didn't care; with Philip, I had seen what passion got you. Having said that, it seems surprising to me to this day that we managed to conceive three children. I told myself I was content, and I settled into an unremarkable domestic life that was exactly the same as the content and unremarkable domestic life that most of my peers had as well. I no longer had to work or worry about the future.

But appearances deceive, do they not? Of all the dull, content, settled people around us, I would have said that Clive was the dullest of them all. Not that I am making myself out to have been a remarkable specimen myself: my oldest child, Deborah, was twelve, and I had long since passed from young and unattractive into aging and matronly, or so I felt. Clive said that was not the case; he said I kept myself trim enough to pass for at least ten years younger and that any man who could not see the unkindled fires banked in me must be blind. But he would say that, wouldn't he? He said a lot of other things, too, things married men say in affairs, but I believed they were true: that Stella, his wife, was frigid and moreover didn't love him. I couldn't have been more different from her, he said, and what he meant was there was almost nothing I wouldn't do for him, and he was right.

He even begged me to leave Bernard. And I might have; I told myself that Bernard, preoccupied with sailing and his accounting work, would hardly notice my absence. We no longer lived as husband and wife; we hadn't slept together since before our third child, Joann, now six, had been born. We even had separate bedrooms. Because I had long ago proved myself to be a poor first mate, too dreamy by far, he hadn't taken me sailing with him in years. It was just as well. I was content to sit on the shore or wade into the shallows with the children. The truth is, I liked the sea less with the children along. There seemed so many more hazards with these tiny, vulnerable people at my side: stinging things, and big waves, and tropical storms and hurricanes, and the sea itself, always pulling away from shore, too eager to take everything with it. The idea of its unfathomable depths, which had once exhilarated me, had come to terrify me instead. I suppose you could say that motherhood made me dull but I would argue instead that motherhood made me *aware*. The world was so full of danger. It was a wonder any of us managed to navigate it for any time at all.

And the sea is terrible in other ways, haunted as well – by millennia of drowned sailors. By pirates and their prey. By captains and their passengers and their crew, by mercenaries and soldiers and lost explorers, by unwary fishermen and swimmers and beachcombers and people who did not notice the tide drawing in. The sea is heaving with corpses and dead souls. It is a stew of old bones and rotten flesh.

It is my single consolation: that wherever they are out there, my children are not alone.

But still they need their mother. All children need their mother, do they not?

I know what you are thinking. That they are going to be horrors when they come in from the sea. That the loving embraces I imagine will be grips of death. That they will be foul, decayed, mad creatures, that they will fall on me with salt-puckered eyes and mouths and suck the life out of me. Or that I am mad myself: old, and mad, delusional, that I ought to have been put into a home long ago, and that I need *help*. *Help you*, hang you, burn you. You are ugly, female, and old: three strikes and you're out, but you are worse, you are alone, you are reclusive, you are not kind and grandmotherly and comforting. Your eyes do not twinkle. We are too enlightened to call you a *witch* but we will steal your life away from you anyway and lock you away and feed you drugs and call it a mercy.

So, you see, this is a risk I am willing to take. And what mother would not willingly give up her own life for her children's?

I would have, you know. What happened to them was not my fault. I couldn't have saved them. No matter what anyone says. I loved them and I lost them but I did not kill my babies.

4

They say that you never really know a person, and they are correct. Case in point: my Bernard. I thought him incapable of passion, save for his love of the sea. I thought the children and I were little more than props in his dull life. I even thought he might be the kind of man to turn a blind eye to the fact that his wife had a lover. What did he care? He didn't seem to want me.

I was wrong. Bernard found out about us, not in a dramatic fashion. He didn't stumble upon the two of us in bed together or anything so crass. He saw a look here, a touch there, noticed an absence or two that could not be explained. He is an accountant, after all, and he added it all up, and he knew.

He need not have done anything. Ours was a business arrangement, I had explained to Clive, but a business arrangement with children involved, and as such, I couldn't think of leaving him, at least not until little Joann was off to college. It wasn't fair to either Bernard or me or to the children, who adored their father.

Why could that not have been enough for Bernard? Why could he not have allowed us to go in living with a small lie within the much larger lie that we were all living, the one that said we were a happy, contented family?

Even now, I do not believe what Bernard discovered inside himself was a passion for me, or for his family. There is a certain type of man who has a passion for the things he believes to be his. His own feelings for the things are not the issue; his ownership of the things is.

I do not know how long he was aware before he took action, but he did not give me any indication that he had noticed anything. One late-spring day, I went to pick up the children at school, only to find that none of them were there. Their father had come and taken them out of class in the middle of the day.

From the moment they told me, an icy lump of fear settled in my belly. *He knows.* I told myself it was something else, something innocent, but I knew better. And yet even then, the worst-case scenario that I could imagine was that he would divorce me and be able to keep the children, because what judge would leave children with an adulterous mother? And then Clive would abandon me as well, and there I would be, middle-aged, alone, unskilled, unemployed, a pariah among all who knew me and with no resources to seek out a new community. My parents were dead, and I had no family left. Where would I go? How would I live? *Why* would I live? What would be the point of anything at all?

I phoned Bernard's office; his secretary told me he was not in. I couldn't bring myself to speak to Clive. It was as though if I did not say anything to anyone, whatever was happening would not be happening, would not be true.

I sat there in our home and I waited. I didn't know what else to do. I didn't eat or drink anything. I didn't read, or watch television. I couldn't. I smoked, compulsively, one cigarette after another. It grew dark. And then I heard the sound of Bernard's car in the driveway, the doors slamming – and the children's voices. I almost sobbed with relief. I had half-convinced myself I would never see them again.

They came tumbling in ahead of him, and immediately it was clear to me that they knew nothing was amiss; moreover, they'd had a fantastic day. All of them were sunburned and windswept, having spent the day on their father's boat, a rare treat, and they were all talking to me at once, and I started to think that perhaps I had been wrong. Perhaps Bernard had had a single unpredictable moment out of his entire life and decided that he and the children would enjoy spending a day sailing, with no ulterior motives or secret knowledge behind it all.

Then he walked in, and I looked at him, and I knew.

He said quietly, "Joann, Kevin, Deborah – go brush your teeth and go to bed. Your mother and I need to talk."

They all stopped short at the sound of his voice, and I remember thinking how much like wild animals children are. Their emotions are one with their bodies, and they had been so excited as they all jabbered to be heard above the others that they were contorting themselves, jumping up and down, making hilarious faces, all long brown limbs and sun-bleached hair and laughter. But at the moment their father spoke, everything changed. They were suddenly as wary and watchful as a deer who has sensed a hunter in a nearby stand. They froze; their eyes twitched; their mouths closed. They knew that of all the moments there had ever been, this was not one to argue.

They hugged and kissed me in a perfunctory way and left the room. At any other time, I'd have scolded Bernard for speaking to them so sharply and cutting off their joy. But I had no speech left in me. I had nothing in me.

Or so I thought. Until Bernard spoke, and of all the terrible things I had imagined in the hours leading up to this moment, I never imagined anything as terrible as what he said to me:

"I took the children sailing today so that I could murder them."

He let that sentence hang between us for a few moments before he continued. And as he did so, I thought some part of him was loving this. Meek, inadequate Bernard had the floor in a way he'd never had before in his life, in a way he'd never dreamed. I was as captive an audience as anyone could ever hope for.

"I thought it would be the best way to hurt you most. And it's still what I want to do to you – hurt you, as badly as I can, in as many ways as I can. I was going to go through with it, and I actually had Joann in my arms, ready to toss her over the side, and do you know what stopped me? It wasn't love of the children. I don't love them and have never loved them, and I want you to be very, very certain of that, because one of the things I want you to know is that your beloved children are going to grow up with a man who does not love them at all. I know how much that is going to hurt you. I think it might hurt you even more than if they were dead, knowing I am going to bring them up, poison them with lies against you, and loathe them because they are the spawn of such a filthy, deceptive creature as you."

He went on in that vein for a very long time. I do not remember for how long, or what all the things he said were, because it was impossible for me to move past that first point. *He was going to kill the children. He was going to kill the children.* And he had not done it today, but what was there to stop him changing his mind in the morning, or in a week or a month or a year? And what was this reservoir of pain and anger and hate that I had never seen in Bernard, who had never so much as raised his voice to any of us? Who was the man I had married?

Looking back, I suppose he was thinking something similar about me.

He kept on like that, haranguing me, and sometimes he would require me to respond, and I would, as best I could. I remember thinking that I had to keep him there, keep him talking, and morning would come and he would have to go to work – because surely he would not allow his routine to be disrupted for a second day in a row – and then I could do something. I didn't know what, but I had to do something. He didn't shout at me; didn't raise a hand to me; in a way he was still my mild-mannered, soft-spoken Bernard, and that was what made it all the more terrible.

Even the most awful things come to an end, and that night did at last as well. Bernard went to shower and dress for work and I went to wake the children for school. Their tired, drawn faces, so different from the elated ones that had greeted me when they burst into the house the previous night, told me all I needed to know about how much they may have overheard and understood.

5

My plan – I did not have a plan, or not much of one. I told the children we were taking a vacation and that Daddy would be joining us later. I do not think they believed me, but they knew something was wrong and they were too frightened to put up a fuss although Joann did timidly ask me once if I was going to tell her teacher why she had missed school. She was only in first grade, and was still very excited about it all. I snapped at her, which I will always regret, and she retreated miserably into herself.

I left Deborah to oversee their packing while I went to the bank. I was terrified that Bernard would make or had made this stop before me, and so as soon as possible after they opened I was there to draw as much money as I could out of our joint account. I remember how troubled the teller, a lady named Mrs. Cook, looked as she counted bills out to me, like she knew that something was wrong. Of course it was; married ladies did not turn up alone and make enormous withdrawals like that without some cause.

I do not like to include this part, but I am trying to be as honest as possible here – I knew there was a chance that shortly after I visited the bank, Bernard might stop in as well, in the interest of vigilance, and find out what I had done. For all I knew, they might phone him and tell him themselves. And I knew that if such a thing happened, he would immediately go home, and all would be lost. This was my one chance, the only chance I would ever have for a decent escape. And so when I returned home, the first thing I did was to make sure that Bernard's car was nowhere in sight; the second thing I did was park my own some blocks away, and walk home from there. And the third thing I did was position myself near the window while the children finished gathering their things so that if Bernard did come home, I would have some warning; I would be able to flee, I would be out the back door and away up the street to my own car before he even realized I was there. I would make my getaway, alone. It was not what I wanted, but it was what I would do if it came to that.

I told myself this was the next best thing. I told myself this was better than being trapped here with the children, that the children would be fine without me, so what if they were taught to hate me, that my presence would make him more volatile and they'd be safer with him and they would be okay. They would grow up okay. They would never know how he felt, or didn't feel, about them. These are the lies I told myself to make it okay for me to abandon my children with their insane father if it came down to it, a choice between them or me.

Other women are not like this, are they? It's documented – it's why women stay in terrible marriages, in deadly situations, in order to protect their young or just to avoid being separated from them. I loved my children more than anything in the world; I loved them so much I found that love almost unbearable; and yet surely there is something wrong with me, that I could do this cold mental arithmetic that would permit me to leave them behind if I had to. But I am not a monster. I said it forty years ago and I say it here, again, I did not hurt my children. I would never hurt my children.

It was the sea; the ghosts; the dead things. The seventh wave.

6

I didn't know what to do, so I just drove. The children were subdued. They knew everything I'd told them was lies. There was no vacation, there was no Daddy joining us later, and something was terribly, terribly wrong. That first day, I was so afraid that I drove for eighteen hours straight, keeping on back roads. I was sure that he would have reported us missing and that law enforcement everywhere would be combing the highways in search of a car of my description with my license plate number. But I was so exhausted that I began hallucinating – imagining people stepping out in front of us on the road – and I finally pulled off and paid cash for a motel room, pulled the car round the back, and piled us all inside where we slept.

We lived like that for a week or more – me, driving until I couldn't any longer and then a motel. I kept heading west. Isn't that where people go to reinvent themselves? I'd never been west of Texas or north of the Mason-Dixon line. I imagined the entire West Coast as a glittering paradise where we would be safe.

I bought spray paint to inexpertly disguise the colour of our car, and somewhere out in the desert, at one of the many low-end, no-questions-asked types of places where we'd spend a night or two to rest up, I asked a shifty-looking desk clerk if there was some way I could get a different license plate for my car. I could barely get the words out; it was such an alien thing for me to do, but he reacted as though customers asked him for things like that all the time, and they probably did. He told me he'd have something for me when I checked out in the morning. After that I relaxed a lot more. Not only were we thousands of miles away from Bernard, but we could not be casually identified either.

Yet I still didn't feel safe. We got to southern California and I couldn't stop; it was as though movement had become a compulsion. I turned north, and we went up through the state and then crossed into Oregon and the Cascade Range. And then we were out of the mountains and by the coast, and it was a sea like I had never seen before. The sea I was used to was on the edge of hot white sands, and it was warm for swimming. This sea was icy, washing up on pebbled beaches or crashing against rocks and cliffs. It was grey and roiling. In comparison to the sea I was accustomed to, it felt wild and untamed.

And I finally felt safe.

Those days were such a blur that I don't know how long we were on the run for. Ten days, two weeks, three weeks? I have never known. But I thought, we can do this, we have done this, I have done this. We can disappear. We *have* disappeared. And I think for the first time ever in my adult life I felt a sense of exhilaration and possibility, that the life that had been written for me was not the one I had to live.

True; the children were disoriented and traumatised; they missed their father, and cried for him and for their lost home. But children are resilient. I would find us a place to live, get them enrolled in school in the fall, and things would be better. I still wasn't sure how I would find work or support us, but I had enough cash to at least buy myself a few weeks, and surely in one of these resort towns on the coast I could at worst get a job cleaning hotel rooms.

It was in that exhilarated spirit that we'd had an evening picnic on the beach. It had been windy, and a little on the cool side for our Southern bones, but the sun sinking into the ocean had been beautiful, and the children seemed almost happy for the first time since that evening they had come in from sailing with their father. They had begun to run about and play on the rocks jutting up from the water. The tide was actually on its way out, and the waves were choppy but not nearly of a size to alarm.

I didn't actually see the moment it happened. I had turned away and was tidying up the remnants of our picnic, was thinking idly rather than in a panicky way for a change about what I would do the following day, that I would start to look for work, when I heard a piercing shriek –

And all of my children were in the water, and were being carried out to sea.

I ran in after them. I tried to save them.

You must believe me.

They must believe me.

People tell a story in these parts about the seventh wave. It is not something I ever heard of in my childhood growing up along the southeast coast. The dangerous sneaker waves that snatch people to their death here do not exist where I come from.

Here, though, the ocean is crueller. These waves come out of nowhere, out of a placid sea. They say that every seventh wave is the one to watch out for, that it is the unexpectedly large and dangerous one.

I read about the seventh wave, all those years ago. I even called an oceanographer at a university here and talked to him about it. I was so distraught for so many years, and I felt that if I could only understand why it had happened, it would lessen my pain. What I learned was that science and superstition do converge, that patterns do exist in which roughly the seventh wave or thereabouts will be the largest. But sneaker waves lie statistically outside even this estimation. They cannot be explained. No one can say when one will rise like a great hand out of the sea and pluck people from dry land and drown them. No one can say why.

I do not know when, but I understand why. The gods and the demons and the ghosts that live in the sea demand human sacrifices. What could be lonelier than being dead? And down there in the ocean depths where pale eyeless things swim, beasts that are nothing but tubes and mouths lurk, where monsters that have thrived since the planet was young and all of evolution's nightmares converge under cover of darkness and deep, deep water, down, down, down they dragged my three babies, creatures of sun and light.

It is so late here. It is as late as the ocean is deep, as dark as the depths of the ocean and the blackness of space.

But, you say to me, *you say you love the sea. How can you love such a terrible thing?*

Have you not been reading the story I am telling you? Have I not always loved terrible things? My love has been nothing if not misguided and unwise. And how could I not love the sea, when my children are a part of it? No matter where I go in the world, I can touch the sea and touch some part of them, the atoms of their being.

On that day, twenty years after I walked into the sea in my attempt to die there, I ran screaming into the sea demanding that it bring back my babies. Ancient and implacable, it did not reply. And it was so calm. You'd have never guessed that such an act of inexplicable violence had just occurred.

Everything came out after that, of course: my flight with the children, and accusations from Bernard that I was unhinged and had killed them. Because of him, they investigated, but they said they found no reason to think that what had happened was anything but a tragic accident. Bernard said he would never believe that. I think it is because he had a guilty conscience. I would never have hurt them. What kind of a mother, what kind of a person would that make me? I am not that kind of person.

All of the publicity was strangely advantageous for me. A local innkeeper took pity on me and did give me a job cleaning rooms. From there, I worked my way up to supervising the maids, and then over to the front desk, and at the end of it all, I was running the inn myself. Somehow, from all that horror and despair, I made a good life for myself. I could never have imagined such a life.

And I travelled the world, and I visited the sea everywhere I went, and every year, on the night of my children's death, I walk down to the shore where it happened and I talk to them. I tell them what the last year of my life has been like and I tell them stories about how their lives would be now. The first few years it was easy, but the older they get the harder it is; I cannot imagine my babies, even little Joann, in their forties and fifties now! They would have families of their own, of course. Their lives would be blessed. I would have seen to it. I would have given them good lives. I would have.

This is the first year I am not able to go down to the beach and talk to them. The weather is too bad, and I have done something to my right foot that makes it difficult for me to walk. I am hesitant to see a doctor about it. I have remained what people call 'surprisingly spry' throughout my older years, and I know how they are, these medical people, how they take one look at you and diagnose you with 'old,' and everything that comes after that is secondary to the disease of 'old,' and the next thing you know they are poking you and prodding you and trying to put you away, and you with nothing to say about any of it.

But I have a little house that is right on the coast, on the edge of a cliff with a path leading down to the shore, and I can hobble out onto my front porch and see the sea smashing against the rocks below. I don't dare go any further than that. This storm is very violent; it feels as though the wind itself could pick me up and toss me into the ocean. They *would* collude in that way, the elements, to get me back to the sea, to do away with me like that.

I have not gone out just yet, though. For some time now the wind has been howling in a way that sounds like the children crying. They are calling for me over and over: "Mother! Mother!

Mother!" Children get so angry, and they must be disciplined. They must not be allowed to run wild and do whatever they like, don't you think? It spoils them, and above all, children must not be spoiled.

It was better for them this way. We saved them from love, saved them from passion, the sea and I. My only lover, my one true love, vast and unfathomable and savage, subject to the whims of the moon and the vagaries of the wind, oh my darling brutal sea.

Something thumps on the front porch. A single thin line of seawater has trickled from under the front door and across my floor to stop now at my foot. Their voices on the wind are so loud now, shrieking for me, and their little fists are beating at my door. My children have come home. Suddenly, for the first time, I feel afraid. *I never meant any harm to come to them.*

Can you believe that?

Will they believe that?

THE PALMYRA CURSE

There are many places on Earth which at first glance appear to be beautiful but on closer inspection turn out to be vile. You can't judge a book by its cover, they say; scratch the shiny veneer and see the foulness that lies beneath, etc. It's a cliché that dates back to the original concept of Eden, the heavenly garden in which a scheming serpent lurked.

If there is any such place on the ocean, it is the superficial 'island paradise' of Palmyra Atoll, located in the North Equatorial Pacific about one third of the way between Hawaii and American Samoa. It is a remote spot to be sure, but from a distance, Palmyra, which actually isn't an island but a circle of volcanic coral reefs, is covered with palms and other rich vegetation. Yet if you land there – assuming you are able to land without suffering a serious boating accident, which is not at all easy – you will find much to dissuade you from staying. And this doesn't just refer to earthly evils, though there are plenty of those on Palmyra too.

To begin with, up close it isn't as pristine as it may seem. Used as a staging post and refuelling depot by the US Navy during World War Two, it is still scarred by decayed ruins – bunkers, buildings, roads and landing strips, all now smothered in creeper and jungle mosses. In addition, the atoll sits in the midst of swirling ocean currents, both northerly and southerly, and as such its beaches are strewn with seaborne rubbish; not just driftwood and the like – cans, bottles and rags are also plentiful, making an unsightly mess and at the same time creating the false and eerie impression that the island is extensively populated. In fact, there is no permanent human presence on Palmyra anymore; occasional visits are made by climate researchers and wildlife scientists, and these are few and irregular.

But trash and litter are very far from the only problems in this wretched place. The 'Palmyra Curse', as it is often referred to, dates back to 1798 and tells a tale of bizarre and inexplicable events, disasters, murders and an overwhelming aura of supernatural evil.

It was in that year when American skipper Edmond Fanning only just avoided the then-uncharted atoll after an intense and disturbing dream woke him in the middle of the night. Fanning ran up on deck, and was just able to steer clear of Palmyra's northernmost reef. However, others weren't so lucky. In an ongoing series of catastrophes, the most recent of which occurred in 1989, countless craft have been lost around the atoll's edges – including the SS Palmyra in 1802, which originated the name – many disappearing completely without trace. Though the waters encircling Palmyra, and even its deep central lagoon, are known for their aggressive shark population, and that may explain why so few bodies are ever found, why wreckage also disappears remains an enduring mystery.

Even those who have made it ashore may face a terrible fate. Rumours of marine monsters slithering up onto the atoll, weird creatures lurking in the undergrowth and ghost-lights flickering during the darkest hours, are frightening enough even if they are standard fare where ocean mysteries are concerned, but some of the actual, undeniable facts are themselves terrifying.

In 1870, a band of castaways made it onto Palmyra after the US ship Angel was wrecked on its shoals. It wasn't long before a relief vessel arrived, a matter of days only, and yet no survivors were discovered. All the men on the island were by this time dead, having been brutally slaughtered. Whether they had killed each other for some reason, or had been murdered by pirates or other forces unknown was a question which to this day remains unanswered.

During World War Two, many US Navy personnel had to be removed from the atoll base after suffering nervous breakdowns, or displaying curious and sometimes violent behaviour, even though they were not at the time under fire. Others reported nightmares, hauntings in their barrack blocks and a desperate feeling of dread and fear.

Three decades later, in 1974, the atoll was the backdrop to a notorious murder case. When Malcolm Graham and his wife Eleanor arrived at Palmyra in their luxury yacht, the Sea Wind, intending to explore and camp, they found it inhabited by disparate groups of ocean wanderers who for various reasons had dropped out of society. The atmosphere was bad, with people scavenging to exist and few trusting each other. Among them was known criminal Buck Walker, and his girlfriend, Stephanie Stearns. This odd duo particularly worried the Grahams (especially as Eleanor had visited a psychic shortly before setting out, and had allegedly been told they would meet someone evil during their trip). And yet for some reason, a short while later, when the other campers had departed the atoll, these two couples were left there alone together. When all radio contact from the Grahams ceased, an investigation was launched. Palmyra was found to be deserted – the four stragglers had vanished. However, when Walker and Stearns then turned up in Hawaii in the Sea Wind, unable to explain what had happened to the Grahams, they were arrested. The bones of Eleanor Graham *were found on the atoll six years later, and Buck Walker was convicted of her murder and imprisoned for life. To this date, the remains of Malcolm Graham have never been recovered.*

And yet, this tragic murder mystery is almost mundane compared to other events.

In 1977, another boatload of tourists arrived at the atoll, only to be menaced by a tribe of filthy 'Mansonesque' hippies whom nobody had known were there. The visitors left quickly, relieved to have escaped with their lives, but when the assault was reported and an investigation launched, the atoll was again found to be empty, with no trace that anyone had lived there for years and years. Similarly creepy were the circumstances surrounding the 1987 discovery of a rudderless craft shunting among Palmyra's reefs and skerries. When the Coast Guard intercepted it, they found its bridge manned by the skeleton of a single man. He was eventually identified, but how he died, and why his absence was not reported sooner – and why he was anywhere near the dangerous vicinity of Palmyra Atoll, sailing solo – were yet more puzzles that would never be solved.

This lonely clutch of rocks in the azure heart of the Pacific Ocean remains an enigma. To some there are explanations behind all its mysteries, most of them involving poor judgement by inexperienced seafarers and/or vicious behaviour by immoral individuals. But to others, it is the absolute epitome of a bad place, a haunted isle, an edge – one of those weird, unexplained points in time and space where our world merges with another one that is far more sinister.

HIPPOCAMPUS
Adam Nevill

Walls of water as slow as lava, black as coal, push the freighter up mountainsides, over frothing peaks and into plunging descents. Across the rolling backs of vast waves the vessel ploughs ungainly, conjuring galaxies of bubbles around its passage and in its wake; vast cosmos appear for moments in the immensity of onyx water, forged and then sucked beneath the hull, or are sacrificed fizzing to the freezing night air.

On and on the great steel vessel wallops, staggering as if up from soiled knees before another nauseating drop into a trough. There is no rest and there is no choice but to rear, dizzy, near breathless, over and over again to brace the next great wave.

On board, lighted portholes and square windows offer tiny, yellow squares of reassurance amidst the lightless, roaring ocean that stretches all around and so far below. Reminiscent of a warm home offering a welcome on a winter night, the cabin lights are complimented by the two metal doorways that gape in the rear house. Their spilled light glosses portions of the slick deck.

All of the surfaces on board are steel, painted white. Riveted and welded tight to the deck and each other, these metal cubes of the superstructure are necklaced by yellow rails intended for those who must slip and reel about the flooded decks. Here and there, white ladders rise, and seem by their very presence to evoke a *kang kang kang* sound of feet going up and down quickly. Small lifeboat cases resembling plastic barrels are fixed at the sides of the upper deck, all of them intact and locked shut. The occasional crane peers out to sea with inappropriate nonchalance, or at the expectation of a purpose that has not come. Up above the distant bridge, from which no faces peer out, the aerials, satellite dishes and navigation masts appear to totter in panic, or to whip their poles, wires and struts from side to side as if engaged in a frantic search of the ever changing landscape of water below.

The vast steel door of the hold's first hatch is raised and still attached to the crane by chains. This large square section of the hull is filled with white sacks, stacked upon each other in tight columns that fill the entire space. Those at the top of the pile are now dark and sopping with rain and sea water. In the centre, scores of the heavy bags have been removed from around a scuffed and dented metal container, painted black. Until its recent discovery, the container appears to have been deliberately hidden among the tiers of fibre sacks. One side of the double doors at the front of the old container has been jammed open.

Somewhere on deck, a small, brass bell clangs its lonesome, undirected cry; a traditional affectation as there are speakers thrusting their silent horns out from the metallic walls and masts. But though the tiny, urgent sound of the bell is occasionally answered by a gull in better weather, out here tonight the bell is answered by nothing save the black, shrieking chaos of the wind and the water it ploughs.

There is a lane between the freighter's rear house and the crane above the open hatch. The lane is unpeopled, wet, and lit by six lights in metal cages. MUSTER STATION: LIFEBOAT 2 is stencilled on the white wall in red lettering. Passing through the lane, the noise of the engine intake fans fills the space hotly and the diesel heat creates the apprehension of being close to moving machine parts. As if functioning as evidence of the ship's purpose and life, and rumbling across every surface like electric current in each part of the vessel, the continuous vibration of the engine's exhaust thrums.

Above the open hatch, and beside the lifeboat assembly point, from out of one of the doors that has been left gaping in the rear house, drifts a thick warmth, as if to engulf wind-seared faces in the way the summer sun cups cheeks.

Once across the metal threshold the engine fibrillations deepen as if muted underground. The bronchial roar of the intake fans dull. Inside, the salty-spittle scour of the night air, and the noxious mechanical odours, are replaced by the scent of old emulsion and the stale chemicals of exhausted air fresheners. A staircase leads down.

But so above so below. As on-deck, no one walks here. All is still, lit bright and faintly rumbled by the bass strumming of the exhaust. The communal area appears calm and indifferent to the intense, black energies of the hurricane outside.

A long, narrow corridor runs through the rear house. Square lenses in the steel ceiling illuminate the plain passageway. The floor is covered in linoleum, the walls are matt yellow, the doors to the cabins trimmed with wood laminate. Half way down, two opposing doors hang open before lit rooms.

The first room was intended for recreation to ease a crew's passage on a long voyage, but no one seeks leisure now. Coloured balls roll across the pool table with the swell that shimmies the ship. Two cues lie amongst the balls and move back and forth like flotsam on the tide. At rest upon the table tennis table are two worn paddles. The television screen remains as empty and black as the rain-thrashed canopy of sky above the freighter. One of the brown, leatherette sofas is split in two places and masking tape suppresses the spongey eruptions of cushion entrails.

Across the corridor, a long bank of washing machines and dryers stand idle in the crew's laundry room. Strung across the ceiling are washing line cords that loop like skipping ropes from the weight of the clothing that is pegged in rows: jeans, socks, shirts, towels. One basket has been dropped upon the floor and has spilled its contents towards the door.

Up one flight of stairs, the bridge is empty too; monitor screens glow green, consoles flash and flicker. One stool lies on its side and the cushioned seat rolls back and forth. A solitary black handgun skitters this way and that too, across the floor. The weapon adds a touch of tension to the otherwise tranquil area of operations, as if a drama has recently passed, been interrupted, or even abandoned.

Back down and deeper inside the ship, and further along the crew's communal corridor, the stainless steel galley glimmers dully in white light. A thin skein of steam drifts over the work surfaces and clouds against the ceiling above the oven. Two large and unwashed pots have boiled dry upon bright red cooker rings. From around the oven door, wisps of black smoke puff. Inside the oven, a tray of potatoes has baked to carbon and now resembles the fossils of ancient reptile guano.

Across the great chopping board on the central table lies a scattering of chopped vegetables, cast wide by the freighter's lurching and twisting. The ceiling above the work station is railed with steel and festooned with swaying kitchen wear. Six large steaks, encrusted with crushed salt, await the abandoned spatula and the griddle that is now hissing black and dry. A large refrigerator door, resembling the gate of a bank vault, hangs open to reveal crowded shelves that gleam in a vanilla light.

Inside a metal sink the size of a bath tub lies a human scalp.

Lopped roughly from the top of a head and left to drain beside the plughole, the gingery mess looks absurdly artificial. But the clod of hair was once plumbed into a circulatory system because the hair is matted dark and wet at the fringes and surrounded by flecks of ochre. The implement that removed the scalp lies upon the draining board: a long knife, the edge serrated for sawing. Above the adjacent work station, at the end of the rack that holds the cook's knives, several items are missing.

Some dripping *thing* was taken from the sink area and out of the galley and along the corridor, and down one flight of stairs to the crew's quarters. Red droplets that have splashed as round as rose petals, lead a trail into the first cabin that is situated in an identical corridor to the communal passage on the deck above. The door to this cabin is open. Inside, the trail of scarlet is immediately lost within the engulfing borders of a far bigger stain.

A fluorescent jacket and cap hang upon a peg just inside the door of the cabin. All is neat and orderly upon the book shelf holding volumes that brush the low, white ceiling. A chest of drawers doubles as a desk. The articles on the desk top are weighed down by a glass paper weight and are overlooked by silver-framed photographs of wives and children at the rear of the desk. Upon the top of the wardrobe, life jackets and hardhats are stowed. Two twin beds, arranged close together, are unoccupied. Beneath the bedframes, orange survival suits remain neatly folded and tightly packed.

The bedclothes of the berth on the right hand side are tidy and undisturbed. But the white top sheet and the yellow blanket of the adjacent berth droop to the linoleum floor like idle sails. There is a suggestion that an occupant departed this bed hurriedly, or was removed swiftly. The bed linen has been yanked from the bed and only remains tucked under the mattress in one corner. A body was also ruined in that bed: the middle of the mattress is blood-sodden and the cabin now reeks of salt and rust. Crimson gouts from a bedside frenzy have flecked and speckled the wall beside the bed, and part of the ceiling.

Attached to the room is a small ensuite bathroom that just manages to hold a shower cubicle and small steel sink. The bathroom is pristine, the taps, shower head and towel rail sparkle. All that is amiss is a single slip-on shoe, dropped to the floor just in front of the sink. A foot remains inside the shoe with part of a hairy ankle extending from the uppers.

From the cabin more than just a trail of droplets can be followed down the passage and to the neighbouring berths. A long intermittent streak of red has been smeared along the length of the corridor, and past the four doors that all hang open and drift back and forth as the ship lists. From each of these cabins, other collections have been made.

What occupants there once were in the crew's quarters all appear to have arisen from their beds before stumbling towards the doors as if cause for alarm had been announced nearby. Just before the doorways of their berths they seem to have met their ends quickly. Wide, lumpy puddles like spilled stew made with red wine, are splashed across the floors. One crew member sought refuge inside the shower cubicle of the last cabin because the bathroom door is broken open, and the basin of the shower is drenched near black from a sudden and conclusive emptying. Livestock hung above the cement of a slaughterhouse and emptied from the throat, leave similar stains.

Turning left at the end of the passage, the open door of the captain's cabin is visible. Inside, the sofa beside the coffee table, and the two easy chairs sit expectant but empty. The office furniture and shelves reveal no disarray. But set upon the broad desk are three long wooden crates. The tops have been levered off, and the packing straw that was once inside is now littered about the table's surface and the carpeted floor below. Intermingled with the straw is a plethora of dried flower petals.

Upon a table cloth spread on the floor before the captain's desk, two small forms have been laid out, side by side, in profile. They are the size of five year old children and black in colour. Not dissimilar to the preserved forms of ancient peoples, protected behind glass in museums for antiquities, they appear to be shrivelled and contorted with age. Vestiges of a fibrous binding has fused with their petrified flesh and obscured their arms, if they are in possession of such limbs. The two small figures are primarily distinguished by the irregular shape and silhouettes of their skulls. Their heads appear oversized, and the swollen dimension of the crania contributes to the leathery ghastliness of the grimacing faces. The rear of each head is fanned by an incomplete mane of spikes, while the front of each head elongates and protrudes into a snout. The desiccated figures have also had their lower limbs bound tightly together to suggest long and curling tails.

Inside the second crate is a large black stone, crudely hollowed out in the middle. The dull and chipped character of the block also suggests a great age. A modern addition has been made, or offered, to the hollow within the stone. A single human foot. The shoe around the disarticulated foot matches the footwear inside the shower cubicle of the crew member's cabin.

The contents of the third crate has barely been disturbed. In there lie several artefacts that resemble jagged flints, or the surviving blades of old weapons or knives to which the handles are missing. The implements are hand-forged from a stone as black as that of the basin that has become a receptacle for a human foot.

Pictures of a ship and framed maps have been removed from the widest wall, and upon this wall a marker pen has been used to depict the outlines of two snouted or trumpeting figures that are attached by what appears to be long and entwined tails. The imagery is crude and childlike, but the silhouettes are not dissimilar to the embalmed remains laid out upon the bed sheet.

100

Below the two figures are imprecise sticklike forms that appear to cavort in emulation of the much larger and snouted characters. Set atop some kind of uneven pyramid shape, another group of human shapes have been excitedly and messily drawn with spikes protruding from their heads or headdresses, and between these groups another plainer individual has been held aloft and bleeds from the torso into a waiting receptacle. Detail has been included to indicate that the sacrificed victim's feet have been removed and its legs bound.

The mess of human leavings that led here departs the captain's cabin and rises up a staircase to the deck above and into an unlit canteen. Light falls into this room from the corridor, and in the half-light two long tables, and one smaller table for the officers, is revealed. Upon the two larger crew tables long reddish shapes are stretched out and glisten: some twelve bodies dwindling into darkness as they stretch away from the door. As if unzipped across the front, what was once inside each of the men has now been gathered and piled upon chairs where the same men once sat and ate. Their feet, some bare, some still inside shoes, have been amputated and are set in a messy pile at the head of the two tables.

At the far end of the cafeteria that is barely touched by the residual light, and to no living audience, perversely, inappropriately and yet grimly touching, two misshapen shadows flicker and leap upon the dim wall as if in a joyous reunion, and then wheel and wheel about each other, ferociously, but not without grace, while attached, it seems, by two long and spiny tails.

Back outside and on deck, it can be seen that the ship continues to meander, inebriated with desolation and weariness, or perhaps it has even been punched drunk from the shock of what has occurred below deck.

The bow momentarily rises up the small hillside of a wave and, just once, near expectantly, looks toward the distant harbour the vessel has slowly drifted toward overnight since changing its course. On shore and across the surrounding basin of treeless land, the lights of a small harbour town glow in white pinpricks as if desperate to be counted in this black storm. Here and there, the harbour lights define the uneven silhouettes of small buildings, suggesting stone facades in which glass shimmers to form an unwitting beacon for what exists out here upon these waves.

Oblivious to anything but its own lurching and clanking, the ship rolls on the swell, inexorably drifting on the current that picked up it's great steel bulk the day before and now slowly propels the hull, fizzing and crashing, but perhaps not so purposelessly as was first assumed, towards the shore.

At the prow, having first bound himself tight to the railing with rope, a solitary and unclothed figure, nods a bowed head towards the land. The pale flesh of the rotund torso is whipped and occasionally drenched by sea spray, but still bears the ruddy impressions of bestial deeds that were both boisterous and thorough. From navel to sternum the curious, temporary figurehead is open, or has been opened blackly to the elements, and the implement used to carve such crude entrances to the heart is now long gone, perhaps dropped from stained and curling fingers into that far below obsidian whirling and clashing of a monumental ocean.

As if to emulate the status of a king, where the scalp has been carved away, a crude series of spikes, fashioned from nails, have been hammered into a pattern resembling a spine or fin across the top of the dead man's skull. Both of his feet are missing and his legs have been bound with twine into one, single, gruesome tail.

GELATINOUS

As a rule, humans aren't frightened of jellyfish. Even though we are aware there are some nasty species out there, the normal response is to give them wide berth, but it's rarely the case that anyone loses sleep where jellyfish are concerned. However, there is a school of thought that jellyfish are not only among the most dangerous creatures on Earth, but that they can also be among the most monstrous, with certain as-yet unidentified species growing to staggering size and able to deliver stings so venomous they will instantly prove fatal.

Chilean fisherman folklore mentions a demonic entity known as the Hide, describing it as a vast sheet of quivering flesh with eyes all around its edges and four in its centre, which hunts its prey – often human beings – by rising slowly and unnoticed from the depths, and then engulfing them as they swim. Researchers have sought to identify this mythical beast with a type of giant octopus, but as octopi only boast one pair of eyes and nearly always attack full-on with their tentacles, it seems to be more akin to a jellyfish, whose mantle is often fringed with sensory organs called rophalia and also possesses four eye-like pouches in the middle of its bell.

Is it possible the legendary Hide is a form of hitherto unknown jellyfish that grows to such size it can easily devour people? Is there any precedent for this kind of thing?

Most folk, swimmers in particular, will no doubt be alarmed to learn the answer is 'yes'.

In 1865, a specimen of the Cyanea capillata, or Lion's Mane Arctic jellyfish, was noted in Massachusetts Bay with a bell diameter of eight feet and tentacles of roughly 120 feet. At the same time, in terms of toxicity, almost nothing on Earth can match Australia's Chironex fleckeri, or Sea Wasp. Victims who have survived contact with this fearsome entity have allegedly gone insane through the pain it has caused. But what of some as yet unknown species that may combine these two traits? Such a monster would be a true devil of the deep, and surely can be nothing more than legend, right?

Wrong.

Several incidents have been reported in relatively modern times wherein sea-going folk have encountered gelatinous monstrosities which rose from the deep without warning to wreak terror and death.

One of the most celebrated of these involved the *Kuranda*, a 1,400-ton steamer, which in 1973 was en route from Australia to Fiji when a heavy wave deposited something onto the vessel's forecastle which at first its crew could scarcely believe. It appeared to be a gargantuan jellyfish, the sheer size of which – the skipper, Langley Smith, estimated it weighed at least 20 tons – threatened to capsize the ship. Though it sounds like something from a 1950s 'creature feature', the battle that followed was described in authentic detail by all the crewmen, as they engaged the horror with poles and axes. According to Smith, the invader's multiple tentacles, some over 200 feet in length, lashed back and forth, packing so poisonous a punch that one deckhand who was stung writhed in agony as his flesh visibly putrefied, and died shortly afterwards. Help finally arrived when a salvage tug, the *Hercules*, sailed 500 miles to answer the *Kuranda's* emergency call, and dislodged the beast with two high-pressure water jets.

Even more unsettling was the tale told by Frenchman Henri Baiselle, who, according to 'The Fortean Times', was arrested by the Bordeaux police in the late 1980s and charged with murdering his wife and two children during a seaside holiday, but maintained hysterically that all three had been taken by a colossal jellyfish, which had risen up beneath them while they were swimming. He never changed his story, even passing a lie detector test.

Perhaps the most frightening story of all comes to us from 1957, when an Australian Navy diver was trialling a new type of deep sea suit in an undisclosed location in the South Pacific. He was several hundred feet down, perched on the top edge of an undersea cliff that overlooked the utter darkness of the abyssal plain, and keeping a wary eye on a scavenging shark – when something happened that would haunt him for the rest of his days. A ghastly object – brown in colour, roughly the size and shape of a hot air balloon, and pulsating horribly – emerged slowly from the blackness below. The diver watched in disbelief as the upper section of its bell had only to touch the shark to induce immediate convulsions and death. The dead shark was subsequently drawn inside the creature, which then descended into the murk again. As jellyfish bodies are loaded with sensory structures capable of detecting the slightest motion in the water, the diver could only thank his stars that at the time the shark had been swimming while he had been sitting still.

Of all rumoured sea monsters, colossal man-eating jellyfish are among the most plausible. Science can neither certify nor discount their existence. Most likely they are denizens of the extreme depths, so interaction with humanity is likely to be a rare event indeed – something we should all probably be grateful for.

THE OFFING
Conrad Williams

Fearne gathered her treasures into the blue handkerchief and picked her way up the beach to where her mother was lying in the shingle. It was early evening – summer's terminal breath – but even so Fearne could see the skin of her mother's arms stippled with goosebumps; she had always been sensitive to a chill in the air. She didn't seem to mind. By her side lay the remnants of their picnic tea: a few pastry crusts from the quiche, an empty packet of crisps, Pinot Grigot dregs gleaming in the base of a sand-blasted bottle.

"What did you find?" her mother asked. Her voice carried traces of sleep, although whether it was that already taken or yet to come, Fearne couldn't be sure. The skin above the collar of Mum's blouse was blotchy, a sure sign she had drunk too much. She always did when Dad wasn't around, as if she was making up for lost time.

For a moment Fearne was reluctant to list her acquisitions. She felt the insecurities of childhood rise up even though she had turned thirteen last birthday; a fear that what was uttered would become desired by the other. Mum shouldn't be interested in bits of sea junk. She loved wine and shoes and hard rock. Fearne sometimes wondered why she had chosen to have children at all. The question alone was a surprise: Mum hardly ever showed any interest in what she was up to. The reluctance remained, however.

"I found some rusting chain. A blue stone. And a fossilised twig."

"Nice," her mother said, but her voice was as flat as the horizon. "That stone isn't stone, it's glass, polished by the sand. And that isn't a fossilised twig, you ninny. It's some kind of coral. White. Which means dead. And you're not bringing that rusty old piece of rubbish home. If it scratches you: lockjaw. I don't think you've had a tetanus shot since you were little."

Fearne had found a shell too, a pretty one that reminded her of the ice cream that Mr Nardini swirled on to the top of a sugar cone at the parlour near the guest house. She hadn't intended to show it to her mum, convinced she would want it for herself, but she felt undermined; she had nothing of worth to show for her search and she didn't want her mum thinking she was useless. She withdrew it from her pocket and held it out for inspection.

"Ooh, that's gorge-o," her mum said, holding the shell up to the hard, midday light. "It wasn't a wasted trip after all. Lovely colour. Very unusual. Carmine, I'd say. Or a cochineal red. Very earthy. Very organic. I could make that up into a pretty necklace if you'd like."

"Okay," Fearne said, knowing full well that she'd not see the thing again. Her mother fancied herself as a craftswoman. Barb the Boho jeweller, she said. She had a little corner of the kitchen set up with various pieces of hardware: pots of glue, a little rotary power tool, a soldering kit, endless tubs of beads. Whenever she got to work on something, it would invariably be accompanied by a large goblet of wine. There'd be more wine than work, especially if one of her wine-by-day friends called for a chat. Jules, say, or Kat, or Loz. The shell was destined to end up as just so much calcium dust when Mum inevitably introduced the Dremel too enthusiastically.

"Although it's a little weird, isn't it, when you think about it? This shell … every shell was once home to something all wet and squidgy. Bit morb-o when you look at it like that."

Fearne gazed out at the compressed edge of sea, like a beaded line of hot solder. It must have been five miles away. The sand was the colour of cooked cream. To the south, the power station skulked, steam rising from its cooling towers like the lazy pre-launch vapour of a sleeping rocket.

She too was tired. Originally she'd planned to march all the way out there to the water's edge. The distance formed a layer on her own fatigue. She imagined striking out to try to meet it before nightfall, the effort it would take, and her posture slumped. She'd never been to the beach by herself or encountered the sea alone before. It was high time, she kept saying to her mum and dad, when they were driving out here. They teased her about that for hours afterwards.

Dad, unpacking his things in a room filled with sailor's paraphernalia: coils of rope, a propeller on the wall, a dressmaker's dummy in a Breton shirt. "It's high time I put my jacket in this wardrobe."

Her mother, fingering the corkscrew already, though breakfast had been only a couple of hours before. "It's high time we thought about lunch."

Very funny. Very *fucking* funny.

She coloured now, as she thought of that prohibited word. She had never sworn in front of her parents; would not dream of it. But she had been angry, and what made it worse was that they registered that and did nothing to placate her.

"Shall we go back to the room?" her mother asked. "It's getting a bit nippy."

"Will Dad be there?"

"I don't know, avocado pip. It's likely. He's been out longer than we have. It'll be time for dinner soon. If he's anything like me he'll be starv-o."

The thought of food made her feel even more tired. She wished they had come here during a proper holiday. Dad's work – he was a wildlife photographer for a number of international travel and nature magazines – meant that they were forever slinking off during school term time. It would be nice to play with some other kids in the pool rather than sit with grown-ups all the time.

The wind began to swell as they trudged back along the sea front. Tiny twisters of sand stung their legs. By the time they got back to the pale blue guest house, Fearne's long hair was matted with silica; it would take an age to wash it out.

Their room was empty. No note from Dad. No camera gear. "He must still be working," her mum said. "I guess the light is better for him at this time of day. Less harsh."

"What does he do at midday, then?" Fearne asked.

"Drink beer. Lech the local talent. I don't know."

"What about dinner?"

"If he misses it, he misses it. But I'm having a shower and a cocktail and then I'm eating seafood until it leaks out of every orifice."

"Ew, *Mum*," Fearne said, but she couldn't keep the smile from her mouth.

They showered together, her mother helping to get the worst of the sand out of her hair. She seemed to grow a little wistful at the sight of her daughter's coltish body, and she complimented her on her long, slender legs.

"Better legs than me," her mother said. "But I've got the best bust, my little cherry stone."

Fearne felt herself reddening again. Her mother seemed to want to steer whatever discussion they had towards talk of her burgeoning sexuality. *Got any boyfriends? Kissed anyone yet?* and once, mortifyingly, *Ever masturbated?*

She exited the shower and dried herself quickly, then dressed before her mother reappeared to pry more about the curves and bumps that were making themselves known in her body. She felt pulled in too many directions at once. Sometimes, she would come to, as if from a trance, to find herself playing with dolls, or reading a comic aimed at children much younger than she. She'd push these things away from her, guilty, embarrassed, but sad too, as if acknowledging that in her resting state she wanted to remain a girl; hormones seemed to be taking the decision out of her hands.

At the window she peered into the distance and wished the sea closer. Her mother said, when she was a child, the tide hardly ever went out beyond the old, weather-bleached groynes. But in the last decade or so, the waters around the coast had steadily retreated, and the shape of the island had changed to the point where all the maps had to be radically redrawn. Doom-mongers talked of fatally damaged eco-systems, unlikely to repair themselves again. The concept of four seasons already seemed like some nostalgic joke.

Where are you, Dad? she asked herself, craning her neck to look up and down the front. She wondered if he was off beachcombing. That irritated her, because he knew how much she loved to do that, and they'd spent many happy hours in each other's company trying to outdo each other. She wondered, not for the first time, if there was some trouble – some serious trouble – going on between her mum and dad. Over the years there'd been some nasty back and forth, but it had mostly been hot air. They loved each other, she was watertight sure of that – although she couldn't for the life of her understand what it was about her mother that secured such devotion. No, his going off like this must be connected to his work. He'd said as much, hadn't he, before they set off? *Busy, busy, busy. Lot on my plate. No rest for the wicked.* Any heartache lost to the easy roll call of clichés.

They ate outside at one of the restaurants that boasted an extension on the esplanade. It was too cold, but her mother insisted. Under a canopy that flapped alarmingly they ordered clams and swordfish and hot, garlicky lobster tails.

"How are the fishermen finding this if the sea is receding? Where are the boats?"

"Maybe it's from the freezers," her mum explained, hoovering up a fantail of opaque white flesh.

The salt on the back of Fearne's hand was like the smear of dust transferred to a fingertip upon handling a moth. She dipped her tongue into it.

"Don't do that," her mother said. "That salt … you don't know what's in it."

The waiter was a young man with high cheekbones, a half-mask of light stubble and a tattoo in burgundy and ochre that peeked out from the rolled-up sleeve of his shirt. He kept yawning and rubbing his eyes. Her mother allowed Fearne a diluted glass of the white Burgundy she was washing her bivalves down with. Each time she heard a boot gritting on the pavement she lifted her head in case it was Dad, but he didn't appear. Her mother flirted with the waiter, her chin slicked with butter. Fearne wanted to be in her room listening to music through her headphones, reading her book, anything else.

"Do you live around here?" her mother asked the waiter. Fearne turned her face away.

"Yeah, just up the road in Mapleton. But I'm aching to get out. I'm busting a nut. I don't trust the power station. I don't trust the sea. This place is a ghost town and nobody here realises that yet."

"What's wrong with the sea?" Fearne asked. Her mother arched her eyebrow, evidently amused that she'd engaged with another human being, and a boy at that.

"It's like a tsunami, only in super slow motion. Tide goes out. Comes back with interest. I don't want to be around come that reckoning."

"Oh don't be so apocalyptic," Mum said. "Guy your age. You shouldn't be worrying about stuff."

"Yeah well," he said, "I've been here all my life. I'm not just a tourist." He seemed about to say more but he pressed his lips together and collected plates instead. "How was the meal?"

"Lovely," Fearne said. "What's wrong with the power station?"

"Nothing," said the waiter. "Guy my age? I shouldn't be worrying about stuff."

"People around here," her mum continued (Fearne recognised the drawl that alcohol lent her voice), "and I've heard them, still talk about the sea as if it should be placated. As if we should be sacrificing our first-born sons or daughters. Flinging them piecemeal into the waves, like rubby-dubby. Like chum. What do you think of that?"

"You don't have to worry," he said, smiling at Fearne. She felt her cheeks burn. "Your daughter is no child."

"She's my little girl," her mum said, archly. "She always will be. My baby."

For a moment Fearne thought her mother might cry, but she cut it off with another gulp from her wine glass. Thirteen years old. On the cusp. Like this place. Her hips were becoming wider, like the bay. Her breasts were swelling, like the ocean. She felt something like the tide pulling at her insides. Childhood was something she had wanted to escape for so long, but now that time was here, she feared it. She wanted infancy back. The comfort and simplicity. The lack of confusion and doubt.

It grew so dark that it was impossible to see the sea any more. Her mother finally paid the bill and they retreated to their room, but not before Fearne had to experience the ignominy of her mother's offer to the waiter of a nightcap when he finished his shift.

She said good night and closed the door on her mother before she became morose and began to tearfully list her regrets, a recurring process that took hours and usually the best part of another wine bottle.

Fearne quickly pulled on her pyjamas and got under the duvet. It was cold in the room; frost was spreading across the window panes. It was more like the Sahara here these days; hot afternoons and bitter nights. She switched on the little portable TV and turned down the sound. News items showed boats stranded in motionless seas where slob ice had turned the water to sludge. She wished she had the shell so she could trace its patterns with her fingertips. Though sleep was some time off, she felt on the edge of a terrible dream. Every surface was hard and flat yet refused the weight of her gaze. Her view slid away and would only hold when it met that uncertain, treacly shift of thickening water.

Things moved within it, agonisingly slowly, black mouths agape in a bid to swallow oxygen that was no longer there. Now sleep was settling, but she had not recognised the shift from wakefulness. She dreamed of creatures beyond the limits of vision regurgitating the brittle bones of animals they had eaten, the slurry of waste filling the seas, condensing them like cornflour added to gravy. Everything was cold and brittle. She thought of the waiter, but even his wolfish beauty was mottled with bruises of frostbite.

She touched herself in the night and she was like a cast of sand, fragile, friable. She was scared to explore more forcibly in case parts of her caved in. At one point, when sleep was secure inside her, she tried to cry out but her throat seemed filled with ice.

Unable to find sleep, she crept into her parents' room. Her father had still not returned. Her mother was snoring, and in last night's clothes, make-up smudged on her face and turning a patch of the pillow the colour of tea. She saw that the wardrobe was opened and feared that her father had returned while they were asleep to pack his things and abandon them. Even as she moved towards the wardrobe door, she knew that would not be the case; he would never do that, no matter how bad things became.

There: his suitcase. She felt guilty to have doubted him. She went to it and pulled it open, not worried about the racket she was making; after wine, her mother could sleep through noise that would have alarmed patients in a hospital for the deaf. Her relief was short-lived, here it was: evidence that her dad had been treasure-hunting without her. The base of the suitcase was gritty with sand. Within it sat objects he had acquired. Intricately patterned shells and polished stones and odd pieces of bleached wood.

She took a handful of them back to her bedroom and studied them in the moonlight. They were strange, jointed things; strange globular things. They hinted and haunted, and she fell asleep with their smooth hollows beneath her fingers, and dreamed of buried skeletons scrabbling through the soil for a gulp of air.

She was wakened by the sound of seagulls shrieking outside the window. She watched a pair wheel around a woman trying to fend them off from the baguette she was carrying under her arm. Last night's trinkets seemed ordinary now. Whatever mystery and magic the night had suffused them with was gone. She still could not identify them, though, in this hard, unflattering light.

She went to wake her mother, but thought it would be much nicer to do it with croissants. Checking her money, she dressed and slipped on her shoes. The bakery was part of a row of shops set back from the road behind a narrow buffer of parking spaces slowly being adopted by weeds. There were no cars. She saw someone move behind the large window of the bakery, a ponderous figure now collecting up the display of cakes, pastries and tarts arranged lovingly on silver trays and bone china platters. Salt caulked the corners of the windows. Drifts of it created brackets at the foot of the door. The name on the awning had been bleached to invisibility.

She reached the bakery just as he was flipping the *Open* sign around to *Closed*. He saw her and stood aside to let her in. The bell tinkled and she was put in mind of icicles dropping to the path at the angry slam of a door.

"Oh," she said, "am I too late?"

"No, no," he said. His lips were chapped and there were shrouds of dry, white skin on his fingertips. Sleep was collected in the corners of his eyes like sticky wads of pollen. "I have a couple of customers in the morning, but that's pretty much it. I was going to shut up shop and get on with my jigsaw puzzle."

"I just wanted two croissants," she said.

"Two croissants it is, young lady."

She breathed an internal sigh of relief when he pulled on a pair of latex gloves to handle the bread.

"Holiday?" he asked.

"Kind of. My dad's taking photographs for a magazine. It's his job."

"Nice. Although nothing much to photograph here, wouldn't you agree?"

She nodded her head. "It's for a geographical magazine, I think. Rugged coast."

"Everyone's leaving," he said, appearing not to hear her. He placed the croissants in a paper bag and tenderly twisted it shut. It

111

was warm in her hands. "It used to be a busy little place, this. But now all the windows are getting boarded up. People are trying to sell their properties. The sand and the salt are coming. It'll bury us, you watch. We're all going to sleep."

"You're still here."

"Not for long. Business is terrible. I'm going to be out by the end of the year. I can retire, at least. I'm going to go north and help my brother. He keeps bees. Makes his own honey."

She felt bad now that she had not ordered more food, but she only had so many pennies. He took them from her now and let them cascade from his dry fingers into the open mouth of the cash register. For some reason she thought of sacrifices.

"Seaside towns die when the sea disappears," the man said, his voice edged with sorrow. For a moment she thought he might start weeping. "It's kind of the point, isn't it? 'I do like to be beside the seaside' and all that. What have you got without the water? It's just a walled-in desert, it's little more than a sandpit."

He walked her to the door.

"Mind how you go," he said.

"What is it?" she asked, impulsively.

"Sorry?"

"Your jigsaw puzzle. Is it a big one?"

"My yes," he said. "Ten thousand pieces. I've been working on it since New Year. A picture of the harbour at Antibes." He stared out of the window at the denuded skyline. "A lively harbour. A place with real get-up-and-go. I miss the sea," he said.

"I'm sure it will come back," Fearne said, but she could offer no logical reason why.

It seemed like a good moment to leave; she didn't like the mild horror that had arisen in his face at her words. She looked back once she'd crossed the road and descended, by way of the stone steps next to her guest house, to the sand. He was stock-still by the window, as if stricken by the salt he had warned her about.

Her mother was not on the terrace; a glance up at their room confirmed that her curtains remained shut. She was about to head inside, eager to surprise her with the warm croissants, when her attention was drawn to a set of footsteps in the sand stretching off into the distance where the sea gleamed like a line of silver thread. She recognised immediately the tread of her father's boots, that and the size of them. *Claude Hopper*, Mum called him. And she would tease him by saying: *If only it were true what they say about men with big feet.*

The footprints moved away from the low sea wall in a large arc, as if he had been on his way back to the guest house only to be diverted by something at the critical moment. Perhaps he had seen something worthy of his lens; a sea bird of some sort, or an unusual play of light on the scenery. She decided to follow the prints, determined to find him and give him some grief for leaving her with her mother for so long. If she left it any later, the prints would be erased by the incessant dance of sand heated loose by the strengthening sunshine. She experienced an unpleasant image of her father becoming lost should she fail to track his prints properly, mummified by the salt winds driving in from the north.

Bit morb-o, she thought, in her mother's voice, and shuddered. *Bit morb-o, my little pineapple ring.*

At least it was not so cold now. Daylight lifted the temperature to a point where her light cardigan was adequate protection. She was worried about her dad though. He had been wearing his short-sleeved shirt yesterday. If he hadn't sought shelter by evening, he would have frozen to death.

Stop it, she thought. *He's not a child. He would have found somewhere warm.*

Of course he would. And of course he would have called to let them know. The fact that he had not done the latter kept her nagging at the likelihood of the former.

She glanced behind her at the properties along the sea front and tried to spot her mother in the window of the guest house. No such luck. Still asleep. She'd be amazed if Mum raised her head before lunch.

From here the guest house looked pretty as a button. It was only when you got up close to it that you saw the cracks and the dust and the stains. A bit like Mum, she thought, and laughed. If it had been her guest house, she decided, she would have given it a name. *Clouds* or *Dunes* or *Breakers*. Something to suggest the coast and holidays. Something a bit dramatic. Mrs McKenzie, who owned it, was as dull and tired as the beige towels that hung from the rails in the bathroom. Maybe she had been enthusiastic, once upon a time. But now she could barely muster a smile when she took their breakfast orders.

Something glinted in the sand. She bent down and swept with her fingers until she had unearthed her father's watch. Now she found it hard to swallow. It was as if the ice from her dream had returned to lodge in her throat again. She felt the prick of tears as fear jangled its nails up and down her back. The watch face was scoured opaque, as if the sand had been working it for years. She held it to her ear; it was still ticking. What to do? She ought to go back. She couldn't understand why but her father couldn't have just

113

simply dropped his watch. He must have been attacked. But his was the only set of footsteps around and there was no sign of a struggle.

"Dad!" she called out. Her voice was ripped from her lips by the eager wind, as if it had been waiting for her to say something. She felt a bizarre urge to dig in the sand, convinced that he had been sucked down. She didn't remember there being any concern about this beach in terms of quicksand, but that didn't mean there weren't any hazards.

She was weighing up the pros and cons of going on or heading back when she heard her mother calling her name.

"Mum!" She raced towards the figure, waving the watch as she weaved through the sand.

Her mother was carrying a bag laden with food. "We'll have another picnic," she said, unaware of Fearne's panic. "It might not be the warmest day of the year, but even scant sunshine means outdoor eating in my book. Right, peach fuzz?"

"Dad's gone," Fearne said. "Look!" She pressed the watch into her mother's hands. The older woman stared at it as if she had never seen it before, but it was she who had bought it for her husband, for his fiftieth birthday. Fearne reminded her of that but the perplexed look remained.

"I'm tired, grape-skin," her mother said. "Can't we just pretend to be having a nice time? Can't we just eat this bread and cheese and sit in the sand and rub suncream on each other's shoulders?"

"But what about Dad?"

"Daddy's a rock, applesauce. This isn't the first time he's gone walkabout. I remember some time in the late '80s he went missing for a whole week."

"But his watch …"

"Maybe he dropped it. It was always a bit too big for his wrist anyway. Sweaty weather. Not concentrating. It happens. Give it to me. I'll look after it for him. Now, I thought we could nip up to those rocks over there and –"

"No!" Fearne shouted. "I'm going to find Dad. You do what you want."

"But pumpkin …"

Fearne ignored her and marched after the footprints, clutching the watch more tightly. Behind her she heard the metallic screw top lid easing off a bottle, and her mother sighing as she reclined in the sand.

Rocks crumbled from the headland towards that gleaming seam of silver, like cake fragments on to a tea-time salver. She searched frantically for some vertical stripe of colour and movement within the still, horizontal mass but could see none. The leaves on the trees were grey with salt. Then, on to the stripe of gunmetal road curling around the bluff, she saw someone running in a pair of black shorts and a lime green vest. Even at this distance she could tell it was the waiter from the previous evening. He skipped down a set of steps, the lower risers of which were disappearing into the sand, and began jogging across the beach, presumably back toward the restaurant.

He slowed when he spotted her, and removed a pair of white buds from his ears. When he smiled at her she was emboldened to ask him what music he was listening to.

"Not music," he said. "It's a recording. Of a lecture I went to in London last month."

"What lecture?"

"Oh, just some stuff about environmental effects on communities. Behaviour. Health. That sort of thing. Linked to global warming. Or the possible dangers of nuclear power plants."

"I don't see any gills on you," she said, meaning it as a joke. He laughed, a bitter little snort, but his fingers absently went to the side of his neck and plucked at the flesh.

Fearne checked behind her; her mother was lying back in the sand, having kicked off her shoes. To her mortification, she had also removed her blouse to reveal a black satin push-up bra that shimmered in the hazy light.

"Is anything wrong?" the waiter asked. Fearne remembered the previous night he had been wearing a shirt with his name on a badge, but the badge was grimy, or the light wouldn't allow her to read what was upon it. She wanted to ask his name now, but also she wanted to know what things he had found in the sand, or whether he was tired all the time, and whether he believed that the nuclear power station was dangerous, or that there really was a tsunami poised to engulf the town.

Instead, she said: "I'm trying to find my dad. Did you see anyone, up on the road?"

"I saw nobody," the waiter said. And then: "I only run for twenty minutes in the mornings, but by the time I get to work, my hair is stiff with salt, and it's in the creases of my skin. It's like being attacked."

"You're scaring me."

"You should be scared. You know we understand more about the moon than we do about our oceans?"

"What could we do if we knew everything?"

He stared at her. Sweat had dried to thin cakes on his skin. A muscle jumped in the shadowed flesh beneath his left eye.

"You're probably right," he said. "The sea comes back. The sea doesn't come back. Either way makes me scared to the point of shitting myself."

"I just want my dad," she said. "Will you help me?"

"I can't. I'm already late. Where's your mum?"

"You'll run straight past her if you go the way I came. So I'd run fast if I were you."

He made a strange, stilted noise, a laugh, perhaps, though hobbled by mild guilt at finding her mother a figure of amusement.

"Okay," he said. "Mind how you go. The rocks can be treacherous."

Fearne watched him settle back into the rhythm of his run, and felt her skin tighten and flush as she caught herself admiring the jut of his buttocks against his close-fitting shorts, his slender, toffee-brown calves. She turned her back on him and marched towards the collapsed headland, angry with herself for becoming sidetracked. The watch in her fist was hot. Her father needed her and she had chosen instead to flirt with a guy who had not one iota of interest in her.

She reached the rocks ten minutes later. At some point there would have been pools here, little bowls of trapped seawater where kiddies would poke around with their nets, hoping to capture a stranded tiddler, or a crab. Now they were only tinder-dry crucibles littered with the translucent bones of sea creatures she could not identify. They reminded her of glass noodles; of thin, fractured patterns in puddles of ice. Some of the creatures seemed deformed, and she thought of what the waiter (Eric, was it? Eddie?) had said about the nuclear power plant. They used sea water as a cheap, readily available coolant, apparently. What came in was eventually discharged. She imagined water warmed by the reactor core going back into the ocean. She wondered if salt water meant that corrosion was a problem. She thought of all that water flushed with scintillas of uranium; irradiated fish spawning for generations. Imperfections upon imperfections. There might come a future where the fish returned to the land to avenge their crippled ancestors.

Maybe they were already in the process. She imagined a great piscine army jealously drawing back the waves. A power station without coolant could not survive for long, and she guessed uranium did not simply have an OFF switch.

Too many prawns before bed, she thought. *How shellfish of me.*

She picked a way through the pot-holes, looking out for any striking counterpoint to the dun landscape. She found a shoe as she was making her way down the side of a rock scarred with what looked like a million tiny ash-white limpets. Was it her dad's shoe?

She couldn't be sure. It was big enough, but it was badly damaged: leather hung like a flap of torn skin from the vamp. Dried blood ringed the collar. She called out for him again but her voice was as dry and cracked as the scenery.

On the other side of the fallen shoulder of land, a bay stretched away to what looked like marshlands, and a narrow, stunted fringe of trees with weather-beaten canopies like back-combed hair. Salt made Christmas of everything. No figures here, though Fearne could see the marks Eric (Ernie? Is the name Ernest still going?) had made in the sand with his prissy gait before angling up on to the bluff.

There were no buildings here either, save a small wooden hut that might have served as a coastguard's retreat but was now dilapidated, its door wailing grittily in the breeze. She approached it anyway. Inside she found a chair with its vinyl seat torn, sunburned foam frothing from it like fat from an opened gut. A newspaper had been whitened to illegibility. Ink from a pen had oozed across a page creating a thought bubble of furious black. The sound of something tapping or flapping against the wood at the back of the hut made her think of restless sails knocking against masts in deserted harbours. The beat matched that of her heart, and, she imagined, that of the tide creaming against a shore many miles away. She remembered wiggling her toes in the crashing waves at anonymous beaches all over the world. Her father with a Nikon in his hand. She remembered a holiday – an assignment – when she was constantly worrying about her parents. It was around the time she began to understand what mortality was. After the reassurances, after the cuddles, her father – never one for sentimentality – had taken her for a walk along the beach.

"The waves are like us, Fearne," he told her. "They move through their short lives placidly, unnoticed, but at the end, near death, they gather pace; they struggle and roar. Never think that death is easy, sugar lump. The body might be tired and old, but it fights like fury. It does not go gentle."

The hasp of the padlock that had kept this hut closed was shattered; anything of value was long gone. She closed her eyes. The smell of the vinyl from hot days gone by had remained in the air. There was a smell too of burnt dust, and of skin that has been touched by the sunshine.

When the tapping became more of an irritation than she could cope with, she stepped outside and walked around to the rear. The rocks had reached this far in their collapse from the promontory. They formed a loose circle. She found her father within it, like a fragment trapped in a ring of teeth. Something had been at him in the night; most of his face was missing. She stared at the pale skin where his watch had been. The wind blew the fastener on his camera bag against the shed's rim joist. She watched that for a few minutes, until the numbness inside her felt too much like the frost creeping across her bedroom window panes. Sand was shifting over her feet, and she struggled to free them. She moved away and the horizon was suddenly closer, as if viewed through binoculars. The sea was returning.

Fearne hurried back the way she had come, and only when she hit the shield of the headland did she realise that she was crying. She pressed the heels of her hands against her eyes and wiped her nose. The surf was alive. It did not move in the way those waves from her childhood had moved. There was no rhythm or poetry to it. It was a shambling collapse, filled with angles and shadows: were they fins? Tentacles? Teeth? She thought she saw a serrated hook on the end of what looked like pistoning white muscle unsheathed from a tube of blood-red chitin. She thought she saw something globular turn in on itself, revealing a skirt of nacreous tissue, like oyster flesh hanging off a bed of shells. The water billowed and foamed with the exuviae of a billion things either dead, or grown too big for what had housed them. The sound of the sea was nothing that she recalled. No ozone crash and hiss; no skitter and chuckle of surf on pebbles. This was a sickly slithering, a jumble of keratin and collagen, a slick of ink and membrane and cartilage. She thought she saw remnants of ancient meals on the barbs and claws of what thrashed beneath the surface. But she could not concentrate on them. They looked too much like fingers. Too much like the things that she'd found in the base of her father's suitcase. Her eyes would not fasten on the eyes that fastened all too readily upon her: they were too soulless, too intent. There were too many of them.

Her mother was half-asleep, singing snatches of a song half-remembered from the radio. Sand had claimed her to the groin. It played in the pleats and crevices and wrinkles of her flesh. Her lips made a ring of dry white elastic; her tongue was a forgotten bivalve on a half shell, desiccating in the sun.

The perils of the cockle harvest. The collapse of a tunnel bored through a dune with cheap red plastic and tiny hands. Quicksand. *A man was dragged from the pier.* Tsunami. Riptide. *The shark attack occurred in just three feet of water.* Bodies still missing. You'd be forgiven to believe that such things as accidents did not occur.

She moved toward the water and her pace increased. She felt herself turning brittle under the cold stare of what shivered just beyond that frothing black tide.

The beach was no place for a child.

BLOOD AND OIL

C*an Nature fight back? Are there times when, in the guise of the raging sea and all the beasts that dwell therein, it might finally strike at those who seek to defile it? Is it possible that our ocean has drunk too often of Man's pollutants, has seen too many of its regions depopulated of wildlife, has swum too thickly with the blood of its most magnificent creatures?*

Is it feasible that on more than one occasion it has retaliated?

In the late winter of 1821, the whaling boat Dauphin was scouring the Pacific for new prey, when it encountered the floating wreck of a 25-foot lifeboat belonging to a fellow whaler, the Essex, which had last been reported sailing out of Nantucket Island, New England, over a year earlier. On boarding the wreck, the Dauphin's crew found what they initially thought were human skeletons – when, to their shock, two of these heaps of bones and carrion began to twitch and groan.

The names of these barely living survivors were George Pollard, skipper of the Essex, and a young sailor, Charles Ramsdell. The two men were gradually revived to the point where they could tell their story – and what a litany of horror it was.

The Essex had embarked in 1819 on a mission expected to last two years, during which time they would collect a king's ransom in valuable whale oil. Spirits were high on embarkation day, the Essex proud of its history of profitable missions, but almost from the beginning of the voyage there were serious problems.

During a challenging journey around Cape Horn into the Pacific and then up the coasts of Chile and Peru, the vessel was battered by squalls, which exposed flaws in the hull caused by its age. Undaunted, when the weather settled the experienced crew began to harpoon whales, but the ship had now been weakened. How badly weakened only became evident in the November of 1820, when some 1,500 nautical miles west of the Galapagos Islands, a long way from land in any direction, the Essex found itself in a furious engagement with a large and aggressive bull sperm whale (they estimated that it was over 85 feet in length, which if accurate would be astonishing). Oblivious to their weapons, the beast continually rammed the craft, finally holing it below the waterline. This had never been known before, but even as the vessel sank, the whale smashed itself repeatedly into the hull as though determined to finish it off. Second mate Owen Chase would later write that it

119

displayed "tenfold fury and vengeance" for the hunting of its relatives.

Bizarrely, the whale disappeared once the Essex had listed below the surface, almost as though it considered its job was done. With only three lifeboats remaining, the crew were safe for a time – but it would soon become apparent that those who'd drowned were the lucky ones. Because after the unprecedented experience of the whale attack (the actual event that would inspire novelist Herman Melville to write 'Moby Dick' 30 years later), a different kind of horror would follow – a horror even more terrible and yet in many ways more familiar to those who lived and worked on the sea.

To start with, the three small craft were light on supplies, and at least 2,000 miles from the nearest land, which was the Society Islands (modern day French Polynesia), and these at the time were inhabited by cannibals. Instead, the men set sail for Chile, a much vaster distance away, 60 days' sailing at least, when they only had a couple of weeks' worth of food and fresh water. The inevitable happened. They were soon ravaged by thirst and hunger, the resulting delirium affecting their seamanship and navigational skills. When a killer whale attacked them, many were stricken with terror that the enraged sperm whale had returned, though the orca did enough damage in its own right. Following that, sharks also pursued the struggling vessels. So disoriented were the men by this time that they narrowly missed the Pitcairn Islands, which they didn't realise were occupied by British colonists descended from the mutineers who had arrived there after stealing HMS Bounty in 1790, and who could have saved them.

The perilous voyage continued, but was now struck by further storms, which blew the boats far apart from each other. Two months later, in the January of 1821, the boat on which Pollard and Ramsdell would later be found was still adrift and still over 2,500 miles from Chile. It was around this time that the men began to eat each other, initially butchering and devouring those among them who'd died from starvation, but eventually turning – because they had no choice – on the living. This part of the tale is particularly harrowing, Ramsdell reluctantly suggesting they draw lots to decide who should give up his life first. A young sailor called Coffin was eventually chosen, and though Captain Pollard volunteered to take his place, the brave lad insisted that fair was fair and allowed the others to shoot him.

One by one the other crewmen went the same way, killed and cannibalised by their shipmates. But even then it was touch and go. When all except Pollard and Ramsdell had been eaten, the two survivors, now too weak and ill to control their craft let alone kill each other, had resorted to sucking the marrow from the dry, shell-like bones of their former companions. When finally rescued – 93 days after they were shipwrecked – even this resource had run dry; the men were insensible, deranged and on the very edge of death.

In later weeks, survivors from the other two boats were also discovered, though they too had resorted to feeding on human flesh. When news reached Nantucket Island, several of the townsfolk who were personally acquainted with the victims are said to have gone insane. The event wasn't even spoken of again, at least not officially, for several decades in the town.

But the story wasn't completely over.

Some 30 years later, roughly around the time when Melville was penning his oceanic masterpiece, another Pacific whaling vessel was attacked and sunk, this time near Hawaii, in a ferocious attack by an enormous bull sperm whale, a beast of prodigious size, whose head was scarred and slashed and hung with broken lances as though it had engaged in numerous other battles with whaling craft. Though the whale died shortly afterwards, news of this latest disaster spread quickly, and though no-one said it aloud, seafaring folk wondered nervously about the numberless disappearances of ships over the intervening years since the attack on the Essex, many of them whalers, which had never been adequately explained.

SUN OVER THE YARD ARM
Peter James

Tony Trollope was a man of routine. He would arrive home from the office at almost exactly the same time every weekday evening, other than when the train from London to Brighton was delayed; kiss his wife, Juliet; ask how the children were and what was for supper. Then he would glance upwards, as if at the masthead of a yacht, and announce, "Sun's over the yard arm!"

That was Juliet's cue to make him a drink, while he popped upstairs to change – and in earlier days, to see their children in bed.

"Sun's over the yard arm" became, to Juliet, almost like Tony's mantra. But she had no idea, any more than her husband did, just how ironic those words would be one day.

After a few minutes he would come back downstairs in an oversized cable-stitch sweater, baggy slacks and the battered, rope-soled deck shoes he liked to slob around in at home as much as on their boat. Then he would flop down in his massive recliner armchair, feet up, TV remote beside him and the latest edition of *Yachting Monthly* magazine open on his lap. A couple of minutes later, Juliet would oblige him with his gin and tonic with ice and a slice of lemon in a highball glass, mixed just how he liked it.

Over the years, as the stress of his commute and his job at the small private bank increased, the quantity of gin got larger and of tonic smaller. And at the weekend the timing of just when exactly the sun appeared over the yard arm steadily reduced from 1 p.m. to midday and then to 11 a.m., regardless of whether they were at home or away on the boat.

"Eleven in the morning was when sailors in the British Navy traditionally took their tot of rum," he was fond of telling Juliet, as if to justify the early hour of his first libation of the day. Frequently he would raise his glass and toast 31 July 1970. "A sad day!" he would say. "A very sad day indeed!"

It was the day, he informed her, that the British Navy abolished the traditional tot of rum for all sailors.

"So you've told me many times, darling," she would reply patiently. Sometimes she wondered about his memory.

"Yes, I know I have, but traditions are important, they should never be allowed to die. Now the thing is," he would go on to explain, "a tot is actually quite a big measure. Half the ship's company would be totally smashed by midday. That tradition was there for two reasons. Firstly to ward off disease, and secondly, as with many military forces around the globe, to give the sailors courage in combat. Historically, many soldiers went into battle totally off their faces on alcohol or drugs. The Zulu warriors were sky high on drugs during the Zulu wars. Half the US troops in Vietnam faced the enemy stoned on marijuana or heroin. Dutch courage indeed! Didn't get its name for nothing."

Tony had never actually been in the Royal Navy, but the sea was in his blood. From the age of ten, when his father had bought him a Cadet dinghy, which he sailed out of Shoreham Harbour near Brighton, he had been smitten with the sea. On their very first date, when he was twenty-three and Juliet was just twenty, he had sat opposite her in the little Brighton trattoria and asked her if she had ever been sailing. She replied that she hadn't, but was game to try it.

The following weekend he took her out into the Channel on his 22-foot Sonata, the entry-level yacht he had bought with a small inheritance from an uncle. She was instantly smitten – both with Tony and with being out on the open water. And Tony was smitten with her. His previous girlfriend had thrown up fifteen minutes beyond the Shoreham Harbour moles, and had spent the rest of the short voyage lying down below on a bunk, puking into a plastic bucket and wishing she was dead. Sitting in the cramped cockpit of the small boat, he fell in love with Juliet's sea legs. And with – erm . . . well – her very sexy legs.

And with everything else about her.

Juliet loved that Tony was so manly. Loved that she felt so safe with him out at sea. He knew everything there was to know, it seemed, about the craft of sailing and seamanship. He taught her how to tie a reef knot, a bowline, a round turn and two half hitches, a clove hitch, and helped her create her very own knot board. She learned from him how to navigate with the satnav and then, far more basic, with a sextant. How to read charts. How to learn from the clouds to predict squalls and rain. Tony seemed capable of fixing anything on the boat, from taking the engine apart to sewing torn sails. Gradually, in their modest little craft, they ventured further and further afield. Down the south coast to Chichester, then to the Hamble and up the Beaulieu River, and then further afield still, to Poole and then Torbay.

A promotion at work, coupled with a large year-end bonus, enabled him to splash out on a bigger yacht, with more comfortable accommodation, and a larger stateroom – or master-bonking quarters – as he liked to call it.

A year later he proposed to her on the stern of the *Juliet*, the Nicholson 27 he had named after her, in Cowes Harbour on the Isle of Wight at the end of the year's round-the-island race. She accepted without an instant of hesitation. She loved him truly, deeply, as deep as the ocean below them.

As his career advanced and he climbed higher up the corporate ladder and salary scale, their boats became bigger. Big enough to comfortably accommodate their three children as they grew older and larger, culminating in his dream Oyster 42 with hydraulic roller reefing. A substantial yacht that, thanks to all the electronic technology, the two of them could easily handle, with or without the help of their youngsters on board.

And then suddenly, without realizing how time had crept up on them, with two of their children at university and one married, they found themselves planning for Tony's retirement.

And his dream. To circumnavigate the world. Spending time in each country on the way. America. Then Australia. Then Asia. South Africa. Up through the Suez Canal. Then maybe a couple of years in the Mediterranean. "Hey, what does it matter how long we are away?" he said to her. "What's time to the Irish?"

"We're not Irish," she replied.

"So?"

She shrugged. It was a strange thing he had said, she thought. And he had become a little strange, if she was honest with herself, during this past year leading up to his sixty-fifth birthday. She couldn't place a finger on what it was exactly. He seemed to have become a little distant. Distracted. Grumpier. He had always been good-natured. She used to tell her friends that they had the best marriage, that they never argued, that their sex life was still wonderful.

But there was a wrinkle. Deeper than the ones that gradually appeared over the years on their increasingly weather-beaten faces. Tony began to joke more and more about sailors having a woman in every port. And in his now senior position with the bank, he had become responsible for its overseas client development, which meant he regularly flew around the world. And with each trip, when he returned home, his interest in making love to her seemed to wane further and further.

She tried to put it down to a natural decline in libido as he aged, knowing from discussions with her girlfriends, and from looking it up on the internet, that a man's testosterone levels diminished as he grew older. Nevertheless, she began to have nagging doubts about what he got up to on the trips, which were becoming even more frequent and often prolonged – very prolonged at times, with some

124

two-day trips turning into a week or even longer. He also became a little furtive, guarding his mobile phone carefully, getting an increasing number of texts at all hours of the day and night, and frequently disappearing to his den to make or take calls.

At dinner one night, with friends, he told a jokey story, but one she did not find particularly funny. "Did you know," he said, "that in naval-base towns like Portsmouth and Southampton, wives of seamen whose husbands were away at sea for long periods of time used to put a pack of OMO washing powder in their front windows to signal to their lovers, *Old Man Overseas!*"

Everyone laughed, except Juliet. She just stared quizzically at her husband, wondering. Wondering.

For Juliet, the day of his sixty-fifth birthday, and the big retirement party the bank held for him in the City of London, could not come soon enough. Because they had planned their round-the-world sailing trip to start soon after, and they were going to spend the next five glorious years away. They would be together for all that time, and Tony seemed really happy and had spent months planning every last detail and provisioning the yacht.

He told her, repeatedly, how happy he was at the thought of the trip and spending all that time together. She began to think that maybe she had misjudged him, and had been jumping to the wrong conclusions. All those long trips overseas in the past few years had, perhaps, been totally innocent after all. He had just been working as hard as hell to justify his worth to the bank. He was a good man, and she loved him, truly, deeply, as much as ever. More, perhaps. She realized that of all the choices that life had presented to her, nailing her colours to his mast had been the right decision. She began to prepare for the voyage with a sense of excitement and adventure she had not felt since she was a child.

And Tony told her, after a bottle of Champagne celebrating their fortieth wedding anniversary, and using one of the nautical phrases that were part of his language, that being spliced to her was the best thing that had ever happened in his life.

She and Tony pored over charts, looking at routes that famous round-the-world sailors had taken. Through the Bay of Biscay, around Spain and Portugal, then through the Med and down through the Suez Canal was one option. Another was to carry on after Spain down the coast of Africa. But the one they preferred was to cross the Atlantic first, cruise the East Coast of America, then head through the Panama Canal, down the coast of Ecuador, across to the Galapagos, then Fiji, then circumnavigate Australia, before heading up to Indonesia, then across to South Africa, around the Cape of

Good Hope, over to the East coast of South America, to Brazil, then across to the Canary Islands, Morocco, then home to England.

*

Finally the big day came. Their children, with their own young families now; a large group of friends, who had sponsored them on Just Giving to raise money for the Martlets Hospice in Brighton; a photographer from the local paper, *The Argus*; a television crew from BBC South, and a chaplain friend, Ish, from Chichester Cathedral, who had renewed their wedding vows on the stern of *Juliet 3*, were all there to wave them off and wish them luck.

The next two years were, for the most part, a blissfully happy time. They had plenty of scary moments, particularly when they lost their self-steering gear during one severe Atlantic storm, and another when they lost their mainsail off the coast of Florida. But, one by one, they made their destination ports and got things fixed or replaced.

Most importantly for Juliet, Tony and she were getting on better than ever. By the time they berthed in Perth, nearly three years into their voyage, she had never, ever, in all their years, felt so close to this man she loved so much. Enjoying the luxury of a hot shower in a deluxe hotel room, then making love to Tony afterwards and falling asleep in his arms in soft, clean hotel bedding, she decided she never wanted this voyage to end – although she did miss her children and grandchildren. He told her that he didn't want it to end, either. And why should it? They were in the happy situation of being able to afford this life at sea – why not continue it for as long as they were both able-bodied?

They only had one real argument. That was when they were in Darwin, three years and six months on, and two more of their grandchildren had been born. Juliet realised that if they did not get back to the UK, at least for a short while, their grandchildren would be total strangers when they finally returned.

It didn't seem to bother Tony, but it was an increasing concern to her. "Why don't we take a straight route back home, spend a year there, bonding with the kids, then set off again?" she asked.

"I really want to go to Singapore first," he had replied. "We've never been and I've always wanted to sail there."

"But you've been there on business," she said. "Several times. And you always said it wasn't that special. I asked you one time if I could join you on one of your trips and you said it was too hot and humid, and I wouldn't like it."

"I did?"

126

"Yes."

He had shrugged. "It's so totally different when you arrive by boat, darling," he said. "Can you imagine what it must have been like for Sir Stamford Raffles when he first arrived there? I'd love to experience that sensation with you."

For the first time in the voyage, Juliet had bad vibes, which she couldn't – or wouldn't – explain. "I want to get back to England," she insisted. Then she pointed at the chart. "We could take that route, couldn't we? Sri Lanka, then across to Oman, then up the Suez Canal?"

Momentarily he had a far-away look in his eyes. "Sri Lanka? I think you'd like it there."

"Didn't you have a client there? You used to go there a lot."

He nodded. 'Yes. Yes indeed." And suddenly his whole countenance lit up. "Sri Lanka's a good plan!"

"So let's do it!"

"Sri Lanka it is!"

Then he pointed at the chart again. "If we're going to sail that route, it's about three thousand, seven hundred miles. At our average speed of six knots that's about thirty days sailing across open ocean, and there's a risk of Somali pirates all the way. We'd have several days out of radio contact with anyone – we would be totally on our own – at the mercy of whatever happened."

"I feel safe with you. And besides, what interest would pirates have with us? They're after big commercial ships – like in that film *Captain Phillips*."

"Not always. They take Western hostages, too. We'd be sitting ducks."

"I want to get home, Tony, OK? I'm prepared to take that risk."

"Right, fine, we'll have to establish a watch routine all the way – like we had to do during some other crossings on this trip."

"Yes, no problem."

For some reason he seemed particularly keen to get this idea of the watches across to her. "It will mean long, lonely vigils on deck," he said.

"I'm used to that."

"Of course you are."

There were a couple of occasions over the next two days, while they provisioned the boat, when Juliet's old suspicions about Tony returned. He seemed to need the toilet on the harbour rather a lot, and always took his satellite phone with him. And he had become particularly irritable with her.

Once, she ribbed him, only partially in jest, saying, "You're going to have a crap, darling. Does your phone help you or something? Do you have a crap app on it?"

He just gave her a strange look as he jumped ashore and strode up the quay.

God, she loved him. But there was something, always something, thinking back throughout their time together, that she felt he kept from her. And she hated that. She had never kept anything from him, not from the very first moment they had met. Her biggest wish was that she could trust him just as much as she loved him.

She stared at the chart over his shoulder and could see it really did look a long way. An awfully long way. They would be leaving Borneo, and then Singapore, hundreds of miles to starboard. There was just a vast, blue, fathomless expanse of Indian Ocean. Of course, they could just berth the boat here and fly home. They'd be back in England in twenty-four hours, instead of three months, minimum. But she thought about the huge send-off they'd had, and all the donations, some per nautical mile covered, that were still clocking up, and she knew they had to arrive home, just as they had departed, by boat.

Three days later they set off. Tony, with his tanned face and beard flecked with white, was at the helm, motoring them out of the harbour while Juliet stowed the fenders into the hatches. It was a calm day, with a gentle force three breeze. Once they were clear of the moles, Juliet, still spritely, energetic and agile, unfurled the roller jib. When it was set, with the breeze on their port beam, she pressed the button to raise the mainsail.

Then Tony cut the engine and they sailed, with smiles on their faces, in the blissful, sudden silence. Just the crunch sound of their prow through the water, the clatter of the rigging, and the occasional caw from the handful of seagulls that accompanied them, hopeful of a snack of any scraps that they might jettison overboard.

After their long stay in port, Juliet moved around the deck, tidying away or coiling loose ropes, and checking for any loose tools Tony had left lying around. Then when her chores were finished, she went aft, leaned on the stern rail and watched the coastline of mainland Australia slowly, but steadily, fading into the heat haze.

Suddenly she felt a prick of apprehension. As if she had a presentiment, which she could not define, of the horror that lay ahead. They faced a long, long, voyage ahead of them. It would be one of the longest times they had spent at sea, unbroken by any landfall. In many ways she had been looking forward to it. On a long sea voyage, routine took over your lives, and she liked that routine. Taking turns on deck at the helm, on watch for other craft, especially at night in bad weather, when you were in the shipping lanes and there was the constant danger that a container ship or supertanker with a lazy crew on the bridge might not spot you, and could run you down without ever even noticing the impact.

Then preparing meals. Sleeping. And plenty of time for her passion: reading. They had a good supply of books, and she had her Kindle loaded with all the books she hadn't yet got around to reading, including *War and Peace* and the complete works of Charles Dickens.

The first two weeks passed without incident, and they had a steady, benign wind on the beam, giving them slightly faster progress than they had expected. If this continued, they could be home several days ahead of schedule. She was looking forward to seeing her family more and more with every passing day – and becoming increasingly excited. About two weeks to landfall in Sri Lanka, then up towards Europe.

The first inkling of what was to come happened while she was asleep in the stateroom with two hours to go until her turn on watch, when suddenly the yacht pitched violently, almost throwing her out of bed. She could hear the rigging clattering more than usual, and the yacht pitched again. It felt like the sea was getting up.

She slid out of bed, made her way across the saloon and climbed the steps up to the cockpit into the pitch darkness of the night, with Tony's face looking grim and paler than normal in the glow from the instrument binnacle. For the first time since they had set sail on this leg of the voyage, she could see no stars above them. "Everything OK, darling?"

"Wind's getting up," he said.

The forecast earlier had said a mild depression was heading their way, but Tony had not been worried. Now he looked a tad concerned. "Take the helm, will you, I want to go below and get a forecast update."

She could feel a strong, warm wind on her face, and the boat's motion was now so violent she had to hold onto a grab rail as she stumbled over to the wheel. The bitumen-black sea was flecked with phosphorescence from white horses. "Are you OK, darling?"

"I'm OK – well – I don't feel that great, to be honest."

"In what way?"

"I sort of feel a bit clammy. But I'm OK."

"Clammy?"

"That curry we had – I think I may have eaten a duff prawn."

"You poor darling. Go below and I'll take over for a while."

"I want to get an update on the forecast. But I'll be fine."

"You don't sound fine," she said, alarmed now. "You sound short of breath."

"I'm OK, really. All shipshape and Bristol fashion! We may have to reef in a bit if the wind gets up any more." He told her the course to stay on, advised her to clip on to the safety wire, gave her a peck on the cheek and disappeared down the companionway steps.

The wind was very definitely strengthening. The boat was heeling over, and pitching and rolling increasingly violently. They had far too much sail up. Reducing the mainsail was a matter of pressing a button and the reefing mechanism would wind it in. If necessary they could lower the main completely, as they had done on several occasions previously, and just sail on under a reduced jib – they could do that from the safety of the cockpit by winding in one of the sheets. In configuring the boat for this voyage, Tony had sensibly ensured that anything they needed to do at night to reduce the amount of sail could be done without leaving the cockpit.

Above her head, the rigging was clacking and pinging alarmingly. Suddenly, in a violent gust, the boat almost went flat on its side. She only just averted disaster by violently swinging the wheel, bringing the prow around into the wind. Below, she heard Tony bellow in anger – or shock or pain; she couldn't tell which. Immediately she obeyed his earlier instruction and clipped herself on.

Moments later he reappeared, his face looking like thunder through the hatch, and blood pouring from a gash in his forehead. "What the hell are you bloody doing, woman?"

"I'm sorry, darling, we've got too much sail up. Let me put some antiseptic on your head and a bandage."

"Bugger that," he said. "Get that ruddy main down, fast! We're heading straight into the eye of a force ten!"

"That's not what the forecast said earlier!"

She didn't like the panic in his voice. Tony never panicked, ever. But he was looking extremely worried now.

"OK!" She leaned over and pressed the button to begin the hydraulic roller reefing. The boom would rotate, furling the mainsail around it. With a force ten imminent, they needed to lower the main completely and take in the jib. The strength of the wind would power them forward just on their bare rigging. And they could do what they had done on two previous occasions, which was to go below, batten the hatches and ride it out. Fortunately they were well past all the major shipping lanes, and they could drift for days, if necessary, without any danger of striking land or rock. They had plenty of what sailors called sea room.

There was an alarming clanking sound from the boom, a loud whirr and nothing happened. The boat keeled over, and again, only her fast reactions on the helm prevented them from being knocked flat by the wind. Then it began pelting with rain, hard needles on her face.

"Get that sodding main down!" he yelled, clinging onto the companionway rail, unable to move with the angle of the boat.

"It's not working!" she shouted back.

"Turn into the wind!"

"I am, I'm trying to hold us there!"

Tony ducked down, out of sight, then reappeared holding a large rubber torch. He shone the beam up the mast, to the top. And they could both immediately see the problem. The very top of the mainsail had torn free, and was tangled in the rigging; the Australian courtesy flag, which they had run up weeks earlier and forgotten to take down after leaving the country, was fluttering hard.

Also clipping himself onto the jackstay safety wire, Tony stumbled across the wildly pitching deck and stabbed at the buttons on the reefing controls. The sail jerked up a few inches, then down. Then up again. They both smelled the acrid fumes of a burning electrical motor.

"Struth!" he said. "Struth!"

He stabbed at the control buttons, but now nothing happened at all.

"What's happened?" Juliet asked.

"Sodding motor – it's either burnt out or fused."

"Put another fuse in!"

"It's not going to help, you bloody stupid woman! It's all a bloody mess of knitting up there! I'll have to go up in the bosun's chair and sort it! You'll have to winch me."

"You can't, darling, it's too rough, I can't let go of the helm!"

They'd had the self-steering replaced last year in Perth harbour with a completely new system, but this, too, had failed in today's storm.

"We don't have a choice. We're going to go over unless we get that damned main down – keep her into the wind while I pull in the jib."

A few minutes later, puffing and wheezing, and looking exhausted from the effort, Tony managed to get the jib completely furled. But with the wind rising, by the second it seemed to Juliet, it was making minimal difference, and she was fighting, with all her strength, to stop the boat being knocked flat. Rain continued pelting, and the troughs into which the prow was plunging were deepening.

Each time it felt more and more like they were shooting down a big dipper. Spray roared over them, stinging her face.

"I've got to go up!" Tony shouted.

He pulled on gloves, climbed up over the cockpit onto the deck, holding on to the grab rails for dear life, and wormed his way forwards towards the mast on his stomach. He reached the webbing harness, which was like a trapeze attached to a pulley system, and managed, with difficulty, to haul himself into it and secure himself with two straps, forming a seat, and one rising up between his legs. Then he clipped everything securely in place and shouted out, "OK, darling! I'm going up!"

He released the safety wire attaching him to the boat, then slowly, inch by inch, hauled himself up the nylon rope by the handle. As Juliet did her best to hold the boat head-on into the wind, the mainsail thrashed at him with enormous force – so hard in one gust he thought it had broken his arm. The boat was pitching and rolling ever more crazily, and there were several moments on the way up when he was convinced he was going to get a ducking.

The boat could ride this out, he was confident of that. Even if they did get knocked over, provided the hatches were all shut, it would right itself. What he was most scared about was losing this mainsail. They didn't have enough fuel to motor the 1500 miles they still had to go to Sri Lanka. And if they had to rely on the jib alone, it would add weeks to their sailing time.

He hauled himself ever higher into the night sky, getting increasingly breathless. Almost at the top now! He was going to sort out this bastard! Then suddenly he felt a stabbing pain shoot up his right arm and his head swam. The darkness turned into a fairground ride. And suddenly it seemed as if a steel tourniquet was being tightened around his chest.

"Darling! Darling? How are you doing?" Juliet yelled. "Are you OK?"

He shone his torch at the tangle of wire and rope. As he did so the boat keeled over violently and the wind ripped at his face and hair. Below him, he heard Juliet scream. The bosun's chair was swinging wildly, and suddenly, despite his efforts, it stopped. Tangled up in the mess, too.

"Bugger!" he shouted out in frustration.

"What is it, Tony?"

There were times when you had to make fast decisions at sea. This was one of them. The companionway hatch, which he had climbed up through, was open. If they did get knocked flat, the sea would pour in and down into the saloon. If that happened, they were doomed. Juliet and he would stand no sodding chance of survival in the middle of the Indian Ocean in the little inflatable life raft with its emergency provisions of a small quantity of water and a couple of bars of chocolate. It was designed to keep them alive for a few hours, or a couple of days at the outside, before they were rescued. There was only one option.

He began to cut the mainsail, stabbing it, ripping it, then moving his knife as far as he could reach. Within seconds, the wind made the tear wider. Then wider still.

"Tony!" Juliet called. "What's happening?"

He tried to shout back, but he couldn't find the energy. Instead he spoke softly into the brutal wind. "It's OK, we're safe!"

"Tony?"

The band was tightening around his chest.

"Tony?"

He saw faces appearing out of the darkness. The faces of beautiful women. All of them were calling out, "Tony! Tony! Tony!"

Somewhere in the distance he heard Juliet's voice, anxiously calling, "Tony? Tony! TONY!"

The yacht was easier to steer now, with the torn mainsail flapping around like laundry on a line above her. But the wind was so intense that whenever she tried to let go of the wheel, the yacht keeled over so sharply she was scared it would go flat, even on its bare rigging. She fought the wheel, trying as desperately hard as she could to keep the prow head-on into the strengthening and constantly veering wind, which seemed as if it was playing a weird game of catch-me-if-you-can, and constantly having to close her eyes against the stinging spray and rain. Again and again, she called out, "Tony! Tony! Tony!"

Finally, without the storm letting up, dawn began breaking, slowly, after the longest night of her life. She kept on shouting her husband's name. As the sky steadily lightened, she could see Tony's silhouette at the top of the mast appear intermittently, as a strip of torn mainsail alternately wrapped itself partially around him, then flapped away. Steadily he became more detailed. He sat up there, silent, strapped into the bosun's chair, his head slumped forward, swinging to port and then starboard with each roll of the boat.

Her voice was hoarse from shouting. The rain and spray had long since stopped and now her eyes were raw from crying. This wasn't happening, please God, this was not happening.

"Tony!" she called again. "Wake up, Tony, please wake up!"

He rolled around like a rag doll in his yellow T-shirt, blue denim shorts and plimsolls, the gloves making him look like some kind of mechanic.

"Tony!" she called again and again, with increasing desperation. The storm was beginning to ease. The swell was still very heavy, though, with the boat riding waves and almost pitchpoling. Over the course of the next two hours, the wind dropped steadily, and as it did, the sea slowly calmed down.

Finally, she felt able to leave the helm. She locked the wheel, clambered up onto the deck, still clipped to her safety wire, and stumbled on all fours to the mast. She stared up at her husband and called out again, repeatedly, her throat raw and her voice croaking, "Tony, Tony, TONY!"

She tried to climb the mast, but each time, swaying wildly, she only got a few feet above the deck before sliding down and burning her hands, painfully, on the raw wires. "Tony! Tony! Tony!"

There was no response. And now in full daylight, as the torn strip of sail flapped away from him again, she could see why not. His eyes were wide open, but he wasn't blinking. They just stared, sightlessly.

Sobbing, she pulled at the wires, trying to free the bosun's chair high above her from the tangle, but all that happened was the burns on her hands became worse. Finally, she gave up, crawled back to the cockpit and went below.

She switched on the radio and tuned it to Channel 16, the international maritime channel. But all she got was a buzz of static. She tried other channels, but the same buzz greeted her. All the same she returned to Channel 16 and sent out a Mayday distress signal. The satnav wasn't working, and she could only figure out their approximate position from Tony's last plot of the chart on the chart table. She gave it and asked for urgent medical help.

The only response she got was more of the same static buzz.

She went back on deck and looked up with a shudder, past her husband's swinging body by the spreaders, close to the very top of the mast, where the radio aerial, transponder and satellite navigation receptors were – and where the yard arm would have been on an older boat. And she saw, to her dismay, that they had gone. Presumably torn away by the tangle of rigging in last night's storm.

She wept uncontrollably. "Tony, please don't do this to me. Don't leave me. Not here. Don't, please no!"

She stared up at the dark grey sky. And then at the expanse of dark green ocean all around them, which stretched out to the horizon in every direction. According to the chart, Christmas Island was a couple of hundred nautical miles behind them. Sri Lanka was still well over a thousand miles ahead of them. Indonesia was several hundred miles to starboard. It would be days of sailing to reach them, days taking her away from the most direct route home.

134

Tony was dead. She had to accept that, she knew. It wasn't going to make any difference whether it was a few days now, or two weeks. Her best option, she decided, was to keep to their course, and hope that her Mayday had been heard. If she saw a commercial ship or another yacht on the horizon, or if a plane flew overhead, she would fire off one of the flares they had on board. Her best hope was that her distress signal had been picked up, but she wasn't confident about that.

Maybe a helicopter would appear? But she was pretty sure they were out of range for one. Then, cursing herself for forgetting it, she swore aloud as she suddenly remembered Tony's satellite phone.

"Of course! How could I be so stupid?" It didn't need a mast! Tony had bought it for emergencies, justifying the expense by telling her that even if they lost all their electrics, they could still use it to call for help.

She clambered back down into the saloon, and found it safely stowed in the cupboard to the right of the chart table. She unclipped it, studied it for some moments, then pressed the power button. After a few moments, the display came on. Several symbols appeared, one showing that there was 80 per cent of the battery life left. Then, to her dismay, there was a request for the code.

And she had no sodding idea what that was.

"For God's sake, Tony," she cursed under her breath. "Why the hell did you need a pass code?"

Then she remembered a piece of wisdom Tony had once given her a long time ago, and that was to never panic. Panic was what killed people, he had said. Survivors of disasters were those who were able to keep calm and clear-headed, no matter how bad the situation they faced.

And bad situations did not get much worse than the one she was currently in.

"Good advice, Tony!" she said aloud. Doing her best to keep calm and clear-headed, she thought about the pass codes they had always used. The one for their burglar alarm at home was the first one that came to mind. Her year of birth: 1954. Whenever they had stayed in a hotel anywhere and there was a code required for the safe in the room, they had used the same one: 1954.

She tapped the numbers in expectantly. But all she got was an angry buzz and the display shook.

Sod it! Why the hell hadn't he used that one? Just to make sure she hadn't made a mistake she entered it again. And got the same response.

She stared at the phone, thinking. She knew there were settings on some phones that only permitted you a limited number of tries at a pass code before locking you out. How many did this allow?

What the hell might he have used? On such an important phone, it must be a sequence of numbers that he would remember easily. What about his date of birth?

She entered 1948, and instantly got the same angry buzz and short, sharp shake of the display.

"Stupid bastard!" she said, out aloud this time. What else? She tried the numbers backwards. Same result. She tried her own date of birth backwards. Same result again. Then she shouted at the phone. "Come on, you are my sodding lifeline! Give me your bloody code!"

It required four numbers. How many sodding combinations of four numbers could there be? She started trying, at random, different sequences. His birth date, day and month: 1607. Day and year: 1648. Then her own. Then 0000. Each time she got the same response.

"Please!" she said. "Oh God, please let me in."

She took the phone up on deck and saw, to her alarm, that they had veered way off course whilst she had been below. She brought the boat back round onto the correct heading, but the wind had dropped so much that she was barely making any progress at all. She needed to get some sail up, or else start the engine and motor, but she was worried about the amount of fuel they were carrying. She had always left that to Tony, but remembered that he had always been careful not to run the engine for longer than necessary. He always told her that they needed to conserve their fuel for charging up the boat's batteries and for entering and leaving ports. *Juliet 3* was a sailing yacht, not a power boat. They did not have long-range fuel tanks. How far would their fuel take her, she wondered?

The mainsail was useless, way beyond repair, one large strip of it listlessly flapping around Tony's body, like a shroud, before slipping away and fluttering around. She would have to sail under the jib, because when she did reach Columbo harbour at Sri Lanka, she would sure as hell need to motor in – she didn't have the skills to go in under sail.

She freed the jib sheet from the cleat, then pulled hard to unfurl it. After a few minutes of exertion, the massive sail was fully extended and filled with the wind that was coming from the stern. She could feel the boat accelerating forwards, and watched the needle on the dial steadily climb from one knot to three. The mainsail, now a huge, tattered rag, flapped uselessly.

Three knots, she thought. How long would it take to get to their destination, sailing with only the jib, making seventy-two nautical miles a day? Somewhere between two to three weeks. She stared, warily, up at her husband's motionless body. Then, in a sudden fit of anger, she shouted up at him, "You want medical help, Tony? Give me your sodding phone code!"

Then she wept again. She had not prayed for years, not since she was a child. But suddenly, she found herself pressing her hands against her face and praying.

"Oh God, please help us. Please help us."

As if in answer, she suddenly heard a horrible, ugly cry above her. "*Aaarrrggghh! Aaarrrrggghh!*" She looked up and saw a gull-like bird with a sinister hooded face, as if it was wearing a mask. Spooking her, it circled the boat several times, unfazed by the sail that continued to wrap around Tony's body then flap away, free, again. After a few minutes, slowly, unhurriedly, it soared away.

Did the bird mean she was closer to land than she realised, she wondered?

She watched it warily, until it became a tiny speck, remembering, suddenly, the albatross in the *Rhyme of the Ancient Mariner*. Was it bad luck to see a gull, too? There was a country superstition in England that it was bad luck to see just one magpie, you needed to see another quickly. Did the same apply to gulls?

Shakily, she went below again to try the satnav and radio once more, but the satellite navigation screen was just a mass of squiggly lines and the radio continued to produce nothing but a buzz of static. She gave up on them and instead tried to study the chart, to see how far they were from the nearest port. But for several minutes, sitting at the chart table, all she could do was cry, her grief pouring out. She felt so alone, so scared and almost as if nothing mattered any more. She had lost the man she loved. Lost their life. The easiest thing would be to climb back up the steps, go to the rear of the cockpit, haul herself over the stern rail and let go.

But then she thought about her children and her grandchildren, and dabbed her eyes, blotted up the tears that had fallen onto the chart and did her best to pull herself together. It was having no one to talk to – no one at all – that was the worst thing at this moment. No one to share her grief or fear with. And the prospect of two weeks like this. Two weeks of sailing, with Tony stuck up there by the spreaders, in the full glare of the sun when it came out. There had to be a way to get him down.

Had to. Please God.

She studied the chart carefully and took measurements. Indonesia was definitely a lot closer than Sri Lanka. Five or six days' sailing instead of about fourteen. But she wasn't confident enough about her navigation skills to risk changing course. She could have programmed the satnav if that had been working, but although Tony had taught her how to plot a course, calculating currents and, where relevant, tides, she didn't trust herself enough to do it alone. And for a start, she didn't even know her exact position.

If the sky had been clear, with the sun or stars out, she might have been able to figure out her exact position from the sextant. But there was only thick, unbroken cloud. Tony had drawn, in pencil, a circle around their last position, which he had plotted yesterday evening. There was no land showing, although she knew that if she just steered a course east she would be almost bound to reach somewhere on the Indonesian coast – the country virtually formed a barrier in that direction.

But that would be taking her off the planned course, and she could not be sure of landfall remotely near anywhere that had an airport. At least if she kept going towards Sri Lanka she would be heading closer to home. And when she reached there she could find an undertaker and fly home with her husband.

Although, she suddenly remembered in her misery, Tony had always told her that he wanted to be buried at sea, and she had promised him that if he pre-deceased her, she would arrange that. How ironic, she thought now, that he had died at sea, doing what he loved, and she wasn't able to get him down and do at least that.

Perhaps, if the authorities permitted it in Sri Lanka, she could arrange it there?

Maybe, she wondered, they were closer to land than she thought. How far could gulls fly from land? Thousands of miles? Perhaps. Some birds flew great distances when they migrated, didn't they? Where had that one, with its sinister hooded face, come from?

She went back up on deck, swung the wheel to bring them back on course, then looked at the broken self-steering mechanism, wondering if there was any way she could fix it. But she could see that a whole central cog had ripped away. Nothing short of welding was going to fix it.

She resigned herself to having to man the helm for as long as she could, and sleeping for as little as possible.

The sun was high in the sky now and, despite the light breeze, it was sweltering on deck. She tried to look up, but the sight of the lifeless body of the man she had loved so much swinging around in the bosun's chair, and the creepy sail that kept furling around him like a shroud, was too much for her to bear. Instead she stared, steely-eyed, ahead, her gaze fixed on the far horizon beyond the prow of the vessel.

After half an hour, she suddenly saw two tiny specks, high in the sky, heading towards her. For an instant her hopes rose. Helicopters? But then, a few minutes later, her spirits sank again; she could see from their motion that they were birds.

And as they got closer still she could see their masked faces. Was it the one she had seen before returning with a friend? Keeping one eye on the compass binnacle, she watched the birds circling, soaring around in a wide loop, then a tighter loop. Then a tighter one still.

She felt a sudden prick of anxiety as they began to circle her husband's body. Tighter and tighter, showing increasing interest.

"Sod off, birds!" she called out.

Then one darted at his face, made a pecking motion and flew away. Then the other flew in and pecked.

"Sod off! Go away! Don't touch him!"

Suddenly she saw more dark specks on the horizon. She counted five, six, seven, eight, ten?

Within minutes there were a dozen gulls swarming around her husband, all pecking at his face.

"NOOOOO!" she screamed. She swung the helm wildly left and right, heeling the boat over to port then to starboard. But it made no difference to the birds. They were crying out, a hideous *caw-cawcaw* shriek, batting each other with their wings, darting in, pecking at Tony's eyes, lips, nose, ears.

"NOOOOOOOOOOO!"

She locked the wheel and hurried down below, opened the locker where they kept the six emergency flares, unclipped them and clambered up on deck with them. There were even more gulls now, hideous creatures with demon faces, all fighting each other for a morsel of his face.

She held up one flare, trying to read the instructions, but her hands were shaking so much the tiny print was just a blur. Finally she succeeded, aimed the flare directly at them and pulled the small plastic ring. There was a sharp whoosh, and it fired, sending something like a firework rocket shooting up, well wide of the gulls, high into the sky before exploding in a sheet of red light. They took no notice at all.

"GO AWAY YOU BASTARDS!" she screamed and seized another flare.

She aimed again, pulled the loop, and this time scored a bullseye, sending it right into their midst. It hit one gull in the belly, then arced down into the sea, exploding as it struck the water off her port beam. The gull spiralled downwards, helicoptering, unconscious or dead, and landed motionless on the water. As if in wild panic, all the other gulls, cawing in anger and confusion, scattered and flew off towards the horizon.

She was shaking uncontrollably. The motionless gull passed by the port side and soon was way behind her. "Bloody serves you right, you ghoul," she muttered.

Ten minutes later the gulls returned, some singly, others in groups. Now there seemed even more than before. She fired off another flare, but she was shaking so much she missed altogether. Ignoring it totally, the gulls were now on a feeding frenzy.

Tears were running down her face, blinding her as she fired off another flare, then another, with no effect. She realized now she had only one left. She couldn't fire it, she needed to preserve it in case she saw a ship on the horizon. It would be her last hope, she knew. The nightmare of Tony dying, which she could not have imagined getting any worse, now had. She had to stop these vulture birds, but how?

She clambered forwards, gripped the mast and desperately, using all her strength, tried to climb the narrow aluminium pole. She felt a splat of bird shit on her forehead. Then another. The din of their cries above her was almost deafening.

She screamed at them, again and again and again. Gripping the mast with her arms and her legs she made it up a few feet, but then, obstructed by the rigging and parts of the ripped sail flapping in her face, she could get no higher.

She slid back down, weeping uncontrollably, and returned to the cockpit. They were heading wildly off course. She turned the wheel and watched the compass needle slowly swing back round. She shouted at the birds until she was hoarse, but it made no difference.

The gulls stayed until there was nothing left of his face to peck, and then, as dusk began to fall, they gradually, some singly, some in pairs, flapped away into the falling darkness.

High up above her, swinging in the bosun's chair, was her husband's skull, with a rictus grin and patches of hair on the scalp.

Her stomach was burning, but the rest of her felt numb. Totally numb. She prayed. Prayed that she would wake up and find this had all been just a nightmare.

The gulls returned soon after dawn. Now they were pecking through his clothes, bits of fabric from his orange Henri Lloyd yachting jacket fluttered in the air as they greedily found the flesh beneath it.

By the end of the third day, Tony resembled a scarecrow.

It was twelve more days and nights before, in the early afternoon, she finally saw the lighthouse, the long, welcoming concrete harbour arms of the port of Colombo, Sri Lanka, and a speed limit sign. She was utterly exhausted, almost out of her mind from lack of sleep, and during the past two days she had started speaking out aloud to Tony, holding imaginary conversations with him. The gulls had long departed, having, she presumed, picked his carcass clean. Some bits of his clothes still clung, raggedly, to his skeleton.

There was no wind on this searing hot afternoon, and fortunately, the strip of sail had once more furled around Tony, almost completely covering him. She was motoring, the fuel gauge on empty, praying there was enough left to get her to a berth in the yacht basin that she had found identified on the harbour chart and marked in red by Tony. She was thankful, at least, for his meticulous planning.

Through bloodshot eyes, behind sunglasses that were long fogged with salt, she watched the bunkering stations pass by, cranes, a huge lumber warehouse and an endless line of berthed container ships and tankers. Then finally, to her relief, she saw a whole forest of yacht masts through a gap to starboard and headed towards them.

Fifteen minutes later, passing a refuelling station, she saw a sign for visitors' berths and, slowing her speed to a crawl, scrambled forward and removed a bow line from its locker, then pulled out several fenders and hung them over the side. She wasn't sure how she was going to manage the actual berthing, though.

Then, to her relief, an elderly man in a battered peaked cap, with the appearance of a port official, suddenly appeared, signalling to her with his arms. She threw him the bow line, which he caught expertly and secured around a bollard. Moments later he caught the stern line and secured that, and steadily, as if he had done it a thousand times before, reeled her in alongside the pontoon.

Sobbing with relief, she did not think she had ever been so happy to see another human being in her life.

She jumped ashore and then, pointing towards the top of the mast at Tony's remains, tried to explain what had happened. But he spoke no English and failed to take any notice of her gesticulations, nor did he look up. All he kept saying, repeatedly and insistently through a sparse set of yellow teeth, one gold and several missing, was "You Passeport? Passeport? You papers? Papers, documentation?"

She went below, found the boat's papers and her passport and handed them to him. Signalling he would be back, he hurried off. She stood on the deck, watching him head towards a cluster of buildings, shaking with relief that she was no longer at sea. As she had sailed in, she had passed several yachts flying British flags. If she walked along, with luck she would find someone who could tell her where to find the British consul, or at least let her use their phone.

But before that, she badly needed a drink. She went below and pulled one of the bottles of rum that Tony had been fond of drinking at sea out of the booze cabinet. Just as she was pouring herself a glass, she heard a female voice above her, calling in broken English, "Hello? Tony? Hello?"

Frowning, Juliet looked up and saw a very attractive-looking Indian woman, in her early thirties, peering in.

"Can I help you?" she asked.

"This is the *Juliet*?" the woman asked. "The yacht *Juliet*?"

"Yes, it is."

"I'm meeting Tony."

Now Juliet frowned again, more severely. "Tony Trollope."

"Yes!" Then she hesitated. "You are the cleaner?"

Bloody hell, Juliet wondered. Did she look that bad after all this time at sea? Without commenting she replied, "Might I ask who you are?"

"Yes, I am Tony's fiancée."

"Fiancée?" Juliet could barely control herself.

"Yes, Tony was sailing here to meet me, to get married here."

"Who was he sailing with?"

"He said he was sailing alone, solo."

A sudden chill rippled through Juliet. Was that why Tony had chosen this route? Three weeks at sea, away from land. Three weeks out of radio contact. Three weeks where anything could have happened to either of them, and no police would have had any evidence that a crime had been committed?

Had that been his plan? To push her overboard and then sail on to a new life with this beautiful young woman.

The bastard.

"What is your name?" Juliet asked.

"Lipika."

"That's a very pretty name!"

"Thank you. Is Tony on board?"

"Yes, he's just a little tied up at the moment. You know what, I think we should have a drink, Lipika, to celebrate your engagement!" She pulled a second glass out of the cupboard.

"No, thank you," Lipika said, and smiled sweetly. "I don't drink."

Ignoring her, Juliet filled the second glass. "You're going to need one, dear, a very large one!"

She carried both glasses up into the cockpit and stared at the woman in daylight. She really was very beautiful indeed. Beautiful enough to kill for?

But what did that matter any more? It was over now. The past. She raised her glass and clinked the young woman's. "Cheers!"

Lipika hesitantly clinked back.

Then Juliet said, "Sun's over the yard arm!" and raised her glass high. "Here's to the happy couple. Tony and Lipika! He's all yours!"

The woman raised hers high and followed Juliet's gaze. And at that moment, a light gust of breeze unfurled the strip of sail that had wrapped around Tony's body, and it flapped free, exposing his ragged skeleton, his skull picked clean apart from a few sinews and a small patch of hair.

Lipika's glass fell to the deck and smashed.

Her scream shattered the calm of the afternoon.

ECHOES OF AN ELDRITCH PAST

'The nightmare corpse-city of R'lyeh ... was built in measureless aeons behind history by the vast, loathsome shapes that seeped down from the dark stars. There lay great Cthulhu and his hordes, hidden in green slimy vaults.'

The Call of Cthulhu (1928)
H.P. Lovecraft

The writings of Howard Phillips Lovecraft were not specifically concerned with themes of oceanic horror, but by necessity the vast and timeless seas of our world came to play a significant part in them. Lovecraft's mythos proposes that mankind is an irrelevant flyspeck beneath the notice of an eldritch race of abominable beings who came down from space in billennia past and now reside in secret places in a monstrous, deathlike sleep.

There is no suggestion, and never has been, that Lovecraft's mythos comprises anything more than a shared fictional universe to which numerous chapters have been attached over many decades, and not just by Lovecraft himself. HPL's stories have no real foundation in world mythology despite his fascination for and frequent referencing of ancient civilisations and their belief systems. At no stage did he imply that he had uncovered some long-forgotten truth which might have terrifying implications for mankind today.

Even so, the imagery he painted has made an unforgettable impression – to such a degree that when certain weird anomalies emerge in the modern world, especially those with their roots in distant antiquity, even more especially those with apparent oceanic origins, we are quick to use terms like 'Lovecraftian'.

For example, in 1997 various hydrophones placed around the southern Pacific rim by the US National Oceanic and Atmospheric Administration detected a curious sound which initially they were at a loss to understand. The purpose of the study was to observe natural phenomena such as subaquatic seismicity, marine animal migrations and the rate and direction of the movement of ice floes. But this new sound – which was of extreme low frequency and astonishingly powerful – was completely unexpected and seemingly inexplicable. As quoted in the actual NOAA report, the noise "rose rapidly in frequency over about one minute and was of sufficient amplitude to be heard on multiple sensors, at a range of over 5,000 km (3106.86 miles)." A variety of plausible theories were offered. Had the system recorded a succession of controlled explosions such as undersea bombs? Did the sound indicate increased Russian submarine activity? Or was it perhaps a series of deep ocean earthquakes? When a proposition was put forward that what the team was actually hearing was organic in origin, in other words a noise made by a living creature, there was general amazement but a gradual consensus that this was possible. The 'Bloop', as it was quickly referred to in scientific circles, matched the rapidly altering audio signature of various known marine animals, and yet was recorded by sensors located almost 5,000 kilometres apart, which meant that it was vastly louder than any blue whale noise ever detected, and up to this point the blue whale was by far the loudest creature on Earth. If all this was true, the Bloop had to represent a beast of such colossal proportions that it's like would be completely unknown in the modern world.

For this reason perhaps, scientific opinion soon shifted away from the animal theory and it was eventually affirmed that, as icequake echoes were predominant throughout the Southern Ocean, this was almost certainly what the survey had recorded. However, not everyone agreed. Certain geophysicists have gone on record to insist that the Bloop resembles no geological sound they've ever heard before, while others point ominously to the actual place where its origin was pinpointed: 50°S 100°W, several hundred miles west of the southernmost tip of Chile, which by pure chance is extraordinarily close to the location of Lovecraft's sunken city of R'lyeh (47°S 126°W) wherein the gargantuan demi-god Cthulhu would occasionally stir in his trillennia-long slumber.

As well as R'lyeh, Lovecraft spoke of Y'ha-nthlei under Devil's Reef in the North Atlantic, while other writers have contributed Ahu-Y'hloa just off the coast of Cornwall, and G'll-Hoo near Iceland – but though no-one is actually suggesting that these ancient undersea strongholds are anything more than fiction, there are many like them that genuinely exist.

A number of bizarre, drowned structures have been discovered in various of our seas. Several have been identified by archaeologists and historians: Agios Andreas and Helike are the sites of ancient Greek cities that collapsed into the Aegean. The same was true of Dunwich, the Anglo-Saxon capital of East Anglia, which was claimed by coastal erosion during the Dark Ages, while Rhacotis was the original Egyptian city of Alexandria, the second most powerful metropolis in the Ancient World after Rome, much of which was swallowed by a tsunami in the Nile Delta in 365 AD.

But others remain enigmatic.

Perhaps the most obvious is the massive seabed Monument near Yonaguni, off the Japanese Ryukyu Islands. Though some argue the

Monument is a natural rock formation, its complexity of pillars, steps, terraces and columns make this unlikely. The top of the Monument lies only 16 feet below the ocean surface, but geological records indicate that it last stood on dry land some 10,000 years ago, which was long before any complex construction was being undertaken by humans in this region.

A similar mystery has been located in a much colder zone, the icy waters of the Gulf of Botnia in the northern Baltic. This one lies deeper, at 183 feet, and takes the form of a large circular building, with apparent paved platforms leading away from it for hundreds of yards and a spiral stairway penetrating its interior. This particular anomaly was only uncovered in 2011, and as yet there is no photographic evidence of it. Some physical assessment by divers has been made, revealing that it is composed of metallic elements, which may or may not indicate natural sediment. While an original human origin for the object cannot be discounted, again this would render the structure thousands upon thousands of years old – making it much older than anything else known to have been built in that region. Some theories hold that it is a discarded battleship turret, or a German experimental aircraft from World War Two, while others point to the stony nature of its appearance and claim that it must be a fossilised alien spacecraft. But at the time of this writing, it remains officially unexplained.

In an age when we like solutions to baffling mysteries, when we so trust science that we almost feel entitled to an explanation for every quirk or oddity that arises, perhaps it's no surprise that some researchers remain convinced that these lowering hunks of murky, seaweed-covered masonry are testimonies to ancient, primordial intelligences now long forgotten, as much a witness statement to an unknown prehistoric age as any eerie, cacophonous cry recorded in the deepest tracts of the ocean.

FIRST MIRANDA
Simon Strantzas

Burning summer windstorms. Sand rattling car windows. Wheels roaring on the road. Chinking gravel. Jules searched desperately for something to say.

"How long has it been?" His voice sounded strange after hours of the highway's roar. Miranda didn't turn.

"I haven't been back in a lifetime. It all still looks the same."

"It's the middle of nowhere. Weird to think you grew up this far from everything."

She looked at him; she was still there beneath the folds and creases. That face that he'd fallen in love with years earlier. Time had treated her better than most – she hardly looked different from when they'd met – so why was it so hard to accept what she'd become? Why had he made such a mess of things?

"My sisters and I were happy. I never thought I'd ever want anything else. None of us did, back then. But time creeps up and soon you're scattered like seeds on the wind."

"Well, I'm glad your seed landed near me." Jules moved his hand from the wheel and put it on hers. The rumble of wheels travelled upward. Miranda turned to the window, limp hand remaining behind like a fallen troop. Minutes passed before she rescued it.

The road to the cottage was a flash on the highway; one exit and it was gone, no way to turn back for thirty minutes. Jules was careful to watch for the signs, but its sudden appearance startled him, and he barely had time to stop. Half-covered by hanging branches, unproved and narrow, it seemed less a road and more something from a dream. But Miranda was proof it was real and led somewhere.

Jules was lucky to have her back. After he admitted what he'd done she had walked out with a warning not to follow. It wasn't the first time she had disappeared when their fights became too much, but even at her most erratic she was never gone more than a few hours. Then again, he had never done something so horrible before. As days and weeks passed with no contact at all, he grew terrified something tragic had happened. He couldn't help himself – the ideas bred and multiplied and overwhelmed him. Brown alcohol and pills could not smother the distant thoughts that chittered beneath his fuzzy blanket of inebriation. But when all seemed lost, and his darkest times bottomless, he cracked open his eyes at the sound of keys at the door, and in the streaming light stood Miranda, again and perhaps for the first time. She looked different, her skin rougher, but it was her – he recognized the look of disappointment on her face.

Miranda's childhood home was small. A single story, flat roof, and peeling white paint, but the front door was secure and the windows were clean. If he hadn't known the house was empty most of the year, he would have suspected someone was there regularly to keep it up.

"Why don't you go inside? I'll get the bags down and bring them in." It was well past lunch and Jules's stomach twisted, but he didn't dare speak. The therapist told him to ensure Miranda's needs were the first in his mind – as though they hadn't been since the day the two of them met. He, on an early morning walk home along the boardwalk; she, sitting on that same boardwalk, watching the ocean, having stopped during her own morning stroll. It was something out of a movie, and had been perfect. Perfect, until it wasn't.

The cottage was bright – in every direction there was more window than wall – and he understood for once how living so far from the world might be tolerable, especially with such a view of the ocean. Jules rested the bags and walked to the glass separating house from shore. Gazing out at the water, he imagined Miranda as a girl, playing in the narrow patches of sand, swimming in the summer water. Laughing with sisters he'd never been allowed to meet.

So many things moved – the waves, the branches, the soaring birds – that he didn't notice anything at first. A blur, a tiny mar on the day, and when Jules clenched his fists and focused he realized it was moving. Swaying side to side, it poked from the water. A pale arm, trying to pull itself free.

"Do you see that?"

Miranda glanced with disinterest.

"It's nothing. It's the water."

"No, there's someone out there. Don't you see her?"

Miranda squinted again, held her position longer, but still came back shaking her head.

And when Jules looked back, it had gone.

*

"I think I might take the boat out, see what's around. Why don't you come along?"

Miranda sat in the front room, sunlight falling across her back and the side of her face. She looked up from her book, her inscrutable expression framed by stray hairs.

"Come on, Miranda. It will be fun. We haven't done anything like a mini adventure in a while."

She appeared to consider it, and he imagined sitting beside her as he circled the boat over its own wake, bouncing the two of them on a short thrill ride. They would laugh as they used to, long before he'd made his mistakes. Long before Miranda had walked out.

"It's okay," she said. "You go on. Have fun. I'm going to catch up on my book."

"Miranda ..." he started, but didn't have the energy to fight. He missed the old Miranda, yet there was no one he could blame.

The boat's rusty outboard motor needed to be primed, but once it coughed it kept on coughing. Blue fumes drifted up, a smog that coated the rickety dock and hung in the air long after he'd eased the motor into reverse and backed the boat away from its mooring. Once clear, he gunned it and waited as the boat sputtered worryingly and inched forward. Then a clunk, a long wheeze, a cough, and the boat accelerated quickly. Jules grinned.

The boat skipped over the waves, its prow pointed into the air as it tried to leap free. Relief from the oppressive house, his unreadable wife, all his mistakes, came immediately. It was behind him, a distant memory as he motored toward the endless horizon. Clouds slipped off the sun in response to his rising joy, bathing him in light. He wanted to live in that moment forever. Everything else faded as he pushed the rattling motor faster.

A small island rose from the ocean a few kilometres off the coast. Jules turned the boat toward it out of curiosity. As he approached the island's narrow shore, the outboard motor grumbled, and he downshifted it to let it cool. The island passed on his right as he circled, row after row of trees with trunks like straight arrows stuck in the ground. Something moved among them, a shadow taking refuge in the thick forest, but his unease lessened when he realized it was simply a refraction of light.

Motor sufficiently rested, he pulled the rudder and aimed the boat back at where he'd come from. The cottage was farther away than he thought – so far he could barely make it out or its drab dock. Without warning clouds drew back over the sun.

The thought of returning to Miranda evoked a deep sorrow. The empty seat beside him was filled with an afternoon of unrealized possibilities, but Jules knew there was no way they could have left their problems on the shore. And the ocean was not deep enough to drown them all.

The waving from the water caught his eye. The arm, long and lithe, moved dreamily, its mate wrapped around a bobbing orange buoy. It hardly seemed real, like the fragment of a dream. He rubbed his eyes but it didn't disappear. Worry stirred. Was someone stuck too far from shore? He pulled the steer, angling the boat toward the buoy.

The boat sputtered as he approached. The arm filled his vision, and in its motion he detected desperation and panic. He raced through the possible scenarios, worried he might be too late, and when that arm vanished before his eyes, that worry grew worse. He eased back on the throttle and scanned the ocean's surface for movement. His eye found Miranda, watching from the distant shore with shielding hand on her brow.

"Do you mind?"

The disembodied voice startled him.

"Hey! What's your problem?"

He peered over the edge of the boat. Three heads bobbed in the water: a young girl in her late teens, flanked by two boys. Her hair was wet, her face round.

"What are you? Some kind of creep?" she asked.

"What? No. I'm just –" He tried to focus on her face, but her pale shoulders glowing under the water distracted him. Was it *her* arm he'd seen?

"Get out of here," one of her olive boyfriends demanded. "Screw off, loser."

"But I was just – Where did you – ?"

"*But I was just. Where did you,*" they mocked.

So much young flesh. He sputtered, awkward, unable to think.

Defeated, he revved the outboard motor and slowly backed away from the laughter. He was both humiliated and aroused, and remained so until he glanced at the shore and saw Miranda retreating into the house.

Whatever she thought she'd seen wasn't right. Nothing had happened or was going to, but she wouldn't believe that, and part of him hated her for it. Despite all the love he offered, she couldn't look past one small mistake made when things were at their worst. He tried and continued to try, but she made it difficult. Maybe it would have been better to give up and go their separate ways.

The boat reached the dock choking on its last breath of petrol. He glided it across the water and threw a line around each cleat before pulling himself onto the dock. He wrestled with what he'd say to Miranda as he walked the narrow path to the cottage, but when he entered through the sliding glass door, she squeezed past

150

him on her way outside, dressed in her yellow one-piece suit and carrying a towel in her hand.

"I didn't do anything!" The words sounded so tiny and foolish aloud. They trailed her back down to the dock. "Miranda, will you stop and talk to me?" he called out, but she wouldn't respond. At the dock's farthest edge she sat and dipped her feet in one at a time before pushing herself forward. He heard the splash, and saw her hazy yellow figure swim off beneath the waves.

His fists clenched. Jules turned and went inside, as though that small spiteful action would communicate his hurt, maybe make Miranda realize she still loved him. He would unpack his suitcase and prepare for the coming nights. With luck, she would remember why they were there, and work with him to fix their marriage, not crack it further.

It took no more than a few minutes, but it gave his anger time to dissipate. He had to try harder, be better, if he wanted to reach her. It shouldn't surprise him her solution to conflict was to disappear – she had lived most of her life on the ocean's edge, isolated from the world. It wasn't a reflection on him.

Jules watched from the window as Miranda swam in the tide with graceful ease. The buoys were visible in the distance, orange markers in the afternoon light. They bobbed as the waves pushed them back and forth, and Jules found himself searching for the girl and her two boyfriends. His heart's rhythm increased and mouth dried as he imagined what they might be doing, what their young arms would feel like wrapped around him. A shiver ran through his spine, and he shook to interrupt the aggregating thoughts. There couldn't be any more mistakes, no proving Miranda right. Still, when he saw the lithe arm rise from the water again, closer to shore, his heart resumed its flutter.

But it looked different than it had earlier. He squinted, leaned forward, and tried to understand why the sight terrified him so. The realization turned him cold.

"Miranda!"

He ran to the dock and leapt without hesitation. Miranda struggled to keep afloat, arms thrashing wildly, gasping for air in the scant seconds she spent above the surface. Jules's legs pumped, propelling him as his hands clawed the water. When he reached Miranda she aggressively fought his rescue attempt; it was all he could do to keep hold of her as he dragged her to shore. Miranda crawled from the surf and hugged the land as though she'd never been there before. Jules staggered out and to her side. Hands on his knees, struggling for breath, he forced the words out.

"Miranda, what happened?"

Wet hair plastered to her forehead, eyes wide and searching, she appeared unfathomably lost. Her skin was pale and lips colourless as she shivered in the orange sunlight. A few feet away her towel lay on the shore, and Jules stepped away to retrieve it. When he turned back, she was running toward the cottage, and he was left alone and confused, holding the towel in his trembling hands.

He followed her back to the cottage, worried about what had happened. Miranda had nearly drowned, and yet still seemed to be harbouring misplaced anger. He didn't know what more he could do to earn back her trust. All her wanted was to hold her and make sure she was safe, but when he reached the bedroom door he found it locked.

"Miranda, can you let me in?"

He jiggled the knob. There was quiet rustling, and a murmur as though she were talking to herself, but the door remained shut.

"Are you okay in there? I'm getting worried."

He waited, then pounded on the door. It still didn't open.

Frustrated, Jules sniffed the reek of fish and algae wafting from his clothes. He wanted desperately to change them, but everything he'd brought was locked behind the door with Miranda.

"I'm going to take a shower," he shouted. "Maybe when I'm done you can tell me what happened."

The odour lingered as her stepped into the bathroom and stripped off his sopping clothes. There was no shower, so he ran the tiny faucets in the tub until the water turned clear and used a hand towel to sponge himself. By the time he stepped back into the front room, Miranda's beach towel wrapped around his waist, the sun had set and the cabin was dark. He lit a lamp, and tried the bedroom door again. Miranda was still locked behind it, nursing whatever anger or embarrassment had driven her away. He pressed his face against the door.

"I don't know what you think you saw out there today, but it was nothing. I was just talking to those kids," he said. "I wasn't saying or doing anything you need to worry about. Miranda, I told you before: I love you. I'm here for you. I want things to go back to how they were." He waited, tried the knob again. His frustration mounted.

"Goddamn it, Miranda. Open the door!"

He banged the flat of his hand against it.

Anger would not solve the problem. He repeated it to himself. She needed space, and he had to give it to her. Jules forced himself to breathe until he was in control again.

"Miranda, I'm sorry. Take all the time you need. I'll be here, waiting."

Jules took a seat on the couch, naked except for the towel he pushed beneath him. Miranda couldn't keep him out of the room forever; eventually, she'd have to emerge, and when she did he would sit her down and calmly discuss what had happened. The therapist told him talk was the only way to heal the rift. The small television was poor company while he waited – it barely received any channels, and the electronic fuzz across them heightened his disconnection. He turned it off and stared at the bedroom door. Miranda may have been in the other room, but she felt farther away.

He drifted off listening to the crickets outside. When he woke, it was in darkness. Faint moonlight dribbled through the bare windows, enough to illuminate traces of the cabin around him. He shivered, a chill crossing his naked shoulders and arms. Something had woken him, and when he heard the rattle come from the kitchen a jolt travelled along his nerves. He looked up at the long pale spectre that approached. Breath caught in his throat.

It was Miranda. She was naked.

Bare footsteps on the wooden floor; eyes drilling into his. Lips full, eyes devouring, she closed the gap. Something stirred beneath his towel.

"Miranda, what are you doing?"

She didn't speak. Instead she pressed her fiery hand against his chest and pushed him down. He reached to embrace her but she brushed his hands away, then parted her legs and sat atop him. She leaned back and unknotted the towel while he ran his hands over her wet skin. She was soaking, and the steam that rose off her as she slid him inside filled his head with musky confusion. He didn't understand what was happening, only that Miranda was as she hadn't been in years. Eyes closed, wrinkled brow furrowed in concentration, she rocked her hips, grinding herself against him, as short high-pitched noises slipped from her pursed lips. Jules's thoughts were washed away, replaced with a warm tide that moved his body autonomously. Back and forth she rocked, Jules's hips jutting in rhythm to hers, and when every muscle in his body tightened, when the intensifying pressure was about to consume him, he gripped the sides of the couch and tried to hold on. But everything slipped away in an explosion of liquid heat. He gasped and fell backwards into his head, plummeting into an ecstatic obliviousness, waves pulsing along his body. It was some time before he was able to open his eyes, and by then Miranda had gone, retreated into the locked bedroom. She left only the impression of her burning hands on his cooling skin, and the unspoken promise of leaving their past behind.

He drifted into oblivion, warmed by the memory of her flesh against his skin, and didn't wake until hours later, when the sound of Miranda's screams propelled him to his feet, wobbling and disoriented, the towel sliding to the floor. She stood where he'd first seen her during the night, but in the morning sun she was clothed and unleashing her fury.

"What are you doing here? Get the hell out, Jules. I don't want you around anymore. Can't you get the goddamn picture?"

He didn't know how to respond. The smell of her midnight sweat lingered.

"Miranda, what's – ?"

"Spare me your oblivious routine. You know damn well what you've done to this marriage. You shit. You stupid, dumb shit. I want you out!"

"Miranda, calm down. I – "

"Oh, shut up for once, you idiot. You good-for-nothing, can't-do-a-goddamn-thing right idiot. Do you know how ridiculous you are? You're a joke. A big fucking joke. The only reason I'm not laughing is because I was too stupid to realize it in time, and I let you screw up my life. You ruined everything, you selfish prick. You ruined it all. Every goddamn thing and now I'm stuck here in this horrible life with you and I want to die. Honestly and truthfully, Jules. You make me want to die."

"Miranda, I – "

"How many times to I have to tell you? Stay the hell away from me!"

She snatched a vase from the mantle and hurled it. It caught Jules's temple with a hollow sound, and he crumpled, head filling with stars. The front door slammed as he tried to push past the pain and follow. He staggered into the harsh sunlight, but Miranda had vanished.

Frustration and anger burned in him. Miranda wasn't the only one wronged. What about Jules, and all he'd had to suffer married to her? The reverence she held for her past – a life with her sisters that was clearly better than any he could provide. Was it any wonder a wedge had been driven between them? As much love as he held for her, even that had its limits, and she'd tested every one, pushed him into straying from her. Miranda ran from the cottage because her first instinct was always to run when things were tough. It was the only solution she knew – to disappear, to return to the ocean and the cottage where she'd started life. If there any surprise, it was that she'd brought him to her sanctum. How it must have bothered her, once her anger flared, that her refuge had been invaded and that she had nowhere to go.

154

Jules strode inside. The bedroom door finally unlocked and open, he retrieved some clothes from the closet and dressed again, sitting on the edge of the sagging bed to pull on his socks. The sheets were twisted together behind him, curled like a desiccated body, and he realized that after all his work trying to get in, he didn't want to be in that room any longer than necessary. It reeked of her hatred.

Jules paced the front room, bothered by Miranda's cavalier dismissal of the work he'd done to build a life for the two of them. Maybe the mistake was his. Maybe he shouldn't have been working to fix their marriage, but destroy it as Miranda clearly wanted – her every action screamed that was the case. And as much as his previous indiscretions were a mistake, they proved he would have no trouble filling the void in his bed. All he had to do was concede his life with Miranda was over.

*

Jules's anger ebbed and his sense returned as he awaited Miranda. It was foolish to think there might be anyone else he'd want or love as he did her. She had always been his anchor when the world went mad. Had it not been for Miranda, he would never have made it through the disciplinary hearings and investigations – she had stood by him even when she could hardly keep from crying. Miranda was too important to lose.

Photographs of landscapes on the mantle, unlabeled pencil marks on the wall. Indiscriminate scratches along the wooden floor. The cottage held Miranda's secret history, but Jules could not break its code. There was a vacation photograph of Miranda as a beautiful teenager, seated on a wooden bench and smiling, her hair straight and well past her shoulders. There was another of her at the summit of a small hill, turned towards the camera, skinny child arms raised in triumph, while a pair of girls who were no doubt her sisters continued climbing to greet her. All he saw were the backs of their heads, but the resemblance was uncanny. There were so many sisters Jules wondered how she'd kept them hidden from him for so long. Then he wondered how so many of them fitted in the cottage when there was only one bedroom for the family to share.

Stars lit the sky as the sun set, and Jules found himself on the edge of the dock, staring into the dark water, running his dried tongue over his lips as he tried to recognize the familiar shape submerged beneath it. Jules's concern grew the longer Miranda was gone. In the city, he would have known where to look for her, but he was lost at the cottage. He waited by the window as the afternoon passed, ignoring the creeping suspicion something was wrong. Miranda had spent the first half of her life on the ocean's shore, and despite her earlier near-drowning he couldn't believe the water had her. But there was no denying it held a secret, one Miranda knew but wouldn't share. Like all of Miranda's secrets, it was sunk deep inside her, resistant to his efforts to dredge it loose.

A flash of light pierced his haze. It was small, barely noticeable, but Jules knew it was Miranda – it had to be, waiting past the line of orange buoys on the tree-filled island. Her faint voice called to him over the water. He didn't know how she'd got there – the motorboat was still moored and unfuelled beside him, but whoever had taken her had left her abandoned. He didn't care about the reason, he only cared about how long it would take to get the spare petrol can from the trunk of his car.

The motor's roar echoed off the calm water as gulls pushed themselves into the sky. The cottage faded the farther he got from shore, until he wasn't certain he knew where he had launched from. Confusion and fear addled his mind, but he pushed them away. Miranda was why he was there. Miranda. He aimed for the orange glow of the sun and the dark island trees outlined against it.

He slowed the boat as he approached and scanned the shoreline for his wife. In the murk of dusk all shadows appeared the same – a legion gathering among the thick of trees and rock crevices as he motored around the small island. He called out for her, hoping she'd hear him over the motor's din, and searched in vain for another flash of light. When he completed his circle, the sky had grown darker still, and those shadows more numbered. But he continued searching.

A dark mass lay on the edge of the shore. Jules squinted. It was shaped differently from the other shadows.

"Miranda?"

The mass did not move.

"Miranda!"

He revved the outboard motor and headed straight for the blackened heap.

Jules ran the boat on to the sandy shore, but before it stopped he leapt out and stumbled across the shore to Miranda. She lay still, waves lapping around her, torso exposed while the rest remained submerged under water. And when Jules reached her he dropped to his knees and grabbed her shoulders, fighting against the panic threatening to overtake him.

"Wake up, Miranda. Please wake up. I'm sorry. I'm so sorry. Please wake up."

But she didn't move, and the sand that clung to her cold face in the falling darkness only made her appear less human.

So much time was lost – time he would have used to fix his mistakes. It was all gone. Miranda had left him finally and forever. He lifted her too-heavy body from the surf to hold against him – one last memory of her skin pressed against his own. It was penance for what he'd allowed to happen.

But even in the dark something looked wrong. What emerged as he pulled her body from the surf were not the pale heavy legs he remembered. Her body was instead blackened like night solidified, and her slippery dark flesh uncoiled in an undulating corpulent mass that tapered to a point. Pairs of thick short stalks dotted her abdomen, a small slit in each like a puckered mouth that hissed as it opened, quiet screams mirroring those behind his horrified stare. What Jules thought was his Miranda was something half-formed, something born from the dark oceanic waters, and when he felt the first spasm of its muscles against his chest, saw an eye flicker open, then another, he ceased to think straight. Feet barely in line beneath, he fled to the boat.

And behind him, the tree-line shook.

Jules shoved the boat into deeper water, struggled to leap inside despite the water grabbing his legs. The thing on the shore, the half-Miranda, was moving as other shadows peeked from between the ancient trees. He landed in the boat on his side, but didn't take the time to right himself before gripping the outboard motor's pull and yanking. It coughed to life, and he swung the boat around and aimed for the shore where he hoped the cottage waited. He resisted the temptation to look back at the island; he didn't want to see a series of indescribable shapes, waterlogged and dark, watching him escape. If he didn't turn around, they couldn't reach him. If he didn't turn around, they couldn't really be there.

The motor screamed across the flat unmoving water like a man who had lost everything. He squinted through the fog of tiny insects at the distant light of the cottage. Wind passed his ears too quickly to let in more than a roar, and yet he couldn't move fast enough to outrun the sense he was being pursued.

Jules was unprepared when the dock reared up from the edge of the ocean. He narrowly avoided hitting it, but drove the boat straight into the ground, the sudden stop pitching him over the prow. Everything spun, the shadow of something crossed behind him, and the ground met his face as all light went out.

Waking was unpleasant. A voice softly cooed as familiar hands stroked his head. His eyes cracked open, but they were swollen and puffy and wouldn't part more than a sliver at first. It was enough, though, to reveal he was back in the cottage. Back in the loving, comforting arms of his wife. So much time had passed since she last held him that he spoke without thinking.

"Am I dead?"

The caresses stopped.

"Why would you ask that?"

He tried to roll over, but it was too painful.

"I feel dead."

His chest was the worst of it – a stitch cut into him with each breath he took. A stinging ghost of anguish left on his face. Miranda cooed.

"Hush. You're all right now. Safe and sound. Everything is going to be okay."

His closed his eyes as fingers raked through his hair. The pain's urgency dulled. Miranda's breath was warm as it whispered in his ear.

"There's nothing to worry about. I'm here."

"Where were you?" he mumbled. "I went looking – "

"I know, love. I know. I'm here now, though. I just walked into town. There's nothing to worry about."

"But I looked everywhere. The island – I even went to the island."

A pause.

"You shouldn't have gone there."

"I went," he said, though the words were getting harder to speak. "I went and I think I saw you. Only you weren't you. You were on the shore, but something was wrong. I thought – I thought you were dead."

Her body shook. Had she laughed?

"Hush now, Jules. Don't worry about that. Everything is fine."

Hands passed over his body, touching the flesh of his leg, the bald spot on his pate. Arms hugged him, pulled him close, warmed him until he forgot himself in the swell of affection. But as Miranda caressed him, something wasn't right. Perhaps it was the smell of the ocean rolling into the cottage or wafting off her clothes; perhaps her skin, rougher and more wrinkled than he remembered. Something peculiar he couldn't make sense of, but knew innately was trouble. Her hands held him close, but they held other things. Too many other things. When he opened his eyes again he found those hands were holding him down, pinning him into place.

"Miranda?"

She shushed him.

"It's time."

The front door rattled, the knob jittered, and the door swung open. Cold night air rolled in, the tang of ocean spray with it, and before he could speak another Miranda stepped into view.

Jules sputtered, bewildered.

Was he was in a dream? If Miranda stood in the doorway, who was holding him?

"Hello, Jules," the second Miranda said.

He didn't speak. He couldn't. She wore the green sweater he loved so much, the one he'd bought for her birthday, the one he was certain she'd lost long ago. Fingers continued to stroke his hair while, behind the Miranda in the doorway, a third Miranda appeared – hair and clothes disheveled.

All his thoughts drowned in a flood of panic.

He emitted a litany of guttural sounds in place of words. Despite what his senses told him, it had to be some sort of trick. None of them could be Miranda, yet they all looked like her. Each carried herself like her. It was impossible. Impossible. Even more so when the glass door slid open and three more were revealed. Jules screamed.

Miranda's hand – some Miranda's hand – stroked his face as calming whispers floated around him. He struggled to make sense of what was happening. The women couldn't be sisters, couldn't be anything but his wife, but it was impossible. And yet he was surrounded, each wearing a duplicate of his wife's face.

"Murderer!" one Miranda screamed, boiling with rage and hatred.

"What is this?" he cried. "Who are you? Which of you is the real Miranda?"

They laughed in unison.

"Miranda is gone." He couldn't tell who was speaking. All their voices were the same. "Miranda tried so hard, but you're not worth the effort. If only Miranda had seen it earlier."

"What are you talking about?" He scrutinized each. They had the same face. The same expression. "Where is she?"

"You know."

"How would I know? What have you done with her? Why won't you let me see her?"

"Miranda was a good wife. But you were not a good husband, Jules. You failed."

"How dare you. How goddamn dare you. Miranda and I had problems, but they were *our* problems, not yours. We were working them out – we *are* working them out. Now where is she?"

"Look outside."

"What?"

"Look outside. What do you see?"

He looked out the large window at the side of the cottage. There was nothing – no figures, no movement. Nothing but moonlight, and beneath it –

"I see the ocean," he said.

"Do you know what comes from the ocean?"

"What are you talking about? Where's my wife?"

"Everything does," Miranda answered. "Have you ever seen a school of fish? One steers the whole school. Without that one, what do you think happens?"

Jules's impatience turned to anger.

"You better tell me where Miranda is or –"

The closest Miranda smacked him hard across the mouth. He tasted blood.

"Without that one, what happens?"

"Nothing," he said, swallowing. "Nothing. Another fish takes its place or something. Nothing changes."

"Wrong," Miranda said. "Everything changes. One dead piece and the whole school rots."

"I don't know what the hell you're talking about. Where's my wife?"

"You know where she is. You put her there."

He put her where? The memory of standing on the edge of dock surfaced. He remembered staring into the dark water. He remembered the familiar shape submerged beneath it. He remembered.

And he staggered.

"No."

"A piece from Miranda was lost because of you, Jules. Miranda brought you here to reclaim it."

"It's time," the Miranda that held him said.

"What do you mean?"

But he knew. His day of reckoning had come. He'd been lying to himself about his betrayal and what he'd done to Miranda. She was never the same and finally he understood why. She was gone. He'd extinguished the last piece of her that loved him. It was his fault. There was no forgiveness left.

The Mirandas converged, a dozen identical hands grabbing his arms, his legs, his head. He kicked and thrashed but couldn't break their grip. The air was heavy and damp, and it grew worse as the Mirandas' fingers clawed into his face, pushed into his nose and eyes, pried open his mouth. Those fingers pulled as he struggled, threatened to tear him apart, and beneath the pain and the screams, those fingers found his tongue and held it down.

The Mirandas hoisted him onto their shoulders and ushered him, hand to hand, body to body, through the cottage in which they had all lived a lifetime. They carried him to the edge of the dock where the world met the vast ocean, where everything both began and ended, and with little effort they heaved him into the air. He sailed over the churning ocean storm below.

From above he saw the silhouette of the tree-lined island, larger and closer than he remembered, in relief against the moon.

He saw the line of orange buoys, dancing on the dark waves, marking the limit beyond which no one was safe.

And he saw the dark shadows of gulls circling overhead, carrion eyes glistening in the night like stars.

Jules saw these things before he saw what lay under the churning waters below. Beneath the tumultuous waves dark oily shadows moved, hundreds and thousands of them, stretched as far as his spinning mind could see. They were formless, and yet from each black mass a single pale limb rose, one after the other until a sea of arms reached toward the sky. He saw their long recognisable fingers – fingers he had felt touch his face, stroke his hair – and watched them as they clawed the air madly, thousands of hands hungering. Jules's flailing arms and legs could not stop the rending to come.

SHARKBAIT

There have been many great fictional horror stories of the ocean, but probably the one that made most impact on a general world audience was 'Jaws', Peter Benchley's best-selling 1974 novel, which detailed the terrorisation of a small coastal community by a rogue great white shark. Stephen Spielberg's movie adaptation, which followed in 1975, was a smash hit and is credited with singlehandedly emptying seaside bathing areas across the Northern Hemisphere despite the scorching summer that year, and in rewriting the civilised world's relationship with sharks, changing their status from varied species of large and adaptable game fish to the very incarnation of evil.

It helped that the movie was superbly well shot, acted and written, though many fans agree that the most outstanding scene of terror in its 124 tension-packed minutes is a single monologue delivered by the actor Robert Shaw in the guise of shark-hunter Quint, in which he recounts his personal experience of the dreadful fate of the USS Indianapolis, a warship that went down with all hands in 1945, almost its entire complement of men then falling victim to waves of voracious sharks. The scene, which was added later in order to extend the movie's running-time, was penned with extreme skill by legendary Hollywood script-doctor John Milius, performed with bravura by veteran screen star Shaw, and assisted massively by Spielberg, who played all kinds of subtle but eerie tricks with lighting during the course of it.

But perhaps the most chilling aspect of the Indianapolis story is that it is almost completely true. There were some factual errors in the script, but if anything, what happened in reality is more horrifying than the fiction.

The USS Indianapolis CA-35 was a heavy cruiser of the US Navy, Portland class, which saw continuous action across the Pacific theatre during World War Two. Among its battle honours, it counted the attacks on Lae and Salamaua, the Aleutian Islands, Tarawa Atoll, Saipan, Peleiu, Okinawa and Iwo Jima, and for much of this time served as the official flagship of Vice Admiral Raymond Spruance, commander of the US 5th Fleet. But perhaps the Indianapolis's most important mission came in July 1945, when it was required to deliver atomic bomb components and a cargo of enriched uranium from San Francisco to Pearl Harbour and then to Tinian Island in the Northern Marianas. Said elements would there be combined to create the nuclear device 'Little Boy', which one *month later would be dropped on the city of Hiroshima, killing 45,000 people in a single blast.*

On July 30, seven days before the bomb was actually dropped, the Indianapolis, the majority of her crew unaware of the importance of the secret mission they had just completed, was steaming back to base in Leyte. Half way across the Philippine Sea, she was ambushed by the Japanese submarine I-85, which hit her with two Type 95 torpedoes. Fatally holed, the ship sank inside 12 minutes, not nearly enough time for her entire crew to evacuate. At least 300 men were taken straight to a watery grave. But in retrospect, those poor souls might have been among the lucky ones. Because some 880 men now found themselves adrift at sea with nowhere near enough lifeboats, buoys or lifejackets. Immediate problems were caused by the searing heat of the tropical sun, shock and multiple injuries, but that latter factor contributed to an even worse outcome, the resulting bloody waves attracting hundreds and hundreds of sharks. The vast majority of these were tiger sharks and oceanic whitetips, two breeds notorious for indulging in spectacular feeding frenzies.

Unimaginable scenes of horror followed, the increasingly exhausted and delirious men clumping together for protection, but the sharks attacking relentlessly. Survivors would later report hideous screams echoing across a boiling, crimson ocean, fins cutting the surface on all sides, one man after another being dragged underneath. Perhaps the most debilitating factor for the men as they fought for their lives and limbs was the uncertainty about when they would be rescued, or perhaps if they would be rescued at all. They certainly could never have known that, despite the speed of their vessel's demise, their senior officers had still managed to send distress calls and that these had been received at naval stations in the Marianas, but that for various reasons none were responded to, a negligence that would later lead to very severe reprimands for a number of senior commanders on shore.

Even without the sharks, the delay this caused would likely have accounted for many lives through thirst, salt poisoning and exposure. It was three and a half days before a passing PV-1 Ventura happened to spot the floating survivors. The alert was sent out, but even then no immediate assistance was available. When a Catalina seaplane arrived, its commander, Lieutenant Adrian Marks, was so appalled by the sight of men literally being eaten alive in the gory waters below that he disobeyed orders and landed on the surface, picking up as many as he could – 56 in total, so many that he could barely take off again – but it was only when other ships and boats turned up later that night that the remainder were saved.

Out of the 880 men who had originally been cast into the waves, only 321 were lifted out again, and four more of these would soon die from wounds. To this date, these terrible losses mean the crew of the USS Indianapolis suffered the most shark attacks ever launched on human beings in one place in recorded history. It is surely one of the grimmest and most terrifying stories of the ocean, and there are numerous witnesses alive today to attest to its absolute truthfulness.

THE DERELICT OF DEATH
Simon Clark and John B. Ford

S
trange things happen at sea. Aye, and some are more sinister than the darkest imaginings of any man. Now my life draws towards its close; my remaining days are few – *Death* advances stealthily. *Death* has stifled my voice, but not my horrific memories. Still I have the ability to write down that which I witnessed in my youth, and may God give me the energy to deliver a warning – about what I have looked upon and what may be to come again. This is a danger I must tell of before it is too late.

*

I remember the time clearly. I was eldest 'prentice aboard the *Jenny Rose,* and with this I was pleased and proud, for I had a penchant for the old windjammers, and here was one of the few still to see service. We were engaged in salvage work, picking this and that from the seabed – anything that would turn a sovereign or two: old cannon, a bit of pewter, copper bottoms from sailing vessels that had foundered a century before.

Our diver was a wiry man by the name of Dodgson, who seemed more at home in the water than out of it. Normally he worked alone but on occasions I was sent down in the second Siebe Gorman suit when there was particularly heavy lifting to be done. I can't say I liked the sensation of waves above me, but I was a dutiful sailor and obeyed orders. Still, what a diver sees on the seabed can rattle a man's nerves. On one of our later dives we entered the hulk of a slaver lying ten fathoms deep. There in the hold were the bones of more than a hundred African men, women and children who'd gone to the bottom still chained to the timbers, poor devils.

At the time we were becalmed in the tropics, with all the lower sails up in the buntlines so as to harvest even the lightest breeze. But there was something uncanny about that area of ocean; something awful in the unnatural silence and stillness of the sea, not to mention in all those bones beneath our keel. Perhaps because of my youthful years, I was more receptive than I should have been to my queer surroundings – for it seemed to me that everything about this place implied menace.

One day, just after I had joined the other 'prentices swabbing decks, I noticed young Adams staring hard at the ocean.

"What's up, Tom?" I asked. "You've not seen a mermaid, have you?"

"Just have a look over there, Will," he said, pointing.

I looked, and beneath the surface of the sea I saw a silver glistening. Even as I watched, many small objects rose up through the water. It looked like a mass slaughter, countless shoals of dead fish rising to the surface.

"What do you suppose is causin' it?" Adams asked.

"I don't know," I replied, "maybe there's some poison in the water or something."

After a while our inaction attracted the wrath of the second mate, but on noticing the morbid spectacle he joined us in amazed silence. Soon it came to the attention of the whole crew, but not one man there could give decent explanation of it. At the same time, the swabbed decks began steaming in the heat of the blazing sun, sweat trickling from the faces of the toiling ABs. All the rest of that day we sweltered in the terrible heat, and not one cloud was there to give us shelter. With the setting of the sun came a sight so weird it brought cries from the look-out: the sky westward flamed with blood-red fire, but forming in the heart of it was an unnatural vision, a hideous blackness mixing with crimson, creating an evil design. I felt a thrill of intense fear. Others of the crew fell to their knees in prayer. For on that western horizon now a clear image had formed, a face, the black voids of whose eyes opened to display a redness beyond.

The first mate turned to me with a look of barely suppressed fear.

"Go below ... tell the captain we have some curious atmospherics I'd ... like his opinion on. *Smart now!*"

When I returned with the 'Old Man', I was able to stand behind him and the mate, so I overheard their conversation.

"What do you think it is, sir?" asked the mate.

"I'm blamed if I know," replied the captain, astounded. "But I know what it looks like! It beats anythin' I've seen in all my years."

"Somethin' to do with atmospherics?" suggested the mate.

"Ain't no atmospherics could ever shape themselves into something like that, Mister! Though if I'm takin' your drift, we'll have to pass it off as some freak kind of weather effect due to the heat ... I see the crew are takin' it pretty bad."

A short while later, the Old Man stood in front of the crew and made a reassuring speech. And though not one man was taken by his explanation, or his manufactured high spirits, still perhaps they allowed themselves a partial belief, for Captain Reynolds was mighty respected by all, seeming like a father even to those older than he.

As any shellback will tell you, it's a fact that down in the tropics the falling of night comes rapidly. This being so, I completed my few remaining tasks and made to go to my bunk, meaning to snatch a few hours' sleep before my watch. That night I was on watch from midnight till four, my stint as look-out for the first of those two hours. So at some time approaching twelve, I was abruptly wakened by Collins. Having just completed his own stint on watch, he seemed in a state of nervous excitement.

"What the devil's up with you?" I asked, angry at being shaken.

"You've just mentioned what's wrong with me," he replied. Then then walked away to his own bunk, in a peculiar hurry.

As I came fully awake, I noticed that the air-temperature, if anything, was even hotter than it had been during the day. I pulled on my clothes and climbed the steps to the main deck, where I halted in shock. The redness of the sky westward had defied the nightfall. Within it, that demonic face still gazed on us with infernal eyes, but now the black void of the mouth had also opened – to reveal an apparent cavern of fire.

Straightaway I noticed there was more activity on deck than usual; the second mate gazed at the thing through his night-glasses, while the bo'sun leant on the taffrail, smoking and talking to Captain Reynolds in a low voice. The sea, meanwhile, remained calm and still – as though waiting for something.

After making a circuit of the decks, I walked to the break of the fo'cas'le head. Here I took my post, pacing to and fro, always watching that dreadful face as it peered at us through the night, eyes blazing with unholy hatred. And yet one hour later, there came a dark outline on the surface of the sea, framed against that gaping, burning mouth. I lifted the night-glasses to give further study, and with this grew greatly afeared – for I could identify the vague outline of a ship. Apparently sailing from out of the flames.

I hailed the captain.

"Ship sighted on starboard, sir!"

"Give me the position, lad!"

"The face, sir," I shouted excitedly, "it's sailing from the flames of the mouth!"

I watched as Captain Reynolds lifted his own glasses to his eyes, and saw his lips mutter an oath. By now the second mate and some of the men had come beside me. The mate lifted his own glasses and studied the progress of the vessel.

"My God! She's been dismasted by the look … no more than a derelict from what I can see. Yet she's moving at speed …"

"Perhaps she's caught in some kind of current," I offered.

"No, she's dead straight, lad. No current would ever carry her so straight. It's almost as though she's set a course ..."

Word spread below to the sleeping crew, and men began to appear above decks, watching in silence as the derelict made its way across the stilled sea. The captain came to join us on the fo'cas'le head.

"What do you make of her, sir?" asked the mate.

"She's not right, Mister," he replied, uneasy. "Not right by a long chalk."

As we continued our observations, it became obvious that the derelict was on a course directly for us. Suddenly a light flickered to life aboard her, and instinctively I trained the glasses on it. What I saw chilled me to the core; standing at the ship's wheel was a black-shrouded figure with a death-white face.

"There's a figure at the wheel, sir!" I shouted.

A murmur spread through the watching crew. But as the captain and mate made an effort to focus on the light, the derelict was instantly blotted out by darkness. The fear inside me grew, became almost personal – for to my mind the 'man' at the wheel had sensed my prying eyes and maybe the open mind of youth. Is that why he had revealed his dread form *only to me*.

The drear outline of the derelict grew nearer, and though I scanned her decks, there was not another sign the vessel was inhabited. It would be at daybreak when she arrested her approach. Soon after, I was ordered by Captain Reynolds to my bunk, for I had remained on watch longer than I should, and maybe he was aware of how my nerves had been strained.

*

I slept for perhaps three hours before waking, saturated with the sweat of nightmare. When I went above decks I began to wonder if indeed half my experiences had actually been nightmare, for the satanic face of flame and blackness had been replaced by the vivid blue sky we had grown so accustomed to. But looking one mile to starboard, I saw a dark monument to the reality of the previous night's events. The derelict repelled the very sun; like a black blotch on the sea, she seemed representative of the greatest evil. Much closer now, large parts of her hull appeared to be covered with thick fungi, a testimony to years of neglect.

Suddenly, I was startled by a tremendous bellow in my ear.

"Mr. Dodgson! Clear the starboard lifeboat!" It was the captain hollering orders. For a solid seafaring man not given to the horrors,

I heard a tremor in his voice. And I reckon he shouted louder than he ought because he heard it himself, and knew that it was a tremor of fear. "Bo'sun, pick out a dozen men! We're going to take a little boat ride across to that damn wreck and treat ourselves to a closer look." He smiled through his whiskers. "You never know, there might be some salvage to be had from her even though she's a queer-looking beast of a thing."

The bo'sun pointed at me. "Jessop, lad, help Mr. Dodgson get the cover off the boat and start bailing her out."

"Aye-aye, sir."

"Oh, and Jessop?"

"Sir?"

"You man enough to take one of the oars?"

"Yessir."

"Good man."

He turned to the crew on the main-deck.

"Men, you know I'm a damn b____, and I don't have a polite bone in my body, but this time instead of orderin' I'm askin'. Hoist those hands up if you volunteer to man the lifeboat so as to take the captain to that devil-ship over yonder." He looked gravely at the faces of the men. "There'll be no come-backs or dirt chores for those not fancyin' boarding her."

The men weren't eager. Nevertheless, there was a good crop of hands.

As I hauled the canvas bib from the lifeboat and began emptying her of the flotsam and jetsam the shellbacks tossed into her when they couldn't find cupboard space below, I let my gaze rove over to the derelict.

Despite that tropical heat, now hotter and more humid than a Turkish bath, I shivered to the roots of my bones; she was an evil-looking vessel all right. Let me tell you, a calm sea mid-ocean can be taxing on the nerves in its own right, stretching out flat and lifeless as some queer plain of death. But that terrible derelict was a dozen times worse. I can only describe her oblong shape, bereft of mast and rigging, as a floating coffin. There was no wheelhouse. The deck was pretty much flat with the exception of the ship's wheel.

Whatever manner of man had stood there the night before, he had vanished below.

But somehow I couldn't picture that dark cowled figure with the white-as-death face tucking into a plate of hot grub.

In no time at all we were in the lifeboat and heaving on the oars.

"Pull away there, men," the captain sang out as he worked the tiller. "Nice and easy does it. See any life on her, bo'sun?"

The bo'sun, sitting with his hands on the prow, shook his head.

"Not a living soul, Skipper."

"The only souls aboard that thing will be those already damned to Hell," murmured Adams beside me.

"Pipe down at the oars there," the captain said. "Hark ... does anyone hear that?"

I heard nothing above the rattle of the oars in the rowlocks and the splash of the blades in the water.

"Vast pulling, all," the captain ordered.

We all stopped rowing.

"Now then, does any man hear that?"

We listened. From the direction of the derelict came a faint sound.

"Sounds like hogs?" the bo'sun replied in a low voice. "It's damn peculiar, sir."

"Damn peculiar indeed," the captain agreed. "You'd not credit any livestock would remain alive on a wreck like that."

"Shall we go on, sir?"

"That we shall, bo'sun. We'll bottom out the mystery of that evil-looking packet once and for all."

*

It took only a few moments to cover the intervening space of ocean between us and the derelict. Above us the sky was a dazzling blue. And away to our stern lay the *Jenny Rose* with the remainder of her crew on deck taking a keen interest in our progress.

Now the bo'sun looked back at the captain.

"There's a fearful stink coming from that b____ hulk."

And truly, the smell was powerful enough to have me swallowing more than once; it had caught in the back of my throat and clung there.

"Perhaps it's coming from the slime?" The bo'sun nodded up at the flanks of the ship which were lathered in something I'd have described closer to fungi than slime. For it was black and silkily smooth, bulging and curving here and there as if it had overgrown the portholes and the like.

"Back-water, all," the captain ordered. "Let's have a look at her stern. Her name should at least give us some indication which port she hails from."

We reversed our stroke, taking the lifeboat sternward. All the time the captain's big grey whiskered head turned this way and that, examining the black-coated flanks of the derelict. I glanced at the faces of the men as they feathered the oars. Their faces were

170

strained and I saw fear writ in their eyes. They had all smelt the odour emanating from the ship. It was more of the pigsty than any ship I'd been near before, the overpowering malty odours of swill overlaying the sharper porcine stench of swine. A hateful smell. And somehow, suffusing it all, a sweet, almost syrupy stink – like human cadavers exposed to the heat of the sun. One man pressed the palm of his hand across his mouth and screwed his eyes shut.

"Let it go, man. You should never strive to keep it in." The captain's voice was kindly. My stomach heaved, too, but I wasn't given to being ill in such a fashion, so reckoned I'd be all right.

"By Gum!" the captain exclaimed as he looked at the black skin of the fungi. "Have you ever seen such a thing? It's covered the ship's name plate. Here, Mr. Holden, pass me your oar."

The second mate hauled his oar from the lock and passed it to the captain. Water dripped from the blade and down the shaft to wet the Old Man's hands as he stood in the stern and scraped at the fungi. The blade of the oar made a slithery sound as he worked at the timber, loosening the black substance.

"It's shifting," he said at length. "It's coming away in sheets …. you know, If I didn't know better I'd swear this ship's hull had been sheathed in pigskin. By Gum! Look at the stuff." He paused to scratch his forehead. "There's even hairs growing from it. Pigskin, I say again. Although if I wrote that in the ship's log-book I'd lose my master's ticket with no shadow of a doubt."

He returned to scraping the 'pigskin' with the oar.

"Ah … I can see a name. It's the … oh, dear God in Heaven …"

He stopped scraping and stared hard at the name exposed beneath the black flaps of that horrible fungoid skin. I looked too, and the shivers ran over my body. And as I read that name – once, twice, thrice – a hog-like squealing seemed to emanate from the bowels of the derelict, but far away, as if echoing from the depths of a deep cave.

The name of the ship was *Death*.

At length the captain broke the silence.

"Rum name for a ship, eh, boys?"

We nodded, mute.

"Perhaps she was a pirate ship," Adams ventured.

"Pray that she was, lad. Then she might be full to the scuppers with rubies and gold."

There was another pause. No one, it seemed, could slip their eyes away from that painted name, which seemed to beat with such a vivid red that it occurred to me blood might run through it. "Well, bo'sun," said the captain. "We won't get rich just by ogling this little beauty, will we?" He laughed. But it was a forced laugh, I judged. "Adams," he said. "You're the nimblest. If you've no strong opposition to my request, will you accept the opportunity to be first on deck?"

"Aye-aye, sir." Adams looked scared to death. But he was a game sailor, never to refuse climbing the rigging on even the foulest of seas. He seized a chain, or a cable, it wasn't possible to tell which for it was sheathed in that same 'hog-skin' and bristling with silver hairs. Then he climbed quickly up onto the deck. I thought he might have paused before clambering over the rail, but he'd slithered over in a moment, kicking his sea boots hard.

We held our breath. The wait wracked the strongest of nerves. My imagination had him confronted by that thing with the white face and deathly black cowl.

"What's keeping him?" murmured the bo'sun. He should – wait!"

Adams's head popped over the rail. He waved.

"Anyone on board?" called out the captain.

"Looks deserted, sir."

The captain rubbed his hairy jaw before looking at us.

"Well, my boyos, shall we indulge ourselves in a spot of exploring?"

*

I was left behind in the boat with the second mate. One after another, the captain and bo'sun, followed by the rest, clambered up the sheathed chain and onto the deck. Shielding my eyes against the glare of the sun, I stared upward. There was precious little to see. One of our crewmen's heads, now and then, would pop over the rail. I heard the voices of the men, but couldn't make out what was being said, except that from the tones of their voices I deduced that there were wonderful – or terrible – things to see.

"What do you think's up there?" I asked the second mate.

He swore. "How the blast should I know? I don't have a twenty foot long b____ neck, do I?"

I nearly forgot my rank and swore back. The tension of waiting as the others explored that strange and terrible ship was all but overpowering. There was a sudden scream.

Both our heads tilted up. Of course we saw nothing. But now screams shimmered on the air in a series of dreadful peals. This time it was the second mate who shot me a startled look and asked, "By Heaven, what's happening up there?"

I reached out to the sheathed chain, ready to scramble up and join in the fight, but the mate stopped me with a trembling hand.

"No, Jessop! There's murder going on!"

"But we ..."

"The captain'll handle it ... the captain will handle it, lad"

The way he repeated the statement suggested to me that he didn't believe what he himself had said. We stood in the lifeboat and listened to the screams. It was only a moment or so before the commotion faded, trailing off as men succumbed one by one. For what seemed a long while we waited there, our little boat resting on the ocean. The shadow cast by the derelict was cool, almost icy.

Presently, the second mate called to the captain; then to the others by name. There was no answering reply. The ship was quiet again; a deathly kind of quiet. The second mate dipped his hand into the sea and wiped water across his face. Then, taking a deep breath, he looked at me and said in a whisper, "They've gone, lad."

"But we could ..."

"No, Jessop. Listen to me. If whatever's on board can snuff out ten hearty sea-dogs in less than two minutes, what chance do just the two of us stand? Take your oar, Jessop, we're going back to our own ship."

He silenced my next protest before it began with a fierce glare. I took my place at the oar. Without another word we rowed back to the ship, and I wondered what fate had befallen the captain and nine men of the *Jenny Rose*.

*

On the orders of the first mate we were all doled out a tot of rum to help darn the fibres of our ragged nerves. I was relieved of my watch duty and ordered to rest in my bunk. Naturally, I could not sleep and lay listening to the creak of the ship's timbers. I knew that with the disappearance of the captain, the first mate had taken charge, and that he and the second were chewing the fat over what should be done next.

I wished our old packet possessed a big enough deck gun to blow the death ship out of the water. As it was, I reckoned they'd soon hoist every inch of sail and try to get away with all possible speed, which wouldn't have been much, for there was still hardly a breath of wind beneath those sultry, tropical skies.

I lay there in my bunk, feeling the trickle of sweat on my forehead. In my mind's eye I saw the captain and the rest of the boarding party on the deck of that grimly named ship, *Death,* and how they struggled with whatever slithered from the hatches below ... And I was drifting into an uneasy doze when I felt a hand on my arm. Turning my head, I saw a death's head swathed in black cloth.

The hand was mere bones, a spider scuttled from the thing's eye-socket. I opened my mouth to scream out to sweet Jesus in His mercy ...

"Jessop ... Jessop? Easy there, lad. I didn't mean to startle you."

I opened my eyes, my heart pounded.

It was the first mate shaking me free of my nightmare.

"What's wrong?" I asked, scared.

"Don't worry yourself, lad. Are you fully awake?

"Yessir."

"We need your help, Jessop."

"Need me? Why, sir?"

"Now then, I'm told you've used the diving-suit before, is that right?"

"Yessir."

"Good."

"Why, what's wrong?"

"You know the diver, Mr. Dodgson, boarded the derelict with the captain and we have to consider him lost too. Now, lad, if you're willing." He looked at me levelly. "I need you to take a look under our keel, because something seems to have a hold of the ship. Something with no intention of letting us go."

*

Within the hour I was being winched overboard in the heavy diving-suit. It was a brute of a thing to wear, for it had lead boots, lead weights on the belt and more lead weights against my chest and back. On my head was the great brass collar on which was screwed the ball of the diving-helmet, also wrought from brass.

It was all I could do to stand on my own two feet on the little timber frame swaying above the deck. Peering through the glass view plate, I could see the men of the *Jenny Rose* looking up at me. The second mate gave me a thumbs up sign, which is the kindliest gesture I'd ever seen him make. And there was old Butterbuck and Frenchie working the bellows. Right away, I could hear the hiss of air coming through the valve behind my head. A couple of men pushed the platform as it swung on its cable and then I was over the ship's rail.

The platform turned a point or two, and I could see the black derelict that was the well-spring of our troubles. It sat there on the sea, looking as if it could draw all that is bright and good out of the world. I thought of the captain and my mates, and I wondered what beastly end they'd met there.

The men on the derrick pulleys let me down toward the sea.

Now, it's a truth that many sailors can't swim, for they have a real dread of the sea; every shellback has heard tales of the things swim that through deep waters, and many have seen them with their own eyes: man-devouring sharks, eels with teeth like band-saws, squid with tentacles as long as a steamer and possessing beaks that can nip a man in half.

As the water swirled over the platform and around my boots, I felt that same wave of horror that I always did on a dive. I hated the press of the water against the vulcanised rubber suit. It was like a hundred hands gripping my legs. Instinctively, I held my breath as the water swirled up and up, for I was certain that it would gush in and drown me.

The sea slapped against the glass faceplate of the helmet, and suddenly the afternoon sunlight had vanished, replaced by the dappling light play of sunbeams filtering down through waves. And there I was in the submarine world. The air whistled through the valve with the laboured sounds of an asthmatic old man. With the ocean surface just a foot or so above my helmet and looking like a wrinkled silver sheet, I peered round. There was nothing much to see in the ocean, for all its vastness; it shaded off into a turquoise mist. Feeling lighter now as the buoyancy supported the weight of the suit, I made a half-turn on my platform so I could see the keel of the ship and maybe discern what held her in place. I waited for a gush of bubbles to pass so I could get the whole picture. But what I then saw sent sheets of ice through me. I pushed my face forward against the glass plate, my eyes bulging, my heart thudding.

Gripping the bottom of the ship like a massive sucker was an amorphous piece of flesh. Pulpy and white, it was; almost the shape of a wine glass, its wide mouth clamped onto the keel as if the creature sucked at the timbers. Beneath that, it became fluted, growing narrower and narrower until a stem little thicker than my own waist ran down into the deeps to be lost in the misty haze.

What manner of creature was this?

It reminded me of a lamprey eel that can batten onto a man's chest and suck him dry. But this thing ran the full length of the keel. And there were no eyes, nor any other features discernible. I checked the axe was still in place in my belt, then gave the line three sharp tugs. That was the signal to lower me deeper still. It occurred to me that if I could find the point where the root of this creature bonded to the ocean bed, then perhaps I could hack it through and free the ship.

The platform descended.

The water darkened. The ship with the strange growth suckered to the bottom dwindled overhead. Down I went, into silence. My

175

ears ached as the pressure increased, and repeatedly I had to tug the line to signal the need for more air. On the deck the bellows-men would be working like navvies to feed the suit.

At twenty fathoms I saw the seabed. The stem of the thing that had snared *Jenny Rose* ran down into an area of weed or kelp maybe seventy by thirty feet. A second stem ran into it also. Although I could not determine exactly where this second one led up to, I guessed it was to the derelict named *Death*. This is when the horrors really got their teeth into me and wouldn't let go, because that's when I really saw what that shape was on the seabed. I cried out, though I knew no-one could really hear me.

That shape on the seabed was not a crop of kelp – but a face.

That same satanic face I'd seen in the atmosphere the previous day.

Again, it was that blend of deep blacks and flame-reds. Fear paralysed me. I couldn't tug the line to order the winch men to stop lowering me. So down I went. Right down into the midst of that face. As before, the mouth was a cavern of fire; the eyes blazing with unholy hatred; and all around it, haloing that unholy head were the silvery bodies of fish killed by whatever poisons emanated from it.

At last I reached out my gloved hand to the communication line. I intended to signal to the winch man to stop and haul me up with God-speed. Instead my hand found the supporting cable of the platform and I yanked uselessly at that. I only noticed my mistake when it was too late – an instant later I was plunged into the orbit of a demonic eye.

Strange though it may seem, *that eye consumed me.*

There was no eyeball in it, but some pulpy, bulked thing opened and admitted me. In a welter of water and dead fish and weed, I found myself dropping down a chute with dizzying speed. Then came darkness; my head flung against the inside of the helmet scattered my senses. When I next opened my eyes, I was sitting in a cavern lit by blood-red light. And I was not alone. Captain Reynolds was helping me to my feet. I saw the concern in his eyes. His bellowing voice made it to my ears through the bronze globe of my diver's helmet.

"Jessop! Is that you in there?"

Still dazed, I nodded.

He slapped me on the arm, pleased to see me. I reached up to unscrew the helmet from its collar, but the captain shook his head, as though such a thing would be folly.

"No! No, Jessop. Keep the helmet in place."

But by now the atmosphere inside the helmet was stifling; I saw that my air hose had broken. Clumsily I clutched at the faceplate and unscrewed it. It came away in my hand, and I breathed deeply and gratefully. The air in that place, though warm, humid, and cloying with a swinish stink, seemed breathable.

"Skipper," I panted. "I was sure you were dead. Are the others ..."

"The others, boy. They're right behind me."

I looked over his shoulder. In a line stood the rest of the men who'd boarded the derelict that morning, including the bo'sun and Tom Adams. Their faces were grave, but there was no panic; for these were brave men, men of iron.

"Skipper, how did you find yourself down here? You know you're beneath twenty fathoms of water?"

"Aye, lad, we guessed something of the like."

My heart swelled with pride. I was overjoyed to see the captain and his men safe, and to know that the Old Man had mastered himself and was no longer afraid.

"What we must do now, lad," he said, "is get you away from this devil and back to safety."

"No, surely, skipper. We must all escape. Look, I have my axe."

"No, lad. We'll be staying here."

"Here?" I looked from face to face. "Why?"

The captain gave a grim smile. "Because I reckon we're beyond saving."

"Skipper ..."

"Take a closer look, boy. We aren't what we seem."

I glanced from his face to his body. I saw the same barrel-chested man. Nothing was amiss. Then I looked down at his legs, and from his legs to his booted ...

I saw what he meant.

"Skipper ... my good lord!" I cried with horror. "What has it done to you?"

The captain's feet – and all the men's feet! – were sunk to the ankles into a reddish, fleshy material. A skin-like substance, apparently flushed with blood, not only encircled their legs, but had become one with them, joining to the tissue.

"We're part of it now, lad," the captain said, still without panic or terror.

He explained how they had climbed on board the derelict and how they had been rushed by black-shrouded figures with faces of death. These figures hadn't moved like men, they'd budded from the decks in the way anemone tentacles spring out from the body, and all through the fight had remained attached by black, flesh-like stems to the ship. The fight had been brief, the hideous beings seizing the captain and his men, and then melting and flowing over them, enveloping them the way press-gangs sack their victims.

The men found themselves drawn down a slippery, membrane-like tube, through the ship and into the unknown depths below. At last they found themselves here, their legs rooted into the red floor.

"Take a look at this place," the captain said. "This has happened many times before."

I did as he asked.

I saw no figures rooted to their ankles, like these men. But I saw heads on the cavern floor. In fact, they covered it, like cobblestones on a street. I saw ears with gold rings, bearded faces, bald crania, some still wearing bandanas, even one old gentleman in spectacles, though only the top half of his head protruded from the pulsating red mass. Worse yet, each head was still in some way alive, moaning or sobbing. Their harrowed faces gazed on me, pleading silently for help, tears of blood trickling from eyes filled with endless suffering.

"You see," the captain said. "We are slowly being consumed."

"But you can't stay here to be eaten alive!"

"This is our fate now, boy." He gave a grim smile. "Now leave us be, so we can make our peace with the Lord."

"But I can't leave ..."

"Yes, you can. Until your bare skin touches this red stuff, it can't get a hold of you."

"No, sir, I meant ..."

"And no, you cannot help us either. Now, go while you have the opportunity."

"But sir ..."

"Replace the faceplate, Jessop. That's an order."

"Aye aye, sir."

He watched me gravely as I screwed the face plate back into the helmet, and then he mouthed the word: "Go."

I knew I must obey the captain's order, not only from obedience to him, but to tell the others what had befallen the boarding party. Maybe we could then find a way to smash into this submarine cavern and free the men of the *Jenny Rose.*

At that moment the captain tugged my sleeve. His eyes shot me a warning look and he said something I failed to hear through the thick helmet. But one backward glance painted a clear picture of the danger. Moving quickly, gliding smoothly, almost like ice-skaters, came those damned figures in black with their skull faces. Whether they moved independently of that red floor or were part of it, I cannot say.

There was one certain truth: they were coming for me.

I glanced at the captain. He nodded in gratitude for my attempted rescue of him and his men. Then I was off. I moved as quickly as I could in those weighted boots, though they were cumbersome. More than that; I had to run across those slippery cobblestones composed of human heads. How many I trod on and broke with my lead soles I do not know. But as I struggled along the cavern, I pulled free my axe. Ahead, the way was sealed by a membrane of white. I slashed at it, breaching a hole through which I could wade. Everywhere, faces peered up from the floor and even from out the walls: their rolling eyes watched me as I stumbled past.

When I trod on the areas of floor clear of the doomed men's heads, it clutched at me as if I was stepping into molasses. Once I brushed a wall with my elbow and it rippled and sucked. Pulling myself free was no real difficulty but I knew that if my bare skin had touched it, it would never have let go. A black garbed figure loomed from a side chamber and grabbed at me. Its hands were mittened in white skin, showing no splay of fingers. I felt the palms of those hands adhere to my chest, sucking; the death's head face stared into mine. Its hog-like eyes glared with the purest evil.

With a swipe of my axe I cut the monster down.

Ahead lay another membrane, like a tautly stretched curtain. With a downward sweep I cut it from top to bottom, and this time a wall of water rushed in at me. I'd breached the outer skin of that demonic thing. Instantly, I was beneath the sea again. At that moment I remembered that my air supply had been severed. In the space of five seconds I dropped the axe, pulled off my lead boots, my weight belt, my chest and back weight.

With the suit inflated with air, albeit foul air, it was as light as a cork. In a geyser of bubbles I rocketed upward. The speed was dizzying. That demonic face receded below ... I looked up to see the under-surface of the ocean hurtling toward me. Then a series of pains spiked me from head to heels and I plunged into unconsciousness.

*

There my yarn comes to its end.

Aye, I reached the surface – half suffocated, yet alive. And when I had no help from the men of the *Jenny Rose*, I managed somehow to swim to her and haul myself onto the deck. But what of the crew?

Gone. Every man-jack of them.

Although in a terrible state, the bends boiling the blood in my veins, I suspected the entire ship's company had been drawn through the fleshy stem battened to the keel of the *Jenny Rose,* and sucked down to that devil face on the seabed.

In a thousand agonies, I managed to wriggle out of the suit. It was a miracle the bends didn't kill me there and then; I had surfaced too rapidly. I felt the joints of my arms and legs lock; my torso twisted like the trunk of an olive tree; the bends even found the part of my brain that services human speech and destroyed it. I've never spoken a word from that day to this.

Suffering though I was, I watched the derelict retreat into the fiery face once again resting on the sea. I then lay comatose in my bunk until a passing steamer put a party on board and found me.

These past forty years – though a human derelict, you might say – I've survived purely by the Christian charity of a good man called Parson Willis, and in that time have posted various accounts of the loss of the crew of the *Jenny Rose* to Admiralty House and Lloyds' of London, quoting exact longitude and latitude, and begging them to warn ships away from the area. I've received no reply and conclude they dismiss me as some old shellback with a tot too much rum in his belly. But this morning Parson Willis read to me from *The Times*, as is his good, honourable custom, whiling away half an hour with the crippled mute he shelters in his home. He read to me about ships reported missing in a part of the tropics I know only too well.

Good men have gone down.

And now, I daresay, they are satisfying the appetite of that thing, which was made neither by man nor God, but which beats with a hell-fire heart all of its own somewhere deep on the ocean floor.

HORRIFIC BEASTS

Throughout the history of mankind, the ocean has been the closest and most visible of all the Earth's elemental forces. With its typhoons, tidal waves and water-spouts, there is no human society that makes its home close to the sea that has not felt its fury at one time or another. Even Britain, whose encircling waters are relatively calm, has seen coastal cities collapse into the waves, inrushing tides demolish acres of farmland, and entire fleets go down in the midst of raging tempests. Little wonder perhaps that so vast, amorphous and destructive an entity – so much of which is unknown to Man even now – has reputedly bred demonic children, horrific creatures spawned with a single purpose: to annihilate every living thing in their path.

In all the legends of all the civilisations on Earth there are hellish sea-beasts. We aren't just talking about mysterious serpentine forms glimpsed from a distance, or white whales bristling with harpoons, but monstrosities so unimaginably vast and terrible that their mere existence in reality would threaten the survival of Man.

The **Leviathan** is surely the most famous of all these aquatic horrors, so much so that its very name has now been standardised to mean some colossal and terrifying thing. The creature is first referenced in the 'Tanakh', the original canon of the Hebrew Bible (which provides the basis for the 'Old Testament'), particularly in the 'Book of Job', where it appears as the ultimate chthonic monster, a shape-shifting fishlike abomination some 300 miles in length and around whom the Mediterranean Sea – its home patch – literally boils. It is so powerful that its destruction will only be accomplished by God himself at the End of Days, when it will literally be torn to pieces and fed to the faithful. In the meantime, it will wreak untold devastation, a ghastly reputation for which would persist into early Christian times, when it was upgraded from the rank of monster to that of devil, in fact the actual devil through whose gaping mouth all evil souls would be sucked into Hell.

The modern view of the Leviathan is that ancient societies conceived of it as an archetypical chaos monster, a metaphorical being which served to illustrate Man's inherent weakness and the utter futility of his resistance to God.

Jormungandr was another primordial sea-dwelling entity of such astonishing strength and ferocity that it had world-ending potential. A staple of Norse mythology, this fabled beast, also known as the Midgard Serpent, was effectively a snake, but so massive that when lying along the ocean floor it circled the entire world and was able to grasp its own tail in its mouth. According to the earliest skaldic poets, it was born of the evil god Loki and the giantess Angrboda, and it became the nemesis of Thor, whose main role was to protect mankind against it. These two fearsome foes had several violent encounters before meeting once and for all on the day of Ragnarok, the last battle between gods and monsters. The serpent, in a final desperate effort to wipe out Odin's children – men – rose from the sea and spurted fountains of venom, the idea to poison the waters and sky, to literally eliminate humanity with a storm of chemical weaponry. Thor struck it dead with his great hammer before it could finish the task, but died in the process.

In Jungian psychology, Jormungandr is held to be a representation of the 'dawn state' of human development, or the Ouroborus – an apparently unending and unchanging condition (childhood, if you like), which eventually must be broken, inviting the misery of mortality but at the same time, progress.

The **Umibōzu** is a deadly force of Japanese origin that is not widely known about in the West, yet there are few marine monsters more frightening. It appears most impressively in the artwork of the 18th century woodblock painter Utagawa Kuniyoshi as an immense, cloudlike humanoid rising dark and featureless from the waves to menace passing ships, with whose crews it might sometimes negotiate, though in most cases it would not be happy until it had drowned them all. Such tales featured regularly in Japanese folklore, the Umibōzu allegedly representing either the souls of drowned Buddhist priests or those of ordinary lay-folk who had not received proper burial and thus had sought sanctuary in the sea. Technically, it was a ghost rather than a monster, which may go some way to explaining its evil reputation, spectres in Asian culture often having a more belligerent role than they do in European.

The origins of the Umibōzu have to an extent been lost under a recent mass of Japanese pop art and animation, in which they figure prominently, but they are almost certainly drawn from the ranks of the Yōkai, a caste of supernatural beings in the oldest Oriental myths who employ a range of methods to either help, bewitch or harm mankind.

But perhaps it is in Greek mythology where the twin monsters, **Scylla** and **Charybdis**, present us with the most recognisable of all ocean perils. Though separate entities, in the annals of the Ancient World these two beasts formed a symbiotic relationship in their efforts to depopulate the Strait of Messina, the narrow strip of ocean lying between Sicily and mainland Italy. Scylla was a many-

armed, many-necked aberration – a gigantic hydra-type thing, which, while it didn't live in the sea as such, fed from it; it lurked in a cave under a rock on the north side of the strait and would swoop down at passing ships, snatching six men at a time and devouring them alive and screaming. Yet this grotesque opponent was often regarded as the lesser of two evils, for to sail within reach of it meant that ships could avoid Charybdis, a colossal, flippered bladder, which lay on the seabed on the south side of the strait and through an unquenchable thirst for saltwater would suck down the ocean at least three times a day, creating a gargantuan whirlpool in which all craft were obliterated. Both creatures appear repeatedly in the myths, encountering among other heroes, Heracles, Jason and, most famously, Odysseus, though their ultimate fate is unrecorded. They were reputedly the descendants of earlier primeval monsters, though typically of the Greek tales, there are alternative origin stories in which they were once beautiful nymphs who were punished by the gods for different reasons but in the same cruel way: transformation from loveliness to horror.

Scylla and Charybdis are seen today as a simile for the difficult choices we face in life, and yet at one time they were believed to be real entities, with some evidence to support the claim. Whirlpools do appear on the south side of the Strait of Messina, though they are only a danger to small craft, while the waters under the 'Rock of Scilla' on the Calabrian coast have long been known for their larger-than-average specimens of octopi.

THE DECKS BELOW
Jan Edwards

The Chief Petty Officer swung Captain Georgianna Forsythe the barest of salutes, which told her exactly where she sat in the Royal Navy of His Majesty King George VI's scheme of things. Of the civilian salvage ship's skipper there was no sign, but that was to be expected. Her job tended to make sane people somewhat nervous.

"Captain Barlow sends his compliments but he's over on the other side." The CPO waved toward the pontoons awaiting the submarine HMS M2 when she was finally raised. "He says you're to wait here until we've secured the boat and towed it back to harbour."

Georgi held back the more colourful comments that sprang to mind. Jobs handled by the Department were never easy – easy wasn't what the Department did – but some grudging co-operation was the least she expected. She rubbed the line of blue scales around the third finger of her left hand, the indelible legacy of her encounter with Nyarlathotep. Meddling in the doings of gods had both marked her *for* life and marked *out* her life; as the hand of Nyarlathotep's enemy, Nodens, her life had become one long line of such doings. She put the memory aside and plastered on a smile for the CPO, despite his insolence toward her pips. *Charm*, she decided, *will be a better calmer of this particular beast.*

"Sorry, *miss*. This lot are *red dusters*." He said. "Always hard, dealing with civvies, but we've got Admiralty orders. Naval personnel only inside that boat until we tie up at 'Blockhouse' docks."

"This boat? What about the submarine?"

"No, Miss. *This*!" He stamped a booted foot on the deck. "*This* is a ship." He jabbed a finger toward the stretch of choppy water between salvage ship and pontoon. "The *boat* hasn't been brought up yet."

"You mean the submarine?"

"That's what I said." The Chief gazed at her blandly and Georgi just knew he enjoyed playing naval word games with outsiders. She sank her head a fraction further between her shoulders; struggling to keep a lid on her temper in the teeth of Nelsonian obstinacy. The CPO was not alone in his hostility. She knew by the looks coming her way from crewmen close enough to matter that she was not just a curiosity but an unwelcome one.

From all around her came the clank of marine industry. Salvage gear under duress and voices bawling over that mechanical mayhem, and beyond that a rising clamour of wind and waves. She had boarded with reasonable confidence because her deity-touched hand had given no premonition of danger lurking on board, except that it was not the Department's standard model in monsters that were making life difficult right then. She glanced back at the motor launch already heading for Portland Head. There was no other sign of shipping in the teeth of a rising heavy swell. Even the ubiquitous gulls that habitually haunted Lyme Bay, were absent; doubtless wheeling inland to pester the ploughmen. "I have my orders from a lot further up the chain," Georgi replied. "You realise we do know about the Sonar research? And ASDIC." She allowed time for the knowledge that the Navy's most secret of secrets were not nearly so secret as they had obviously thought. "Chief ... The Department knows it's the duck's quack, believe me," she added. "And they are not interested in filching it. So, leaving all that *fluky* naval gumph aside, why not tell me what *you* think is going on." The CPO's jaw whitened and Georgi sighed. "The Brass don't call me in for tea dances and alibis. This is important. Not just for me, for Whitehall, or the Admiralty. It's the lives of your crew. I need to know ... come on. You've got the goods on them. Show me the CPO who doesn't know twice as much as any brass-hat."

The Chief removed his cap and ran a hand through his oiled hair. "M2's sinking were no accident. I knows that much." He glared at her, daring any contradiction.

Georgi was not cowed. She had faced down gods and won. "I've heard rumours. What have your chaps seen?"

The Chief shrugged, his attention flickering toward the roiling water and criss-crossing chains marking the spot where the stricken submarine was due to surface. "First off I thought the dive-crews were playing daft buggers ... if you'll excuse the language, miss. But then we had a *Bubble-head* near on ripped out of his suit." He glanced at her, plainly wondering how she would take his assertions. "Not just ripped," he said, "Cut. Like a cod's gizzards."

"Did he survive?"

"At a hundred feet?" He let out a bellow of derision. "Drowning, blood-loss, sheer bloody fright. Any one of them would've took him, and ... I've seen things hit by a motor-prop as caught less damage."

"No chance it was just that?" Georgi asked.

"None. Only a *boat* could reach that depth. And apart from the M2 there were none down there."

"So what do *you* think it was?"

"The old stories always have roots. There's a dozen tales about things that lives in this bay. Creatures as lure men to their doom."

"Mermaids? Those girls are all about having a good time."

"Not female. Things that control the minds of tars and whores the same." He frowned. "You're not playing about are you?" he said. "You really believe in these things."

"Given the rum coves I work for? It rather helps if I do."

"Aye." He snorted. "It would that. Then I'll tells you this much. The creature as haunts this bay is no man as God intends, nor female neither. It's a monster."

"And you're just as serious aren't you?" she said. The CPO made no reply beyond a wry smile and she nodded. "Thanks for speaking plainly, Chief. It really is appreciated."

A sudden burst of noise grabbed their attention. "Stand clear, Captain, Ma'am ... Sir. She's on her way up," he said.

"I'm first in," Georgi replied. "Orders direct from the Admiralty. They trump any trivia your barge skipper dreamt up." She leaned in. "He's just a civilian. So really? You're in charge."

"In a manner of speaking I s'pose I am. All right, Miss. But a quick decko's all you'll get time for."

She was aware that it was more than the balance of the ship that had shifted. "Thank you, Chief. I am in your debt."

"That's as maybe," he replied. "But I'm not doing you no favours. Be ready to slip aboard, and ready to get out again the moment I shouts you up. That boat's bin' up 'n down like a tart's kni ... like a fiddler's elbow. There's a big blow coming in."

Georgi tried not to flag up the implications of 'cod's gizzards' as she stationed herself near to where the aft crane dangled hawsers into the deep. She stared moodily at the water and her hand twitched a warning. Losing a finger to Nyarlathotep, and having it restored by Nodens, had turned her world into ... what exactly? Was she more than human? Less? It was a question that occupied much of her thoughts.

Compressors hissed, pumping air to divers already surfacing from around the wreck, and also into the ascending hull; driving out water and lending it buoyancy. Chains and hawsers clattered around iron drums as the cranes winched. Bawled out commands and men answering with time-honoured aye-ayes. A bellowed, "broaching depth," brought her to the present. Boom arms creaked under the shifting weight as the boat surfaced. The M2's conning tower and its cumbersome bolt-on hangar rose from the waves like a strange

186

walrus peeking above an ice flow. It lay heavy amongst a web of steel lines, crusted with rust, and already speckled with concretions of sea creatures from its year beneath the brine.

A gangplank was extended and Georgi nodded thanks to the CPO before edging her way out to the plank's tip, just a few feet above the sub's swaying deck, all of the crew's attention was fixed on her, willing the outsider to succeed and also to fail in equal measure. *This is it*, she decided, *walking a pirate's plank.*

She set foot on the M2's deck, between the plane's launch tracks, using them to haul herself into the hangar where the Peto seaplane was firmly bolted; wings folded back, a resting bird that would never fly again. Georgi sidled past the plane to the bulkhead hatch and grasped the hatch wheel, took a deep breath, tugged it open and shone her torch down into the void. The air that met her reeked of sea water and diesel, and, less tangible but no less cloying, the stench of corruption, which seemed to permeate the very structure.

She descended the ladder into the boat and paused at the bottom of the companion ladder to gain a feel for her surroundings. The ceiling crowded in on her, close enough to touch, as were the walls. *It's a military womb*, she thought. *For the projecting of torpedo offspring at any enemy its commanders cared to name. No, not even that. It's a tube. An armour plated cigar tube. One with every inch of its insides slathered in beige shit.*

Georgi ducked through the low hatchway to the Control Room. She was not squeamish, yet was reluctant to touch the silty blanket coating every surface until the boat tilted violently and she was forced to steady herself against the nearest control station. Water sucked at her calves and sluiced noisily around the cabin. Then – nothing but the dun-coloured silence. Her hand was throbbing now. Not the fierce warning she expected from the presence of arcane enemies, yet still an insistent awareness that was not to be ignored.

Away from the feeble light that filtered down from the hangar companion tube even her enhanced vision struggled to pick out detail. The torch she carried was small, with a narrow beam. She played it around the confined spaces noting the pipes and cables and controls, highlighting drab, muddy fittings crammed in close from either side so that she could touch to left and right with only a slightest of leans should she be so inclined.

Little room to manoeuvre for a crew on duty and less still for a novice who was so unused to such close quarters. Unfamiliar with the layout, and in near blackness amongst loosened cables which hung bare inches from her head, she fought down a moment of

187

claustrophobic panic. The comparison with Nyarlathotep's burial vaults in the Valley of the Kings could not be ignored.

She was backing toward the exit when the torchlight picked out sporadic dabs on convenient handholds that were not her own. Someone had been this way before her. Impossible in theory; except that her job so often asked her to ape Dodson's White Queen and "believe six impossible things before breakfast".

The lightest of zephyrs brushed her face, bringing with it another waft of fuel and fish and the stench of stagnation that she tasted as a sour darkness grasping the back of her throat. A rasping hiss came loud in her ears as she was hurled backwards, slamming into the steel surface before sliding into putrid water. "What in hell?"

She caught a glimpse of a skinny figure in the same moment that a voice called from above.

"Miss Forsythe? Captain, Ma'am!" The sub dipped wildly to scoop another deluge through the companion-way. She looked up to see the Chief's round head silhouetted against the block of sky. "Come up, Captain." He bellowed. "Orders just in. We're to put in to port immediately! Captain Forsythe?"

A nebulous string of notes from out of the darkness took her attention.

"One minute, Chief," she shouted as she hauled herself to her feet. "I'll be up in one minute."

"I'll come down ..."

"No. Stay out there! That is an order!"

The notes rose from whisper to warble. "A wailing," she muttered. "No. A song." A melody of sadness and longing shimmered across her senses as a silken blanket of reassurance. The boat lurched, flinging Georgi against the bulkhead where her temple connected with the metal rim of a hatch and she fell to her knees. Cold water arced across her face like a slap, returning her to her senses; and to a roughly humanoid in shape framed in the doorway.

Its arms seemed too long, with webbed hands clutching the hatch edge. Its legs were bowed and short. A ridge of bone rose across its skull, which was narrow, with eyes set more to the sides than was human. The mouth was wide, with a pronounced peak to a thin upper lip, giving a beak-like appearance. The creature did not possess all of the physical attributes of a Deep One but instinct had her step back and raise the Webley. The fact that her gift from Nodens gave only the faintest twinge did not mean the creature was benign.

Dark strands frilled around its jawline fluttered with the strange song filling the space between them. It stopped abruptly and swallowed several times before showing twin rows of decidedly carnivorous teeth in some semblance of a smile.

"Captain Forsythe!"

The creature looked toward the voice, wary but not afraid.

"Captain Forsythe!" The Chief shouted again, sounding as close to anxious as his kind ever came.

The creature looked back to her. "Forsssythe," it purred, the voice as soft and bubbling as its song. The dark 'beard' gave Georgi an impression of 'male', though no sex was immediately obvious.

Georgi tapped her chest. "Forsythe," she said and then pointed back at the beast.

"Veassst ..." it replied.

From outside came the muffled but unmistakable rattle of gunfire. Georgi held up her hand, ignoring its warning burn. "Chief?" Georgi waded across to stand beneath the companion ladder, squinting up at the dull winter light that was harsh against the wanton blackness of the boat's interior. "Chief!" She grabbed the ladder, and fell back with a yelp as a spasm shot through her left hand.

There was barely time to register the implications before Veast was dragging her back through to the section beyond the control room. "Cef," he hissed.

"Cef?"

"Cef." He waved his hands, plainly frustrated at the shortcomings in language. More hand waving and a bubbling foment of noise that was melodious yet unmistakably angry. Georgi had travelled the world and come across many languages, many of them not human, and it occurred to her as an inconsequential aside that profanity was unmistakable no matter what the source. "Daughter." His hands flapped frantically and calmed enough to indicate something of some size. "Of Great Mother," he said. "Hydra?" Webbed hands were slapped together.

"Oh hell. And the prize for setting up right behind the wrong place goes to the girl in wet boots." Veast gazed at her, his head tilted in query, and Georgi indulged in a little hand flapping of her own. "In a mess?" she said. "Trouble?"

"Cef killsss many," he agreed.

"Now why does that not surprise me?" Georgi looked around the gloom-ridden space. "I take it you found no other way out?"

He shook his head. "Cef wasss waiting ..."

She could understand his reluctance to leave. When a creature such as Veast was so evidently in mortal fear the implied presence of Deep Ones in the vicinity seemed far less improbable.

The only puzzle was in why her early warning digit had barely reacted to Veast until he had touched her. She had come to rely on its accuracy as a barometer of endangerment, and if he were correct then it had let her down this time around. "You have nothing to do with this Cef?" she said. "Is ..." The unmistakable rattle of gunfire scurried around the surface world.

Veast began to 'sing'; the ruff's oscillations around his neck synchronising with the eerie sound. Georgi felt her conscious mind falter under its spell. What was he? A siren? A merman? *The Portland* merman? She had read the legends even before the Chief had touched on it. Nothing she'd heard now or then was encouraging. She rubbed at her scaly third digit and reeled equilibrium back into her skull, where it belonged. As she came back to reality she caught another glimpse of those rows of ivory teeth, far closer now, just inches from her face. She floundered backwards, waving the Webley in his general direction.

"Back up, siren, or whatever you are," Georgi rasped. "Start charming whatever it is that's coming to get us."

Veast's song cut off abruptly. "Cef," he said. "Knowsss why. Knowsss what." He looked feral, hunted, and there was no mistaking his agitation.

Noises of fighting, of shots fired and of mortal screams, were drawing closer to the conning tower. The periscope hanging down in the centre of the bridge shook a cascade of silt onto the water. Georgi looked up, and imagined this creature Cef peering down the lens. It made her feel a little queasy. She had not heard of Cef but Mother Hydra was all too familiar. An Old One. Maybe the oldest. A tentacled terror of far-off ancient times and scourge of the Pacific Sea. So what in hell was her daughter doing in the cold waters of the English Channel?

Rifle fire continued sporadically, with the occasional clank against the hull. There was no danger such small shells would pierce the hull but logic dictated there had to be a target somewhere on the boat that was drawing fire.

Georgi had no idea what form this Cef creature would take. She might be no bigger than herself or Veast ... Or the size of a whale.

They waited, motionless, eyes raised as if to a god. The fighting has ceased and only the ocean noises battered the hull; then a violent blow shuddered through the vessel, shivering silt down from the upper ledges. A second impact, which Georgi pinpointed at the conning tower, sent fresh vibrations fore and aft. "Sounds big," she observed.

Veast fluttered his hands, his gill-frill fluttering.

190

Georgi took it to indicate agitation, if only because her own pulse ratcheted up more than a few notches. The sounds of knocking moved further toward the hangar deck. Just a matter of time before the deep, dark, creature known as Cef found the open hatch.

Avoiding the daughter of an ancient and monstrous sea goddess in a space little more than a man's wide-armed span, cluttered and strewn with cables and debris, in total darkness, was not going to be simple. Georgi moved into the shelter of the bulkhead, clipping the torch's end tag to her belt and switched it off, freeing her right fist for the comforting smoothness of the Webley's grip. The darkness was a challenge even to her preternatural vision, so she aimed the barrel toward the companion ladder. Her hearing, sharpened by blood mingled with that of higher beings, picked out a gentle fluttering of breath close to her side. She made out Veast's pale outline as the source, as her night vision took charge.

She tilted her head, as though fine tuning signals from a crystal set; the better to catch any sound emanating from the for'ard section. Each of her six, and possibly the seventh, senses jangled in expectation of the being prowling the outer hull.

Cef's arrival came as a physical assault on all those senses. Georgi felt it as a blast of air and energy, and also as a piercing sensation radiating from the blue-scaled ring around her finger, and as a throbbing in her chest and pulsing in her skull.

It was as if the entire force of the ocean had entered His Majesty's vessel M2. Not seeing, or more possibly ignoring, the hangar route, the maelstrom of flesh and energy descending into the space in a bare second.

Georgi had not known what to expect from any daughter of the Hydra. A many-headed beast perhaps? Tentacles, slime and scales? The slim creature that stood swaying in the shaft of light from the hatch was the least of her expectations. In some respects Cef resembled Veast; smooth-skinned and be-gilled, with a patina of fine filaments on her head and down her back that glowed with the colours of fire; vibrant oranges and scorching reds. As Cef raised her clawed hands folds of thin cerise coloured membrane could be seen to flutter from her arms like some exotic denizen of the southern ocean reefs. Her features were as un-disguisedly alien as Veast, but as undeniably beautiful as he was not; aquatic streamlining that was taut across slender bones, with huge round night-eyes that were set wide on her slight skull. She was not camouflaged for the sea depths as Veast was. Cef was as unlike any of the tribes of Old and Deep ones as Georgi had ever seen – except in one respect. The salvager's entire crew had apparently been silenced in a few sparse minutes. In that respect she was very much akin to the rest of her kind. She was deadly.

That startlingly exotic beauty turned toward her and howled a hostility and rage that Georgi felt she did not deserve. Veast stepped neatly behind her, using her as a shield. His proximity, his breath on her neck and his body touching hers, made her shudder. A sharp sensation shot up her left arm, though she barely had time to think about it.

Cef lunged, cobra-quick; her mouth gaping wide, a dark oval lined with tiny double rows of needle teeth glimmering pearlescent white, screeching as she came in for the attack.

Georgi dived away and fired off two rounds. Cef's shrieks turned to howling and Georgi knew she had hit. She did not hang around waiting to see where and how. Georgi leaped toward the next compartment, running blind in near total dark. Something shot past her and she doubled back. But ducking through the low hatchway she grazed the top of her head. Pain wavered through her and she staggered, splashing across the small space to hit the far wall.

Cef was a fraction behind her, hissing in the old tongue. Georgi whirled around, her left hand extended toward the furious waves of sound. Her entire hand was engulfed in fire and ice, and blue radiance flooded from her, illuminating the small area and its occupants with absolute clarity.

Cef had backed up against the wall adjacent to the hatchway, a cowled arm thrown up against the flare of intense light.

Of Veast there was no sign.

Georgi pinged off two more rounds. At point blank range she could not miss, and yet the beast seemed not to sustain any kind of impact.

The sub pitched and a deluge cascaded down the shaft, so that Georgi was forced to drop her guard and grab for the ladder. By the time the wave had spent she was up to the hangar level and securing the hatch and was casting about for something to fasten it. She ripped a broken strut from the Peto to insert into the wheel and across the adjoining structure. It would not hold for long, but with luck it would not need to.

She staggered out of the hangar and struggled across the bucking hull to the conning tower. She had no idea whether Veast remained inside the M2, and though she had no connection to the mer-creature it seemed wrong to entomb him with the Deep One – but that thought lasted for only the briefest moment.

Georgi whipped off her Sam Brown and lashed the heel of the fastener to the stem. It would not hold any longer than the hangar door; she hoped it would be long enough, and slithered back along the M2's length to the gangplank.

The salvage vessel heaved in the grip of the storm and all was grey in the scudding wind and rain. She lurched across to the deck and bent to examine the bloodied remains of two crewmen. Both had been killed as if by a phalanx of flying Kukri. Georgi turned the other over, knowing before she did so that it was, had been, the Chief Petty Officer. His eyes were glazed, staring in anger at his last vision, his face bleached pale beneath his sea-weather-tan, his throat below it – missing; only a pulpy mess remained, seeping remnants of blood still pooling in his gullet.

The boy had fared less well than the Chief. Half his chest was missing; viscera puddling to one side of his cooling corpse. A civvie diver by the grubby white gansey sweater visible through bloody gashes in his waterproof jacket, and the non-naval haircut on his partially detached head. There was nothing to be done for either of them, but something maybe to end it with a sort of justice.

The ship had a sizeable compliment plus naval personnel; close to fifty men, but she could neither see nor hear a single one living. Ravaged bodies littered the deck, and the evidence of more in the fast-reddening wash around the ship. Georgi ran for the winch room and arrived in front of the boom arms' controls with no sign of pursuit. She blew out a long breath. The array of controls held a veritable plethora of possibilities and little indication as to which did what, beyond a few letters printed beside each section. A control panel built solely for the initiated. Georgi always found it paid in any emergency to push, pull or turn absolutely anything that was labelled in red. Button, lever, handle, it made little difference. Red was the key, and to the right of the controls was a double set of scarlet D-handled levers that looked highly promising.

She watched HMS M2 roll in her web of hawsers, vanishing periodically as the rising storm sent ever-larger breakers crashing across its bulk, expectant of pursuit. And there, indistinct through the spray-murked windows, Georgi spotted the athletically sculpted Cef emerging from the boat. The sea-creature stood on the viewing deck's edge, riding the bucking, heaving sub with the unconscious ease of a circus stunt rider – and stared straight toward the winch room for the count of two before dropping from view.

In the moment that the demi-deity slipped into the water Georgi left the controls, skittering back into the midship array of cabins and corridors. She was not averse to confrontation, yet there had been a gun battle clearly heard and Cef had shown no sign of injury. The creature had seen off the entire ship's crew and more, and had taken fire from Georgi at point blank range without a scratch to show.

Most of the dead were civilians, not fighters, she thought, *but that makes the waste all the more tragic. The slaughter of so many* ... She barely needed the slice of warning pain in her left hand to tell her that Cef was close. A sudden rush of air from an opened doorway told her as much.

There were few places to go on such a small ship, and little time to formulate plans. The walkway furthest from the salvage web was two strides away, and Georgi took them, sidestepping into the windward side of the salvage pontoon; and the teeth of the gale.

Cef appeared at the far end of the walkway, oblivious to wind and water and rolling deck.

Georgi fell back the way she had come, grasping the pitted white rail to stop her headlong flight.

A flurry to her right through the spray, and Cef materialised like a writhing knot that straightened out as if she had never moved a muscle, and advanced, sashaying with all the grace and intent of Garbo's Mata Hari.

Georgi stepped back into the cabin corridor and headed up to the pilot deck. Since Cef was too fast for her to outrun the only option was to make a stand. And the only place for that would be the bridge. She took the steps two at a time and lurched into the cramped confines of the salvager's hub. The door was missing, torn off and hurled who knew where. Beyond that a good half of the floor was taken up with a fresh corpse. Lacerated around face and neck, just like the others had been; an officer by the cap laying close by, but a civilian one. The warning stab of approaching menace in her hand told her time had already run out. She scuttled over the body and placed herself to the far side of the chart table, just as her nemesis flowed in through the open door.

Georgi raised her left hand with palm outwards.

The creature paused; those limpid black eyes glistened anticipation and curiosity, nostrils flared and her lips parted as she scented the air. She flicked a prehensile tongue across her lips and nose and almost up to her rounded eyes. "What are you?" she hissed.

"I am the hand of the god Nodens," Georgi replied. "His warrior. You, on the other hand, are one of Hydra's spawn. Ten a penny."

Cef hissed air inwards and raised her chin. "I am different," she snapped. "Not a slave, like the rest."

"Well you are not as pug-ugly as some I've seen. I will grant you that much."

The beautiful monster paused to gaze at her opponent, shifting balance to compensate for the sea swell, but making no attempt to advance; apparently perplexed by the implied compliment.

Georgi tensed, wishing she had taken time to reload the Webley. She hoped her god-touched hand was not trembling from the outside as much as it felt from within. It was currently her only defence. Cef's webbed hands were twitching, claws extended fully like a scaly cat and Georgi had seen what that home-grown weaponry could do. "Why?" Georgi asked. "Why such death?"

"I defend myself. As you would." Cef shrugged. "They were not worthy of note. But you ..." Her tongue flickered, tasting the air, and she smiled, displaying those teeth all over again. "You have not the scent of any common land creature. I understand why Veast spared your life. You are the one called Georgah. The bride of Nyarlathotep. Veast thought you a match against my power."

"I am the hand of Nodens. Not Nyarlathotep's bride. I did evade that hell."

Cef shrugged, edging a little closer. "Nyarlathotep claims otherwise, and you cannot deny the ceremony took place. He and I have reluctant – absent – spouses in common." She laughed a low, sibilant derision.

"Your what ...?"

"Veast escaped our nest a long while ago. He is a dangerous creature."

Georgi glanced at the captain's body. "Veast? But ..."

"Mark this, Georgah, I did not begin this slaughter. It was not I who sank your vessel for the morsels that lay within. I wish only to return home with my property. Yet know I will finish it if I must."

Cef whipped forwards like mist in a gale. Faster than anything Georgi had ever faced previously. She allowed instinct take the slack, sending the cold fire of Nodens to wrap around the blurring figure like chiffon scarves in the wind.

The demi-god was knocked back but grasped at the frame, her claws piercing the metal as if it were formed in warm bread and not cold iron. Cef lunged yet again, throwing Georgi into the wall. Claws raked for vital organs, neck, heart, lungs; found purchase in just shoulder and arm; spilling blood, noise and profanity in more or less equal measure.

Georgi rolled free, kicking out against her attacker, making contact with taut flesh and pushing against it with a bone jarring stab, sending Cef far enough across the space that she could scrabble for a weapon. A navigator's T-square was the only thing that came to hand. She sent it, with a knife throwers' flick of the wrist, into her opponent's face It was a pathetic weapon but served as a 'sand in the eyes' resort; gaining a portion of time to raise her hands and pour another slather of icy fire into Cef's torso. The cold flame hit hard and set off a high screech, which was echoed from outside by Veast's warbling siren song. Georgi rolled into the cover of the chart table to ram shells into the Webley and would have emptied them into the prone body had Cef remained there a fraction longer. But, writhing briefly like a stranded eel, Cef flipped around in her own length and vanished through the door before Georgi's fingers could tighten around the weapon's stock.

Georgi peered out across a silent ship but found no sign of the demi-deity. From somewhere the siren song, cutting across the noise of wave and wind, changed tone.

The M2 swung still in its cat's cradle, as silent as the sister-salvager holding the strings on the far side. The squall had lessened, though cold spray was thickened now by the wetness of driving sleet. She sat back, struggling to finish reloading the Webley with wet hands that were rapidly numbing with cold. Fully armed once more she crept down to the gangplank that was still extended out to the M2's foredeck.

She slipped across to survey the boat's buckled hatch wheel. The inside was no more inviting than it had been the first time she had entered. Perhaps less so knowing what lay within. She listened intently, reluctant to enter that claustrophobic space without need. "Veast," she called. "Come up."

Silence from within.

"Veast?" Enhanced hearing detected a swirl of water, as though something were being hauled through it. "Veast? Cef told me a few interesting things. Are any of them true?"

The silence deepened. Not even the lapping of water moving with the waves. Yet she knew he lived, and listened. If he was spouse to a near-goddess, and his cover was blown, then his refusal to answer said all she needed to know. She did not doubt his intent was hostile.

A paleness in the gloom, caught her eye, moving rapidly up the companion way, a flurry of hissing speed, preceded by tooth and claw, homing in on her like a cold, sinuous torpedo.

She fired once, twice. Still he came, uttering bone-freezing howls of malevolence. "Damn you for a web-footed little schlepper!" She fired twice more, directly into the gaping, tooth-filled maw. Blood splattered back across her outstretched arm, and into her face. She fired one more round; and then one final time on an empty chamber. Georgi lowered her right arm and stepped back, raising her left in readiness to pour blue fire at anything that moved.

The merman lay with his lower half still dangling inside the M2, his skull reduced to a bloody crush.

Georgi took a few deep breaths, struggling to breathe against adrenalin distress. Once her heart beat slowly enough to think she unceremoniously heaved the body into the chute. It seemed fitting to give marine monsters a sea burial. Navy teams could seal the coffin on the sea bed once the storms abated.

She hurried back to the salvage ship's winch room and set those twin red handles loose; watched as cables and chains stretched to their limits in fighting boat and elements; cracking like whipcord at their sudden release. Some ran free, others snaked up and back on the rigs, thrashing octopus arms of steel; and then the submarine surged upward, briefly, before it plunged between the salvage vessel and pontoon like a huge porpoise.

HMS M2 reappeared briefly before vanishing stern first into the boiling water. As the wind dropped and surface calmed, Georgi swore she caught a hint of orange; brief and bright.

THE FLYING DUTCHMAN

"At 4 a.m. the *Flying Dutchman* crossed our bows," wrote John Neale Dalton, Canon of Windsor and tutor to Prince George of Wales, later to be crowned King George V, during a cruise up Australia's east coast in 1880. Dalton added: "A strange red light as of a phantom ship all aglow, in the midst of which light the masts, spars and sails of a brig 200 yards distant stood out in strong relief as she came up on the port bow, where also the officer of the watch from the bridge clearly saw her, as did the quarterdeck midshipman, who was sent forward at once to the forecastle; but on arriving there was no vestige nor any sign whatever of any material ship to be seen either near or right away to the horizon, the night being clear and the sea calm. Thirteen persons altogether saw her ... At 10.45 a.m. the ordinary seaman who had this morning reported the Flying Dutchman fell from the foretopmast crosstrees on to the topgallant forecastle and was smashed to atoms."

This amazingly detailed witness statement pretty well fits the usual bill for sightings of the legendary Flying Dutchman, which is regarded as the ultimate portent of doom on the high seas; a sure sign if you see it, that catastrophe will shortly follow.

The name 'Flying Dutchman' is known all around the world, especially among seafaring nations, and the common perception of it – though invariably this is drawn from imagination – is much the same from one country to the next: a ghostly galleon, wind-battered and skeletal, but sailing hard towards you, usually in the teeth of an oncoming hurricane, manned by the damned souls of wretched, long dead seamen, and captained by a demonic figure who roars with laughter from the prow.

Alleged real sightings of the Dutchman are somewhat less dramatic, as exemplified by John Dalton's account above, but also by the captain of a German U-Boat during World War Two, who was so convinced the phantom ship was real that he had it in his sights and was all set to launch torpedoes when it suddenly vanished – the same sub later took terrible damage in a duel with a genuine enemy. The ghost ship was even allegedly spotted by a number of sunbathers on a South African beach in 1939, none of whom had ever seen a 17th century sailing ship before, but all of whom described the vessel with astonishing accuracy. Shortly afterwards, there was a mining accident in the area, and several deaths resulted among relatives of those self-same bathers. It may *surprise many that there is so much apparent evidence of this death-ship's existence – there are few portside towns where it is taken as a joke – but the origins of the story are shrouded in an oceanic fog of folklore and fiction.*

References to the Flying Dutchman were first committed to paper in George Barrington's 'A Voyage To Botany Bay' in 1795, in which he describes an English warship's nightmarish journey across the Southern Ocean, where it is struck by one terrible gale after another and dogged all the way by the spectral shape of a ship whose name he was advised by veteran seamen to be "the Flying Dutch-Man". From then on the fearful name appeared sporadically in other documents – so-called factual reports alternating with poems, novels and short stories, the latter contributed by authors who would go on to gain legendary status in their own right: Walter Scott, Samuel Taylor Coleridge, Washington Irving and Edgar Allan Poe.

Despite this mass of sensationalist literature, it is still possible to pick out the salient details and gain some insight into the genesis of the story.

It seems that in the early 18th century, a Dutch barque skippered by a certain Hendrik Vanderdecken was renowned for the speed of its cargo runs from Rotterdam to Java, and for the wealth Vanderdecken accumulated as a result. One rumour suggested that black magic was part of this success story, another that the ambitious skipper was not above a spot of piracy if he encountered any smaller, poorly defended craft en route. Later tales asserted that he controlled his crew with extreme brutality and thought nothing of shooting men dead if they were insolent. It seems there was never any danger of mutiny on the Flying Dutchman, but then stories concerning villainous individuals who later meet their just deserts often grow with the telling. During one particularly stormy run, Vanderdecken overruled his crew, who didn't want to risk rounding the Cape of Good Hope. By all accounts he swore that he would navigate this perilous stretch of sea even if it took him until the Day of Judgement. Needless to say, the ship went down with all hands, but that was only the beginning of the horror – because now Vanderdecken had to make good on his vow, sailing the seven seas until the end of time, taking his cursed crew along with him and always bringing horrendous squalls of the sort that had sent him to his watery grave.

Though the Flying Dutchman has all the hallmarks of a grand Gothic romance, it isn't easy for sceptics to dismiss the plethora of reported sightings, though many of these would undoubtedly have been caused by the phenomenon of the Fata Morgana, an impressive type of mirage typical of vast open spaces, in which bending rays of light create the illusion that objects – such as a ship on a far horizon, or even beyond it – are nearer than they actually are, and even that they are hoisted upward, in effect travelling through mid-air. Perhaps unsurprisingly, these astonishing illusions also have the potential to simply vanish from plain sight.

But does this explain everything? Certainly not those particularly lurid accounts in which ragged, bone-thin figures on the Dutchman's decks have supposedly screamed and begged for help from passing boats, or those occasions when witnesses have themselves sought contact with these damned souls, asking for news about loved ones in the afterlife, even attempting to send messages to them. And why, if all this is nothing more than an optical illusion, is disaster so often recorded as having followed on the heels of such sightings?

There are more questions than answers in the story of the Flying Dutchman, primarily perhaps because those in a position to know are usually dead soon afterwards, swallowed by roaring foam, their broken, bloated corpses sucked down into the briny depths.

HELL IN THE CATHEDRAL
Paul Finch

I didn't quite know what the German couple were expecting, but they'd geared up as if they were on some deep sea diving mission. Spear-guns, flippers, harnessed oxygen cylinders, the lot; even a pack of underwater sodium-flares. They looked the part too. He said his name was Dolph, his wife Heidi – both of them were leonine blondes, deeply-tanned. He was trim and firmly-muscled; she statuesque and incredibly handsome in the traditional Teutonic way. Inevitably of course, they both spoke impeccable English.

They made Karen and myself, neither of us speaking a word of German and equipped with only snorkels and goggles, feel small and insignificant. Add to that our alabaster-white complexions – we'd only been in Sicily two days, after all – and it was the usual case of the Brits abroad standing out like sore thumbs. I was only glad I wasn't dressed in rolled-up pants and string-vest, with a knotted handkerchief on my head. I was even embarrassed about the hamper we'd brought, with its packs of sandwiches and multiple bottles of beer.

Not that Carlo, our guide seemed worried. He also spoke good English, and chattered idly to the four of us as he steered the little outboard around the various rocky coves. Ironically, he was clad in a ridiculous old vest, flip-flops and baggy khaki shorts, but somehow his plump physique, olive-brown skin and thick tangle of blue-black hair, made it alright on him. He was a local, after all. Locals could dress how they pleased.

Now he wore a straw cowboy hat as well, to shield himself from the midday sun, which as well as blazing down from above was also glaring back up from the sea. Even out there, off the coast, rounding one headland after another on a generous swell, the heat was terrific. Both Karen and myself were heavily greased-up in factor eight, but already we could feel our shoulders and backs itching.

When he'd first tapped us up on the beach at Taormina and offered us this day-trip for what seemed like an incredibly reasonable price, he'd never mentioned being exposed to the sun for quite so long; but to be fair, neither had he said we wouldn't be. He was taking us to what he mysteriously referred to as 'the Cathedral' – a fantastic cave system, accessible only from the sea and by narrow boat. Neither Karen nor I had ever heard of it before, but

Carlo assured us it was worth seeing. Apparently it knocked the Blue Grotto into "ow you say ... cock-hat, no!"

Dolph and Heidi, who we'd only met that morning when we'd first arrived at the jetty, reckoned they *had* heard of it. By all accounts it was as exhilarating to look at from under the water as from over it, which explained their diving equipment. I had to admit, I was getting the bug quickly. As a coastline it was spectacular: an endless succession of deep coves, titanic arches and narrow channels between volcanic outcrops. The sea rose and fell with its usual intimidating power, froth spraying up through the nooks and crannies. For the Mediterranean, the water was relatively clear, and you could see a long way down into the rippling shadows. We stuck closely to the shoreline, but I still got the impression of extreme depth.

On impulse, I asked Carlo about it. He shrugged. "Hey ... maybe sixxy, sevenny feet ... good for diving!"

I mumbled to Karen that I wasn't so sure about that, but she told me to be quiet and not to show her up in front of the Germans, both of whom were checking their pressure gauges and looked up eagerly every time we chugged around another headland. Fleetingly, I wondered if they really had heard about the Cathedral, or were just saying that for appearance's sake. It did seem odd that something as allegedly spectacular as this had to rely on freelance boatmen to take you there. I say 'boatmen' because I assumed that Carlo was one of a number, but even though we'd been out with him for several hours by this time, we hadn't seen any others – either on their way there or on their way back.

*

For all my doubts, the Cathedral was worth waiting for.

From the outside it wasn't too impressive: a triangular opening in the cliff-face, dark waves chopping and foaming inside it. But the moment we actually sailed in, it struck me how well named it was. A high, multi-coloured roof arched above us, the waves reflected on it in sparkling liquid-patterns. There was a big ocean swell, but the sense of space was mesmerising. I think every one of us must have gasped aloud in delight.

The sunlight beaming in through the cave-mouth behind us came up from the sandy floor fathoms below in rays of luminescence, turning the water swimming pool blue.

"Can we swim here?" Karen asked excitedly.

Carlo shook his head curtly. "No yet, lady. Good place inside ... I promise."

202

For minutes on end we went deeper into the system, crossing one chamber after another, all as vast and airy as the first, many hung with stalactites. It was quite a network. Occasionally, we followed narrow channels with roofs so low that we all had to crouch down. They were more like something from the River Caves than the Blue Grotto, but always they fed through into new immense caverns.

It got cool quickly of course. And dark. We were still chugging into the labyrinth when it struck me that there wouldn't be much point in swimming if it got any darker. I mentioned this to Carlo, but he insisted that not far ahead there was "good place".

Karen hissed at me to stop worrying. This was part of the experience, she said. We were probably making our way through to the other side of the headland. I tried to put a brave face on, but wasn't entirely convinced. We were now so far in that even the ocean swell had dwindled. Daylight had almost deserted us and the water was black. That was when Carlo cut the motor, and we found ourselves drifting. He began fiddling with some equipment under his bench. It was a portable arc-lamp. He hefted it up and switched it on, just as we cruised through into the next cave. It would have been a void in there had he not done so, for this was a truly gargantuan chamber with no natural light and water as still as any inland lagoon. Even with the strong electric light, we could not at first see the encircling walls.

Carlo trained the light upward. "Fantastic rock formation, no?" he said proudly. We followed his gaze; countless feet above us hung innumerable dripping stalactites. "Even better down there." He swept the light over the surface of the water. Powerful as it was, it didn't penetrate far underneath.

"You've got to be joking!" I said.

There was a blinding flash beside me, and I had to cover my eyes. It was Dolph, striking the first of his sodium-flares. It threw a searing glare to the farthest corners of the cave. Both the Germans were fully rigged out: cylinders in place, spear-guns loaded. Dolph was wearing a kind of bandolier-belt, with the remaining eight flares fitted into it.

"Good place to swim," Carlo went on, nodding brightly.

Heidi swung her supple body over the side, and lowered herself gently into the water. Dolph followed. He gave us the thumbs-up before sliding under. The flare was clearly visible, and we could see them both flippering their way down. With such a bright light below, the water no longer seemed so menacing. Twisted granite outcrops were discernible, albeit at some considerable depth.

"They're more adventurous than I am," I told Karen.

She gave me a withering look, then stripped off her T-shirt and picked up her goggles and snorkel.

"You're not going down as well?" I said.

She slid quickly over the side, cringing at the brief chill. "For God's sake, Rob ... it's just the sea! We're not in some flooded pot-hole!"

She pushed herself away, swimming out over the lagoon with dolphin-like grace. Finally, she dived under.

I looked around at Carlo, and grinned awkwardly. "It'd be ... er, it'd be marvelous if they'd put some lights down there."

"You no swim?" he asked, confused.

"Er ..." I didn't really know what to say, but was thankfully interrupted by Karen breaking the surface twenty yards away, whooping with delight. She lifted her goggles. "Oh Rob," she shouted. "You've got to come down. It's fabulous. The mineral formations ... you want to see the different colours."

She vanished again. In the deep glow of the flare, I could see her frog-kicking strongly down towards the two Germans. She'd always been a much more confident swimmer than me, but even so, I wondered at the sense in this. I put my goggles on, stood up in the boat and tentatively stuck my big toe into the water, wiggling it about. As I'd expected, it was very cold.

That was when something detonated against the back of my skull.

There was an explosion of thunder, the world turned upside down and an icy mantle of water enveloped me. In my rush of dazed thoughts, I heard a motor start up.

For seconds I was only half aware what was happening. I broke the surface with Karen's arms around me, gasping, a splitting pain at the back of my head. Everything seemed to have gone dark, and then, from the corner of my eye, I saw Carlo's arc-light fading away down the vaulted tunnel at the other side of the lagoon.

"What ... what the hell ..." I stammered, starting to tread water. Brine slopped into my face, and I coughed. Karen was still holding tightly onto me, but I eased her off. "I'm ... I'm alright!"

"What's he doing?" she said, voice shaking.

A strong light rose up from beneath. It made the blackness in the cavern press down even harder. But seconds later Dolph and Heidi emerged beside us, the flare chasing away the shadows, inviting new ones in below.

We trod water together, telling them what had happened. They were as baffled and amazed as we were. "Is this not some kind of joke?" Dolph wanted to know.

Karen, growing angrier by the minute, showed him a handful of blood from the back of my scalp. "This is no joke! I don't know what he used, but he could've killed Rob, hitting him like that."

"We shall go to the Carabinieri when we get back," Heidi said, wide-eyed.

"We have to get back first," I replied.

I don't like always being the prophet of doom, but at that moment I had to remind them all that we must have been half a mile in – and that was assuming we could find our way straight out again. Even when we reached the open sea, how far along the coast would we need to swim to find a suitable landing-point? As I remembered, it had seemed like sheer cliffs in both directions.

The flare began to fade, so Dolph tossed it away and lit another one. We were all now shivering hard. A slight swell seemed to have come from somewhere, and we felt chill currents around our feet.

"We may have another problem," Dolph said. "This cave-system is of course tidal ... it may be that with high tide, some of these passages become impassable."

The terror of that thought gripped us like a vice. "Let's go now!" I said urgently. *"Now!"*

We moved in a group towards the tunnel, at a steady breast-stroke – but not before Dolph handed us two flares each in case any of us got separated from the rest, though we were only to use them one at a time. The two Germans were proving themselves good companions – they both took off their flippers and fastened them to their harness, so as not to get too far ahead. As we swam, Karen came up beside me and asked if I was sure I could make it. I could have laughed. What choice did I have?

I could never have imagined however, just what a feat of strength and endurance was required even to make it out of that deepest chamber. Anyone who has ever tried to swim against a rising tide, even in shallow water off some pleasant beach, will know how difficult it is. For every three yards we made towards the black crevasse that was our first exit, the current pushed us back two. We gasped and grunted and strained every muscle, yet at the same time we knew we couldn't afford to overtax ourselves. Just thinking about the distance between us and the outer world was unbearable. Mind you, I doubt in that particular moment that any one of the four of us knew the real meaning of fear.

One second later, we did.

It was Karen who first saw it coming up behind us. She was in front of me and had glanced around, concerned that I was dropping behind, when I saw her face change. She gave a shrill, prolonged scream. I looked around too, and had a fleeting vision of some vast shape barrelling towards us under the surface.

Before I could cry out, a huge object – squashy, rubbery, freezing cold – bundled into me with such force that I was catapulted out of the water and into the midst of the others. I hit Dolph squarely in the back, knocking the wind from him, causing him to drop his flare, and then crashed beneath the surface.

Stunned, I gazed into the blackness below.

Through the chaos of bubbles and by the descending glow of the flare, I saw a mass of threshing, writhing limbs, a gigantic body, shapeless and black. It plunged down into the shadows, then turned sharply about in classic octopoid fashion and came straight up again. When I broke the surface, my terrified shrieks were lost amid all the others. Total darkness had descended, and I splashed around in a frenzy of foam, not knowing which direction I was swimming in.

"Twenty feet!" I shouted. "It must be twenty feet long at least!"

There was another searing light as Dolph lit a second flare, throwing everything into stark relief. We were close to the tunnel mouth, but were widely dispersed from each other, and riding a terrific swell owing to the passage of the vast body below us. Waves crashed against the rock walls. Everyone was still shouting and screaming, unable to communicate. Then the demonic thing reappeared, now in the middle of us, tentacles arching out of the water like immense saurian necks, their sucker pads the size of tea-cups. The head followed, a vast gelatinous bulk, black as coal.

The horror of that second was almost more than I could manage.

My sanity was literally teetering.

As fast as it had arrived, it re-submerged, foam hissing on the surface behind it. We began plunging towards the cave mouth. Both Dolph and Heidi had unslung their cylinders and were swimming for their lives. Karen and I hammered after them, legs thrashing. It only took seconds to reach the next cavern, but the distance across it was heartbreaking. Daylight glimmered from the four arched cave-mouths on the far side, reflecting on the water in pale blue streamers, though that made the rest of the lagoon as black as night. We each realised that we could never make it across there and at the same time outrun this thing from Hell, so when Dolph cut sideways along the cavern wall, we automatically followed.

We swam desperately but nowhere could we find a ledge, just sheer rock, thick with weed and salt. All the way we were conscious of that bottomless gulf beneath us, but we ploughed noisily on, unconcerned about stealth, anxious only to locate a footing.

Karen was the first to succeed. She gave a choked cry and began pounding ahead of us. In the flickering light, I saw a tooth of rock standing up from the water, about a yard from the cave wall. No more than one person could have stood upon it at any single time, but it might have been the tip of other rocks only just submerged. Anything would do, anything we could plant our feet on. Dolph was the first there, and he hoisted his gleaming body up effortlessly, quickly turning to help Karen. As she scrambled up, she looked back to see where I was – and let out a wild cry.

I looked over my shoulder. Heidi was just behind me, and just behind her the thing was rising again, a huge shining bulk approaching with shocking speed. Heavy tentacles rolled over it and crashed down on Heidi's head, knocking her under.

One snaked across my legs, and, with desperate shrieks, I kicked and splashed myself away from it. I could hear Dolph screaming something in German. I looked up at him. He had given Karen his flare and spear-gun and now was hunched forward, eyes straining as he scanned the frothing waters. Heidi burst out of it again, but rose up to impossible height, thick fleshy coils wrapped around her neck and torso. A gargle of agony was locked in her throat as it twisted her out of shape. For seconds it held her there, suspended above us like a criminal on the gibbet.

Dolph dived full-length at it, but more suckered limbs swung up to meet him, slamming into his head, sending him cart-wheeling into the water, and then diving down after him like snakes.

A split-second later it had vanished, an enormous swell left behind it, bubbles fizzling on the surface.

I clambered hurriedly up onto the rock, beside Karen. We were shivering violently, our teeth chattering. Karen's face had twisted with disbelieving horror as she gazed down into the ink-black water. Gradually silence descended.

"What ... what in Christ's name is it?" she finally stuttered. There was a faint, eerie echo. Suddenly we seemed terribly alone.

"Octopus," I whispered.

She looked round at me in slow disbelief. "Octopus? Are you mad!" Suddenly, unexpectedly, she began screaming. "That's no octopus, it's some kind of monster! You stupid bloody half-wit ... don't you know a monster when you see one?"

I slapped her, hard. Her head dropped and she began to sob. I was too cold and frightened to try and console her. "Giant octopus," was all I could say.

Yet as I said it, old schoolroom memories flooded back to me – about an ancient legend concerning this particular coast of Sicily. How, according to Homer's *Odyssey*, it had been haunted by a duo of terrible monsters: Scylla and Charybdis. The latter of the two was supposedly vast and lived on the seafloor, but the other was described as having many legs and arms, and living among the rocks on the shore. I shook my head in disbelief; had we uncovered an origin of that fable?

"I wonder how long it's been down here," I found myself saying.

She glanced up at me again, bewildered.

"How long do they live?" I asked no-one in particular. "A hundred years? A thousand? No wonder it's got so big ... with Carlo and his maniac friends feeding it."

The flare began to die and I hurriedly struck another. Now we only had three left between us.

"We've got to get out of here," I said quietly.

She regarded me with fascination. "And how do you propose we do that?"

"Swim. How else?"

The eyes widened in her face. "That knock on the head must have driven you mad!"

"It's the only way!" For once in my life, I felt quite definite about something. I suddenly knew for certain that to stay where we were was to *invite* death. "Nobody's going to come here, Karen. The only people who know about this place probably know about the octopus as well. That's why it's a secret,"

"You really *are* mad." She edged away from me over the rock. "I'd rather stay here and starve than chance that water again."

"Unfortunately I don't think it'll come to that. That thing's tentacles are as long as a bus ... you think it couldn't swipe us off here any time it wanted? The only reason it's not attacking now is because it's taken Dolph and Heidi back to its lair."

That thought was a hideous one and Karen groaned as she covered her face with her hands. "Oh my God. Oh God, help us, please ..."

"Which means that right now is probably the best time," I added. "Karen, this is not some *evil* creature. It's just an animal ... a thing of habit and instinct. If it's eating, it might leave us alone. It might not even notice us."

"Can't we get around the walls or something?"

It was worth a look, I had to admit. But it was impossible – sheer all the way around. And in any case, the distance would have been far too great to make with naked fingers and toes.

It took me another half-hour to talk her into coming with me. Even then, she insisted on having the spear-gun at the ready, despite the fact it would slow her down. Only the thought of being left on her own, at the mercy of the beast, made her finally leave her perch. We paddled across the lagoon as quickly and quietly as we could, all the time dreading that silky, feathery touch on the souls of our feet, not even thinking about the huge, empty spaces below. Within minutes of course, we were wheezing and grunting with the effort, but we made it to the far side without incident.

Where a new terror confronted us.

Which way?

Four different tunnels led off, all with faint glimmers of daylight filtering through them. To take the wrong one could be a potentially fatal mistake. Karen shivered violently as we trod water. None seemed familiar; none to possess a greater tidal surge than another. The wrong path might lead to a dead-end, or some wide circumnavigatory route beyond our physical endurance. Then again, it might lead us into the waiting coils of the octopus. The thought of the monster was enough to propel us into the first of the tunnels, and for several minutes we swam down a progressively lower and narrower passage until eventually we were ducking low to avoid striking our heads on the rough ceiling. We'd have had to turn back had we not suddenly broken out into another vast, church-like chamber, though this one was possessed of an ocean roll.

That brought a small sense of relief, even though it was several hundred metres to the other side. We struck out gamely; in the far corner, faint aqua-blue light rippled on the water. There had to be an exit to daylight of some sort, even if only a cleft in the rocks. But our limbs were leaden, our joints stiffening with cramp. Several times we had to stop and hang onto each other, gasping, simply floating there. We weren't half way across when my flare began to burn down. Karen struck one of hers. She was physically fitter than I was, and now that her early panic had subsided, was more her steely, reliable self. She suddenly gave a cry of joy and pointed across the water. I turned, and saw what looked like the hump of a sand-bar perhaps only fifty yards away.

"At least ... we can rest," she stammered, swimming tiredly towards it.

I was about to follow, when something occurred to me. I grabbed her ankle to stop her. I don't know much about oceanography, but I do know that sand-bars don't *rise and fall with the swell*.

It struck us simultaneously that what we were looking at was the octopus. Idling there, biding its time. I imagined two baleful eyes just above the surface, rivetted on us.

With a *whoosh* of spray, it went under.

Hysteria seized us. We began floundering towards the light, still an impossible distance away.

Only seconds passed before a tentacle tip broke the water ten yards to our left, rising slowly, cutting a V-wash behind it. With shrieks, we veered away. It followed, and with a titanic surge of water, the beast passed right under our bellies, at a depth of no more than fifteen feet. I had a vague impression of it, spread out starfish-like, skimming below us and vanishing into the opaque depths.

Then suddenly, blackness was all around us.

I called out to Karen, screamed at her to keep swimming. I received no answer, and with mounting horror, pulled up and looked around.

I was alone.

I dragged my goggles up over my eyes and plunged under. And there – far below, by the light of her receding flare, I had a last glimpse of my wife's despairing face as the horror hauled her down into the shadows. A split second before she vanished, she placed the spear-gun under her chin – and crimson flowers bloomed around her.

I crashed back up through the surface, wailing, but determined that her sacrifice would not be in vain. I swam feverishly for the light. I was close enough to it not to need another flare, which was a relief as I only had one left. By her death Karen had bought me vital time. I was certain I could make it, though I still couldn't see an exit.

Soon the light was all around me; that shimmering blue light so typical of Mediterranean sea grottos. But where was its source? Only a solid rock wall faced me. No cave mouth had come into view, no cleft or high natural window. Then I realised the truth … and my heart sank.

It came from below.

As I neared that farthest wall, I saw a great curve of rock numerous fathoms down; a huge arch from beneath which daylight was streaming, illuminating the sand and weeds on the seabed. It was a tantalising sight – so tempting to imagine that on the other side of that arch, only a minute away, there was open air and freedom. The reality of course, was that it probably led into an underwater tunnel, which might run for hundreds of yards.

I trod water frantically, tearing my hair with consternation. The only way to truly know was to try, but to try and be proved wrong was unthinkable. My problem was solved a half-second later, when a seething wave burst over me from behind.

It was the octopus.

I swam down and away as hard as I could. But it was no use. The brute was so big it seemed to fill the lagoon, and it bore down remorselessly, pressing me further and further under. Its limbs coiling around my legs and torso – one minute like soft, oozing muscle, the next like flexible iron, crushing flesh and bone with terrible force, the suckers fastening to and ripping skin so that blood was soon billowing around me.

I writhed madly, but to no avail. Its strength was awesome and unrelenting. Fleetingly I saw a white, palpitating underside, and in the middle of it a beak, an immense bird-like beak with serrated edges. But there was still something else. Something even more horrible, something which proved I was in a world of nightmares rather than reality. For an immense glassy eye opened beside me – a huge and perfect sphere, filled with opaque liquid, blinking repeatedly at me as I drowned.

And then inspiration struck. Seemingly from nowhere.

I pulled the last sodium-flare from my trunks and struck it. The glare was blinding even to me, who'd expected it. But to the giant mollusc, which normally dwelt in a world of near blackness ...

That huge alien eye rolled white with shock. And I jammed the blazing torch straight into it. The sphere burst, but I rammed the flare in all the harder, grinding it into the socket. A second later I was flung high into the air, spinning like a top, my head almost bursting with the pressure change. Below me, the monster thrashed around in an orgy of pain and bewilderment. I slammed back into the water hard, the wind knocked from me, but I was free of it. *Free of it.*

Without a second thought, I filled my lungs with air and dived down, kicking hard for the undersea arch. I have never swum harder in my life. I could feel the beast raging blindly behind me, its tentacles swarming around it. But it wouldn't catch me now, I told myself over and over. Not this time. I had foxed it.

And it seemed that I had, for in less than a minute I had passed under that great vault of rock and was arrowing upward towards a rippling surface sparkling with sunlight.

However, I was not out of the Cathedral yet. Not quite.

I broke into the air, drinking it avidly, the sounds of gulls and breakers singing in my waterlogged ears. But when I looked, I found that I was in the entrance cave, and there was no immediate escape from it. Coming in through the triangular gateway, perhaps thirty yards in front of me, was Carlo. He had cut his motor and was drifting.

I rode the swell exhausted, watching him warily. He was standing up in the prow, legs apart, scanning the surface and brandishing a long boat-hook. Scouring for incriminating evidence, I realised; shreds of bathing costume, maybe the odd snorkel or oxygen tank.

At that moment, I felt a unique kind of hatred for him. He had just condemned four people he didn't even know to an unimaginably horrible fate, and now here he was, calmly clearing up as though it were all in a day's work.

My wife ... a day's work!

I plunged across the cavern towards him at a fast crawl, my weariness forgotten. He looked round sharply, then threw the boat-hook aside and reached down to his feet. To my horror, I saw him pick up a pump-action shotgun. I recognised the model from my shooting club days back home. A Winchester twelve-gauge. In the traditional Sicilian style, it had been cut down to half its length and fastened with a shoulder strap. Such a weapon would pack devastating firepower.

He trained it on me, but I pulled my goggles up and dived under the surface, intending to swim beneath the boat and capsize it. The breakers on the cliffs thundered in my ears, so I don't know whether he fired or not, but in any case a far more terrible danger was now presenting itself. A few fathoms below me, a black shadow was spreading over the seafloor, and I saw the giant, gelatinous bulk of the octopus sliding under the arch, its tentacles still thrashing the water in a frenzy of pain.

I turned about and kicked for the open sea, acutely aware that I'd first have to pass close by Carlo's boat. My lungs were already fit to burst, but there was a terrific swell and progress was even slower than before. Having made hardly any distance, I was forced up to breathe. I emerged ten yards to the side of the outboard, gasping. Even in the echoing cave mouth, the boatman heard me and glanced around, taking aim immediately.

I ducked wildly under, knowing that from this range only immediate depth would save me, but in that same instant I found an unlikely ally. The octopus was wheeling up towards the boat, a vortex of sand and bubbles swirling around it.

I broke the surface just in time to see the treacherous Sicilian screaming and flailing as the sea began boiling around him. His flimsy vessel was knocked sideways, and he staggered and dropped the shotgun, before toppling backward over the gunwales. Mesmerised, I dived beneath and saw his fragile form kicking frantically as the monster's thick, muscular coils rolled around it.

Which meant the boat was free.

I surfaced and swam towards it, swinging myself up and over the side. Our hamper and various items of clothing and equipment were still in there. I threw them overboard for purposes of speed, before yanking several times at the ripcord of the motor. At last it churned into life, and, leaning on the tiller, I swung the outboard around. I chugged laboriously into the cave mouth, seeing sunlight, sky and blue luxurious waves beyond it. I hardly dared to believe that I had really escaped.

Which was a good thing.

For I hadn't.

I was still hanging on the tiller, willing myself to go faster, when I felt a mammoth surge in the volume of water underneath. Then the octopus struck the boat – with terrifying force, lifting it bodily into the air. Flinging it twenty or thirty yards out over the waves. It landed with a deafening splash, but miraculously stayed upright, rocking wildly. With a crack and sputter, the motor died. I was thrown down hard into the bilge, but at least I was still aboard.

To my immediate left, a great fleshy mass of tentacles went soaring past under the surface and down into the gloom. They seemed to go on forever. Fleetingly, I saw Carlo's broken corpse tangled up in them. I knew another attack was only seconds away, and scrabbled desperately for a weapon – an oar, the boat-hook, any kind of weapon. It was only by divine grace that my hand closed on the cold, smooth barrel of the shotgun.

I grabbed it and clambered to my feet, bracing my legs against the gunwales. Thanks to Carlo, the gun was already fully loaded and I pumped a shell into the breach – just as the monstrosity came ballooning up again. The turbulence threw me off-balance, and a huge rubbery head, bulbous and shining with sea-water, broke the surface. Three sinewy tentacles fell across the outboard.

I got off one good shot immediately, the barrel-load crashing clean through the first tentacle, severing it in half. Black-yellow ichor spurted from the stump, but more of the hideous arms swung up to engulf me. Timbers cracked and the boat tipped precariously, sending me heavily onto my knees. I'd pumped in another cartridge however, and this time jammed the barrel hard into the slippery, spongy mass of the creature's head. From that range the red hot payload had a ruinous effect, blowing out a huge crater of flesh perhaps a foot across, spattering me with meat and sickly fluids.

The thing literally convulsed away, its tentacles writhing madly. When it submerged, it left a cloud of ochre fluid behind it.

I knelt there, panting, the boat still swaying in the chopping waters. A second passed, before I scrambled back astern to see if I could start her up again – only to find the motor and its blades a mangled wreck.

For several minutes I was unsure what to do. Around me, the sea had gone eerily quiet. Had I killed it? I didn't know. By my understanding, I'd blown a hole clean through its brainpan; but did an octopus even have a brain? I had certainly wounded it. Even if I hadn't killed it, perhaps I'd incapacitated it to such an extent that the battle was over. Maybe even as I sat there, tilting on the gory waves, the monster was slithering painfully back into the depths of the Cathedral.

It wasn't.

A second later, it exploded out of the surf right in front of me, flopping its massive bulk onto the prow of the outboard, almost up-ending it in a single motion. As I fell headlong towards it, I opened fire with the shotgun again and again. Tentacles were torn to fragments; the sole-remaining globular eye shattered like glass; the gross, sac-like body shuddered at the repeated impact of shot, the black, rubbery hide shredding open like rotten fruit. The stench of foul fish was overpowering, but I knew that I was winning.

The boat righted itself again as the dying creature slid heavily off it, leaking vital fluids from a dozen livid wounds, each one the size of a dinner plate. I cracked the shotgun open and shovelled more cartridges into it. When I looked up again, the octopus was drifting away like a mass of pulsing seaweed, the stumps of its tentacles twitching feebly. I didn't care. I slammed several more barrel-loads into it – pulping it, eviscerating it, splattering it literally to mush.

When I'd finished and the smoke cleared, the unrecognisable heap of tattered flesh was sinking slowly from sight, trailing a gray fog of guts and blood behind it.

*

I am now adrift on the southern straits of Sicily, my vessel listing badly.

My body is covered in circular wounds from the creature's sucker pads, many of which are so deep they are still bleeding. There's the distinct possibility of blood-poisoning. Did it inject me with some sort of venom? I don't know. But that would certainly explain my exhausted, listless state. It's funny how after triumphing over inconceivable odds, in a battle for my very survival, I feel no sense of exultation or even relief. If anything, my main emotion is disgust … self-loathing for being the only survivor. My wife Karen and those other poor wretches went to deaths more horrible than a normal human could even imagine. No amount of rejoicing will change that, or expunge the ghastly memory from my mind.

And so here I am … in my flimsy, leaking boat, watching the sun descend in embers, and darkness creep on the wine-coloured sea, and I'm unsure what to do next or even how to do it. And, for the moment at least, I couldn't care less.

FROM THE HADEAN DEEP

*I*t is perhaps a sobering fact that the most terrifying monster in the whole of the world's mythology is probably real. From the earliest days of civilisation, all cultures on this planet with a sea-going tradition have spoken of gigantic, multi-armed sea-beasts – from Scylla of the Greeks, to Hafgufa and Lynbakr of the Norse – which would rise from the stormy ocean and take down entire ships, and in the process prove impregnable to human weaponry.

Of course the generic term for this unstoppable devil fish is 'kraken', a word which originated in medieval Scandinavian sagas, though it entered more common usage when first included in a scientific document of the 17th century, in which the beast was described as being a mile in length and, when it wasn't lying on the bed of the Greenland Sea awaiting its next prey, floating on the surface, sometimes being mistaken for an island by mariners looking to put ashore and subsequently claiming many more lives by accident rather than design.

In modern times the most likely candidate to have been so misidentified in antiquity is either Architeuthis, better known as the 'giant squid', which can grow to 46 feet in length, or even more likely, Mesonychoteuthis, the 'colossal squid', which has been known to reach 60 feet. Science was well aware of these creatures long before 2004, when a Japanese underwater research team first filmed a live giant squid in its natural habitat, 3,000 feet down off the Ogasawara island chain, or even more sensationally in 2007, when a New Zealand factory ship accidentally snared one in the freezing waters of the Ross Sea – in the latter case, the entire encounter was caught on camera, and the world watched agog as the crew struggled to overpower the aquatic giant while it thrashed and struggled on their lines.

However, big though they were, in neither of these cases were the animals of sufficient size to pose a serious threat to modern vessels, or even, one might think, to well-built ships of an older vintage – which seems to contradict the numerous frightening stories that dock tavern seadogs have passed down through the ages. So is there a chance that a vastly more stupendous squid still lurks beyond the known limits of ocean science?

Not everyone discounts the possibility.

In 1802, French malacologist Pierre Dénys de Montfort recounted the tale of a merchant ship, which the previous year had been attacked just off the coast of Angola with massive loss of life as

216

sailors fell screaming through the splintering decks into the clutches of a gargantuan beaked mollusc whose tentacles reached higher than the mizzen mast. A similar fate had allegedly befallen other smaller craft of the 17th and 18th centuries, wild-eyed survivors spreading hair-raising tales that would later inspire the vivid sequence in Jules Verne's novel 'Twenty Thousand Leagues Under The Sea' (published in 1870) in which Captain Nemo leads the fight against a whole school of immense 'cuttlefish' (giant squid). But evidence has emerged in more recent times too. In 1924, a rotted, tentacled carcass grounded itself on the shores of Natal, South Africa, measuring 115 feet in length; a couple of years earlier, a similar 80 foot relic had been found on a beach in New Foundland. During World War Two, crewmen of a US warship stationed in the Maldives reported a squid floating alongside them in harbour which was at least 175 feet long. More frightening still, circular scarring has been identified on the hides of sperm whales and even the underside hulls of large battleships, which implied suckers at least two feet in diameter – and these could only belong to a squid of 300 feet or more.

The cryptozoological community is certainly impressed by these calculations, even if ocean biologists are hesitant to endorse them. The crypto crowd points out that the giant squid itself, though guessed about from the fragments of it that occasionally washed up, officially existed outside science until as recently as the early 20th century. Part of the reason for this is the astonishing depth at which the creature normally dwells. Though it ranges through all the oceans of the world and evidently surfaces now and then, it prefers the abyss – that sunless Hadean void between 3,000 and 10,000 feet in depth, where the water is ice-cold and the crushing pressure intolerable for anything not born and bred there, but where an absence of vegetation means the entire population consists of predators, and, thanks to the factor of 'deep see gigantism', outsize predators at that.

At the end of the day, science cannot deny the existence of the kraken, and in fact will not try. We know its smaller cousins thrive and multiply in those terrible depths; we also know that the realm it calls its own is over 90 percent unexplored and so hostile to normal life that many accepted rules of the natural world no longer apply.

The truth is certainly out there. Just pray you never encounter it.

HUSHED WILL BE ALL MURMURS
Adam Golaski

S trings, *Tabula Rasa* at the right ear; sirens and horns, close at the left. A blank page to walk across.

Two men drag a rowboat. Their footprints are erased by the boat-hull. Half-way to the shore, Andrew quits. "Okay?" Joseph asks. Andrew nods. "Okay," Joseph says. He doubles his effort toward the shore. Andrew offers to carry the oilskin satchel. Joseph stops, adjusts the strap, says, "No." The fog is empty, itself the terror.

Endless fog. From the bow of the ten-foot aluminum boat the stern is invisible in it. Joseph relies on sound to guide him to the shore, but the downward slope of the beach, too – sound, in this fog, is often misleading. The bell-ring from the buoy could be in front or behind. Andrew can't hear anymore. If he does not stay close to the boat, he will be lost.

A wave breaks over Joseph's shoes – he's startled, relieved. He pulls the boat into the water, stands calf-deep, holds the boat steady as he can for Andrew. The boat knocks against Joseph's legs; he is swayed by the waves.

"This air," he says. "I remember ..." Memory, all there is. A cold day at the beach with his young mother. So much rot. His mother's seaweed-creature joke turned briefly frightening when a bright blue crab shook free. She screamed. Terror over, laughter. Flavored ice. Neither men take especial pleasure in their memories.

Joseph fantasises he might row himself and his friend out of the fog. What he did for his family, not a mercy at all.

If the fog were to lift, what would be the world?

A fantasy only.

Andrew heaves himself into the boat. Joseph waits for Andrew to get situated. "Okay," Andrew says; Joseph lingers in the water – this is what the ocean feels like, he thinks, then steps into the boat, picks up the oars and rows.

Andrew says, "I'm near stone today." He means deaf. His hearing, it comes and goes – before the fog, doctors tried to figure out why. After, Andrew's loss just another.

"Nothing to hear," Joseph shouts.

Not true, Andrew thinks: if only water against the boat, the thump of Joseph's boots (muffled by the deep beneath), the breeze

Andrew feels, his own goddamn thoughts free from incessant howl – just another problem.

Joseph rows. Past the first buoy, the next.

Joseph can't row anymore. "Now?" he asks.

"Catch your breath," Andrew says.

"All this fog – " Andrew gestures with his arms – "came from the head of one man."

Joseph listens.

Andrew, who cannot hear himself speak, says …

*

From the jetty to the cliff, a wavering line of frozen sea foam. A man in his middle age descended a short set of steps onto detritus, mostly rocks. A pink crab claw and carapace, the brown glass bottom of a beer bottle. He climbed over the boulders of the jetty – he was rather agile, though hardly 'in shape'. Gulls bobbed. Knots of rockweed crackled underfoot. He wasn't at the little beach for any good reason, a canceled appointment, it was on the way, sort of. He pictured himself wind-swept and contemplative. Wind-swept indeed. Too cold for contemplation. His thoughts, though all over the place, all day inevitably lead to a memory, recently recalled: to Annalisa, a once-crush from high school, to their only date. It was a date, he realised in retrospect, but then, thirty-two years ago, when she leaned over for a kiss, he didn't know what to do, and simply patted her on the head, a reaction that today leaves him flush with embarrassment.

He walked with his head down. The water ate at the shore and left behind plateaus of wet sand which froze into thin wafers. He kicked them apart with his shoes – stopped, stood hands in pockets and looked out across the bay. In the shallows, the water was pale green, like a bit of sea glass, he thought. How clever of me to think so, he thought. The sky was overcast – blank, he thought. A wind brought tears to his eyes – he turned his back to it, and a black stone on the beach caught his eye.

He ambled toward the stone. It appeared to be covered in seaweed. From its direction came an odor of rot, which, the man did not realize, should not be emitted from an object that must be frozen. He was startled when he understood it was hair, not seaweed. A dead animal. Not a dead animal. A human head. Set on the sand.

He stumbled, he crab-walked backward, away, a comic spectacle for the gulls and the wind. He should call the police, he thought, and he might've done, had Annalisa's head not opened its eyes. He sat on his ass.

"Free me," said Annalisa's head.

He said not a word.

The flesh on Annalisa's head fell off, left muscle, bone; her hair slipped off with her scalp. He blinked, and her flesh was restored.

"David," Annalisa's head said. "Free me."

"How?" A breath, hardly spoken. She offered no guidance. So he did not a thing. He could pat the top of her head. I'm a jackass, he thought. The cancelled appointment, he thought. It wouldn't have made a difference. He crawled to Annalisa's head and touched the sand beneath her chin. Annalisa's head opened its eyes. She's buried to her neck, he thought, I need to dig her out. Timid, he brushed the cold sand from around her.

"My lips," said Annalisa's head.

He touched her lips with a sandy finger. She giggled! And her head grew.

"My lips," she said.

Again he touched her lips – she touched his fingertip with her tongue.

"Annalisa," he said.

"My lips," she said.

He touched, he lingered, she bit.

"Hey!" He yanked his hand back, but Annalisa's head didn't let go so easily; she kept a nubbin of flesh between her white teeth and a smear of blood on her cheek.

"What was that for?" he asked.

Annalisa's head fell over in the sand. She's not buried to her neck, he realised. Her body's not attached to her head, he thought, a thought that sucked the pain from his finger. That thought, and the fact of Annalisa's growing head. In all its lovely proportion, the teenage head of Annalisa grew.

David, finger in mouth like an insecure child, saw only the growing head before him, and not the dramatic waves in the otherwise calm bay, nor noticed the circle of froth that took shape a few yards from the shore. Annalisa's head grew. In the midst of the froth emerged two hills – shoulders, of course, each white as Pelops's.

The head, grown big as David, muttered excitement, its eyes rolled madly, its ears twitched beneath its lustrous hair. Behind it, the body emerged, dripping, Annalisa's teenage body, naked as David had never seen it but in his most lurid fantasies, and tall as the lighthouse perched a mile off-shore. When David looked at her body as it walked out of the water, he was blinded by its whiteness except – all he could look at was her pubic hair, wet, curled to a black hook between her legs.

With dignity, the body bent at its waist and reached for its head, which it lifted to its trunk. Annalisa, as David remembered her, but giant. With a gesture, she indicated he should take off his coat. He did. She pointed to his pants. Oh, he thought, and he took off his pants. Once more she gestured, and he nodded, he understood, he took off his clothes, all of them – are we going to have sex? he wondered.

"Come inside," said her head.

"How?"

A colossal eel poured forth from her vagina, swam down her leg and slipped into the sea.

Annalisa considered his question. She took a step and stood over him. David's world was her genitalia. Just as it occurred to him he might be expected to climb her leg and to crawl inside, another eel issued forth – it dropped onto David and knocked the wind from his lungs with its icy weight. She knelt, picked up the eel and tossed it onto the snow where it seemed to David to sizzle; he felt an intense heat from her vagina.

"Why not kiss me now?" she asked.

He opened his mouth – he must've meant to speak – and she opened her mouth – she lifted him from the beach and ate him.

The eel dissolved. A black line of jelly in the snow.

Annalisa, whole and sated, returned to the sea.

Snow fell. The tide rose, left foam to freeze at the snow-line. Moon. Sunrise. Annalisa again emerged from the sea. She squatted on the beach and with a single push birthed a human skull. She returned to the sea.

A gull landed on the skull, but squawked and flew away when, from the eyes and mouth fog poured.

*

"Why?" asks Joseph.

"Why anything?" Andrew says. "Why not nothing? Why is the way of the world." Andrew touches the oilskin satchel. "Okay?"

Joseph takes the satchel and removes from it a revolver. He shoots Andrew in the head. He shoots himself.

From their wounds, fog.

MER-KILLERS

All the mythologies on Earth include fascinating tales of sea-beings, intelligent aquatic humanoids, often with fishlike appendages, who have watched our development on land from their secret realm beneath the waves, and have occasionally, for better or worse, sought to make contact with us.

The explanations behind this are legion and often self-contradictory. For example, a modern theory that the iconic mermaid – a desirable female who lolls sensually on coastal rocks, calling to men and swishing her sinuous tail – is a contrivance of the medieval Church, a lesson concerning the eroticism and evil of womankind, is basically false. Alluring but dangerous creatures that were half-woman and half-fish, or indeed half-man and half-fish, date far into the pre-Christian past. From the nereids and tritons of the ancient Greeks to the havman of the Vikings and the ningyo of ancient Japan, Man managed to convince himself that a strange species of sea-folk – mysterious, handsome, superficially playful but inherently deceitful – were never far from our shores.

But it was in relatively recent times that the image we are familiar with today was constructed. In the 19ᵗʰ century, a plethora of romantic artworks and children's fairy tales softened the legend, painting an image of the mermaid as a poor mute creature, beautiful and lovelorn, yearning for a happier existence on dry land (something that exists nowhere at all in the original pantheon of myths). Another aspect of antique mermaid lore removed during this Victorian 'makeover' was her innate deadliness. Because in all the older sources, the mermaid is a predator.

One of the best examples of this can be found in the Celtic murúch or merrow, a scheming green-haired 'sea-maiden' who in the earliest tales of the Irish and Scottish would prey on sailors, lulling them to sleep with her magical music and then dragging them to the ocean's depths, where they would drown and be eaten. One ugly folk tale, fictionalised by Irish romanticist Thomas Keightley but native to Cork and Wicklow before Keightley was even born, maintains that whatever the fate of these unfortunate victims' mortal remains, their souls would also be captured by the merrow and kept in cages on the ocean floor with no possibility of their ever being reprieved – which achieved the near-impossible feat in the early days of sail of making a long sea voyage even more frightening than it already was.

However, the most terrifying of all the world's mermaid myths originates in the Mediterranean, and was made famous by Homer in his epic poem, 'The Odyssey', first penned around 800 BC, though this legendary monster was famous in that region long before then.

Debate still rages as to whether the dreaded Sirens were actually mermaids at all, some scholars pointing to their habit of awaiting their prey on coastal rocks and never actually swimming. But their feminine allure, their angelic singing, the fact they were at least partially aquatic in appearance, and the sole purpose of their existence – to attract men and eat them, cements them firmly into the mermaid tradition as it was understood in the Ancient World.

Both Greek and Roman authors wrote extensively about the Sirens, treating them as real beings and an enduring peril in the Tyrrhenian Sea, which lies between modern-day Sardinia and south-western Italy. Their lair was a pile of isolated rocks known as Sirenum Scopuli, and their modus operandi was to sing to passing ships in such delectable fashion that these craft, their crews entranced, would steer too close and be wrecked on hidden reefs. All the dead who were washed ashore, along with any unfortunate survivors, would then be seized on by the Sirens and greedily devoured.

The Sirens themselves were said to be three in number, their names Peisinoe, Aglaope, and Thelxiepeia, and in some accounts they were daughters to the sea god Phorcys. More importantly though, there are no romantic diversions in this tale. They were merciless, feasting on shiploads of men for centuries. Hideous descriptions are given of their bone-strewn habitat. In 'The Odyssey', the enchantress Circe speaks of them as inhabiting an inland meadow surrounded by hundreds of rotting, half-eaten corpses. They were also said to be invincible. Many famous personages encountered them, among these Jason, Orpheus and Odysseus, though the only victory these resourceful heroes ever managed was to survive, Odysseus deliberately exposing himself to the Siren song by tying himself to the mainmast while his men, unable to hear because their ears were plugged with beeswax, rowed on. Allegedly, the wily skipper almost went mad with desire, and it was months before he recovered (though one post-Homeric source tells how the Sirens themselves died shortly afterwards, unable to live with their grief at having failed to lure what would have been the greatest prize of all).

Theories abound as to the origins of the Siren story, ranging from a rumour that in tribal days Sicilian shoreline brothels would advertise themselves with attractive music and female singing (and perhaps robbery and murder would follow), to a belief espoused by

17th century writers Cornelius a Lapide and Antonio de Lorea that the Sirens were once real creatures, possibly a kind of lesser fallen angel whose new role was to harm Man physically.

But when it comes to true mermaid horror, the crème de la crème comes not from the distant past but from the 21st century.

In May 2012, the Discovery Channel screened a sensationalist docu-fiction called 'Mermaids: The Body Found', which implied that a team of US scientists had uncovered fossil and video evidence of an entire civilisation of fish-tailed humanoids, which had evolved under the ocean on a parallel track to their cousins on land. Though a drama rather than a real documentary, it briefly reignited pseudo-scientific interest in the concept of the so-called 'aquatic ape'. As before, in the 1960s, all such proposals were finally killed during the peer review process, one paleoanthropological group ending the debate by creating a virtual impression of what a real-life mermaid would have to look like in order to survive the deep ocean: a vast, blubbery monstrosity, flippered and grotesquely bloated, with barely recognisable human features and a blowhole in the top of its head. But at least this abomination would have one thing in common with the femme fatales of ancient myth: it would be a carnivore, a voracious hunter and eater of any human being unfortunate enough to swim into its path.

Think on that the next time you're taking a dip in the sea.

AND THIS IS WHERE WE FALTER
Robert Shearman

i

The church sits high on the cliff top, and by all accounts is an impressive sight far out to sea. So I am told. I have never been to sea. A sailor once, I can't remember his name, but I'm sure he would be dead now, he said to me that seeing the little spire come into view as he neared land was the point he'd allow himself to believe he'd safely reached home. It seemed quite a touching thing to say, or so I thought at first – but he went on to tell me what really stood out were all the gravestones studded along the cliff like teeth. "Enormous teeth, biting into the grass!" he said, and then he laughed. I didn't quite know what to make of that.

Matthew said not long ago that he hates digging graves on the cliff. He said that he's always afraid that he'll dig that bit too deep, and that he'll inadvertently chop right through the whole escarpment, and bring it all crashing down into the sea – the cliff face, Matthew, the church, everything. I think Matthew would have to dig a lot harder and a lot deeper to do any serious damage to the cliff, and if anything, he'd been getting lazy of late. Six feet deep, I tell him, that's what people expect, that's the Christian way. Some of his recent graves have been very shallow, you can see the mourners exchanging disapproving glances as the coffin is lowered inside, it's not right. I should reprimand Matthew, but I haven't the heart to do so, he's been here for years. Why replace him when he'll probably die himself soon? It'd seem unkind.

The church was built in the fourteenth century. It's not a pretty church, but it does its job, and I'm fond of it, and I like to think that my parishioners are too. The people in this village are of the sea, and they go back generations – sailors or fishermen for the most part, and like the church they're simple and weather-beaten folk, and they won't thank you for politeness and they won't thank you for frills. And if it's the church they spy when they're out at sea, then it should present itself to them honestly – it should be a blunt and plain church. Because life isn't easy, and it never was, and it's not the church's job to pretend otherwise.

I don't know whether my father was disappointed in me. I imagine he was. He was not the sort to have said so. He was never a kindly man, but he was never cruel, neither by hand nor by tongue.

225

He was a fisherman. His father was a fisherman too. *His* father had been an honest to God sailor, had transported teas and spices from as far as the Orient. And I know I had a great great-uncle who had been in the Navy and fought the Dutch. A whole ancestry of men who lived upon the waves, my father had liked to say there was salt water in our veins. Though it must be said there's something less glamorous about being a fisherman than being a merchant sailor or a marine, I rather fancied that the salt water had been thinning somewhat as the years went by. As for me, I was expected to be a fisherman too. I refused. From childhood I refused, I would scream if Father took me to his boat, I'd scream if I so much as stood at the harbour and looked out to sea. That huge unending mass of it. Father said, well, if I wasn't going to sea, I'd either starve or end up in the Church – and I think he meant it as a joke, but even so, I followed his advice, and took the latter option.

They assume I'm afraid of drowning. But it isn't drowning. I have seen many a drowned man, and they look hideous, of course, all bloated and fish-pecked. But you have to remember by the time they get to me and the eternal absolution I can grant them, they may well have been under the water several days. I think, on balance, drowning is rather a peaceful way to go. There must be a point where you just stop struggling. Where you can let the stronger force win, and with no shame, or regret, or loss of pride. That final letting go, it must be a comfort of sorts.

I have only been in a boat once as an adult, and it did not go well. And the embarrassment was, it was not even at sea! I had taken Clemence Lincoln to the park in F___; it was a train ride away, and she had never been, and nor had I, and I suppose I was trying to impress her – she was the first girl who had ever looked at me, and I thought she was beautiful, and I couldn't quite work out what on earth she could see in *me*. (Looking back, I still can't. I should have asked her at the time. Ah well!) F___ is a very genteel town, and I felt I stuck out there like a sore thumb, but I was dressed up smart as best I could, and Clemence was wearing a bonnet I recall, and I hadn't seen it before, and she looked every inch the lady. "Look!" she said, and she took my arm. "Pleasure boats, on the pond!" And there were all these dapper young men in waistcoats and straw hats, I have never for the life of me seen the purpose of a straw hat. And they were rowing their ladies, they were pulling on the oars whilst the ladies laid back, they looked so gallant, they looked so proud. I hesitated, of course, but Clemence had taken my arm in her excitement, and I had been attempting to contrive some little physical contact of that nature all afternoon, and I was reluctant to squander it now. She picked a boat. I paid the man. We embarked. Straight away I knew something was wrong. It was the way that the boat bobbed on the surface of the water. There was nothing solid to it – I had never quite realised that before – that the water was so infirm and we could slide through it at any moment, we *should* slide through if gravity had its way, and it was only a few planks of rude wood that kept us from defying it – it sounds ridiculous, because the pond was only a few feet deep, but I felt a sense of vertigo far keener than I had ever experienced on the cliff edge, even as I stood right at the precipice, even as I dared myself to look down. The bobbing of the boat, the little swell caused by the other boats rowing past, the way it made us rock back and forth. There is no control here, I thought, you have lost control – nothing beneath you is real, everything you rely upon has gone. (How could I ever have coped with a real wave on the sea? How could anyone?) And Clemence didn't seem to realise my discomfort, she was laughing and being silly, and I had wanted that ease all day long but not like this, not *now* – she wasn't keeping still, she was rocking the boat all the more. I snapped at her, I know. I told her, *begged* her, to stop playing the stupid clown. To be still. To *stop*. I asked her why she had to make things so much worse. Why did she make me feel so bad, why did she make all my thoughts so very topsy-turvy? And I lost one of the oars, I think. And I panicked. I admit it. All that bobbing, we had no power against the whims of the water. We were not safe. The boat gave us the *illusion* of safety, and isn't that worse? I think it is worse. And I was now the one who was rocking the boat, I was standing up, I was climbing out. Better that I stand in the middle of the pond with my feet on solid ground than be at the mercy of something so inconstant. I turned the boat over. I didn't mean to. I was standing in a shallow pond with the water barely higher than my knees, and even children were rowing past, and were laughing, and the woman I loved (yes, I loved her) was lying drenched in the water. I helped her up. She was crying. I was embarrassed. I'm rather afraid I slapped her.

Clemence Lincoln and her family moved away from the village shortly afterwards, though that had nothing to do with me, her father had found another job elsewhere, I think in a shop? Not many people left the village. I know I was jealous.

I was not a vicar then, of course. It was just as well. The thought of a vicar standing in a pond, it's barely conceivable!

I do not like to lose control. I cannot stomach more than a single tankard of ale (I have to drink a little, the men here will not trust you if you do not drink). After that, I can feel my legs wobble beneath me, and my head begins to swim, and it's like I'm bobbing about on that pond again. Up and down, from side to side. Some men like to lose control. Many seek to. I do not. Emphatically, I do not.

The wind cuts a pace on the cliffs at night, and the way it whips between the gravestones can sound like howling. The children like to play up there at night and pretend they hear ghosts. Matthew says I should chase them away, but there's no harm in it. The view out at the sea is breathtaking, but who enjoys the view when you are a child? They need to play, and there's nothing to do in the village, except grow old and go out to sea. Let them have their fun, I say. Let them have their ghosts. It does no harm to anyone.

*

I have long been sensitive to the vagaries of the weather, I have known even the change of breeze to affect me most ominously! – but, even so, I somehow slept through that dreadful storm that brought my great-grandfather back to the surface.

By the time Matthew woke me, banging on my front door, the weather was calm (or as calm as it ever gets here), and there was no sign of the storm he was babbling about, and I assumed though it was early morning that my sexton was drunk. He may even have been so. I could smell liquor on his breath. But he nonetheless persuaded me that something was awry, and that I should dress and follow him to the churchyard directly.

An oak tree had fallen in the night. I felt strangely sorry for it lying there, dead – it was older than anyone buried beneath it. It was a mercy that it had not fallen upon the church itself – and there was more mercy yet that no other trees had been brought down with it. The only damage was the pit that had been gouged out of the grass – that, and the single coffin that was clutched in the exposed roots.

I told the sexton I didn't understand what the problem was. The coffin would have to be buried again, and the pit filled in. It wouldn't be hard to rebury the coffin. The hole was already there without the digging, and deeper than the six feet he usually shirked so blatantly.

"The coffin is split open," he said. "You can see it." The sides were smashed, and the lid hung loose from its hinges. "And there's something else." He climbed down amongst the roots, reached out for my hand so I would follow. In spite of myself, I did.

You can set a gravestone as a marker, but the truth is, once the coffins are in the ground, they soon become anonymous. All cramped for space beneath our feet. And so it should be – from dust we are made, and as dust we return, and in my opinion, giving identity to the scraps of the body that escape decomposition is not only a meaningless pursuit but an arrogant one. Let the gravestones do their work – and clear off the mildew so you can read the names clearly, and leave flowers by their side for remembrance if you must. But let's not pretend that what happens to our flesh after death has much to do with us any longer, let's set all that aside. I was surprised that the broken coffin Matthew showed me had a brass plaque upon its lid – that was very rare, and expensive, and I would certainly have dissuaded any widow from purchasing such a thing had this body been interred when I was vicar. The coffin was of good hard teak, not the cheap planks that were the common lot for dead fishermen. This had been a gentleman's coffin, maybe, or a landowner – but no one owned land hereabouts, what was the point of owing land when the sea was where you made your fortune?

I read the plaque. I was staggered when I recognised the surname as my own – and the first name, Ezekiel, that had been my great-grandfather's. A man, or so I had understood, of no great repute, of no wealth, of no distinction whatsoever.

"If we need a new coffin," said Matthew, "then the family will have to foot the bill." And there was something sly about the way he said it, was he mocking me? I think he was.

"Pull the bits of coffin free," I said. "Carefully, so we can gather the remains." And so Matthew got right down into the soil, with very bad grace, and heaved away at the wood. I admit, I felt a strange thrill, anticipating what it would be like to see even a small part of my ancestor's remains. I know I believe that the dead should be anonymous, but what of that? I had never met him, and he knew nothing of me, we were separated by over a century, but there was still kinship there, I felt, of a sort. He had lived so that my grandfather might live, and grandfather for my father, and father for me – my life was a consequence of his, and my existence gave his life purpose. And I vowed for respect's sake that I would give Ezekiel a decent burial, he deserved that. A plain coffin, of course, but maybe we could preserve the lid.

There were no bones inside to gather. No skeleton, no grinning skull. Not even, as far as I could tell, any dust – maybe it had run out when the coffin had been smashed, maybe all that was left of my great-grandfather had been blown out to sea in the storm. And maybe that was as it should be.

Matthew was open-mouthed in confusion, as if he couldn't understand the magic of a long dead body disappearing into thin air – he was used to dealing with the newly dead, of course, that are as solid and as fat as the living, and whatever happened to them afterwards was perhaps a mystery. I was kind to him. I wanted to laugh, the fellow did goggle so! "It's all right," I told him. "There's no need for further work. Let the dead rest in peace." – But he said, "No, sir, no, it's not that. Look!" And with a strength I thought had long since dissipated with age and drink, he grasped hold of the loose coffin lid, he wrestled with it for a moment in his arms, and he turned it over to show me.

The first thing that was curious about the carvings in the underside of that coffin lid was how precise they were. The marks were so tiny that at first I thought them the work of termites – but there were patterns to the etching, and I quickly realised this was intelligent design. And as I peered closer I could see that these repeated patterns were letters of the alphabet, and that the letters were collected together in words.

As vicar I have heard all sorts of graveyard tales. Of coffins opened up years after burial, and the horrors revealed within. Of men who had been buried alive, and woken up beneath the ground, and in their suffocating panic cried out for help. And if no one could hear you calling, what then? Would you scratch at the lid just above your face with your fingernails? Would you scratch out a last desperate message before the air ran out? – No, of course not. These were spook tales for children. The fact is, even if you *did* awake in a coffin, not only would there be no air, there would be no light. And there would be no room. You wouldn't have the space to move your hand up to the lid pressing down upon you, you would be locked fast into a world that was entirely tight and dark and there you would perish.

The words that my great-grandfather had carved into the lid (I assumed it was his handiwork) were not done in blindness, nor in desperation. The lettering was so small that I could barely read it, but it was composed in considered thought, and I could see that the essay (for that's what it was! This was long enough to be a damned essay!) was peppered with punctuation. Punctuation! What dying man gasping for air bothers with semicolons, of all things! The handwriting seemed to flow easily, as if it had been written by quill, not scratched into heavy wood – every 'i' was dotted, every 't' was crossed, and there was a silly flourish to the tails of the 'f's and 'g's that looked positively foppish.

And what was still more astonishing than this – than the deliberation of the words, and the intricacy with which they had been carved – what was more astonishing still, was that they filled the entire coffin lid. From the head to the toe, every single inch of the wood was taken up with writing, there was not a gap wasted. The impossibility of it – into my head swum the sudden vision of my ancestor contorting his body into every conceivable direction so he could continue with his scribbling, cracking bones to do it,

230

cracking his spine as he sat up in a space that could never allow him to sit up, cracking his very neck as he somehow reached down to his feet. I had the image of a man breaking every single solid part of his body and turning it into something fluid. Something like soup.

"Did you do this?" I demanded of Matthew. "Is this your work?" But the man was terrified, he could see the impossibility of it as well as I – and besides, he couldn't write. "You tell no one about this!" I said. "You tell no one!"

I ordered Matthew to bring the coffin lid to the vicarage where I could peruse it more carefully, but he refused. He ran. I was angry then, but I no longer blame him. I heaved it out of the pit alone. Alone I got it home, I dragged it back along the cliffs. I got it safely indoors where nobody but me could see, and I laid it on the floor of my study, and I fetched a light and the strongest of my spectacles, and I began to read.

I picked out the words the best I could. It was slow going. It took me all day, but not once did I rise from the floor, not once did I think to sleep or eat.

*The weather in Shanghai is good, & the master has secured the consignment of tea without the anticipated difficulty. ** The Chinees helped us to load the cargo. I like the Chinee for all that he is small & strange; he smiles & he is a hard worker & the work was finished swiftly. ** 5,000 crates of tea, & the ship sank deeper into the water with the weight. I like a good full ship, I like to see the water level rise higher up the side of the hull, then we are at one with the water & I feel closer to the sea.*

*

The weather in Shanghai is good, and the master has secured the consignment of tea without the anticipated difficulty.

The Chinees helped us to load the cargo. I like the Chinee for all that he is small and strange; he smiles and he is a hard worker and the work was finished swiftly.

Five thousand crates of tea, and the ship sank deeper into the water with the weight. I like a good full ship, I like to see the water level rise higher up the side of the hull, then we are at one with the water and I feel closer to the sea.

The first mate pulls me aside. Look, he says, there's something I want you to tell the men. He knows I have the ear of the men, if there's something to tell it had best be done by me. I have made this journey five times and made an enemy of no man yet.

He says that we will be joined by two passengers for the journey back to England. I am that surprised at that, we've never taken passengers before, and the master is not the type. The first mate shrugs at my surprise, says it has nothing to do with him. I ask where they will sleep, because I do not think the crew will like it if we have strangers to bunk with; the crew is twenty-six men strong already, we have no room for others; the first mate tells me not to worry. Our guests will sleep below decks with the cargo. I look surprised again, because that would hardly be a comfortable arrangement, and the first mate is annoyed and repeats it is nothing to do with him. Nor me besides. Our guests want to sleep below decks. This they have specifically requested, and no matter there's no sense to it.

Are they Chinees, I ask, and no, turns out they're regular folk like him and me.

I tell the crew, and there is a little curiosity, but no one seems alarmed. The men are full of the journey ahead, of the families they have waiting home, of the money they will be collecting there. They leave us alone, we leave them alone, that's what they say. I explain that the passengers do not want to be seen and that they will embark the ship only at the dead of night and that they will be led below deck directly and that we will have no further dealings with them. One man to lead them aboard tonight, and that is it, and that man will be me, does anyone have objections to that? There are no objections. Bobby can't understand why British men would be boarding a ship for Great Britain, wouldn't they already be in Great Britain to start with? He is properly confused. He is an apprentice and wants one day to be an officer, but I think it unlikely, he has no brains and his head is full of sawdust.

I meet the passengers on the quay past midnight. The moon is hidden by cloud, I find them with a candle. The larger man does all the talking. I'll carry this bag, he says, you may take the others. I take him for a butler, he tells me he is employed as secretary to the silent man he refers to as 'our mutual master'. I do not like that. This man is not my master. For all I carry his luggage. I choose my masters. Don't look at him! – snaps the secretary, but I steal a glance anyway, bundled up as he is, and he looks like a man in his twenties, and handsome too, lordly even, the very sort who might indeed have a secretary.

I lead them on to the ship. As ordered, my crew keep themselves scarce. I take them to the lower deck, and promise that food will be left for them at the top of the stairs each day. Pea soup and salt pork one day, salt pork and bread the next, potato pie at weekends. The secretary seems irritated by the detail, yes, yes, yes, he says. I find them blankets to sleep on amongst the tea chests, I leave them the candle but tell them not to use it once the ship is underway.

It feels to me a hideous place to sleep – it is hot, and cramped, and dark. I even feel sorry for them. And I rather expect them to think better once they see their quarters. But none of that – the secretary takes out a purse, and counts out three gold sovereigns, and drops them into my hand as if they were mere coppers, and tells me to leave them. So I do.

We set sail for Southampton the next morning.

True to our word, we do not see our passengers. But we talk about them. Some say they are spies sent by the king to overthrow the Chinese monarchy. Others claim that the lordly one is royalty himself and fleeing exile. There's talk that the bosun heard from the second mate heard from the captain himself that the man's a gambler, and he cheated the Devil at cards, and now he's escaping with his winnings. It says much that this last story is the most credible.

Either way, no one can believe the strangers can stay cooped below deck forever, and we take bets on how long it'll take for them to crack and break out to the surface. Because it's not just the Devil who likes to gamble, and the voyage is so very long.

It happens in the third week.

I am on deck, I see it all. The sea is a little rough, the ship pitches in all directions. We think at first it is this that smokes them out! For here he is, our mystery man, his arms flung out wildly, gulping at the air, seeming to suck in all the air there is and suck in more besides. And then running to the side. And it makes us laugh, because it is such sport to see a little lordling puking out his guts, who wouldn't laugh at that?

And now he's starboard, staring back at the sea, staring back toward Shanghai as if he wishes he'd never left it. And he screams. I hear it piercing above the wind. Those who hear it stop laughing. This isn't sickness. Or, if it's sickness, it's something worse than a stomach rolling upon the waves. It's a sickness of the head.

The secretary is on deck now too, chasing after his master. No, sir! he cries. No, sir! No, sir! Like a mantra. Like it'll do any good. Because his master is raving now. He shouts, Take it then! Take it all! And he is flinging money into the sea – gold coins mostly, but banknotes too. More money than I've ever seen, or are ever likely to have seen, or will ever see now – and that's true for all of us, and I can see from the crew how some itch to dive overboard straight after it all.

The secretary has reached him, he has grabbed him. He is the stronger, but still he finds him hard to subdue. Some of us at last snap into action, we grab at the man too. I'm not sure we save any of his money. And I hate the touch of the man. He is warm and sticky like oil. We turn him around. We look upon him. And his skin is yellow like a Chinee. Except not like a Chinee neither, their skin is meant to be yellow, that's who they are and we cannot blame them – but the yellow of this man seems to shine from beneath his skin, like it's something thick and evil that's rising up to the surface, and when it does it's going to burn that skin up, it's going to burn through his mouth and burn through his face and burn through his wild darting eyes.

Did I say he was a young man? This is not a young man. This is a man who has lived full lifetimes, and suffered every one.

He is quiet now. The fight has gone out of him. We let go. He slumps. The secretary escorts him back to the cargo hold.

We want to check on the passenger and see that he's well, or as well as can be wished for, and I and Billy and William Bates try to go below a while later. But the secretary bars our access. He says what has happened on deck is a regrettable aberration, and we shall ignore it, and carry on as before, and that he bids us good day.

That is the first night we lose the wind. And we think no alarm of it, we have been riding fast and making good time. But by morning we yet are still, and the sea is as flat as a millpond. We raise all the sails high to the sky, but there is not a breath of air in it.

I have been in the doldrums many a time, but never like this. The stillness hangs upon us heavy, you can feel the weight of it. Three full days we are without movement, no matter what the captain exhorts us to do, and there is no motion to the sea neither, not a wave, it is unnatural. And the sun beats down so hard. And I worry for myself, but I worry too for that sick man below deck, and wonder how he can survive this.

At last the secretary emerges. He is dead, he says, oh my master is dead! No surprise there then. And the secretary, God spare him, he is crying. He cries. And we are embarrassed, and we cannot look at him.

We fetch the body. It is light, and thin like paper. And the yellow in the skin is pronounced now, I fancy I can see his bones beneath, and maybe so I can. On deck the sun seems to shine through him. We wrap him in a blanket to be decent, and I fear that it will be impossible, that his body will break apart and turn to liquid, that it'll soak the blanket and have no substance, but this is untrue. No, you mustn't abandon my master! So says the secretary, but he is weeping still, and he cannot stop us. The captain comes on deck and says a few Christian words of comfort, and we tip the corpse overboard.

It does not even make a sound as it hits the water. It is on the water, it bobs. Then it is under the water, and it is gone.

And then, the ripple.

Where the body sinks beneath, there is a ripple. A little wave, fanning out on the water. But not thin the way a ripple should be, and it cuts a groove across the surface of that stagnant sea, it seems like the sea has a skin and the skin is cracking open, on and on it cracks towards the horizon, the crack splitting darker now and deeper – and then, when it can travel no further, when it seems to collide against that point where the sea and the sky meet, it bounces BACK – the ripple now picking up speed and hurtling its way toward us. And there is wind now in the speed of that approach, and the ripple is a wave, a tidal wave, and I fear we cannot withstand it. Man the sails, lads! Keep the ship steady! And the wave hits us, and we are borne aloft by it, and the water is over the sides but it does not sink us, and the wind is full in our sails, and we are moving, we are moving once again.

We do not know what devilry in our passenger caused the winds to drop, but he is at one with the sea now, and the curse is lifted.

For all that a man is dead, we cheer. The secretary looks first angry, then thwarted, then returns to the cargo hold, and the men say, Devil take him then! And I cannot help but agree.

It is William Bates who is at the stern and spies something strange in the seas behind us. What is that? he says. I say I do not know, it looks like a black spot upon the surface of the water. I am sure that we will lose sight of it soon, fast as we are now speeding, but an hour later we think to look back, and there it still is – it is larger, if anything, it is gaining on us. It is in pursuit. How it bobs about on the waves.

Before sunset it is close enough that we can identify it, and it is a coffin.

A coffin, and not one of your cheap body boxes neither. It is brass handles and brass hooks, and when the waves lift it in the right direction, you can see it has a bloody brass plaque on its top too. We can see it clearly now, it is but a hundred yards behind us. Why is it painted black? asks Bates, and I do not know, but jet black it is, and it may be an effect of the sea but the paint looks wet and dripping. We say, for all the cash he threw overboard, the man has bought his money's worth! Because what can we do but joke? What, except scream, or take fright, or run mad?

There is not much sleep that night for any of us. And I am roused before my shift because I sense something is wrong. It takes me a minute to realise that the winds have fallen again, and the ship is motionless.

Back on deck, and the sea flat once more, the sails hang empty, the very air is dead. If there is one comfort, it is that the coffin has been halted too. But it lies out behind, like a faithful dog at the heels of its master.

And then.

And then we hear the voice of William Bates. High above us, he is up in the rigging. Come down from there, we call, there's no wind to be had! He shouts down. I cannot help it, he says. I cannot help what I do now, but I have such an Urge. Oh, this Urge I feel! Can't you too feel the Urge? It seems strange then, the very word he uses, but in a moment that no longer matters. For the man jumps. And I think he will surely hit the deck – but no – he clears the ship, he is overboard. And as he jumps he gives out such a cry, there is such desperation to it, but something else, something almost exultant.

A hundred foot drop, he hits the water hard, he smacks into it. He is killed instantly, or so I believe, or so I like to believe. The body slowly slides into the sea, as if it's not composed of water, as if it's something thick like treacle.

This time we do not see the ripple. But we feel it, the shuddering of the deck beneath our feet – and within seconds the wind is rising again, and the waves are flowing, and we are once more upon our way.

The coffin follows. It makes no attempt to outstrip us, it is happy to keep its present distance.

And we see now, some way behind it, now that poor William is dead – we see now there is a second coffin, following the first.

The wind holds steady until late afternoon the next day.

We are all on deck, and this time no one is going to leap into the water. On that point we are adamant. And the coffins keep their distance, they wink at us in the sun. We keep our nerve for hours, we even sing songs. We declare ourselves shipmates for life, we profess we shall only ever take to sea again if we do so with this self same crew, down to every last man! What rot we speak. And Simon Cole is singing, and then Simon Cole says he feels so happy, we are brothers all, aren't we? Every one of us dear friends. And the Urge isn't so bad, it's such a relief to give in to the Urge, you can't fight forever. And he begs me to pass a message of love to his poor wife, and he is overboard in a trice, and he is drowned, and the winds pick up, and the waves are behind us again, and there is a third coffin on the seas now, black as pitch like the others. And I didn't even know he had a wife.

The captain summons me to the officers' saloon. He has a bottle of wine hanging on a gimbal above the table, he asks whether I drink, I do not refuse. He inquires of the mood of his men. I do not wish to lie. I tell him that they are all pretty fucking terrified, God beg my pardon. He nods at this. Slow and thoughtful, as if I'd given him a compass reading. This is what we're going to do, he says, and pours us both another wine. You're going to hold them together. You're going to keep them steady, and keep us all afloat. The worst is over. Or the worst will soon be over. Or there cannot be much more that is worst. Then he turfs me out and locks the door.

The next to die is Nick Trott, and then there's daft Bobby the apprentice, he was only fourteen.

We search the lower decks for the secretary, but there's no sign of him. Maybe he has already leaped into the sea, and no one even bothered to look.

And when the wind drops we all gather on deck and we take each other's hands and we hold firm – we will NOT lose another man, we will resist the Urge. We are an unbroken chain. But I hear the men talk. I hear them say how the ship may never move again unless we feed the sea – isn't it better that some men die so that the others reach home? And somehow the chain always gets broken. Somehow there's always a man who gets loose of another's grip, and he makes to the side of the ship, and throws himself into oblivion. And he screams in such fear, but there's pure radiance in his face – a man has found his calling, isn't that a wonderful thing?

Each time the sea takes another man we cannot see the ripple that gets the ship – moving. But we can believe it is there – maybe the cracks are beneath the surface where we cannot see them, maybe the sea is shattered and the world is shattered and we are teetering on the top of it and we daren't look down for fear that at any moment it'll all give way and we'll be lost forever.

I know it will soon be my turn. Better I die than some others. I have no wife. I have no child. I have no one that loves me, or will mourn me when I am dead.

And one day as we work on deck who should come out and join us? The captain, and the first mate, and the second mate – so smart in their braided uniforms – fine British officers to a man. All arm in arm, as if they're dancing like French whores. Help us, they cry. Help us, stop us! We watch them dance themselves over the edge, and we laugh as the seas swallow them up just the same as the common tars.

By now there are a dozen black coffins studding the horizon.

The sacrifice of the officers seems to feed the waters for longer, the winds blow hale and hearty for nearly a week. And some men dare to believe they may reach Southampton after all. The bosun confides in me. He says that though we are sailing, he has no idea where we might be sailing to. We lost sight of land long ago, too long ago, and it makes no sense. There's the sea, and nothing but the sea, there's no end to it. He wants to tell the crew, but I persuade him not to. He wrestles with his conscience over this. They have a right to know the truth, he says. The next time the winds dip the Urge comes for the bosun, so his little dilemma is over.

Oh, how I wonder what the Urge will feel like.

Oh, what a thing it would be to mean something.

We find the secretary. He has emptied out the tea, he has been hiding in the chests. Like a rat!

I demand he tell us what is happening, why this curse has been visited upon us. He will not talk. I threaten him with one of the ship's muskets. He begs me to understand. He DARES not talk. We can have no idea of the consequences if he does. I say to him, what in hell's name could be worse than this? And he stares at me, and he laughs at me, the blackguard laughs. He laughs so long we have to hit him to make him stop.

I'm the one who heaves him over the side of the ship. It isn't even still, the waves are moving, the coffins bobbing behind. No sacrifice is even asked for, but I do not want the man to live a moment longer. He shouts, You dare not kill me! You will be damned! And I rage at him, You think any man here ISN'T damned? You think there can be salvation for any single one of us? And I lift him up by his shoulders, he is lighter than he should be, or maybe there is such fury in me, and I

*

My first instinct, of course, was to find out what happened next.

I turned over the coffin lid. Like a fool, I hoped somehow it was like a book, that by leafing over the page I'd find the next words ready. I knew it was a pointless endeavour – the scratching had been made from *inside* the coffin. But what I had read was already impossible, was it too much to hope the impossibility might be stretched a little further? Apparently so.

It was now night time. It was my turn to wake up Matthew, banging on the door of his little cottage. If he'd been tipsy that morning, by now he was clearly drunk – he blinked at me furious and frightened when he opened the door and he could barely remember who I was. I could hardly blame him. I had not consumed anything the entire day, but I felt giddy too, as if the words I had read had dripped something intoxicating into my soul. "Come!" I said. "We have work to do ! Bring your lantern. Bring your spade." He tried to refuse, and I was forceful with him, I do confess it.

My first hope was that my great-grandfather's account continued on the remains of the coffin still within the pit. Perhaps on the side slats – perhaps on the floor itself. I was so eager to find out I jumped into the pit alongside Matthew, I nearly missed my footing and could have fallen far deeper had he not grabbed hold, I should be grateful of that at least. But I was angry with him when our perusal of the coffin revealed precisely nothing. "The engraving may be faint!" I said – "hold the lantern closer!" Because even then I was trying to find a logic to this, maybe by the latter stages of the narrative my great-grandfather would have been weakening (there was only so much air he had to work with, he must have been so nearly dead). Nothing. Still nothing. I think maybe I swore in my disappointment. Matthew begged I let him return to bed. In the lantern light his face shone with such pathetic hope.

I had an idea. "Dig deeper!" I said. "There must be other coffins nearby!" I did not know how my great-grandfather might have done it, but he would have needed to have continued his story somehow, *anyhow* – or what would have been the point in starting? Maybe another coffin lid would have satisfied his needs. Within only a few minutes Matthew had found another coffin in the soil. "Open it!" I said. It wasn't strong, no rich man's coffin this, it broke easily. Inside there was a skeleton, I couldn't tell whether of man or woman. "Any writing?" I said. "Any message at all?" Matthew said there was nothing, but I didn't believe him, I didn't trust him even to know what writing was. I pushed him out of the way to see, but he was right. "Dig again!" I said. Matthew was crying now, I do not know why, I had no time for that. "I said, dig!" Another coffin prised open, as plain as the last. "Any writing?" Matthew once more responded in the negative.

It was almost dawn. I stumbled home. I was dog tired. I did not yet give in to sleep. I went back to my study, to the coffin lid on the floor. I read it once again. I found myself becoming angry with my great-grandfather. If he had only a limited space to write upon, why waste it describing the flow of ripples, or his sympathy for an idiot apprentice, why waste my time on adjectives at all? Why, when realising he was coming to the foot of the lid, did he not speed up the story somewhat and get to the point?

And I wondered – were these words really my great-grandfather's at all? They seemed like an account of his death – how ever could he escape, how did he get home? But I know he *must* have escaped, if only to be buried here on land – and he must have met a woman, and then had a child who could become my grandfather, who could himself produce my father in turn, and then, him, me: he *had* to have escaped the Devil's curse – somehow – my entire existence was proof of it. Was this why I was so angry I was denied an explanation? I thought so. But it may yet be I just wanted a satisfactory conclusion to a good yarn.

Some instinct told me that these were indeed my ancestor's words. When I fingered at the grooves on the wood, I felt a kinship to them – they were not words of comfort, but still they comforted me. There was no accident I had found them. This was a message for me, written for me and intended only for me – and I knew my great-grandfather had spent the last few gasps of his life reaching out to me. It made me weep. It did. My father had never been a kindly man. But my great-grandfather, surely, he had loved me.

I fell asleep over the coffin lid, and I might have supposed I would have bad dreams – of curses and spooks and deals with the Devil. But the truth was, I dreamed of nothing. My dreams were empty. And they have been ever since.

If this indeed had been a deliberate message, it made even less sense there was no conclusion to it. I woke with the conviction of what I should do next. I went to see Matthew. I explained to him with full patience that we had been digging up the wrong coffins – we needed to find ones like my great-grandfather's, teak and rich and with a brass plaque upon the lid. I said that I knew instructing him to dig up the graveyard looking for such coffins was beyond the everyday confines of his job, and I would be prepared to pay him a generous supplement. He professed himself to be most reluctant, and I regretted how brusque I had been with him the night before. I put on my most calming vicar voice to reassure him, and I doubled the supplement too. One or the other won him over. I told him to start digging that night, once it was dark.

I do not know that I believe in God, but I believe in the Devil. I believe in the need for God. That is not the same thing. I believe in faith, I believe in the need for order and moral rectitude. We strive to find God, and that strife is a worthy pursuit. But I never see God, and I see the Devil at every turn. God is like the solid ground beneath our feet. But the ground isn't really solid. Because underneath this thin crust of the earth there flow waves we cannot see, we are bobbing about on all sides, look how we bob.

People began to complain about the content of my sermons.

I heard nothing from Matthew about his progress. One night I went to see him. He was in bed. I hauled him out, on to the floor. I said I didn't pay him to sleep, I paid him to dig. I stood over him all night as he set to work unearthing more old coffins in the graveyard. He found four, and none of them were any use.

I do not believe in God. I believe in the Devil. Bob, bob, bob.

I go back to see Matthew. "Get up!" I roar. He does not get up. He is dead. He has, quite literally, drunk himself to death on my money. There is something like a smile on his face. I believe it is a smile.

I leave his cottage. I close the door, nice and respectful. You have to respect the dead.

It is cold now, and oh so dark. And on I walk, past the church, past the gravestones. One foot in front of the other, and each time the foot goes down it is met by something solid, the ground is always there to catch me – this step is safe, and then this, and then this one too – but for how much longer? For at some point I shall have gone as far as I can go, I will have reached the end, and everything I believed is solid will have disappeared from under me. When I reach the edge of the cliff there will only be thin air and the fathomless sea below.

I can see nothing, and I can feel nothing, and all I can hear is the cry of gulls and the crash of waves, and soon I cannot even hear them, all there is is the my own breath and the beating of my heart.

Still I walk, and then I stop walking, I stand stock still, and something wet spatters light across my face. I wonder if it is rain or sea spray. I lick at it. I cannot taste. I cannot tell whether it is salt.

I know now I will never read the end of my great-grandfather's message, but that is not why I am going to die. It is a silly reason to die. This is not disappointment, no fit of pique. Is this the Urge? Am I at last feeling the Urge, as the crew on the ship felt it – something greater than their little lives, greater than all life itself? No. No. This is not the Urge. This is not an urge at all. This is not anything. This is the very absence of feeling. Why can I not experience that same frenzy? Am I not good enough? What is wrong with me? I could walk on, I *will* walk on, and soon I shall run out of ground to walk on, and then I shall fall, and then I shall be dead. And there will be no difference between that one state and the other, oh God. I do not believe in God. They assume I'm afraid of drowning. I am not afraid of drowning. I do not fear. I do not fear. I am afraid of nothing. Nothing is what I am afraid of.

Oh, what a thing it would be to mean something.

The moon breaks out from behind the clouds, just for a few moments. And I can see I'm at the very peak. One step forward, all is over. One step to the left, to the right, all over, all of it done.

I look out to sea. I still cannot hear the waves. There are no waves. The sea is still. I fancy the sea is frozen still.

And I think I see it. Out in the distance, pitched high upon one of those unbreaking waves. I think I see the coffin.

The moonlight is gone. It is pitch black once more.

Oh God.

I cannot feel, I do not feel. I begin to shake.

I need to see the coffin again. I need to make sure. I need another moment of moonlight.

I wait. I shake. I worry that the shaking is so violent it will tip me over the edge before I am ready.

It is so dark.

So dark, and I realise if I die now, I will never see anything again, the last thing about me will be this blackness, and that isn't good enough – the blackness is supposed to come afterwards, it isn't good enough.

I will never read the end of my great-grandfather's message. I will never know how he made it back to land, how he found life and found love. Did he trick the Devil? Did he strike him a deal? It may not matter. This is the message – that somehow he got away, when all seemed lost. He lived long enough to write me the message at all.

I wait for the moon. I can wait no longer. I want to see the coffin. I dread to see the coffin, out at sea, expecting me. And now, now I can hear the sound of the waves, and they are loud and angry and they will crush me if they can, they will take my body and they will break it if I give it to them, and now I hear the gulls and their cries are mocking laughter.

I dare not turn around. Turning around might be enough to pitch me into oblivion. I step backwards. And again, and again, until the waves seem further away.

I go home. I go to bed. And still I cannot dream, I have no dreams within me. My mind is like a millpond, there are no waves, there's not a ripple on the surface. But still. Still, it is a new beginning. And I can learn to hope.

AND THIS IS HOW WE FALL

ii

There are such things as second chances after all!

Redemption is there for the very weakest of us, by the grace of God, and oh, I have been so weak. I did not seek redemption. I did not think myself worthy of it, and I never prayed for it. I prayed for those in my parish, not for myself. And redemption was granted anyway, and I have seized it with both hands.

Clemence Lincoln has come back to me.

This is how it was: she returned to the village. She no longer works in a shop in a town, her father died – praise the Lord! – and so she returned whence she came. Do we not all do that eventually, return whence we came, dust to dust? But Clemence has returned to me not yet as dust but in all too corporeal form, and I am blessed by it. And the best of it, she is not a married woman. And the better still, she is beautiful, more beautiful than before.

I saw her sitting there in church, as I was giving a sermon. I lost my place in the text, I repeated an entire paragraph, no one seemed to notice. I recognised her straight away. Sometimes it takes being presented with the full reality of a person for you to realise they have been in your mind every day, you have never stopped thinking of them, though you did not even know it! I do not think she recognised me. She hadn't expected me to take holy orders. "You look older," she said. "Your hair has turned grey." But I do not think it displeased her for she blushed as she said it, and when I asked if I might call upon her she assented.

I have begun to dream again. For three long years my head has been dark and empty as I slept, and there was a strange numbed torture to it, but I was resigned to it, I thought it was my due. I told Clemence I dream now, that I dream of her every night. She took my hand and said I was a poet. She cannot know the half of it. She cannot know how much she has saved me.

I proposed to her after church one day, when she had stayed behind to help me collect the hymn sheets. It was a thing of impulse, I hadn't even got a ring to offer her. She didn't mind. We were married in F___, we went there by train the very next week. I did not want to marry Clemence in my own church. The day was happy.

She is devoted to pastoral duties as much as I am, and she has given me two children. John, we named after her late father. Ruth, we named after the Moabite who wedded Boaz. My dreams are now filled, not only with a wife but with family.

Oh, and I have a new sexton too. After Matthew's death the position fell vacant for many months, and had I been in righter mind I would no doubt have found that very irksome. One day a young man came as applicant. He told me he could dig, and that he believed in Christ, and that satisfied the two main conditions quite neatly; moreover, he was the very son of Matthew, my previous sexton; moreover, his name was Matthew as well! I had no idea that Old Matthew had had any children, and though they do not look alike, I sometimes see some of that same slyness around the eyes. Young Matthew fills his father's shoes well, he digs the graves deep and respectfully, and he never drinks. But for all that, somehow, I preferred his father.

*

Ruth had always been as strong as her brother, and neither Clemence nor I took the illness seriously at first. I know Clemence blames herself bitterly for that; she won't talk about it with me, but I hear her sometimes crying in the night. It's the first time something has come between us. Is it wrong to say, however much I grieve for my daughter, it's for that easy intimacy with my wife I grieve the most? I just hope Clemence can share her grief with God, and it gives her the comfort she no longer seeks from me.

Ruth did not take the illness seriously either. She said she had a sore throat, but she did not make great complaint of it – said rather it was a tickle than a pain. But by the Thursday she was too weak to move from bed, and by Sunday she was running a fever, and the red spots around her face and throat were livid.

That Sunday was the first time I went to church without my wife in six years. Clemence told me to ask for special prayers from the congregation, but although I offered up private prayers of my own, still I felt it wrong to impose my own domestic matters on to others. I am supposed to be their shepherd. I am supposed to be their rock. If I was wrong, then I was wrong. If I failed Ruth, then so be it. Clemence does not need to know it, and poor Ruth never will.

John, for his part, was disconsolate. "Is Ruthie going to die?" he asked me. How can you answer a question like that? And still, he kept on – "If Ruthie dies, who will I have to play with?"

We tried to keep Ruth's temperature down the best we could. She babbled. Her fever seemed at least a happy one. She always smiled. Clemence wanted to take her to the doctor in the town by train, but I feared it was already too late for that. On the evening of the Friday, Ruth gave out a breath that was so sudden and profound I think it emptied her quite. It seemed she put all of her life into that breath. And then she closed her eyes. And then she was dead.

Clemence that night closed the door upon me, and I did not blame her because I knew she was suffering, and by the next night the door was opened to me again and the matter was not spoken of.

That Sunday at church the congregation all wore black, and that was a kindness I had not looked for. We all feel it when a small child is taken into God's care.

Matthew came to see me. He was full of condolence, and if there was a brightness in his eyes I didn't like, why then, bright eyes are a sign of youth and can't be helped. He told me he had a coffin all ready for me. It was a good piece of work too, I couldn't fault it, even though I felt a pang it was plain boards. "This is your first, isn't it?" he asked, and I thought the question was a strange one, the man knew how long I had been married, he knew how many children I had. "Why then, we'll make this funeral the best it can be!" And he took me to the graveyard, and he showed me exactly where he intended to dig, and it was a peaceful spot in the shade of one of the old oak trees. And it seemed odd to be standing on earth that I knew would soon be enveloping my daughter's remains.

Clemence chose the hymn, I wrote the eulogy. We stood by the graveside together, John was with us too, and we looked like a family strong enough to survive anything. The coffin was gently lowered into the pit. John looked scared and confused. My heart went out to him, but still, he irritated me.

I threw down the first clump of soil, and it scattered across Ruth's coffin lid. More soil was thrown down to join it.

I looked at Clemence, and her eyes were wet, and damn it if my eyes weren't wet too. She reached for my hand and tried a smile, and she looked so brave. And I smiled back the best I could, and I knew then we were going to be all right, in spite of all, everything was going to be all right.

I looked back down into the grave.

The coffin was no longer plain; it was black.

Another clump of soil buried the last of the brass plaque twinkling idly at me in the sunlight.

I looked back at my family, at Matthew, at the small gaggle of villagers who had come to pay their respects. No one but me seemed to have noticed the transformation.

The coffin lid was all but buried now. I wanted them to stop throwing soil down upon it. I wanted to shriek at them. All eyes were upon me. I threw another handful in myself.

It was over, it was all over. What was left of my family walked away from the grave. I held Clemence's hand, I held on to John. They were both shaking. I tried not to shake.

The coffin. There are such things as second chances after all.

*

And once night fell, and my family were asleep, I left the vicarage and went back to find my daughter's coffin. I hoped that her grave had not yet been filled in – with Old Matthew I'd have had no cause for concern, but his son was frustratingly conscientious. I was in luck! – I was blessed! I got into the grave, and threw off the soil that obscured the coffin. I hadn't imagined it; the coffin was the finest teak; there was a plaque, and engraved upon it was my daughter's name and the dates that spanned her pathetically brief life. I prised open the coffin. I refused to look at the body of my daughter. Instead, I looked to see if there were any words carved into the underside of the lid. There were.

Once again they filled every spare inch, running from head to toe. I recognised it was the same handwriting. The intricacy of the punctuation, the grandiose loops to the tails of the 'f's and the 'g's.

It made a sort of grim sense that my great-grandfather only passed on the message through his descendants. That was where I had gone wrong before, thinking any old coffin would do! This was personal. He wasn't to know that at the time I read the first part of his story I had no other family. It was a matter of great luck that I later had a daughter, and that she had died. I could hardly contain my joy.

I did not know what I meant to do. Take off the lid and drag it home where I could read more carefully? I must not be caught here. But I couldn't wait – I pressed the lantern as close to the writing as I dared, squatted down in the soil, and began to read.

*

dare not kill me! You will be damned! And I rage at him, You think any man here ISN'T damned? You think there can be salvation for any single one of us? And I lift him up by his shoulders, he is lighter than he should be, or maybe there is such fury in me, and I throw the secretary overboard. He hits the water, he goes straight down, we all crane over the sides to look, there is not much sport to be had in these cursed days, we take our pleasures where we can. But no, he breaks to the surface, gasping for breath and spitting out water, he has swallowed a skinful. The crew jeer at him. I do not jeer. I do not want to mock him. I just want him to die. He flails about, he goes under once more – he cannot last longer surely – and as the ship sails past we all scurry down the deck to watch his final struggles. But then the struggles cease. He seems to find resolve, I can see the look set hard upon his face, and I have seen that look before, in a storm, in desperation, when a sailor decides whether to fight and live or give in and die. He is going to live. And he finds the strength to swim, he swims away from the ship. He swims towards the coffins. The waves crash against him. The waves want to stop him. He pushes the waves aside with his arms. And I know, suddenly, I KNOW, he must not reach the coffins. He must not. I cry, Fetch a musket! Hurry! The secretary is weakening now, as any man might, but he will not give up – that first coffin bobbing upon

246

the sea is the only little chance he has. I have the musket. I fire wildly. God damn it, I shout. I load again. I pray to God. I pray that the next bullet will hit him. He has nearly reached the coffin. The coffin seems to push towards him, it WANTS him close. My next shot splashes by him in the water, for a moment he panics, he goes under, he gasps for air. He swims on. And I abandon God. I pray to the Devil. Make my aim be true! I make the Devil a wager. The Devil loves to gamble. If I shoot this man, I am yours, I am yours forever, and all that I have will be yours, and all that shall come from me will be yours. I fire once more. The secretary grasps hold of the brass handles of the coffin. I think I must have missed. Long seconds seem to pass. And then there is an explosion of red that seems so garish against the blue sea, a plume of blood from his chest, he is hit! The secretary contorts his face. In pain. No, in laughter. He laughs at me. He tries to haul himself up on to the black coffin, he does not have the strength for it – even now he will surely drown, and his life blood is spilling out into the water, how liquid it looks, he is composed of liquid – he heaves, one last effort, he is aboard. He lies upon the coffin, panting his breath away, and I see how his guts are leaking thick upon it, but he doesn't care, he is RIDING that coffin, he has a little ship all of his own. And then, and then I see the lid of the coffin shudder. It breaks open, first a crack, and then widening. Something is escaping from the inside. And I should shoot again, but I do not have the power to hold the gun any longer, it drops uselessly upon the deck. With the secretary now having to scrabble upon the side to stay afloat, and all my crew watching, we cannot turn our eyes away. And from within that coffin there extends an arm, and the arm is so thin and so yellowed. And at the end there is a hand that seems to beckon – at the secretary, at us, we cannot tell – and on the hand there is one single finger and there is no skin upon that finger and the finger is of the whitest bone

*

And here too is where the narrative ran out, every space on the coffin lid had been filled. And I screamed in my frustration. And I cursed my daughter that her body had been so young and so small, if she had died but half a foot taller then I would know how the story ended! And I cried out for any means by which I could finish reading what my great-grandfather wanted me to know. And by the time I reached home my wife was up fretting, for my little boy was coughing and pale, and rubbing hard at the scarlet blotches snaking round his chest and throat.

247

It was a wonder to see how fast my son sickened. His skin grew rotten, all over it pustules bobbed to the surface. We are all truly slabs of meat, and when we stop to salt them, then we go off.

In his fever he would sometimes say such strange things, and I listened closely, but he said nothing of any revelatory import.

We prayed for his recovery. By which I mean, my wife prayed. I did not pray. I made the signs of prayer, I played the part, but I kept my mind as still and empty as a millpond and I did not speak to God. I did not, would not, pray *against* my own son. Withholding prayer is not the same thing. I know it is not as bad.

My wife sat by him day and night and mopped at his brow, but it seemed to me that the waves of heat that rolled off him could never be quenched by water.

I went to visit Matthew, and I told him that soon I would be needing another coffin. "One of your special coffins," I said, and Matthew agreed. He did not waste time on saying sorry; he was not sorry. "You might make it half a foot bigger," I said, and at this he winked and nodded.

My wife caught the train to town to visit the doctor. My son was too weak to travel. She found little comfort. The fever would grow worse. If he were strong enough to withstand it, he would live. If he weren't, he would die. We could only wait.

I looked at my son, and really, he didn't look strong enough to withstand anything. Had he ever been strong? My grandfather lived so that my father had lived, my father had lived so I could be born, all my ancestors converged into a single point and that single point was me. Did I now live only so that my son could live? I did not think so. I must have stronger sons.

I did not want my son to die, but where better than in the care of loving parents? I did not want my son to suffer. But we all have to suffer.

"This may be his last night on earth," said my wife. John cried out for his mother that night. I do not know whether he cried out for me.

Clemence woke me the next morning. Her eyes were wet with tears, so I supposed the worst was over. I made to commiserate – I saw she was smiling. "Oh, my love," she said. "Oh, my dear! He's better. He's getting better. I dare believe it. John will live." I told her not to get carried away.

We went to see my son. His face still was swollen, the red marks were all over. But his skin was cooler, I could see that even without touching him. He was sitting up, and speaking, and asking for food.

"It's a miracle!" she said. "Praise be to God!" Why answer her prayers and not mine? Why always the prayers of others, and *never* mine?

"Go to bed," I told her. "You've been up all night, and you will make yourself ill too. I shall watch over our son."

I sat by John's bed, and held his hand until he slept.

When he was still, I took off the sheets covering him, and I took away his pillow. Wet with sweat, lain outstretched, flat like a dead fish.

"God speed," I said, and I placed the pillow over his face. I pressed down.

I do not know how long I pressed down for. I intended to count the seconds, but I forgot to do so. I thought it was a minute. It could not have been a minute.

I would like to say that something happened to stop me. That God appeared in burning glory and urged me to show mercy. That the Devil came, and I found the courage to rebel. Or that my poor son struggled, or cried out to me, or told me he loved me, that he did something to melt my heart.

Nothing happened. Nothing.

I pressed down for as long as I could bear it.

I took the pillow from his face. John was still breathing. The breaths were shallow, but no weaker than before.

I held the pillow for a long time, but I did not press it over his face again. And at length I set it down upon the bed. And at length I moved it back underneath my son's head.

I sat by John, and took his hand again, and I think he squeezed it. But he was asleep. I may have imagined it.

In the morning, I told my wife I was going to the church. She asked if I were going to give thanks to God for sparing our son, and I said that it was certainly something I was giving proper consideration.

She hugged on to me.

She said, "I love you."

I said, "I know."

She said, "I forgive you."

I said, "I do not want your forgiveness."

I said, "You do not have the power to forgive me."

I left.

In the night there had been a storm. Trees all around had been uprooted, everywhere deep pits had been gouged out of the earth. I had not even noticed. And it's strange, because I have long been sensitive to the vagaries of the weather, even the change of breeze can affect me most ominously.

*

I told Matthew that the coffin would no longer be necessary. He smiled, and led me inside his cottage. There he had a coffin all ready prepared, and the teak was painted thick and black, and the plaque on the lid seemed to shine. And the coffin was not for a child, it was for a full grown man. And the name on the plaque was mine. "I have been waiting so long," said Matthew. And inside me something seemed to click, like understanding – but it wasn't understanding, because really I was as stupid as before.

*

The coffin is comfortable. I had not expected that. Matthew has planed the wood well, it is smooth against my back. I tell Matthew he has done a good job, and he seems delighted by this, how he whoops and claps his hands. I am pleased he is pleased; I have to ask him to stop whooping, it unnerves me.

We review our arrangement. I shall be buried within the coffin for no longer than fifteen minutes. At the end of that time, or if I pound against the lid sooner, Matthew will release me. I shall see for myself the rest of my great-grandfather's story carved into the wood above my head. I shall see the story finished.

Matthew says yes, yes, and all will be as I've said, and he nods his head so eagerly, and I wish he'd close his mouth as he does so, his tongue lolls about in such a wild manner it is quite disconcerting. I wonder whether I should change my mind. I wonder whether I should stop. And I can feel a certain madness lift from me – I do not need this – I can shrug off this mania, and let it go, and live well with my wife and my son – and then the lid is on, and I can hear Matthew banging in the nails to keep it secure. And there is a relief to that. No, no, this is as it should be.

I knew it would be dark. It is dark. I suspected it would be hot too. In that matter, at least, I am pleasantly surprised.

I expected too to feel immediately claustrophobic. That I would be demanding release before giving the experiment a chance to work. But I feel safe. My limbs are secure, I can barely move. There is nothing for me to do. There is nothing for me to worry about.

And then, I feel it. That the coffin is being lowered into the ground. And that makes no sense, because the coffin is already in its grave. Matthew and I put it inside one of the pits produced by the storm. But here it is – a certain sense that I am sinking, and sinking ever deeper. And I get the mad thought that if I were to speak my voice would come out as an echo, as if I were now in a vast cavern, and I try it, "Hello-o," I try softly, and my throat is dry and all I can do is croak.

No matter.

No matter, and I hear the thrum of blood in my head. It sounds like waves. It sounds like the sea. And I think of Old Matthew, and the way he hated digging into the cliff for fear he would hit the water below. And I hear it now, the sea seems all around me. And it's a comfort, with the sky now so far above to have the sea so close.

Because we are of the ocean. My father used to say my family had salt water in our veins, and so it is: I should have been a fisherman, I should have been a sailor, I should never have gone into the Church and wasted my life on God, I have never been with God, that bargain was struck long before I was born.

We are of the ocean, and I am the ocean.

I wonder how the writing will appear. (I wonder how I will see to read it – it is so dark! I thought that in fifteen minutes I should be set freed, and then I could look at the carvings that had appeared in the light – but fifteen minutes was an age ago, there is no time here, it is absurd to think of time, the sea has no concept of that.) Will the story appear by magic, as to Daniel at Belshazzar's feast? Or will I have to carve it in the wood myself?

I try to trace some words into the lid with my forefinger. I misjudge the distance, my shoulders cramp, the lid is too close for my finger to bend back. Still, I rub at the coffin lid, I wait for my great-grandfather's words to appear.

And still, the coffin sinks. I wonder whether I shall ever reach bottom.

My body starts to cry out against its confines – and the wood *isn't* as smooth as I'd thought, and the coffin *isn't* comfortable. It's all this flesh I have, of course it cries out, it hasn't learned how to flow yet. But I am water, and I can flow anywhere, and if I remind myself of that none of it hurts quite so much.

My finger against the lid. Still rubbing at it, I want my great-grandfather to speak through me, I want *something* to speak through me. To be part of something greater. Oh, what a thing it would be to mean something! I have such an urge for it. Rubbing, faster and faster now. I can feel my fingernail break clean off, and I cry out – but think water, think of the water – I rub the very skin off my forefinger, the skin comes right off and now all that's there is bone. And bone is good and sharp, it'll be just perfect for carving words

251

into wood, I am so pleased. The bone is pure white and gleams in the dark, it is good to have a little light.

Something wet dribbles on to my face, and it might be sweat, and it might be blood.

Now, at last, the words start to come.

The coffin hits the bottom, wherever the bottom is – is it Hell? Have I reached Hell? Surely not, for it feels so gentle here, I am being rocked from side to side like a baby in a cradle.

The handwriting isn't mine. The 'f's and the 'g's are too florid. I scratch them into the word, so precise, so *deep*.

Matthew will not release you, it says. *Matthew felt the Urge! He is over the cliff now, over the cliff and far away, and he was happy to jump, because his task has been fulfilled. He was happy, because it is good to satisfy an Urge! And Matthew is dead, and everyone you know is dead and everyone who ever loved you is dead, no one is coming to help. Your wife, dear Clemence, oh, she felt the Urge! And little John, what an Urge he had! Your wife held the pillow over his head and he laughed all the while, and then she took a knife and she cut her throat, oh, the Urge was fast upon them! Can you feel the Urge? Can you feel it? We are not dust here. We do not return to dust. Do not speak 'dust to dust' to us. We are of the ocean, and we are the ocean, we are but little drops in the roaring sea, can you hear them cry to you, can you hear as they Urge you on?*

And I wait for more writing, I wait for the story to continue, but there is no more story, and nothing else will ever be written.

I do not feel afraid.

I hear the waters, they are all about me, I am bobbing up and down, my coffin is riding the waves. I am at sea, as I was always meant to be – oh, father, you would be so proud! Oh, my ancestors, I am coming to you!

I am in my little ship, and I feel such peace, letting go is a comfort of sorts.

And somewhere far away I think I hear three little pops like shots from a gun, and then I feel my coffin tip as something outside grabs hold, something hauls itself up on top of it. I still do not feel afraid, I am afraid of nothing. Nothing is what I am afraid of. The lid comes open. Just a crack, but I can pull the lid off. There is sunlight. There is spray and there is salt water. There is freedom. I stretch my arm far out of the coffin, and my bone white finger crooks as if it is beckoning.

SOURCES

All the stories in 'Terror Tales of the Ocean' are original to this publication, with the exceptions of *Lie Still, Steep Becalmed* by Steve Duffy, which first appeared in 'At Ease With the Dead' (2007), *Sun Over the Yard Arm* by Peter James, which first appeared in 'A Twist of the Knife' (2014), *The Derelict of Death* by Simon Clark and John B. Ford, which first appeared in 'The Derelict of Death' (1998) and *Hell in the Cathedral* by Paul Finch, which first appeared in 'The Shadows Beneath' (2000).

FUTURE TITLES

If you enjoyed *Terror Tales of The Ocean*, why not seek out the first eight volumes in this series: *Terror Tales of the Lake District*, *Terror Tales of the Cotswolds*, *Terror Tales of East Anglia*, *Terror Tales of London*, *Terror Tales of the Seaside*, *Terror Tales of Wales*, *Terror Tales of Yorkshire*, and *Terror Tales of the Scottish Highlands* – all available from most good online retailers, including Amazon, or you can order directly from http://www.grayfriarpress.com/index.html.

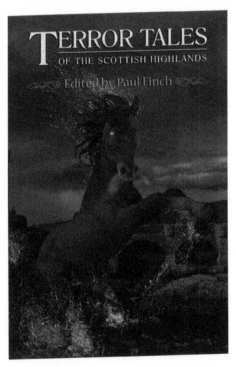

In addition, watch out for the next title in this series, *Terror Tales of Cornwall*. Check regularly for updates on this series with Gray Friar Press and on the editor's own webpage: http://paulfinch-writer.blogspot.co.uk/. Alternatively, you can follow him on Twitter: @paulfinchauthor.